The Brothers

The Brothers
Michael Hastings

PIATKUS

Copyright © 1992 by Michael Hastings

First published in
Great Britain in 1992 by
Judy Piatkus (Publishers) Ltd of
5 Windmill Street, London W1P 1HF

**The moral right of the author
has been asserted**

*A catalogue record for this book is available
from the British Library*

ISBN 0–7499–0141–1

Typeset in 11/12 Linotron Times by
Computerset Ltd, Heathrow
Printed and bound in Great Britain by
Butler & Tanner Ltd, Frome

Preface

In the winter of 1949 Stalin's secret police arrested the leaders of the Anti-Fascist Writers' Committee. The Committee was an association of Jewish writers that had been established during the Second World War, in order to gather support for Stalin's war effort among Jews in Russia and abroad. The most prominent Jewish writers, poets, and philosophers of the Soviet Union had been among the founders of the Committee. Their representatives had even visited the United States, where Albert Einstein and other personalities had pledged support for their initiative.

When the war was over, Stalin was worried by signs of budding Jewish nationalism in the Committee. Chairman Solomon Mikhoels, the poets Fefer, Halkin and Professor Lina Stern had presented him with a petition asking for the settling of Jewish survivors in Crimea; they also asked Stalin to condemn antisemitism in the USSR.

The furious Soviet dictator moved to crush the Jewish nationalists. The Committee Chairman, Solomon Mikhoels, was brutally murdered during a visit to Minsk. A few months later all the Committee members were arrested, tortured and condemned to death in a mock trial.

Some of them were shot immediately. The others were executed in January 1953, shortly after Stalin initiated one of the most hideous frame-ups in his bloody career: the Doctors' conspiracy. The paranoid dictator accused the leading Jewish doctors in the Soviet Union of a plot to assassinate him and other communist leaders. He even claimed that the Jewish doctors, obeying orders from Washington, had already assassinated party chiefs Zhdanov and Shcherbakov. The late Mikhoels had allegedly been the intermediary between the evil doctors and some American Jewish organizations.

Before the Doctors' trial started, all the surviving members of the Jewish Anti-Fascist Committee were shot in the inner court of Lubyanka prison, in Moscow.

Stalin died on March 5, 1953 and the execution of the Jewish doctors was called off.

This book starts on January 23, 1953.

It ends today.

Part One
YOUTH
1953–1967

Chapter One

A cold, bitter night had settled over Russia, and snow was falling on the sleeping city of Moscow.

Watching the lacy snowflakes dance outside the barred window of her cell, Tonya thought, Tomorrow Moscow would look like an enchanted kingdom. The Red Square will be covered with an immaculate carpet, the Spasskaya tower will loom, tall and dazzling, like the Ice Castle in the fairy tale; white patches will gleam on the onion domes of St Basil's, and lie thick on the ramparts of the Novodevichny monastery. In Gorky Park, the small pine grove will turn into a forbidding forest, and children will anxiously trudge into its dark, cold shadows, looking for the Winter Queen, while by the frozen pond others will play with snowballs and build white giants with carrot noses and eyes of black coal.

She loved the white Russian winters; they always made her feel like a child again. One of her most famous poems was 'My White Kingdom', describing Moscow in the snow. She had once read it to the boys, but only Alex had seemed to understand, Dimitri was still too little. But she knew she would never write again, and never again see her enchanted kingdom. By the time the first child galloped into Gorky Park tomorrow, she would already be dead, shot in the base of her skull and buried in an unmarked grave, like all the others killed by the KGB in the inner court of Lubyanka prison.

She didn't want to look at the snow any more, and turned the other way. The narrow cot smelled of urine, tobacco and disinfectant. How many people, she wondered, had lain on this cot before her, turning and tossing on the last night of their life, waiting for the firing squad? A single bulb illuminated the corridor, and faint yellow light crept into her cell underneath the iron door. The walls were covered with names, inscriptions and dates, engraved in the mortar by the former inmates. 'Revenge!' somebody had scratched on the far wall. 'Stalin murderer', another wall proclaimed. 'The blood of a communist . . .' an inscription started; the author had probably been dragged to his execution before completing his thought. The guards hadn't bothered to erase the graffiti, and for a good reason: all those who had read them had carried their knowledge into the grave.

On the far wall somebody had scratched a Maggen David, a Jewish star. She raised her hand to her throat and touched her thick gold chain with the same emblem that her sister Nina had given her before leaving Russia. Her forefinger followed the contour of the three Hebrew letters engraved upon the old symbol of her religion.

Tonya had almost no ties with the faith of her people. Her communist teachers, back in Kiev, had taught her to despise religion; when she was a teenager she regarded her father's prayers and her mother's kosher cooking as backward customs of a dying world. Yet, when the KGB officers had stripped her of her possessions – watch, bracelet, earrings – she had asked to keep the chain. After she died, they could give the chain to Morozov; but as long as she was alive, she wanted to hold on to something tangible that would remind her who she was and where she was going.

In a few hours it would all be over, she thought. Her blanket was thin and threadbare but she didn't feel the cold. She didn't feel anything, just an immense emptiness, a crushing lassitude. She had hoped until the last moment that something would happen, and the execution orders would be revoked. Perhaps Morozov would get through to Stalin himself. After all, Stalin couldn't let innocent people die just because they were Jewish.

But yesterday evening, when they had brought her the children for a last goodbye, she had realized that all hope was lost. She had been taken to a bare office on the ground floor by a sour-faced KGB matron; the boys were already there, standing by the far wall under a faded picture of Lenin. It was as a special favour to Colonel Morozov, the matron had said. Visits were never allowed in the Lubyanka. Yes, the colonel himself had brought the children but she wasn't allowed to see him. She'd better kiss the children, the matron said, Colonel Morozov had to take them back.

Tonya had hugged the boys hard, one after the other. Alex was wearing his new grey coat with the rabbit-fur collar, of which he was very proud; Dimitri was huddled in Alex's old sheepskin, that was still too large for him. Alex must have sensed something, with that amazing instinct children have, and had started to cry. 'Are you coming home with us, Mummy?' he had asked repeatedly, and she had mumbled, 'Soon, Alyosha, very soon.' Dimitri hadn't said a word, he had barely started to speak five months before; he just clung to her, burying his face in her skirt and clutching her forefinger in his tiny hand. Even the matron seemed to be moved; when she herded the children out, she had avoided Tonya's eyes.

And now she lay here, alone with her memories, waiting for her executioner. In the nearby cells waited her comrades, the greatest Jewish writers and thinkers of the Soviet Union, who were to be shot with her at dawn. Why, God? What had they done? Hadn't they faithfully served the Soviet Union? Why had she deserved such a fate? She so intensely wanted to live, she had so much to tell, there were so many unwritten poems in her heart!

She felt the tears welling in her eyes, and bit the coarse blanket to muffle her sob. Her guards shouldn't hear her crying, she wouldn't give them that pleasure. Perhaps it was only a nightmare, and she would wake up in her house, with her family. After all, only three years ago she had received the Mayakovsky Award, and her poems had been read in schools, factories, army camps; the *Literaturnaya Gazetta* had printed two of them together with her interview; she had even been mentioned as a candidate for the Lenin medal. And here she was tonight, waiting to be shot for some nebulous crime she had never committed.

It had all happened because she and her first husband, Victor Wolf, had joined the Anti-Fascist Writers' Committee during the war. That foolish step had sealed their fate. But they hadn't had any choice actually, the government had urged them to join. Stalin in person, Victor said, had suggested he create the Committee. It was in 1941, exactly a year after she had run away from home and married Victor. They were so much in love, both young, both poets, totally involved in the socialist society, dreaming of a new world they would help build as soon as the war was over.

The Committee had been created at the darkest hour of the war, when the Germans were already on the Volokolamsk road, barely fifteen miles from the Kremlin, preparing for their final onslaught on Moscow. One night Victor had come home, very excited, and told her of the Anti-Fascist Committee, that was to group the most prominent Jewish writers and philosophers of the Soviet Union. The Committee's purpose was to gather support for the war effort in the Jewish communities abroad. They had asked Victor to be one of the founders. He was so flattered. He was only twenty-eight years old! He had accepted, and they had both been elected members of the board.

Victor had also participated in the first delegation the Committee had sent to the United States. On his return, he had brought Tonya news from her elder sister, Nina, who now lived in New York. Nina had also sent her a frilly white blouse and three big bars of chocolate – she knew Tonya's weaknesses. Victor was thrilled. In America he had met professor Albert Einstein, who had pledged support for the Committee's work.

The troubles had started after the war. Some of their friends had suggested that with hostilities over, the Committee should disband. 'We are members of the Soviet Writers' Union,' she remembered Slavin saying, 'we don't need a Jewish organization.'

But Slavin was in a minority. Most members of the board thought that on the contrary they should even intensify their activities and speak for the Jewish community. 'The Soviet Jews need moral leadership!' their Chairman, Solomon Mikhoels, had said at the plenary meeting and everybody had cheered. Tonya remembered Victor's passionate speech in support of Mikhoels. Looking back now, she felt they had become intoxicated with their success in Russia and abroad. They had forgotten that the Kremlin resented nationalism of any kind, especially Jewish.

In September 1948, on the day Victor had been appointed lecturer at Moscow University, the Committee had taken another step down the road to their doom. Mikhoels and his deputy, Professor Sapojnikov, petitioned Stalin to settle Jewish survivors in Crimea. They also asked Stalin to condemn antisemitism in Russia.

They had gone too far. They should have realized this, when writer Ilya Ehrenburg, known for his close ties with the Kremlin, resigned from the Committee. Another bad omen they disregarded was that Stalin didn't answer the petition. Tonya and Victor didn't worry; they were too busy furnishing the tiny apartment they had got through Victor's connections at the Ministry of Culture. But in January 1949 they were shaken by a strange incident: during a visit to Minsk, Mikhoels was brutally murdered, apparently by young hoodlums. His wife failed to find out exactly how he had died.

Odd, alarming rumours started circulating among the Committee members. Mikhoels's killers were not hooligans, the rumours said, but officers of the secret police; the murder had been ordered by the KGB. An obituary, scheduled to be published in *Pravda*, was removed from the paper at the last moment. A Committee meeting called to commemorate the Chairman's death was cancelled by orders of the *militzia*, the state police; no explanation was given.

Victor didn't believe the rumours; he told Tonya such things couldn't happen in Soviet Russia. Still, an uneasy tension pervaded the Anti-Fascist Writers, and some of them voiced grim forebodings.

'I have the feeling that a noose is tightening around my neck,' Yasha Slavin told them one night, after a meeting with French communist poets. Slavin, a gangling youth with a huge Adam's apple and brooding black eyes, was their best friend. He knew Politburo member Mikhail Pashko, a party high priest. 'Pashko says Stalin was beside himself with fury when he received our petition.' There was fear in Slavin's eyes.

Victor shrugged. 'Come on, Yasha, these are not the dark ages,' he said without conviction.

But Tonya knew better. In eastern Europe, show trials were being held, and democratic leaders hanged for 'conspiring against the state'. In Russia people disappeared without trace. According to some, millions were imprisoned in labour camps beyond the Arctic circle, and thousands more were being executed. Tonya and Victor never spoke about this. Perhaps it was out of cowardice, perhaps they didn't want to admit that their red flag could ever bear the slightest strain.

Still, Tonya was deeply shocked when her downstairs neighbour, a stout Ukrainian woman always dressed in black, confided in her one rainy Sunday. She had just returned from church – the authorities didn't prevent old women from going to churches – and Tonya found her by the door, crying. Her big flat face was puffy, and her mouth quivered; she kept wiping away tears with her podgy fists. Tonya made her some tea, and the Ukrainian told her about her son. He had been taken prisoner by the Germans, and spent two and a half years in a POW camp. Two months after his release, at the end of the war, he had been shot by a Red Army firing squad.

'They said my Pavka was a traitor, Tonya Alexandrova, would you believe that? My son – a traitor! His only fault was to be taken prisoner. Do you shoot somebody for that? And let me tell you . . .' the wretched woman bent towards Tonya, lowering her voice; there was fear in her furtive eyes, fear and secret knowledge, '. . . he is not the only one. They say that our little Father' – Tonya nodded at the allusion to Stalin – 'has ordered thousands of former prisoners to be shot. Our own sons! He calls them traitors. I think that he himself . . .' Then she had bitten her lip, realizing she had said too much, hastily crossed herself and disappeared into her small dark room beneath the staircase.

A few weeks after Mikhoels's death a man came to the Wolfs' house and asked to speak to Victor. He was dressed in a civilian grey suit – government issue – but introduced himself as Major Boris Morozov. He was tall and strong with wavy brown hair, a broad face and a quiet, matter-of-fact voice. He had a pugnacious chin, a full mouth and straight eyebrows. Tonya was struck by his black eyes, sheltered in dark sockets. They were imbued with profound sadness and carried an oddly tormented look.

That evening they were not expecting anybody. Tonya had opened the door. The stranger had stood quite still on the doorstep, staring at her intently. After a moment Victor came over, and the Major introduced himself. He spoke at length with Victor, in the living room, while she sat in the kitchen, sorting the old baby clothes her sister-in-law had sent her; she was four months pregnant. She was deeply worried. What did a major want with her husband? Worse, a major in civilian clothes – that could mean only KGB. She had the feeling she had seen that man before, at the monthly committee meetings which were open to the public. He might have been one of those who had asked for her autograph, after she had read her poems. She had been troubled by the man's haunted eyes.

Tonight she entered the living room twice, to bring the men tea and some biscuits; both times Morozov stared at her so openly that she felt embarrassed. When he was about to leave, Victor called her and she came to the door. Morozov made his goodbyes, formally shaking their hands. He stared at Tonya a last time before vanishing in the dark staircase.

When they were alone, she turned to Victor. 'Did you see how he looked at me?' she asked. But Victor didn't even hear her question. He was badly frightened. Morozov, he told her, was a KGB investigator. He wanted to know about the Committee. Did they have contacts with Jews in America and in England? Did they meet Western diplomats? Did they engage in activities against the regime?

She was astounded. 'But that's . . . preposterous,' she stammered, 'we only had contacts with the Americans when the government asked us to. Why didn't you tell him that?'

Victor was shaking his head. 'I told him that the last time we met an American was during the war. He didn't seem to believe me.'

'But he must, Victor, he must! Go to Fefer, right away, and tell him about this man!'

'Major Morozov said that several officers are talking tonight to the board members. The KGB suspects we are involved in an imperialist plot against the Soviet Union.'

'My God,' she said. 'If he thinks so, then . . .'

'. . . then that's the end of us,' Victor whispered.

Victor spent the night huddled in the living-room armchair, chainsmoking his Bielomorsk cigarettes. Early the next morning, without even bothering to shave or eat breakfast, he rushed to see the other members of the board. A violent storm was raging outside, and howling winds swept the frozen city. This wasn't a day to walk the streets, but Tonya had to see her doctor, it was her monthly check-up. When she stepped out of the house, a dark figure emerged from the bleak, swirling snow curtain, and approached her. Only when the man was at arm's length did she recognize him. It was Major Morozov. White frost had formed on his eyebrows.

'Do you mind if I walk with you, Comrade Wolf?' he said. He stood bent forward against the strong wind.

She shrugged, her feelings a mixture of fear and helplessness. 'But I'm going to . . .'

'I'll accompany you to the doctor and back,' he said, and she winced. He knew where she was going – of course, the KGB knew everything – and still he sounded awkward, ill at ease.

She expected him to question her, but he walked beside her in silence, staring at her with the same tormented expression she remembered from last night. He was a man of about forty, which made him barely four or five years older than Victor. His sturdy build and broad face made him look older. When she entered the clinic he vanished, but when she came out he was quickly beside her again. At the doorstep of her house, he took two parcels from the large pockets of his heavy sheepskin. 'It's for you,' he said. 'Some smoked ham and a jar of honey. It will be good for your baby. And some chocolate – you'll like it.'

She stared at him, astounded. 'I cannot. I mean . . .'

'Take it, Tonya Alexandrova,' he said softly. 'One doesn't refuse food in Moscow these days.'

He was right; she hadn't tasted smoked ham for months. She was a little scared, though. How did Morozov know she was so fond of chocolate? Was this mentioned in her KGB file? He had addressed her as Tonya Alexandrova, which meant he knew the name of her father. What else did he know about her? And why was he taking such interest in her? Perhaps he was attracted to her? She knew she was beautiful. She recognized the hunger in his eyes; but no man had stared at her before with such pain and intensity.

She accepted the food only because it came from him, a KGB officer. It created a sort of complicity between them, it made him her friend; perhaps he would also help her and Victor in the investigation. She wanted to ask him about it, but couldn't. The next morning, when she went to the foodstore, he was there again. She saw a ZIL sedan at the corner, he must have been waiting for her to come out. At the store he flashed his special card and she was given twice her regular ration without having to wait in line. The women queuing before the fish and meat counters shot venomous looks at her but didn't dare open their mouths; they knew a KGB officer when they saw one.

For the next couple of weeks Morozov kept miraculously appearing beside her almost every time she left her house. By the few words he exchanged with her, she realized he knew all about her work and had read some of her poems.

She finally found the courage to ask him about the investigation. Victor had spoken to all the Committee members, who had also been questioned, but nothing had happened since, and her husband had calmed down somewhat. Morozov, though, wouldn't comment on that. He only shook his head and stared at her with his haunted eyes.

One morning, barely five minutes after Victor had left, there was a knock on the door, and there was Morozov with some parcels of food and a package that turned out to contain a piece of fine woollen fabric.

'I cannot accept that,' started Tonya. 'I am very grateful, Major Morozov, but . . .'

He didn't listen. 'Can we sit down?' he asked, and without waiting to be asked walked into the living room. She hastily removed a clothesline that had been stretched across the room for her washing to dry. At this time of year it was impossible to hang anything outside.

'Would you like some tea?' she asked awkwardly, but he shook his head. He sat facing her, joining his hands on the table. She was already familiar with his tense silences, but today he seemed different, more preoccupied. 'This morning,' he said slowly, 'my colleagues arrested Fefer, Halkin, Slavin and Gurevitch. They didn't pick up Sapojnikov because he is on a lecture tour in Romania. The Securitate will take care of him. All the people we arrested are accused of being enemy agents. We have solid evidence about their contacts with the imperialist powers. They will be tried and probably executed.'

She felt a sudden chill and her hand jumped to her throat. 'But that's not true! I know them, they haven't done anything!'

'The orders came from above, Tonya Alexandrova,' he said placidly. In slow, measured movements he lit a cigarette and inhaled deeply, holding the cigarette in his cupped hands, the soldier's way. 'But there is worse news. Your husband, yourself, and the other members of the board will be arrested during the night. You too are going on trial.'

'But for what?' She was choking. 'On what charges? We haven't done anything. I haven't, and I know that Victor hasn't.'

'Your husband is dead meat already, Tonya Alexandrova,' Morozov said quietly. 'They all are. When we get orders to arrest

10

somebody, it means that the evidence is there. Nobody I've arrested has been found innocent. Ever.'

She slumped in her chair. The room was spinning around her. Morozov went into the kitchen and came back with a glass of water. 'Drink this,' he said to her, in a gentle, but firm voice.

She gulped down the water. 'Why are you telling me all this?' she stuttered.

He shrugged. 'It is not a secret. What can your husband do? Or you? Run away? There's no escape. You're under surveillance twenty-four hours a day.'

He suddenly seemed at a loss and sat silent for a while, frowning. 'I am telling you this' – his voice was different now, rather more hesitant – 'because I think I can save your life.'

'My life?'

He nodded, his eyes searching her face.

'How?' she uttered, but he only shrugged silently.

'I don't believe you.'

He didn't speak, stubbornly staring at her, so she leaned over and grasped his arm. 'And Victor? What about him?'

'I told you, your husband is finished. There is nothing I can do for him. But I can save you. You went to very few meetings, you are a woman, and you're pregnant. I can protect you.'

The question burst from her mouth before she could even think. 'But there's a price, right?'

He held her eyes. 'I want you to divorce your husband and marry me.'

She looked at him, speechless, then buried her face in her hands. He was trying to buy her, spare her life if she became his property. And if she left the man she loved. A wave of indignation surged inside her. She couldn't believe all this was happening.

'I know these are not the right circumstances for a declaration,' Morozov said quietly, 'but I am very fond of you.'

'How can you . . .' she started, but he was already on his feet, reaching for his coat.

'Think about it,' he said. 'Talk it over with your husband. Yes or no, he will be tried and sentenced anyway. The only question is your fate. And your baby's. Do you want to have the child? Do you want to die or live? You've got to decide. I don't demand that you love me.'

Slowly she got up. Her knees were shaking.

Morozov stopped at the door, his shoulders slightly hunched, looking oddly vulnerable. 'You don't know me, Tonya Alexandrova, but you must believe me – I know you love your husband. I never wanted to propose to you in such a way. This is a sad situation, and you don't deserve to be humiliated like this. You are a fine woman. I am embarrassed to talk to you like this. But I care about you, and you have no other way out.'

'He is right, you know,' Victor said that night.

She had come to meet him at the Turgenevskaya underground station. Since Morozov's visit she hadn't had a moment of peace. She felt she was slipping out of her mind. What could she do? Dear God, was there no hope for them? Your husband is dead meat, Morozov had said. She was suffocating in the empty apartment; she had run out of the house and wandered in the streets for hours, oblivious of the freezing cold, till the exhaustion and the falling night had chased her back. Morozov's voice kept ringing in her ears: Your husband is dead meat.

Victor came of the station in a crowd of merry schoolgirls with ribbons in their hair, wearing the red scarves of the Communist Youth. The girls swept by them, eagerly chattering, and their happy, careless laughter trailed behind in a silver wake in the crisp evening air. She shuddered. Victor hugged her. He looked distraught, continually glancing around him. She realized Morozov hadn't been lying. Victor apparently knew about the arrests. They didn't exchange a word till they were home. Then she told him about Morozov's offer. It was disgusting, she said, disgusting and degrading, as if she were a slave one could buy and sell.

'Disgusting or not, he is right,' Victor repeated, his voice barely a murmur. She looked at him. His face was white as a sheet. They were standing in the kitchen, and through the paper-thin wall they could hear their drunken neighbour yell at his wife.

'What he told you about the arrests is true,' Victor went on. 'They picked up Halkin at the university. I saw them. One of my students said Fefer was arrested in front of his house.'

She stared at him, stunned, refusing to believe he was saying this. 'You want me to do as he says?'

He shrugged, and suddenly reached for her, pulling her close to him. 'It's your life, Tonya, don't you understand? They'll kill you like a dog. They'll kill all of us.'

'But I love you,' she cried out, as tears flooded her eyes. 'I love you, I don't want to live without you.' She buried her head in his shoulder.

'I love you too,' he whispered. 'You're all my life. But there is no other choice, don't you see?' He was stroking her hair, his fingers trembling. 'Do it for the child, my love,' he said. 'For our baby, Tonya.'

'How can you say this?' she revolted. 'Can you bear the thought that I'll let Morozov kiss me, undress me, sleep with me?'

Victor cupped her face in his hands and stared at her. He was crying too, the tears leaving glistening paths on his ashen skin. 'Do it for our baby, Tonichka,' he repeated.

They didn't sleep all night, lying on the bed, fully dressed, their unsolved dilemma like an invisible wall between them. She stared at the shadows crawling on the ceiling, and her memories carried her back to her youth in Kiev, to the day she had seen Victor for the first time, directing his bashful, disarming smile to her class at the Kirov High School. 'I am your new literature teacher.' And the same shy, handsome youth metamorphosing before her eyes into a charismatic poet, passionately reciting the verses of Pushkin, Mayakovsky, Lermontov, and his own. Then and there, she was infatuated with the young dreamer. On her way home she thought of nothing else but his black eyes, the proud bearing of his head, the delicate hands that gracefully moved as he spoke, accompanying his powerful performance.

She recalled the first time he had looked at her, the first time they were alone, the first time he had touched her. She thought of their secret meetings by the Bogdan Khmelnizki statue, his husky voice and trembling lips when he murmured, 'I love you, Tonichka.' Their decision to elope still seemed unreal, like a dream. She remembered her flight from home, their marriage, the exhausting train journey to Moscow. She loved him so deeply, so totally, and now he was asking her to leave him, to save her own life.

She got up and walked to the window. It was a starry Moscow night, and their snowbound street stretched before her, serene and calm. Morozov was nothing but a figment of her imagination, a character out of a bad dream; soon it would be morning and she would wake up. But she heard Victor move restlessly behind her. He wasn't sleeping. Like her he was frightened. It was at that moment that she made up her mind. She would do anything, anything in the world, to save him. If he died, she would die too. She returned to her bed, reached for Victor and clutched his feverish hand, pressing it to her cheek.

Shortly before dawn, there was a knock on the door. Victor opened it. Morozov entered, escorted by two uniformed KGB lieutenants. 'You're under arrest, Comrade Wolf,' he said softly. Victor grabbed his coat and stepped outside without turning back. Morozov closed the door behind him, looking at Tonya.

'I am sorry,' he said.

She clenched her teeth. After a short silence he spoke again. 'Have you thought about our conversation, Tonya Alexandrova?'

She got up from the bed and went to the window. A big black car was parked by the pavement, its exhaust pipe spewing thick white smoke. She had to make her decision. 'I have one condition,' she said without looking at him. Her throat was constricted. 'I'll do what you say if you promise that Victor will not die.'

'I cannot promise such a thing,' Morozov said coldly. 'There's going to be a trial.'

'I know all about your trials.' Down in the street, she saw the KGB officers pushing Victor into the black car. A woman passing by quickened her pace, looking away. 'You can have Victor sentenced to a prison term,' she went on. 'You have connections. If you sentence him to death, I'd rather die with him.'

She heard Morozov's steps, then he seized her by the shoulders and made her turn back. His eyes burned with anger and his mouth was a thin line. She shivered.

'If he isn't executed, he'll be sent to a labour camp,' he said. 'Is that what you want? It's worse than death. He won't last more than a year, he's so frail.'

'In a year, a lot can happen,' she said stubbornly.

'Not to him,' Morozov said knowingly. Then he added: 'But I can't promise that. He is accused of treason.'

'Then you'd better take me with you,' she said.

'That's a foolish thing to say,' he snapped, shaking his head.

'You are dealing with a foolish woman.'

He stepped back and lit a cigarette, his eyes never leaving hers. 'And if I manage to save his neck?'

She didn't answer.

'I'll see what I can do,' he muttered, and walked out.

The trial started on July 1 and lasted three days. Except for KGB clerks and officers nobody was allowed to attend. Tonya spent most of the time in the cold waiting hall of the Seventh District Popular tribunal, together with the families of the other Jewish writers. They barely spoke; they were badly scared, and Fefer's wife warned her to keep quiet. 'There are KGB agents among us,' she whispered, wringing her hands.

At the end of the third day, eight out of the ten members of the Committee board were found guilty of treason, and sentenced to death. They were executed after their appeal was rejected. The only survivors were Victor Wolf, who was condemned to life imprisonment in a labour camp, and Tonya Wolf who wasn't brought to trial at all. The KGB report established that she had been unaware of the Committee's illegal activities, therefore couldn't be accused of crimes against the state. The seventeen members of the Committee council were severely reprimanded, but not punished. The Committee was disbanded and its archives seized by the KGB.

Tonya had divorced her husband shortly after his arrest and resumed her maiden name, Tonya Gordon. A month after the trial she gave birth to Victor's child, a boy whom she named Alexander, after her father. In the early autumn of 1949 she married Boris Morozov.

The sound of heavy steps approaching her cell made her start and she propped herself on her elbows, cold sweat breaking on her forehead. Were they coming for her already? But the steps faded away, and she closed her eyes, letting out a deep breath. The faces of the boys sailed out of her tormented memory, followed by Victor's gaunt profile, the way she had seen him last, three years ago. It was an evening in mid-July, and the humid breath of summer was smothering the city of Moscow. Tonya had waited for hours outside the Yaroslavski railway station where the political prisoners were herded aboard a Siberia-bound train. She had barely recognized Victor when he trudged by, in chains, in the middle of a group of prisoners. He was bareheaded; his skull had been shaven. He looked old and withered without his shock of black hair. She called his name but he didn't hear, and she suddenly realized that she would never see him again.

She couldn't write to him. Morozov had warned her that if she maintained any contact with her ex-husband, the KGB prosecutors would come after her like bloodhounds; he wouldn't be able to protect her. She heard about Victor only once, from his old mother who lived in Leningrad. He had contracted tuberculosis and was in a critical condition at the camp's hospital. That was more than two years ago. She had mentioned it to Morozov, hoping he could help, but he only shook his head. 'I told you,' he said gently, 'Vorkuta is the living hell. They don't last long over there.'

She wouldn't give up, and had secretly asked her brother Valery to write to Victor; friends and relatives could write to the prisoners once every three months. But Valery's letter had returned with the word 'Unknown' stamped in purple over the address. The purple stamp meant that the prisoner was dead. Poor Victor. At least he didn't suffer any more.

With Morozov she'd had a few years of sheltered existence. He had been good to her, and treated little Alex with tenderness, like his own child. Ten months after their wedding, Tonya's second child was born: Morozov's son, Dimitri. Neither boy was circumcised, for his own sake.

Morozov was very much in love with her, and could refuse her nothing. They lived in a modern apartment on the Kalinin Prospect, and the KGB car with the driver was at her disposal all day long. She shopped at the special stores for government and party officials; food was abundant in their home, and she could buy clothes she had never before dreamt of. One summer they holidayed in a guesthouse for high-ranking officials in Sochi, on the Black Sea; she tasted caviar and champagne for the first time in her life.

After Morozov was promoted to full colonel, they received a six-room dacha – a country house – by the Biserovskoye Lake, barely a two-hour drive from Moscow. They spent most of their weekends and holidays there, and the children couldn't have been happier. Occasionally Tonya herself would even recover enough peace of mind to return to her writing, for a few hours. But her poems were different now, bitter and cynical, full of contained anger.

She had a good life with Morozov, but she didn't love him. Victor had been her only love and she remained faithful to him, at least in her thoughts and feelings. She did her best to conceal her pain from her family. The first time Morozov made love to her, she lay cold and inert as a corpse under his heavy bulk. As she felt the hot spurt of his sperm inside her, she scurried to the bathroom and threw up, disgusted, feeling like a prostitute.

When she returned to bed, she didn't find him; he spent the rest of the night in the other room. But the following night he took her again, making love to her very patiently, very tenderly. She clenched her fists, trying to restrain herself, but her body instinctively responded to her husband's lovemaking. She was swept by self-hatred for her own weakness in betraying Victor. But she was young, lonely, she desperately needed love and tenderness. And Morozov was the only person who could release her from her agonizing solitude.

Victor, however, never left her thoughts. During the day she still behaved more or less normally, but as she put off the bedroom light and closed her eyes, she was assailed by terrible nightmares, the memory of him haunting her dreams. She was obsessed by feelings of guilt for still being alive while he was already rotting in some mass grave in Siberia. When she became pregnant again, she thought she would go mad. Inside her a child was growing – not Victor's but the child of a stranger. This was her ultimate betrayal, she thought, as Morozov's seed grew in her body. Victor kept returning in her dreams, night after night, his caressing voice haunting her, his dark eyes a silent accusation. Quite often she woke up screaming, and found herself in the arms of Morozov, who watched her in silence. He never asked why she screamed; he knew.

His compassion couldn't dispel her loneliness. Besides being her husband, Victor had been her best friend; they had no secrets from each other. Morozov was different: a reserved man, he spoke rarely, and refrained from discussing his work. He told her very little about himself and seemed unwilling to reveal even the most banal episodes of his life. When he would finally divulge a trivial detail from his distant past, he would behave as if he were parting with a fateful state secret. Perhaps it was because of his profession, she thought; information is power, and you never disclose information unless absolutely necessary.

He reluctantly revealed that he was a worker's son from the village of Shepetovka in the Ukraine; he had enlisted in the Red Army before the war, and gone to the Frunze Military Academy. Yes, he had fought in the war. Where? Oh, here and there, in Poland, in Russia, abroad . . . He had married very young, but his wife Marina had been killed during the war. Yes, there were also children. Two little girls, Natasha and Vera. They had died too. At that point he would abruptly stop, his eyes would acquire a distant look, and he would withdraw into himself. That was the moment when he would heavily step towards the old cupboard in the living room and take out the bottle of vodka, which he would drink alone, his head bent low over the glass, a deep frown etched in his forehead.

Yet on the few occasions he had a reason to rejoice – such as when she announced she was pregnant, or at Dimitri's first birthday – he would discard the shield of self-control, and an utterly different man would emerge, lively, spontaneous, totally uninhibited. He had a surprisingly warm voice, and when he sang golden specks would dance in his eyes. A couple of times, when Ukrainian *kazatchok* had blasted from their old radio, he had danced before the children, shouting and whistling, bellowing with laughter, sticking his thumbs in his belt, slapping his boot heels with his open palms; as the mass of undulating brown hair roguishly swayed over his forehead, and an impish smile fluttered on his mouth, he looked suddenly young and mischievous. Here is Morozov for you, she thought, pleasantly surprised. Still, he never told her what had transformed the young Ukrainian with the melodious voice and the infectious laugh into the lonely tormented man she had married.

Lately Morozov had changed. He had never raised his voice to her or the children before; now he became tense, preoccupied. In the evenings he would sit for hours by the table, the bottle of vodka at his elbow. Often he would enter the boys' room and stand by their beds, watching them sleep. Tonya sensed his anguish and kept asking him what was wrong; he stubbornly refused to answer.

Until that night, a couple of weeks ago, when he had woken her up. He looked distressed, and for the first time ever she discerned a note of despair in his voice.

'Something terrible is happening,' he started, and she jumped out of bed, alarmed. She shivered in her thin nightgown. He lapsed into silence, apparently trying to collect his thoughts. 'Lately the Kremlin is waging a war against the Jews. We have been secretly arresting Jewish leaders all over the country. The orders come directly from Stalin. He has become obsessed.'

She stepped towards him, gauchely tying the belt of her robe. He had never spoken like this, not about Stalin whom he worshipped.

Morozov's breathing was shallow, he spoke in short outbursts. 'Stalin is not himself any more,' he went on. 'He is convinced there is a Jewish plot against his life. An international plot. Concocted in Washington. Controlled by the American Jews.'

She was stunned. 'This is insane,' she said.

'Last night we received direct orders from Stalin to arrest nine doctors, in Moscow and Leningrad. All but one of them are Jews. Stalin accused them of planning to assassinate him and some other communist leaders. Beria even has a witness.'

'A witness? I don't believe it.'

He nodded slowly. 'Dr Lidia Timashuk. A former KGB agent who used to work at the Kremlin hospital. She says she has proof of the conspiracy, she heard the doctors planning the assassinations. She also went through the files of high-ranking patients, and can prove that the Jewish doctors gave them the wrong treatment, in order to cause their deaths. She will testify against the Jews.' He touched her shoulder. 'Your brother is among them.'

'Valery?' She shivered. Valery Gordon was one of Russia's leading haematologists. 'Valery planning to assassinate Stalin?'

Morozov nodded. 'Valery, yes. And Professor Kaplan, Professor Rodoy, Kozlovska . . .'

'This is insane,' she repeated, her heart thumping wildly. 'Nobody will believe this rubbish. Stalin believes that?'

'Stalin wants them shot,' Morozov said bluntly. 'Claims that they have already poisoned Zhdanov and Scherbakov.'

She was overwhelmed by the enormity of the accusation. 'But they . . . they're long dead,' she stammered. Both party dignitaries had died of natural causes.

'Stalin says the Jewish doctors murdered them on orders from Washington. He also says' – Morozov hesitated a second – 'that the intermediary between the Jewish doctors and their American manipulators was Solomon Mikhoels.'

'My God,' she murmured. Mikhoels had been the Chairman of the Anti-Fascist Committee; his murder by the KGB, three years ago, had triggered the Committee liquidation.

'The Jewish doctors will be tried and shot in the next few weeks,' Morozov said, then averted his eyes. 'But there is worse. Stalin ordered us to arrest all the surviving members of the Anti-Fascist Committee. All the former council members.'

She suddenly understood and looked at him in horror.

He slowly nodded, his face livid. 'You too. They'll come for you tonight or tomorrow. I have no power in this affair. Beria has taken the matter out of my hands, and charged the First Directorate with the entire operation.'

The First Directorate, Tonya knew, was in charge of operations abroad. Counter-espionage inside Russia was under the control of the Second Directorate, of which Morozov was deputy-director. 'I tried to stop them,' he said, 'but they wouldn't even talk to me. This time I am helpless.'

'My God,' she murmured. 'And the children? What about the children?'

Morozov looked at her, then shuddered, as if under the impact of a physical blow. A shrill, desperate wail burst from his chest, and his huge body was shaken by hoarse, spasmodic sobs. He leaned on the wall, turning his back to her, crying. Tonya saw a broken man, whose faith had shattered to pieces.

They had come for her last Sunday, four KGB officers. Morozov stood in the living room, head shrunk between his shoulders, watching them take her away. She knew this meant the end for him too, in a few weeks, perhaps a couple of months. First he would be kicked out of the KGB, then arrested and probably shot. In Russia they didn't do things halfway.

They brought her to the Lubyanka, and threw her in this cell. She was supposed to be isolated from the other prisoners, but one of the guards told her that all the Jewish writers were in the same block. Her brother and the other doctors were in another prison.

She wasn't even brought to trial, and in a way was grateful to the KGB for that. She was relieved at the thought she wouldn't have to go through that same charade, the way they had done with Victor. She was ready to die. She had got used to the idea years ago, when they had taken Victor away. But the children? Good God, who would take care of the children? They were so small! She loved them both, but feared most for little Alex. Boris would protect Dimitri, he was his child, perhaps he would send him to his mother; but Alex, a Jewish boy of three, would be thrown on the street! What could she do, how could she help?

She got up and approached the near wall. Boris had told her once about a heroine of the French Resistance, Suzanne Spaak, who had covered the walls of her cell at Fresnes prison with more than three hundred inscriptions, all intended for her husband. After her death, Claude Spaak had found the messages. Morozov would remember that story. He'd certainly ask to examine her cell. She removed the Star of David from its chain, and with its sharp point etched in the mortar her last message for her family.

'Boris,' she scratched, 'save the children Nina can help with Alex love love to you all . . .'

But before she signed her name, the sound of marching boots filled the corridor and the door of her cell squeaked on its hinges.

Shortly before dawn, the guards led them into the east court of the Lubyanka. The blizzard had finally died, and the courtyard was covered with pure virgin snow. The guards herded them toward the far wall, where they stood in line, facing the rough irregular stones. They were not allowed to look back. The stones were pockmarked with a multitude of black scars and grooves. Bullet marks, Tonya thought. So many bullets had ricocheted from the stone wall, after accomplishing their grisly task.

She shivered. On her right, she heard low, muffled sobbing. She turned her head. Bodenkin was standing beside her, holding his baggy pants with his hands, his coat open; tears streamed down his unshaven face. He looked so helpless, Tonya thought, so vulnerable. She remembered his powerful verses, his moving 'Ode to the Unknown Soldier'. She recalled the fire burning in his eyes, and his ringing, defying voice, echoing in Moscow's Taganka Hall as he read his electrifying poems.

Beside him she made out a humped shape. Laufer. And farther down Segal and Belkind and Ribitzky. The gentle Bronstein, the gaunt, brooding Halperin, and of course Plotnikov, the cancer-ridden philosopher. They were all here, the greatest Jewish writers and poets of the Soviet Union, destined to die a traitor's death at the hands of a paranoid dictator.

Perhaps it was at this very place that the KGB officers had also shot Fefer, Halkin, Slavin and the other members of the Committee board after their mock trial four years ago. Would the story of this infamy ever be told? Would they be remembered?

She stood ankle deep in the snow but didn't feel the cold. She tried not to think about what was going to happen. On her left, Horowitz had started to pray, swaying back and forth. 'Shema Israel,' he chanted loudly, 'Adonai Eloheinu . . .' Other voices joined him, hesitant at first, then confident, defiant.

She didn't know how to pray, she had never been in a synagogue in her life; Lenin had said that religion was the opium of the masses. But now she joined the chorus, trying to repeat the unintelligible words after the men. 'Shema Israel,' she murmured, turning for the first time in her life to the ancient God of her nation. God, have mercy on the children, please help my children, they are so vulnerable, please protect them, they carry me in their blood, and Alex is Victor's son.

A shot echoed on her left and she heard the soft thud of a body in the snow. Her heart leapt wildly in her chest. The execution had started.

Chapter Two

From a barred window on the third floor, Colonel Boris Morozov was watching the inner court of the Lubyanka. His eyes were riveted to the slender woman facing the execution wall, her long golden hair spilling over her shoulders. He had been waiting by that window since midnight; he had seen Tonya coming out of the cellars, together with the other prisoners. In a few minutes she would be dead. He shuddered. God, how he loved her! She was the second woman he had ever loved, and the second one he was going to lose.

He had married Marina, his first wife, two and a half years before the war. Boris Morozov was then a young officer in the NKVD, the Soviet security service, with brilliant prospects for the future. He was a fervent bolshevik, an admirer of Stalin, willing to devote his life to the defence of his country and the triumph of communism. He owed the party everything he had achieved: the house by the railroad depot, his education at the Shepetovka High School and his training at the Frunze Officers' Academy.

Actually he owed all this to his father, a burly railroad worker and dyed in the wool revolutionary, who had been killed in 1917 during the assault on Tzaritzin, the Royal city. Tzaritzin was now Stalingrad, and his dead father a hero of the revolution. As the family of a fallen hero, Boris and his mother, Varvara, enjoyed special privileges: a pension for her, free tuition for him, and a decrepit wooden house expropriated from a Polish merchant, who had escaped across the border, only twenty miles away. Shepetovka being a border town, it had a mixed Polish-Ukrainian population. During the civil war and the following Polish-Soviet conflict, the region had passed from hand to hand several times, and many people had relatives on the other side of the border.

Boris had known Marina Arbatova since their childhood. She was a willowy, mischievous girl with irresistible dimples in her cheeks.

Marina's mother was Polish; after the Polish-Soviet War of 1920 her brothers had escaped to Poland. One of them, Henrik Leshchinski, had joined the Polish army as a career officer.

For Boris, Marina was the prettiest girl on earth. And he was the happiest man when she agreed to marry him, shortly after his posting to the local headquarters of NKVD border intelligence. Their marriage had been a three-day-long feast, with guests flocking from all over the Ukraine. Through his connections Boris had even arranged a special visa for Marina's uncle, Henrik, who was serving with a Polish border garrison. Henrik came in civilian clothes; none of the guests suspected he was a Polish officer.

After the wedding Boris had brought Marina to his mother's house. The slender, blue-eyed girl with the silvery laugh and the heavy golden braids had given him two children, two little daughters. The day Boris's younger daughter, Vera, was born, Hitler had attacked Poland and the Second World War had started.

Then the Red Army had invaded Poland on its turn. One night Boris and Marina were awakened by the roar of engines; from their window they had watched the clumsy T-35 tanks race through the unpaved streets of Shepetovka, heading for the Polish border. Only later was Boris to learn about the secret pact between the USSR and Nazi Germany, dividing Poland between the two countries. Boris was thrilled. The radio of the Ukraine, broadcasting from Kiev, announced that Stalin was getting even with Poland, which had treacherously attacked the Soviet Union after the revolution.

The radio commentators kept warning the nation about the danger of a foreign aggression against the motherland. The day of the first winter storm, Boris reported to NKVD headquarters at Gorodok and was dispatched to Moscow. There he was assigned to the 700-men strong Battalion 121, made up entirely of NKVD officers. An old barracks of the Tzar's dragoons in Petrovskoye Forest served as the battalion's headquarters; the camp was heavily guarded and the battalion's very existence shrouded in secrecy. Boris was elated; he was now a member of an elite unit.

Morozov had joined the NKVD, driven by a burning ambition to make his way to the top. The pay was much better than in the regular army; officers who won the trust of the Kremlin could be swiftly promoted, achieve high status in the party and even reach the holy of holies of the Soviet regime, the Politburo. Besides, Morozov had been always thrilled by the secrecy of intelligence work. The NKVD's formal status was merely a government ministry, dealing with internal affairs. Actually it was the most powerful organization in the country. It had swallowed the former secret services, the revolutionary Cheka and the bloody GPU. The NKVD activities tracked down enemies of the State, and carried out secret operations abroad. The organization was headed by Stalin's trusted companion, Lavrenti Beria.

Beria was dreaded. His name was never pronounced aloud, but always whispered; he was feared even by the members of the Politburo. He controlled the secret police, the militia, parts of the army and the secret services; he ruled over the prisons and the labour camps. Beria was rumoured to be a ruthless master-spy, who wouldn't hesitate to kill with his bare hands for Stalin. Boris had seen him when he came to inspect the battalion: a short, balding man in general's uniform, with a sallow face, wire-rimmed spectacles and thin, bloodless lips.

In August 1940, Battalion 121 was dispatched to White Russia. The officers were ordered to remove their epaulettes, medals and officer's stars from their uniforms. They were issued revolvers and submachine guns; heavy crates of ammunition were loaded on the trucks that were parked outside their barracks. Boris and his companions could hardly hide their excitement: they were on their way to a top-secret mission.

Their journey lasted more than four days. In the early morning of the fifth day, after passing through several roadblocks and taking a bumpy dirt road, they reached their destination. As the engine was turned off at last, Morozov impatiently pulled aside the tarpaulin that covered their truck and looked around, stretching his arms. His whole body ached from the long journey. They had stopped in a large clearing, in the middle of a forest. Several tents stood in the shade and a couple of soldiers were cooking thick yellow porridge in a field kitchen. Boris jumped down, enchanted by the beauty of the awakening forest in a summer dawn; in the luxuriant foliage birds were singing.

Boris lit a cigarette and inhaled the acrid smoke. 'What's the name of this place?' he asked a soldier who was learning on a tree.

'Katyn, Comrade,' the soldier said. 'The Forest of Katyn.'

They spent the morning setting up their tents. They didn't know yet why they had been brought here, in such secrecy. In the afternoon they were assembled in the middle of the clearing. All other personnel – soldiers, drivers, cooks – were ordered to leave the area. Colonel Gregoriev, the Battalion commander, came to face his men. He was a wiry man with a hawkish, pockmarked face. He was accompanied by a cadaverous civilian in a leather jacket.

'We are here to accomplish a task for the motherland,' he said curtly. 'It is not a pleasant task, but it is a vital one. Very shortly, a number of Polish officers will be brought over. They were captured in Poland during our recent operations. These officers have fought against our country and are dangerous enemies of the Soviet nation. Since 1920 the Poles, helped by an international capitalist conspiracy, have been trying to smother the socialist revolution. We are here to assure that they will never again lead their soldiers against the Soviet Union.'

Boris and the officer standing beside him, a young Armenian, exchanged baffled looks. What did Gregoriev mean? But their commander went on, in the same dry, matter-of-fact voice: 'Each platoon has been assigned its part of the operation. Your platoon commander will brief you on how to proceed. Dismissed!'

'What does he mean?' Boris asked the Armenian.

'Don't you understand?' a third officer intervened, grinning. 'We're going to bump off the bloody bastards.'

Good, Boris thought, excellent. It's time to get rid of the Polish sonofabitches. As a Ukrainian he knew how treacherous they were. He recalled the revolution years, when the bloody Poles had received with open arms any enemy of the Reds who crossed the border; they had let the Whites use the Polish territory as a springboard for their assaults on the Ukraine. And after the civil war, when Russia was on her knees, the Poles had stabbed her in the back, starting a war against her. It was a privilege for him, a Ukrainian, to help settle his people's account with the Poles.

In the evening, the Polish officers started arriving in covered trucks, escorted by Soviet soldiers. They were dressed in the mud-stained uniforms in which they had been captured. The operation was carried out with utmost efficiency. The Katyn Forest was divided into large lots, and each NKVD platoon was assigned several locations. As soon as a truck arrived at the clearing, a platoon would take charge of the Poles, tie their hands behind their backs, and march them to one of the lots. Then the NKVD men would position themselves behind the prisoners, their weapons drawn, and wait.

At every hour, on the hour, they would shoot their prisoners in the back with automatic weapons, and finish them with pistols. At those moments, burst of gunfire would reverberate throughout the forest, as if a formidable battle was being fought. There were strict orders not to fire a weapon at other times, in order to prevent rioting among the prisoners, who didn't know what fate awaited them; they had been told they were being transferred to a new camp. The bodies were left where they fell, to be buried by other units. Then the platoon would return to the clearing, to receive the next shipment of prisoners.

The operation lasted for three days and nights. Boris Morozov accomplished his task to the best of his ability. The first time he had hesitated, just for a split second; he had never killed a man before. But he had quickly recovered, and shot the Pole, a young boy with dishevelled blond hair whose shoulders were shivering; he had guessed he was going to die. Boris hoped nobody had noticed his hesitation. After the first, the rest were easy.

For three days he behaved like a robot, herding the prisoners from the clearing, arming his weapon, killing, and killing again. He knew he was doing the right thing; at the NKVD school he had heard rumours about mass executions of enemies of the revolution, not only foreigners but even Russians. That was a necessary evil; the Red Terror was the self-defence of the revolution. Even Lenin had said that class enemies should be mercilessly annihilated.

Still, he felt oddly confused: he hadn't expected the Polish officers to be so numerous, they were killing them in thousands. Most of them were young, almost kids; they didn't look like enemies of the revolution. But he kept his thoughts to himself. An NKVD officer from Company 3, who had questioned the orders, had been court-martialled and shot by Colonel Gregoriev himself, in front of his comrades.

On the second day, new orders were issued. The killings couldn't be concealed from the arriving prisoners any more; bodies were strewn all over the forest. The Soviet officers were instructed to force the Poles, at gunpoint, to run to the closest lot, and shoot them without delay.

In the morning of the third day, while the forest was echoing with gunfire and desperate cries for help, a lean, swarthy officer emerged beside him. 'Are you Morozov?' he asked.

Boris nodded.

'You'd better come with me, somebody wants you.'

They ran across the forest, between the heaps of freshly killed bodies. Giant bulldozers were digging common graves and shoving the corpses inside; soldiers from an auxiliary unit were pouring quicklime over the dead; it was summer and the bodies had to be buried quickly, to prevent the outbreak of epidemics.

'Here we are,' the officer said, short of breath. They were both sweating profusely.

In a small clearing, about twenty bodies were strewn in the grass, apparently shot only minutes before. But another Pole, a major, was squatting under a tree, guarded by a couple of Russians.

'That's him,' the swarthy officer said.

One of the Russians, a big fat man, turned towards Morozov. A cigarette was dangling from his lower lip. 'You're Morozov?' he said.

'We've got a surprise for you. This guy here kept yelling your name, so we decided to save him for you.'

Morozov stared back in astonishment. 'My name? How did he know . . .'

'He didn't,' the fat Russian said. 'He kept yelling: Morozov! Boris Morozov! Does anybody know Morozov? Sacha, here' – he pointed at his friend – 'said that there was a Morozov in the Seventh Platoon, so we sent for you. You know him?' He approached the Pole and kicked him, none too gently, making him turn. The prisoner raised his face. His cheeks were covered with bristle; a purple welt ran from his left eye to the line of his jaw. His lips were cracked and his eyes filled with horror. They suddenly lit up as he saw Morozov. 'Boris!' he groaned in Russian, 'Borka, it's you! Thank God!'

Morozov froze, thunderstruck. The man was Henrik Leshchinski, Marina's uncle.

'Borka dear, tell them who I am!' Henrik tried to get up, but the fat Russian hit him viciously and he fell back, blood trickling from the corner of his mouth.

'Yes, who is he?' the Russian asked, suddenly suspicious.

Morozov stared at Henrik, unable to utter a word. He recalled Henrik's warm hug at his wedding with Marina, the beautiful vase of fine Dresden china he had brought them. They had drunk for hours, then danced the Gopak, arms on each other's shoulders. In a flash he saw Marina in her long white dress and colourful Ukrainian hat, clapping her hands and laughing.

'Borka, help me,' Henrik implored, his voice breaking. 'For Marina's sake. God will bless you, please!'

Feverish thoughts raced through his mind. Henrik was Marina's uncle, he was family, he wasn't an enemy of the Soviet Union! But he was a Pole, he had seen the massacre at Katyn. He had to die. Nobody could save him now. And what about me? Morozov thought. What about Marina and the children? If it was reported that a relative of his was a Polish officer he would be exiled to a prison camp, or even shot as a security risk. And Marina, too, would be taken away and never seen again; he knew how these things were done. He felt a sudden surge of hatred toward the bloody Pole, who was threatening his career, his family and his life, by popping up right now. You bastard, he muttered inwardly, you shouldn't have joined the Polish Army in the first place. You've asked for it. And he reached for his gun.

'Well, what is he to you?' the fat Russian repeated, his porcine eyes gazing at him suspiciously.

Henrik understood what was going to happen. 'For the love of Christ, Boris, don't do it!' He joined his hands in prayer, tears streaming down his face. 'God will never forgive you, Borka, I beg you . . .'

Morozov pointed his gun at Henrik's distorted face and squeezed the trigger.

Late that night they completed their grisly task. A convoy of trucks was waiting for them at the camp site. Before boarding the vehicles, they had to line by a long table and sign Oath of Secrecy declarations by the flickering light of petrol lamps. According to Boris's friends, they had shot between twelve and fifteen thousand Poles. When their trucks left the forest, the bulldozers were still at work, burying the bodies, layer after layer, in the black Bielorussian earth.

Inside the dark truck an ebullient atmosphere reigned. Boris's friends were joking and singing, releasing the tension that had built inside them in the last few days. He didn't take part in the rejoicing. Henrik's desperate plea, and his imploring eyes, kept haunting him. He shuddered, recalling Henrik's last words. 'God will never forgive you!' He wasn't a believer, of course, only his old mother believed in God; still, he couldn't overcome his torment. He had murdered Marina's uncle, a man who had done him no wrong. And all the others he had killed, were they all enemies? What had the young kids done? If there was a God, he thought, he would be punished for his crime.

These maddening thoughts kept haunting him during the long, bitter years of the war. They didn't leave him a moment's peace when he served in Latvia, where the NKVD was laying its security networks; when he was attached as a counter-espionage specialist to Koniev's Army after Hitler's invasion of Russia; when he became intelligence officer of the autonomous Smolensk partisans, following the Viazma débâcle; and when he marched into the ruins of Shepetovka with Zhukov's victorious forces, in the spring of 1944.

The Ukraine had been under German occupation since the summer of 1941. Morozov hadn't seen his family for almost five years. He gunned his American-made jeep along the black, gutted houses of Shepetovka, tortured by dark forebodings. The railroad depot was a heap of rubble; most of the houses behind it had been razed. His own house, though, had remained miraculously intact. He ran toward it, but stopped at the threshold, alarmed by the silence. A house with children couldn't be so silent.

'Borka? Borka, is that you?'

At the top of the narrow staircase stood his mother, older, bent, dressed in rags, yet apparently healthy. She had survived! But he only had to cast a look at Varvara Morozova's face to understand that his darkest premonitions had come true.

Marina had been hanged by the Nazis a few weeks after they had occupied Shepetovka, his mother told him that night. A traitor had informed them she was the wife of a NKVD officer; they had shot his little daughters too. There was not even a grave to visit, Varvara Morozova whispered, wiping her tears; all the civilians murdered by the Nazis had been buried in mass graves outside the town.

Boris listened in horror. In a strange way, his mother's story only confirmed something he had known all along. He hadn't expected to find his family alive. He didn't tell his mother a word about Katyn, that was a secret. But deep in his heart, he felt that the death of Marina and his children was his punishment for the murder of Henrik Leshchinski. In spite of his atheism, he couldn't escape this feeling. And he knew he was going to be haunted by his deed for the rest of his life.

It took him three weeks to track down the man who had betrayed Marina to the Nazis. He was Genadi Arkhipenko, one of the Ukrainian traitors who aspired to create an independent Ukraine with German help. Morozov found him hiding in a barn outside the village of Polyanka. He settled his score with Arkhipenko using a sturdy bayonet he had taken from a dead German soldier.

Soon afterwards he left Shepetovka, determined never to return; he wanted to wipe out that chapter from his life. He asked to be attached to Smersh, the top-secret unit created by General Abakumov. Smersh was an abbreviation of the words *Smiert Shpionam* – Death to the Spies. Smersh had been charged with tracking down spies, traitors and collaborators with the enemy, and liquidating them without mercy.

Boris, now a captain, plunged into his new job with fanatical devotion. In Russia, then Poland and Germany, his unit advanced with the Red Army, and combed the liberated lands for Russian traitors, Polish fascists, SS officers on the run. Boris was particularly keen on hunting down Ukrainian traitors; he felt he had to avenge Marina's death on each and every Ukrainian collaborator. Marina's memory haunted him wherever he went; he never touched a woman.

After the war ended, he spent some time in Berlin, hounding families of Ukrainian traitors that had been sent over by the German authorities; he dispatched the women and the children to prison camps in Siberia. Back home, he was promoted to major and assigned to the hunt of Ukrainian counter-revolutionaries.

After a crash course in English Morozov was sent to Western Europe, to track down Ukrainian emigrés, planning to set up subversive cells in his native province. He personally chased two Ukrainians who were on their way to America, to establish an organization financed by the CIA. He followed the two traitors on to the Paris-Le Havre train and shot them in their compartment.

His next task was to set penetration routes and communication systems for Soviet agents tracking Ukrainian exiles in the West. In 1948 he operated in New York, posing as the driver of the Soviet Consul. This chapter in his career came to an end when his cover was blown by Yuri Sossnov, one of the first KGB defectors. Morozov escaped to Mexico by the skin of his teeth.

Back in Moscow, he was summoned to the office of General Takachenko in the Lubyanka KGB headquarters. Takachenko, an old Chekist with a hollow chest and a dropping moustache, was in charge of the Second Chief Directorate. He had a deep, dry cough that seemed to rip his frail body. 'We are creating a department of Jewish Affairs,' Takachenko said, and went into a coughing spasm. 'Comrade Beria expects some trouble from that direction.' He didn't specify what kind of trouble. 'We want you to head the department.'

He accepted the appointment rather indifferently. He wasn't interested in Jews and had had little to do with them in the past. As a child, in Shepetovka, he used to drift with the other kids through the streets where the Jews lived, throw stones at their windows and taunt the bearded men in the funny hats; or pull the sidelocks of children, who ran away screaming in a strange language. But he had never gone beyond that.

One of the first assignments of his department was to investigate the treason charges against the members of the Jewish Anti-Fascist Writers' Committee. The instructions had come directly from Beria's desk, accompanied by a thick file. Actually no investigation was needed; all the evidence had already been diligently gathered. Still he had put his men on the job, and being a field man himself, had directed the inquiry in person.

And one night, at a public meeting of the Anti-Fascists, he thought he saw a ghost, Marina's ghost: a young woman with the same golden hair, the same smile, the same lithe body. For years he had thought a part of him had died, and he would never look at a woman again. But that night he didn't sleep; as old wounds reopened, and the old pain pierced him as a knife, he also felt, for the first time in years, a faint glimmer of hope. The woman he had seen was a Jewish poetess. Tonya Gordon-Wolf.

The following morning he sent his secretary to buy Tonya Gordon's books; and stayed in his office until late, bent over the small volumes. He liked Tonya Gordon's poems; but the reading turned into a torment, as Marina's face kept emerging before him. Her voice echoed in his ears, reciting the verses printed on the white pages. He could hear Marina's voice ringing with youthful enthusiasm when he reached the poem praising the heroes of the National War; it huskily whispered in his ear when he turned the page and plunged into a passionate love poem; and broke into thousand chimes of crystalline laughter as he read the funny children's tales. Boris even imagined hearing the gleeful laughter of his little daughters, echoing their mother's delight.

In the following days he put his hand on every poem, tale or essay Tonya Gordon had written. He sent a KGB photographer with a concealed camera to her address, and made him wait in the street for hours until he got some pictures. When the photographer brought him a batch of glossy portraits, he studied them for a long time, drinking in every detail of Tonya's face. He put most of the photographs in his right hand drawer, but kept four of them on his desk. In one of the pictures, his favourite, she was smiling at somebody while the wind playfully blew her long hair across her face; and for him it was Marina smiling at him again, Marina laughingly pulling aside the strands of her golden hair.

He requested Tonya's file from the department's archives, and found out all about her: her childhood in Kiev, the departure of her sister for Palestine and then America, her brother's medical studies and present employment at the Vassiliev Hospital in Leningrad; Tonya's elopement with Victor Wolf in 1940, their marriage and move to Moscow, which had probably saved their lives. Two months after their departure, the Nazis had occupied Kiev and brutally slaughtered its Jewish population.

It dawned on him that he had become obsessed with Tonya Gordon. He caught himself inventing excuses to justify – to himself! – passing by her house on Kirova Street almost every day. At the meetings of the Anti-Fascist Committee he listened to her reading her poems; he even dared to ask for her autograph. She agreed with a smile. No, she didn't have the same dimples as Marina, nor the same silvery laughter. Yet she was poignantly beautiful; and in her eyes, her voice, her work, he discovered a romantic streak and a shrewd intelligence that Marina had never had.

And he realised that he would stop at nothing to win that woman.

Standing now before the window, he passed an unsteady hand over his hair. He had won Tonya using all the tricks of his trade. First, to earn the confidence of his superiors, he had volunteered to carry out the liquidation of Mikhoels in Minsk; he had driven the huge Gaz truck that had run the old man over on Oktyabrskaya Street when he was on his way to his cousin's home. After delivering the writer's dead body to KGB headquarters, he was given free hand in the Anti-Fascist Committee affair. He never told Tonya, of course, that he was Mikhoels's assassin.

But the most terrible secret he kept from her was his role in her husband's downfall.

The truth was that Victor Wolf was as white as the driven snow. In the files Morozov had received from Beria there was not one shred of evidence against Victor and Tonya Wolf. Their names weren't even on the list of suspected Jewish writers. That was bad. As long as Victor Wolf was free, Morozov couldn't even dream of possessing Tonya Gordon. If he wanted to conquer the woman, he had to remove the husband. He spent some sleepless nights planning his scheme and fabricating false evidence against Victor Wolf. He planted in the Jewish writers' file fake reports of Victor's contacts with foreign diplomats, fake letters supposedly exchanged between Wolf and Jewish leaders in America. Morozov got the false documents from the forgers of Service A, First Chief Directorate. He only had to tell them what he needed, and they delivered the goods. Nobody questioned the orders of a KGB colonel.

In less than two weeks, he had built an ironclad case against Victor Wolf. The frame-up was perfect; when the file was transferred to the Prosecutor General, Victor was accused of treason and arrested. Morozov was too excited by his success to dwell on the moral aspects of his deeds. What counted was that Victor Wolf had been removed from the scene. And Tonya, alone, pregnant and frightened, had dropped into his hands like a ripe fruit.

He wasn't so young any more. The years, the war, the loss of his family had made him a bitter man. Even his promotion to Deputy Director of the Directorate hadn't dispelled his melancholy. But Tonya's presence at his side made him happy again, although he knew she didn't love him. He treated little Alex as a son, perhaps because he had sent his father to Vorkuta. When he came home in the evening, he liked playing with the little fellow. And when his own son Dimitri was born, his joy knew no limits.

He had managed the impossible: to pick up the pieces of his shattered life. He had a family again, a beautiful wife, a little son. When Dimitri was two years old, they had travelled to Shepetovka, to visit his old mother; Boris wanted her to meet her grandson. He looked forward to that trip with a mixture of exhilaration and secret apprehension; he feared the surge of painful memories of the past. How would he face the places and the nights that were so closely connected with Marina's memory? But to his surprise nothing happened. When he saw the old house at the end of Goats' Lane – since renamed Red Cavalry Street – he felt a slight pang, no more. And he realized with wonder that Tonya had gradually supplanted Marina in his heart.

But just when his suffering seemed to be over, the troubles had started. Like distant thunder, heralding the storm, the first bad omen had appeared far away, in Czechoslovakia. The former Foreign Minister, Rudolf Slanski, and twenty other men, most of them Jews, were arrested, tried and found guilty of spying for the British. Most of them were hanged. The communiques stressed their Jewish origins. Zorin, the KGB liaison officer with the Czechs, told Morozov the trial had been remote-controlled by the Kremlin.

A few weeks later, the anti semitic wave reached Moscow. On arriving in his office one morning, Morozov found out that all the high-ranking KGB officers of Jewish origin had been arrested. They included General Raikhman, Head of Counter-Intelligence, General Grauer, Deputy Director of the Fifth Chief Directorate, and Colonel Gorsky, who had handled, in London, the famous Kim Philby. The same day Mikhail Borodin, Lenin's old companion and Chiang-Kai Shek's Soviet adviser, was thrown into prison where he was later to die; his son was incarcerated in the Lubyanka cellars.

'It seems, Boris Artemovitch,' General Takachenko said to him between bouts of coughing, 'that somebody' – he looked up, then lowered his eyes – 'has declared war on the Jews.'

Morozov nodded, acknowledging the mute allusion to Stalin. 'I didn't know . . .' he started.

'No, you didn't,' The skeletal general was staring at him oddly. 'And that's rather disturbing, my boy.'

'We should be the first to know,' Morozov said. 'After all, I'm in charge of Jewish Affairs.'

'The matter is out of your hands.' Again the odd, meaningful stare. 'Perhaps somebody doesn't trust the department any more.'

The meaning of Takachenko's hints hit him only when he returned to his office. He had fallen from grace because he had married a Jewess, a former member of the Anti-Fascist Committee.

Besides, like any other KGB priest, he had his enemies; officers who held a grudge against him for something he had done, others who coveted his position. They needed only a hint that his loyalty was suspect to throw themselves upon him in a wolfpack. They had certainly noticed the signs: he wasn't trusted any more, they could tear him to pieces.

His suspicions turned to certainty in the following weeks. A wave of anti-semitic measures swept the country, but Morozov's department was the last to learn of every one. The Jewish theatre, Jewish newspapers and restaurants in Moscow were closed, and many Jewish employees of state bodies fired. The Jewish wives of Soviet officials were arrested; among them was Zhemchuzina Molotova, the wife of Stalin's former Foreign Minister.

Morozov learned of it from bits and pieces of gossip reaching his office. He was kept out of the operation. All the arrests and the dismissals were carried out by the First Chief Directorate, although its ostensible function – espionage abroad – had nothing to do with Jewish affairs. For the first time in his life, Morozov felt a pang of fear. In the KGB, being bypassed by one's superiors was equivalent to a first step towards the gallows.

What could he do? he kept asking himself. How could he save Tonya and the children? And his own neck? But there was nobody he could turn to. The only possible way lay in defection to the West. But he knew that he would never turn traitor to his country.

While he was helplessly wondering what blow would come next, the affair of the Jewish doctors exploded. Then came Tonya's turn.

Desperate, he requested a meeting with Beria who flatly refused to see him. And Morozov understood what this refusal meant: soon after Tonya died, it would be his turn.

Yesterday, after the children had seen Tonya for the last time, he had taken them home, then returned to the Lubyanka. He had spent the night in his office, slumped behind his desk, swallowing glass after glass of fiery vodka. As a faint grey light had crept into his room, he had woodenly stepped to the window. And now, at the outbreak of dawn, Tonya was going to die.

Morozov tried to look away. When they had given him this office, the intendance officer had joked about the 'show' that he could watch once in a while from his window. No twisted mind could ever have imagined, though, that the 'show' might turn into the most painful torture ever inflicted on a man – having to watch his beloved's death. He could turn his back to the window, or go out, but he wouldn't . He was morbidly drawn to the sight down below, as the hare is mesmerized by the deadly stare of the snake.

He closed his eyes, then looked down again. The execution court was small, sunk in deep shadow. Several officers were moving behind the prisoners lined against the wall, leaving deep tracks in the snow. A colonel came out of the building and stood in the middle of the court. He must have said something, for the soldiers quickly retreated. A sturdy Georgian officer approached the prisoner on the extreme right and drew his pistol.

Morozov leaned forward and felt the cold glass against his burning forehead. There she was, the woman he loved with such passion, with such despair. And he couldn't do a thing to save her. God, he felt so helpless, watching her as she stood facing the wall, waiting for the single shot in the base of her skull. They had taken her only, they hadn't dared to touch him. But he was living on borrowed time. Soon they would come for him as well.

He looked down again. The execution was under way. Several bodies lay in the snow, their limbs twisted, red stains spreading around their heads. He swayed as the squat Georgian officer trudged through the snow and stood behind Tonya. She must have heard him for she straightened up, defiantly throwing back her head. The Georgian raised his pistol. Morozov swallowed painfully. He was paralysed, unable to move, unable to utter a sound. He didn't hear the shot, the double windows were too thick.

He saw Tonya shudder, then she slumped slowly, almost gracefully, the golden hair fanning around her head, her blood trickling onto the pure white snow.

He reached for the table beside him for support. Tonya is dead, he said to himself. Tonya is no more. It is not a nightmare, it is real. Tonya is gone. Soon he would be gone too, perhaps the same way – a bleak dawn, at Lubyanka prison.

Hours later a hesitant knock on the door made him start. He had been sitting in his armchair, shoulders sagging, eyes unseeing, sunk in black torpor. He got up painfully; he felt as if every drop of energy had been drained from his body. 'Come in,' he muttered, and turned to the window.

The stone-paved court was empty. The bodies had been taken away, the snow swept clean; nothing indicated that a bloody execution had taken place down there a couple of hours ago. A wild thought flashed through his mind. Perhaps it had all been a nightmare? Perhaps Tonya was still alive? As the door behind him opened the routine sounds of a day in the office invaded the room – phones ringing, footsteps on the staircase, the distant laugh of a young man. Perhaps it had been his sick imagination only?

But as he turned back, he saw his orderly, the cadaverous Arkadi Dookhin, standing awkwardly at the door, avoiding his eyes. 'They said I should give you this, Comrade Colonel,' Dookhin said. In his outstretched hand gold dully gleamed.

He took from Dookhin the heavy gold chain with the Star of David. Tonya's star. She had worn it until her last moment. He absently fingered it, when he suddenly noticed that one of its edges was slightly twisted, and some grains of uneven grey dust had stuck to it. He stared at the piece of gold, crushing the tiny particles between his fingers. Then it all came back to him: his conversation with Tonya about Suzanne Spaak and the inscriptions she had etched on the walls of her cell. 'I'll be back,' he mumbled, shoved Dookhin aside, and hurried to the elevator.

A few minutes later he was standing in Tonya's cell, reading her last message. 'Boris save the children Nina can help with Alex love love to you all . . .'

He clenched his fists, a fierce determination taking shape in his mind. Now that Tonya was dead, he had a last duty towards her: to save her child.

And he knew how.

Chapter Three

Chased by the bitter February winds, Nina Kramer stopped in the cold lobby of her Brooklyn brownstone to catch her breath. As she wiped her spectacles, she noticed an envelope sticking out of her broken mailbox. She rubbed her frozen hands and picked up the envelope. It was stamped with the logo of the Jewish refugee relief agency. Inside there was a stencilled form, with the empty spaces filled in in square block letters. Mrs Kramer of 49 Elm Street in Brooklyn was asked to come to the agency headquarters in Manhattan on a matter concerning her nephew, Alexander Gordon, age three, born in Moscow, Soviet Union, to Tonya and Victor Wolf.

Her heart pounding, she scurried to the subway station on Flatbush Avenue. She couldn't understand the letter. What did the refugee agency have to do with her sister's son? He was supposed to be in Moscow. Something must have happened to Tonya, something very bad, otherwise why would they want to talk to her about Alex? All through the ride she kept racking her brains for a possible explanation. She reached the agency offices at Park Avenue South a few minutes before closing time, haunted by grim premonitions.

She was received by Mr Lipshutz, a small, bald man who obsequiously offered her a chair, sat down behind his decrepit desk, cleared his throat, suggested a cup of tea, and finally broke the horrible news. Her sister was dead, Mr Lipshutz said, then lowered his voice, although they were alone. According to the agency sources, Tonya had been shot for treason. Her husband, Morozov, had arranged for the child to be sent to America.

It took her a moment to digest the meaning of the man's words. 'No,' she cried out, appalled. Her mouth went dry. 'You don't know my sister. Tonya isn't a traitress, this is all a lie!'

Mr Lipshutz was nodding compassionately. I understand you,' he said softly. 'But we have good sources in Russia, you know. We check every visa application. Your sister's husband pulled quite a few strings to obtain an exit visa for the boy. I understand he is your sister's child from a former marriage. Is that correct?'

She didn't answer. She suspected Lipshutz's story was a lie, but why should he lie to her? Perhaps it was an FBI frameup, yet what purpose could it serve?

'Alexander is three years old,' the elderly clerk was saying. 'He is in Vienna now, and our people are taking care of him.'

'When is the boy arriving?' she stammered, rising heavily from her chair. Her knees were shaking.

'By the end of the week,' said Lipshutz, offering her his small, cold hand. 'We'll bring him to your apartment.'

Three days later, Mr Lipshutz himself knocked on her door. He held a little boy by the hand and carried a small suitcase. Nina took the child into the living room, where he stood awkwardly, shyly studying her. He was pale but robust. Feeling her eyes on him, he looked away, clenching his fists. He seemed lost in his frayed coat made of rough brown fabric. He wore high black shoes and a visor cap, two sizes too large for him.

'Now, Alexander, tell me – what did they call you at home?' Nina asked in Russian with forced cheerfulness.

The boy didn't answer.

'They called you Aliosha, didn't they?' she went on. 'Well, we'll call you Alex. Alex Gordon.'

As she unbuttoned the child's collar, her fingers touched the gold chain. She clutched the Star of David, her heart thumping. She recognized it; she had given it to Tonya on the eve of her own departure from Russia. Looking the other way, she clumsily wiped a tear from her cheek.

Later, as evening shadows spilled into the cold, silent rooms, Nina sat in a chintz-covered armchair watching the little boy sleep. She had no spare room – her husband Samuel slept in the far bedroom and she used the tiny alcove by the kitchen – so she put little Alex to bed on the sofa in the living room. The exhausted boy was asleep before she even started to undress him. As she removed his clothes, she kept speaking softly, although the child wouldn't hear. After Samuel's stroke, that had turned him to a dumb and deaf invalid, she had acquired the habit of speaking to herself, to dispel her loneliness.

'Aliosha, *golubtchek moi*, my little dove,' she kept mumbling, recalling how she used to undress his mother, little Tonya, when she took care of her back in Kiev; her small sister, with her long blonde hair and starry blue eyes had looked like a little angel. She was a blue-eyed angel, indeed, although Nina used to call her a naughty devil. Nina remembered the way Tonya used to hug her, clinging to her with her supple body; and tears, so rare in her, so ruthlessly suppressed for years, gushed from her eyes.

After taking off Alex's clothes and shoes, she gently laid him between a couple of crisp linen sheets she had brought from the plywood cupboard, together with a large fluffy pillow. The sleeping child yawned, rubbing his eyes with his little fists, then curled up and buried his face in the pillow. He had long, silken eyelashes like his mother, and her delicately arched eyebrows.

'You have your mother's face,' she said. 'You know that, Aliosha?' She covered him with her own eiderdown; she should get used to a rough woollen blanket from now on. Once the child was tucked between the sheets she sat by him, studying every line of the little face and comparing it with Tonya's features in her memory. And with another child's face, inert and chalk white, that she had all those years tried to erase from her mind.

So immersed was she in the contemplation of her nephew that she almost missed her daily ritual which took place at nightfall, when the streetlights came on and the Brooklyn kids ended their softball game on the pavement, hurrying home to dinner. She turned off the lights, stepped to the window, pulled the curtains aside and looked down to the street. The FBI automobile was there, as every night in the past four months. It was a tan-coloured car – the boys who lived downstairs said it was a Plymouth – with a dented fender and a patch of brown paint on the forward left door. But this time there were two men in it, not one, she could tell by the two cigarette tips glowing inside. Why two? she wondered, alarmed. Could that be because of Alex? Because of Morozov? Did they know?

Tonya shot for treason, she thought. Tonya had betrayed the Soviet Union. It was a disgusting lie, of course. Tonya was a wonderful poetess, a source of pride for the Soviet Union. Nina had always admired – and envied – her sister for her beauty and her talent, but mostly for her participation in the building of Marxism. She hadn't seen her since she left Russia in 1928, but had met her first husband, Victor, back in 1943. He had visited the USA with the Soviet Anti-Fascist Writers' Committee and had brought her a book of Tonya's poems, with her sister's affectionate dedication: 'To my beloved Ninochka, from your little devil.' She had hardly contained her tears, reading the inscription.

After Victor had left, she would often read the book, until she knew all the poems by heart. She would visualize her sister in military uniform, her bright eyes sparkling, her long blonde hair blown by the wind, reciting her uplifting verses to young Red Army soldiers on their way to the battlefield, during the darkest days of the Great Patriotic War.

She'd envied her, Nina admitted. She too had wanted to be there at Russia's fateful hour, fighting the Nazis. But Tonya took part in the war effort, while Nina sat in an office in Brooklyn and scribbled in ledgers. She had made so many mistakes, Nina thought, while her sister had chosen the right path. Tonya had taken the road that Nina should have chosen. Tonya's life was the fulfilment of Nina's secret dreams.

About three years ago, a letter from Tonya had brought her astonishing news. Victor had been arrested and sentenced to a life term of hard labour for crimes against the Soviet Union. Tonya had divorced him and married Boris Morozov, a KGB colonel. She was carrying his child. The letter had been cautiously worded, hinting at various events, not all of which Nina managed to figure out. One hint she had understood, though. Tonya wrote: 'Boris comes homes every night, although he watches unrelentingly over the security of our nation,' Nina had understood: Morozov was with the KGB.

She had dispatched Tonya an anguished letter, full of questions, but it had remained unanswered. She couldn't believe that Victor had betrayed the Soviet Union. But some of communism's worst enemies came from the hard core of bolsheviks. True, Nina couldn't imagine Victor committing any crime against his country. But who could have imagined that Trotsky, Zinoviev and Kamenev would also turn into enemies of the revolution? Perhaps Victor, too, had slipped; perhaps his visit to America had turned his head.

Nina hadn't heard from her sister since, until that day at the Jewish relief agency. What had happened? What had Tonya done? Why had Alex been sent to America?

The news about Tonya all but made her world crumble. Nina was a communist, a staunch believer in the new gospel of Marx, Engels, Lenin, and the fourth surviving giant, Yossif Vissarionovitch Stalin. Never in her life had she doubted the just cause and the sublime ideals of her native country. She had fervently hoped to see communism triumph all over the world.

But today she was deeply confused. Even her own total devotion to communism couldn't make her buy that nonsense about Tonya having betrayed her country. Nina's only explanation was that Soviet justice had committed a monstrous mistake; and Tonya had died for nothing. Errors did happen, even in the Soviet Union. In the historic events that shook her country individuals didn't count; they were nothing but oil on the revolution's wheels. Lenin himself had said: 'When you chop wood – splinters fly.'

Still, she couldn't digest the idea that her lovely sister had become such a splinter, an ugly mistake of the Soviet bureaucratic machine. And what about Victor? Had his conviction also been a bureaucratic mistake? Could both he and Tonya be traitors? For the first time ever, she was at a loss; her faith in Russia was shaken. There must be an explanation, she said to herself, there must be a reason for this tragedy. She had written a letter to their brother Valery in Leningrad, but he hadn't replied.

She stared down at the tan Plymouth. Alex had been officially admitted to the country, therefore the authorities were bound to know about him, about Tonya and Morozov. One more reason for the FBI to stick close to her. Turning away from the window, she tiptoed to the kitchen to make herself some herb tea. While the kettle was softly purring on the gas-ring, she sat erect at the kitchen table, her hands joined before her.

A few months ago, the *New York Daily News* had printed a picture of her in that posture, face drawn, forehead ploughed by a deep frown, eyes magnified by the wire-rimmed glasses. The headline above the picture said: 'Suspected communist Nina Kramer testifying before House Committee on un-American activities'.

She had never done anything against her adoptive country, of course, although MacCarthy's gangsters had accused her of being a Soviet agent. They had finally let her go. Her lawyer told her she was small fry, she wasn't worth the effort. Nevertheless, she was forced to resign from her position as a bookkeeper with the Department of Health. Soon after, she found a job at Spiegel's Furs and things quietened down.

She was glad that her spell of notoriety was over. After her photograph had been printed in the paper, several people had yelled at her in the street, shaking their fists; a store owner had thrown her out, calling her 'a bloody communist'. It took a while until people forgot about her. But the FBI didn't forget. Since the proceedings, she was kept under surveillance. They followed her openly, and watched her house from their parked automobile. What did they expect, to catch her handing documents to Soviet spies?

Tonight, because of Alex's arrival, she had skipped a meeting of the Peace Movement. There was talk of a march on Washington, to demand the President's clemency for the Rosenbergs. She was ready to go. The Rosenbergs were not spies. If they had delivered nuclear formulae to the Soviets, they had done it for peace. But American imperialism had decided to murder Julius and Ethel Rosenberg. Truman was determined to drag them to the electric chair.

She suppressed a sigh, and glanced at a picture of the couple, that she had cut from a newspaper and fastened to the wall with thumbtacks. Ethel looked so gentle, almost pretty, in her buttoned-up coat with its fur collar; she wore a pointed, coquettish little hat. Julius was bent towards her, with a smile on his lean face. He was wearing glasses and had a small moustache. There was a wire mesh between them. The picture was perhaps taken in court, or in the van that carried them back to prison. One could sense, even from this grainy picture, the deep bond between Julius and Ethel. Nina wished she could have met the Rosenbergs and told them how much she admired them. She couldn't suppress a pang of envy. They had not only believed in communism – they had taken action for the cause. Not like her.

The water was boiling. She poured the steaming brew into a glass, then sat down by the kitchen table and drank it slowly, sucking it through a cube of solid sugar she had placed between her front teeth, the Russian way.

Her habits hadn't changed, although she had been an American citizen for more than twenty years. She still thought and counted in Russian, her English was broken and inadequate, the bookshelf in her tiny bedroom was laden with the works of Dostoyevski, Tolstoy, Lermontov and Lenin. Every morning she bought *Russkoye Slovo*, the Russian daily, at Hershie's kiosk on Foster Avenue. She hated the reactionary ideas of the *Slovo*, but couldn't overcome her desire to read a Russian newspaper. She didn't read American newspapers and books, never went to the theatre, rarely saw a movie. Once in a while she went to a concert, or to the ballet; she didn't need English for that. She kept pleating her hair in a tressed bun on top of her head and wearing dark, buttoned-up dresses and square-heeled shoes, those unmistakeable trademarks of middle-aged women in the country of her birth.

After twenty-four years in America, she remained a stranger in this land. She disliked Brooklyn, with its incessant din and bustle. She had heard about the Dodgers but had no idea who they were; she had never ventured as far as Coney Island or Manhattan Beach. Jazz and rock'n'roll were alien to her ears. Her palate didn't agree with the American foods, she disliked hot dogs, hamburgers and meatloaf. Once a week she walked all the way across town to the Russian grocer in Williamsburg, to buy salted herrings, country sausage and black bread. Her days were divided between her work at Spiegel's Furs and tending to her invalid husband. But her nights were hers to dream of the life she could have had. If she had only dared.

Her whole life, she often reflected, had been divided between her reluctance to become involved in risky underground work – and the burning desire to join the frontline of communist activists. The result of those contradictory impulses was a maddening frustration, and she was constantly haunted by the feeling that she was wasting her life and deserting the battlefield.

She sipped her tea, watching Alex. The child stirred, blinked a couple of times, then stretched his arms and sank back into sleep, his face calm and serene. She bent over him and rearranged his blanket. 'What's the matter, my little one?' she murmured. Then, 'Sleep well.'

He had the blond hair of his mother, but not her eyes. The child's eyes were grey with a greenish hue, strikingly luminous. Alex was thin and pale, he looked small for his age, but seemed to be in good health. She wondered if he was as fond of chocolate as Tonya. Nina used to queue for hours before the Narodnii foodstore on Leninskaya Street to buy Tonya a bar of chocolate, hard and dry, but chocolate all the same.

'Tomorrow,' she whispered to the sleeping boy, 'I'll draw you a bath and scrub away all that filth you've collected during your trip. I'll make you look like new, *golubchek*.'

She must also do some laundry, perhaps go to Polack's used garment store; Alex had nothing on his back but a heavy roll-neck pullover, worn-out pants and a coat. The pants were made of the same rough fabric from which her mother used to cut the clothes of her younger brother Valery thirty years ago.

Her thoughts took her back in time, to the far provinces of her past. She belonged to the ill-fated Russian generation that was old enough to understand the October Revolution, but too young to take part in it. She was in her early teens when Czar Nikolai was shot, and the Bolsheviks seized power in Russia. A student in the renowned Pobedoneszev School for girls in Kiev, she breathlessly followed the revolutionary events, the Brest-Litovsk peace negotiations, then the civil war. At school, passionate debates broke out between the girls. She voiced her admiration for the Reds, who wanted to erect a new brotherly society on the ruins of backward, reactionary Russia. She and her friend, the dark, intense Katya Tiomkin, spun dreams of joining the legendary Red Guards, who included many women, even in commanding positions.

But when a Red Cavalry battalion briefly stopped at Kiev, Katya was the only one to leave with the fiery horsemen. Nina remained behind to take care of a wounded soldier, Sasha Kolodny. This had been the moment, Nina later realized, when she had made her crucial mistake. She should have followed her impulses, left with the Red Guards, and taken part in the revolution. But she had stayed in Kiev, and her choice changed the course of her life.

And yet . . . she was only sixteen at the time, a small, chubby girl with a rather plain face, a strong chin, a large forehead and long silky hair. She was proud of her hair, and secretly enjoyed watching it in her bedroom mirror as it darkly cascaded upon her shoulders; it gave her something of a dreamy look. Like one of Chekhov's young heroines, she thought. But she never dared to wear her hair that way; when she went to school she pleated it in severe tresses on the top of the her head or drew it back in a tight bun.

No man had ever looked at her before, nobody had suspected that behind her homely features romantic impulses burned fiercely. Nobody could guess either that the quiet, plain girl longer for all-consuming, passionate love. But when she and Katya had gone to visit the wounded Red Guards, at the Military School's stables, and Sasha Kolodny had squeezed her hand and looked at her with his gentle grey eyes, she had cast aside all her revolutionary dreams.

She had stayed with him for the following three weeks, until Sasha recovered from the bullet wound in his thigh. On the day he limped out of the stables, leaning on her shoulder, the Red battalion had left town. She brought the young man home, something she wouldn't have dared to do before. But these were revolutionary times. The young made the rules and the old had no choice but to comply. Her parents meekly capitulated and agreed to give Sasha the maid's small room behind the kitchen. Their maid had returned to her village after the outbreak of the civil war.

Two weeks later Sasha and Nina moved to Zhitomir and settled in the expropriated house of a fur merchant who had been executed by a revolutionary squad. They shared the upper floor with four families of factory workers; Nina found work in a rope factory, and very rarely travelled to Kiev to visit her parents.

They became lovers the first night they spent together but Sasha didn't mention any plans for the future until three years later, and then in an odd, disturbing manner. He was an odd young man altogether. Stocky, rather heavy-set, with curly blond hair, a heavy jaw and calm grey eyes, he was the most self-controlled boy she had ever seen. He wasn't talkative, and weighed carefully every word before pronouncing it. He had been very polite with her parents, and had told them he came from a Jewish family living in Omsk. He was kind and gentle with her; in bed, he was an eager, passionate lover. But even in those moments of closeness Sasha wouldn't completely open up. He was a secretive youth, suspicious and ungiving. He reminded her of a conspirator against the Czar, a character out of a novel; one of those shady, silent men who had turned *knospiratzia* – conspiracy – into a way of life.

When Sasha fully recovered from his wound he didn't return to his former unit. Instead, he was assigned by the party to the Zhitomir Narkom, the people's commissariat. Once Nina glimpsed, hidden behind a pile of his clothes, a German Nagant handgun. A friend of hers who was a secretary at the Narkom told her Sasha was with the Cheka, the newborn security and intelligence organization. But when she asked him he just smiled.

She soon realized that she would never get to know all about her lover. There was a part of Sasha's life which he wouldn't reveal to anybody. He would often go out at the oddest hours, in the middle of the day or night; he would meet her inquiries with a blank stare and an absent smile. When the civil war ended he would disappear for weeks, even months; a couple of times he brought her presents – a rabbit-fur hat, leather gloves, a pair of boots. He had bought them in Moscow, she could tell by the names of the stores, stamped in purple on the cheap cotton lining. She kept asking him what he had been doing, but he would only smile in his gentle, disarming manner.

One winter night he came in late and woke her up. He had been absent for six weeks. He was wearing his old military coat, and its shoulders were covered with snow. He looked excited. 'Nina,' he said urgently, 'I am going to Palestine. Let's leave together.'

She stared at him in dismay. 'Palestine? What shall we do there? Have you become a Zionist, Sasha?'

He shook his head. 'It will be better for both of us.'

'You're a communist,' she had murmured. 'You have nothing to do in Palestine. Our future is here, in Russia.'

He took a deep breath. 'Trust me,' he said.

But she persisted in her refusal. She couldn't tell him she was pregnant, and expected his child by the following spring. He had told her many times that he didn't want children, they were nothing but a burden for a communist in this era. And she feared he would be angry with her, or worse might regard her pregnancy as a cheap trick to force marriage upon him.

True, he kept repeating to her that for all purposes they were already married, and didn't need to go through the decadent ceremonies of a dead era; still, she nourished a secret dream of a white wedding, she wearing the magnificent silk dress of her mother, Sasha in his long black jacket and shiny tall boots. A couple of girls from the rope factory had married in a bride's dress, and nobody had protested. Yet she had never dared to share her dream with Sasha. He might dub her a bourgeois and a reactionary.

Finally, he left for Palestine by himself. 'If you change your mind,' he said to her when they parted, 'come. I'll be waiting.'

His train had barely pulled out of the station when she started having second thoughts. Perhaps she should go with him? she thought. But how could she, with his baby already kicking inside her? She had no other way, she had taken the right decision. As soon as the child was born she would write to him, and he would understand.

The baby, a boy she named Vladimir – there were many Vladimirs those years, all of them named after Lenin – was born in March, in the first week of the thaw. He died a year later, as the Great Famine swept through Russia, leaving millions dead in its wake. Vladimir expired in her arms; during the last days of his life he didn't even have the strength to cry, and kept staring at her with his big, inflamed eyes, in which she read a terrible accusation.

As she rocked the emaciated corpse of her little son, Nina felt she was going out of her mind. She had loved the child with all the fire burning inside her; but she hadn't been able to save his life. Other mothers had managed. She had failed her little Vladimir, and failed Sasha too, by letting his son die. The terrible feeling of guilt never left her, remaining her faithful companion until this very day.

Tormented by grief and remorse, Nina returned to her parents' home. She feverishly devoted herself to the raising of Valery and little Tonya. When her pain subsided and she was able to reason again, Nina decided to join Sasha in Palestine. By then, however, the Soviet Union had sealed its borders and would grant no exit visas. It was three years before she finally sailed to Palestine on a rusty Italian steamer, to search for her lost lover.

Lost, for he hadn't written to her once. Lost again, for when she arrived in the Promised Land, Sasha Kolodny had vanished. He had entered the country all right; she discovered the proof in the immigrants' lists kept by the Jewish Agency. His name was in a black ledger she perused in a dusty office in Jaffa. Sasha Kolodni, born in Omsk, 1898, arrived February 27, 1925. Those details were couched in a foreign hand, but the signature was Sasha's – big, square letters, the K massive and wide, the y ending in a long upward stroke, the entire name underscored by a thick line, etched in the white paper.

But Sasha wasn't in Jaffa. He wasn't in Tel Aviv, or in the famished settlements throughout Galilee and the malaria-ridden kibbutzim of the Izreel Valley. For months Nina traveled the country, living in utmost misery, subsisting on one meal a day, searching for him.

As she wandered throughout the land, Nina met Russian immigrants who knew him, mostly young left-wing radicals. A couple of Muscovites had worked with Sasha in a Judean orchard; an old man had approved his application to the Palestinian communist faction; a Haifa docker had been arrested with him by the British for subversive activity. The docker, though, gave her the most disturbing piece of news: Sasha Kolodny had been expelled from Palestine by order of the British High Commissioner. The British claimed that he was a bolshevik agent, sent to Palestine by the communist International, to put in place a subversive organization.

'I saw Kolodny brought to Haifa under police escort,' the docker said. 'They put him aboard the first ship leaving the country. I think it was a French freighter.'

The longshoreman's story explained quite a few things. Sasha had decided to go to Palestine not on a sudden whim, or because he had embraced Zionist ideas. He had been sent on a mission. He was one of the myriad young communists dispatched all over the capitalist countries, to lay the ground for world revolution. Now that she knew the truth about him, Nina lost all hope of seeing him again. He was somewhere in Europe, or back in Russia, probably engaged in another dark scheme.

In a pioneers' camp in Galilee Nina met a gentle, frail youth named Samuel Kramer. His health was bad, and his body weak; he had a rather awkward manner, and seemed unable to cope with the hard life in Palestine. Perhaps she was attracted to him because he was so helpless, and stirred her motherly instincts; or because he was the opposite of Sasha, and didn't have his confidence and self-control. One month after they met, she married Samuel and sailed with him to America. It was her declaration of defeat; failing to find Sasha Kolodny, she had given him up.

She couldn't pretend she was in love with Samuel; for her, it had been a marriage of convenience. She didn't want to stay in Palestine, she couldn't go back to Russia, and in Europe fascist regimes were taking over. Samuel was her ticket to America. He had American citizenship, his parents having emigrated to Buffalo in the eighteen-eighties. He had come to Palestine with the Jewish Legion, that had fought alongside the British in the First World War.

But he was an only son, and rather spoiled; he had lost his Zionist faith after falling sick with malaria. Drifting to the left, he became a Marxist and now wanted to go back to America and help organize the workers. As for Nina, she thought that after losing Sasha, she might as well patch together a new life. She and Samuel shared the same ideals; love and affection would come later.

They had sailed to America together, but soon after they had moved to the small Brooklyn apartment, Samuel had suffered a massive stroke and turned into a salivating, grinning idiot, unable to move. For years now he had been lying on the large bed in their former bedroom, soiling his sheets, panting, sighing and moaning.

He had lost all his hair and his teeth, was unable to speak, and could only utter squeaky, unintelligible sounds. She had to wash him, change and feed him for the rest of his wretched life.

She assumed responsibility for their existence, and found a job as a bookkeeper. During the day, when she was at work, an old woman from across the street took care of Samuel; but Nina suspected she stole a part of his food, and never cleaned him as she should. Very often, coming back from work, she would find Samuel lying in his urine-soaked sheets, grinning foolishly. But sometimes he would grasp her wrist with his right hand – he had a remarkably strong right arm, the left was just a withered bough, hanging beside his flank – and stare at her with intelligent, wise eyes. It was the sanity and the despair she suddenly perceived in the pale blue eyes that drove her mad.

Were it not for Samuel's malady, she often said to herself, long ago she would have joined the struggle for communism. But deep in her heart she knew this wasn't true. She knew her shortcomings; she knew there wasn't enough steel in her backbone, enough dedication to the cause, to drop everything and go.

She was gnawed by the feeling that great historic events were passing her by, and she didn't budge. When the Second World War broke out, she became restless. She could go back to Russia; she could enlist as a volunteer with the Women's Auxiliary Forces of Great Britain or Canada. She knew people who did, ordinary people like herself. She even found out the address of the British recruitment office, and once spent a couple of hours standing on the opposite pavement, watching young people enter through its massive wooden doors. But she was unable to cross the street, and after a while she went home.

Another option was to sail to Europe. Before Pearl Harbour, Americans could travel freely in France, help establish underground networks, smuggle refugees out of the country, carry documents. Besides, Nina had a secret reason to go to Paris. A letter she received carried news that should have prompted her to catch the first boat to the continent. It had been dispatched by Emily Mayer, an American communist, who was in France helping the anti-fascist movement. Sasha was in Paris, the letter said.

'Come,' Emily wrote to her, 'I saw your Sasha, he is worth the trip, this man is a dream!'

But it was to remain a dream, and she didn't set foot out of Brooklyn. Her frustration with herself knew no limits.

Samuel groaned in his bed. He wasn't asleep; the poor wretch rarely slept. Sooner or later she would have to take Alex to his room, and make him meet his uncle. She hoped it wouldn't be too traumatic for the little boy.

As she watched Alex sleep, it occurred to Nina that he could change her existence. Alex could bring her sweet Tonya back to life; he might become the little son she had lost. He could give a new meaning to her life, instil new strength into her withered body. She could raise him, plant her ideals in him, mould him into the person she had so desperately wished to become. She could live again through him, a new, different life.

Yes, she thought with sudden determination, she would make Tonya's little boy a worthy son of his family, a Russian patriot, a communist in the pure tradition of Stalin.

Morozov heard of Stalin's sudden death from two KGB officers who pounded on his apartment door on the night of March 5, 1953. He woke up immediately. He was all alone in the apartment now, and his light sleep was regularly assailed by the same grisly nightmare, where he would see Tonya, her golden hair fanned on the bloodied snow. He couldn't get used to his loneliness. One of the children was already on his way to America. He had sent the other to the Panfilov Orphanage in Leningrad, an institution for the sons of fallen Soviet heroes. Little Dimitri, the principal reported to him over the phone, had quickly made friends with the other children in his class.

The officers kept hammering on his door till he opened, shivering in his old dressing gown. At first he thought they had come for him, as they had come for Tonya. But the young captain at the door only said he was to report to KGB Centre immediately. The car sent for him darted through the sleeping streets of Moscow. Morozov saw troops in combat gear jump out of trucks and take positions by major government buildings. Other units were setting roadblocks at several intersections. When he got out of the car, at Dzerzhinski Square, Morozov heard the distant rumble of tanks.

KGB Centre was illuminated like a Christmas tree, with phones incessantly ringing, orders thundering in the loudspeaker system, messengers running along the corridors. Military automobiles discharged high-ranking personnel at the Lubyanka gates. The massive doors, whose brass coating was engraved with the hammer and sickle emblem, weren't locked as usual; for the first time Morozov saw them wide open. Every KGB officer from second lieutenant to lieutenant-general seemed to have been summoned to headquarters.

At the armoury, automatic rifles were issued to everybody present. Truckloads of junior officers were rushed to the Kuznetsky Most annex and to the Radio Moskva complex, while most superior officers were ordered to deploy around the Kremlin. Officially, the operation was meant to protect the vital government centres from a takeover by hostile forces, but Morozov suspected Beria of following a secret plan that would give him absolute control over the Soviet Union. Beria himself was now speaking at an extraordinary session of the Politburo, assembled in the Kremlin.

By sunrise, though, it became clear that Beria's action, although swift and brutal, hadn't been swift and brutal enough. The KGB officers were instructed to hand back their weapons and resume their regular duties. Morozov was shaving in his office when Takachenko came in with the news. The politburo had elected Georgi Malenkov as the new Soviet leader. 'Malenkov is a good man,' Takachenko said cautiously. 'A moderate. Do you know him?'

They looked at each other, communicating with their eyes what they couldn't say aloud for fear that the office might be wired. Beria and the hard-liners, their eyes said, had apparently suffered a defeat at the Politburo meeting.

One of Malenkov's first decisions, Morozov noted, was to put an end to the witch-hunt against the Jews. Barely a fortnight after Stalin's death, the Jewish physicians who had allegedly participated in 'the Doctors' plot' were released from prison. Among them was Valery Gordon. Dr Lydia Timaschuk, the chief witness against the doctors, admitted publicly she had fabricated the evidence, in order to achieve promotion.

Morozov felt a surge of fury. The war against the Jews had ended, but eight weeks too late. If Tonya's execution had only been delayed, she would be safe now, probably released from prison. Only eight weeks, he thought, and his family would have been spared. But Tonya was dead, the children were gone, and their apartment was empty and silent as a tomb. Every night, on returning from the office, he would open a fresh bottle of vodka and drink in silence, till he slumped unconscious on the kitchen table.

Still, for the first time since Tonya's death, Morozov felt a flicker of hope as far as his own fate was concerned. Things were changing in Russia. Jewish affairs were back in his hands. Nobody spoke to him about Tonya, as if she had never existed. A couple of friends awkwardly asked how the children were, and he vaguely answered that they were staying with relatives. This seemed to be an adequate response. Everybody knew that his mother lived in Shepetovka and Nina's brother in Leningrad.

Morozov wasn't harassed, there was no surveillance on his apartment and nobody interfered with his work; he started to feel secure again. In the Centre corridors strange rumours wafted, saying Beria was in disgrace and his life hung on a thread. Perhaps a miracle would happen, Morozov thought, and he would survive.

But that was to disregard the irreversible motion of the KGB's machinery. Since Tonya's arrest, Morozov had been labelled an enemy; and an enemy had to be destroyed by the KGB machine, no matter who was running it. Morozov was a doomed man. He had a last surge of hope in June, when Beria was arrested by his cronies and shot in the Lubyanka, like so many thousands of his victims. The operation had been meticulously prepared; Beria was dead before his closest aides even learned of his arrest.

Morozov's hopes of survival were unfounded. Even after Beria's death, his former subordinates kept diligently following his bloody decrees. A month after Beria's death, Colonel Boris Morozov was arrested. He had just visited little Dimitri in Leningrad, and received news that the other child, after safely reaching Vienna, had been admitted to the United States. He lived now with Nina Kramer in Brooklyn.

A KGB inner board – not even a court – stripped Morozov of his rank and sent him to the maximum security camp in Vorkuta. A year later, his mother received official notice that her son was dead. No further details were given.

Varvara Morozova was a pious woman. Braving communist law, she slipped into the deserted Pravoslav church and lit a candle for the soul of her dead son.

Chapter Four

Alex realized he was different from the other children on his first day at school. As he stepped into the classroom, he was amazed; he had never been in the same room with so many children of his own age. The first grade teacher was a silver-haired lady named Miss Murphy. She was wearing a neat grey dress with a starched white collar and shiny black shoes, and had a pleasant voice. She told the students to sit down, then asked them to state their names and the places where they were born. When Alex's turn came, he said: 'Alex Gordon, Moscow.' Everybody looked at him strangely, even Miss Murphy.

After they introduced themselves, Miss Murphy asked the students various questions to help them get to know one another. The most popular question was: 'Name the sports team you prefer.' Most of the children announced: 'The Dodgers!' to the sounds of loud hand-clapping and some catcalls. The Dodgers had won the World Series at last. Some kids said: 'The New York Yankees,' and only a few timidly applauded. When it was Alex's turn, he said: 'Dinamo Moscow.'

Silence fell in the classroom. The children eyed him suspiciously. 'What did he say?' a little girl with pigtails asked, surprised; the boy sitting behind her threw his arms up in the air in mock despair, triggering a ripple of laughter. 'Who are these guys?' he quipped. 'Never heard of them.'

Miss Murphy looked perplexed.

'Where is Moscow anyway?' wondered another girl.

'It's in New Jersey,' a boy with slick hair and a fat behind said knowingly.

'What do they play?' Miss Murphy asked Alex encouragingly. 'Baseball or football?'

'Soccer,' Alex said, and sat down amidst stares of bewilderment.

That was all for that day, but the following morning, before class started, three boys barred Alex's way. One of them was large and strong, with a protruding chin and small black eyes; Alex remembered his name was Ralph. He had short-cropped reddish hair and a snub nose. The second boy's name was Stacy; he was small, wiry, with bleached hair and a large mole on his left cheek. The third kid, Burt, was thin and pale, with a narrow face and a small, colourless mouth. He was wearing a red baseball cap.

'My daddy said Moscow is in Russia,' Ralph said, 'and you are a connu . . . connu . . .'

'Connumist,' Burt helped. Several children clustered around them, listening.

'And my daddy said,' Ralph went on, 'that you want to fight us and kill all Americans.'

'Aren't you American?' Burt asked, peeping behind Ralph's back; but before Alex could answer, Ralph hit him in the face. Stacy stepped forward and menacingly shook his fists, trying to kick him in the shin. Blood gushed from Alex's nose, and his attackers ran away, Burt chanting: 'Connu-mist! Connu-mist!'

Alex entered the classroom and went straight to his seat, followed by the hostile stares of his classmates. He was in pain, and clenched his teeth to stop himself from crying. He tried to wipe the blood off his face with his sleeve, but the child sitting behind him, a neat boy with a freckled nose and candid blue eyes, gave him his starched white handkerchief. 'Here,' he said kindly, 'clean your face.' As Miss Murphy entered the class the little boy whispered: 'My father is from England, and he says soccer is the best game in the world.' Then he added, seeking reassurance: 'You aren't a connumist, are you?'

The boy's name was Joey. He was the only one who spoke to Alex that day. The other children looked at him awkwardly and kept their distance; Burt, Stacy and Ralph had spread the word. When he went home Alex knew he had made his first friend; still, he was utterly miserable. He had so much looked forward to the day when he would go to school with other children. He wanted to make many friends, and hoped to be liked by his fellow students. Now he felt he was going to be lonely.

It was nothing new for him. He had always been a lonely boy. Aunt Nina didn't like him to play with other children. She said the kids in the neighbourhood were stupid little brats and he shouldn't waste his time with them. She didn't let him play softball with the boys in the street, and he could only watch their games longingly from the living-room window. He left the house only with his aunt when she went shopping; twice a week she took him to the children's playground on Myrtle Street, and sat upright on a bench, knitting, watching him play.

These were the only times when he could meet children, but Aunt Nina didn't like him talking to the other kids, so he didn't stay with them long. He loved his aunt more than anything in the world, and didn't want to displease her. Even when Aunt Nina was at work, he wasn't allowed to go out by himself. Old Mrs Schneider would fix his meals, and he would spend his days in the living room playing with the few toys his aunt had bought for him.

Aunt Nina was the kindest person. She devoted most of her time to him, teaching him Russian, arithmetic, geography and history; she told him marvellous stories about animals. She always had a severe look on her face, and very rarely smiled, but she spoke to him kindly and never spanked him. She sat with him throughout the evening, and took care of his sick Uncle Samuel only after Alex went to sleep.

Alex was afraid of Uncle Samuel and hated the sight of his twisted body, the sounds of his mumbling and retching, and the bad smells that filled his room. He himself tried not to go near it. Sometimes, in his nightmares, he would see his uncle get up and come towards him, his outstretched hands trembling and his mouth twitching. With his bald head, toothless mouth and pinkish, hairless skin he looked like a grotesque, old baby turned into a monster.

When he had those bad dreams he would wake up, screaming, and in seconds Aunt Nina would be beside him, hugging him, soothing him with words of affection, spoken in soft, caressing Russian. At these moments her morose face would light up, and her eyes would fill with warmth, sometimes even well with moisture; he would hug her closely, breathe her fresh smell, and cuddle into her embrace. He loved her so much, she was like a mother to him.

His real mother and father, she had told him, had been killed in an automobile accident in Russia. He was born in Russia, in Moscow, and had a brother, Dimitri, who was a year younger. He and his brother had survived because they were not in the car the day of the accident. Dimitri had stayed in Russia, with some relatives.

Why hadn't Dimitri come to America like him? Alex asked. Well, his aunt said, Dimitri's relatives didn't want him to go abroad. How come, Alex kept asking, they didn't have the same relatives? They were brothers, weren't they, and brothers always have the same relatives? Actually Dimitri was only his half-brother, Nina explained, because they were both of the same mother but didn't have the same father.

'Which of our two fathers was in the automobile the day of the accident?' Alex pressed on. 'Mine or Dimitri's?' He was secretly hoping it was Dimitri's father who had died, and his father was still alive.

For a moment Aunt Nina seemed upset, but then she said curtly: 'Both your fathers are dead, *golubchek*.'

Alex wanted to ask if both their fathers had died in the same accident, it seemed rather strange, but Aunt Nina looked very nervous so he decided not to ask her. He thought he dimly remembered Dimitri, though. In his vague memories of their house back in Moscow, he recalled another child playing with lead soldiers on the wooden floor – a quiet boy with a shy smile and almond-shaped black eyes.

He also remembered his beautiful mother, her smiling blue eyes and her long blonde hair; or perhaps he was imagining things because the photographs that Aunt Nina had shown him. His aunt had a few of his mother, and he had pasted one onto cardboard and put it beside the sofa where he slept. She was so beautiful! It made him proud. He was sure that none of his classmates had a photograph like this by his bedside. He also saw photographs of his grandparents, wearing dark clothes; and of his mother when she was still a baby, held in the arms of a giggling plump girl who turned out to be his aunt. Those photographs, some of them yellowed by age, were arranged in an old album that Nina kept in her alcove.

Nina – she wanted him to call her 'Nina', not 'Aunt', or 'Auntie' – was his mother's sister. She told him she had actually raised his mother, back in Kiev. She used to dress her like a doll, then plait her golden hair. She bought Tonya chocolate and sweets; his mother had craved candy exactly like Alex.

His mother and father had both been poets, Nina said. They were Jewish. His grandparents had died during the war, murdered by the Nazis. Only Nina's brother, Valery, had survived. He was a doctor and lived in Leningrad. As he grew up Alex repeatedly questioned Nina about his family collecting every bit of information that she would disclose, although at times she seemed reluctant to answer.

His most precious possession was an old book of his mother's poems that his father had brought to Nina when he visited America, many years ago. Almost every night, before going to bed, Alex would read a couple of the poems. He knew several of them by heart. The one he liked most was 'A Soldier's Letter'. It was a ballad about a young soldier writing to his beloved before going to fight for Russia and die in battle.

Alex didn't care very much about love between men and women; the subject rather bored him. Yet, reading 'A Soldier's Letter', he was moved by his mother's intense romanticism, which bestowed upon her an air of eternal youth. Another poem he liked was 'My White Kingdom', depicting Moscow's white winter. It spoke of towering castles and palaces, of valiant princes and fair maidens, of the Winter Queen, the Kremlin fortress, and the evergreen firs in Moscow's parks, caressed by the North wind. He longed to be there, to see the beautiful ancient town: 'A legend dressed in white, a city in a cloud, a dream for pures at heart . . .'

Thanks to Nina's limitless patience, he knew how to read and write in Russian even before he learned to read English. Nina didn't know English, really, and they always spoke in Russian; but he picked up some English from Mrs Schneider, from the children at the playground, and from listening to the massive radio set that looked like a chest and stood in a corner of the living room. When Nina was out he listened to sports broadcasts and talk shows. When she was at home she would tune the radio only to stations that broadcast music.

He had no writing of his father's, only five poems that Nina had cut out from Russian literary magazines and glued to long sheets of white paper. His father's poems were different, more austere, more concerned with freedom, the fight against oppression, and social justice. He still didn't fully understand them, he was only a child after all, but there was a verse that impressed him deeply:

I'd gladly die a thousand deaths,
and hang from thousand trees,
or burn in thousand fires –
if then my bones, my heart, my soul,
into an iron fist would turn
to crush the chains that man has put on man.

Victor Wolf, Alex thought, had been a man of strong convictions, devoted to the truth, respectful of his fellow man. His poetry wasn't as moving as Tonya's, but his ideas were much more powerful. They conveyed a passionate desire to change the world. Sometimes Alex felt angry with his mother for having taken a second husband. She should have remained faithful to Victor Wolf.

Alex had no photograph of his father. He often tried to imagine how Victor Wolf looked, and nagged Nina with questions about his height, his clothes, his face, the shade of his hair, the colour of his eyes. She told him Victor was thin and pale, with a high forehead, abundant black hair, and large brown eyes that expressed 'an inner torment'. Alex didn't understand what inner torment meant exactly, so Nina explained that there was sadness in his father's look. 'He was very handsome,' she summed up, 'a handsome dark man.'

Alex looked at himself in the mirror and was disappointed. He saw a blond boy with bright grey eyes. He so much wanted to look like his father, but Nina said he had taken 'almost everything from his mother, except perhaps the mouth'. Alex often tried to visualize his father, over there in Russia, writing his poems in an obscure study at night, or teaching his students at Moscow university. Sometimes he imagined him reading his poems in the Red Square to a crowd of workers and peasants, in the Russian tradition.

He knew exactly how Red Square looked. He could describe with his eyes closed the Kremlin wall, its turrets and gates, St Basil's church, the Lenin Mausoleum, the huge Gum department store across the square, the gently sloping avenue leading to the Moskva River. From reading magazines and books, Alex had become more familiar with the sights of Moscow than he was with those of Brooklyn. Nina said that he knew about Russia more than many Russian children.

He had learned to read at the age of five, and swallowed scores of books that Nina kept bringing from the Russian library in Gravesend. He knew by heart many Russian songs, especially those performed by the Red Army choir. Nina would play their music almost every evening on her hand-powered record-players, which he was not allowed to touch. At the age of six Alex already knew to sing the workers anthem, the 'Internationale'. He knew about the October Revolution, the victorious struggle of the Russian people against its oppressors, the Great Patriotic War against the Nazis, and the heroic effort that had turned Russia into a paradise for the peasants and workers. And for the children too. He longed to grow up like the children in Russia, wearing the red scarf of a pioneer, a member of the national youth movement.

Brooklyn was unimportant. Alex was a little Russian boy, speaking Russian, and growing up in a Russian house that might have been transported to America by the touch of some magic wand, across lands and seas, soaring mountains and forbidding forests, like in Tonya Gordon's poems.

When Nina came back from work, the day of Alex's fight with Ralph, Burt and Stacy, her nephew was waiting for her in belligerent mood. 'I don't want to go to school anymore,' he said sullenly. 'I don't like it.'

She took off her coat and hat, and sat down on the sofa beside him, hugging him gently. 'Now, *golubchek*, your face is bruised. Tell me what happened.'

Alex narrated the incident with Ralph. When he described the taunting and the chanting, his eyes welled with tears. 'Afterwards, when I got into the class, a boy called Joey . . .'

'What do you mean afterwards?' she asked, feigning surprise. 'You let Ralph get away with it?'

Alex looked up at her, puzzled. 'What do you mean?'

'I mean that when somebody hits you, you should hit back,' Nina said firmly. 'You shouldn't let yourself be bullied. No matter who hits you, you should fight back. Instead, you run away and come home crying like a baby!'

'But Nina, Ralph is much stronger than I am!'

She shrugged. '*Nu*? In a couple of fistfights, he might win. But the following time you may, or else just hurt him so badly he won't want to fight you again. So he'll let you be. And the other children would learn to leave you in peace, because you could be dangerous. Go now,' she abruptly ended the conversation, 'go read something. And think about what I told you.'

Alone in her tiny room, she wiped a tear from her cheek. Poor little Alex! This was the first time, but certainly not the last. Today it had been Dinamo Moscow, tomorrow it might be the principles of communism. For the rest of his life Alex was going to be different, and he was already suffering for it in his first days at school. It was not easy for a child to be different; children tolerated nonconformity even less than adults. The boy must learn to fight and defend himself. Otherwise he might just give up, discard everything that she had taught him, and try to become like the others, one of the herd.

The next evening she again found Alex with a bruised face. She pretended to ignore the scratches on his cheeks and the ugly welt above his upper lip, and the boy didn't say a word about it. He looked even worse the day after. But on the fourth day, although he had a black eye, he hurled himself upon her in triumph as she walked in. He hugged her and kept jumping around her in excitement. 'Ralph hit me today again,' he announced, 'but I fought back. He was wearing shorts, so I kicked him right in the kneecap. You had to see him wriggling in the dust, crying and twisting like a worm!'

'Good for you,' Nina said. 'Now he won't bother you anymore.'

Ralph didn't bother Alex again, and nor did the other children, who grudgingly learned to tolerate their odd classmate. He didn't make any friends, though. Except for Joey Simpson, a bright, curious child, the son of a teacher. He was fascinated by the strange boy who seemed to live in a world so different from his own, wearing those funny clothes, able to read Russian and tell amazing stories about Russia, and above all – a fan of Dinamo Moscow! Joey and the Russian boy became inseparable friends, and Alex didn't feel so lonely anymore. But Nina soon discovered that a danger far worse than loneliness was threatening her nephew.

Slowly, imperceptibly at first, school changed Alex. Nina had been worried about his going to an American school. Now she realized she had been right. For the child had emerged from the protective cocoon she had woven around him and was now exposed to the temptations and distractions America could offer. The boy was spending his days with American children, speaking English, learning about America, her values, her people, her breathtaking beauty. He was fascinated by history, and brought home a pack of brochures about the *Mayflower*, the Revolution, the Civil War. Listening to Alex as he enthusiastically described the highlights of American history, Nina felt a pang of anxiety. At these moments, Russia wasn't present in his mind at all. The child could drift away, she feared, and then nothing would bring him back.

And after all, he was just a child, so easily tempted! He played softball with his schoolmates, read books in English, and was spellbound by the first movie he saw: *Robin Hood*, starring Errol Flynn. He saw Jewish boys with skullcaps and sidelocks, and for days on end pestered Nina with questions about his origins.

'What am I more?' he would ask seriously. 'More Russian or more Jewish? Can I also be an American?' He was still a fan of Dinamo Moscow, but now he also liked the Dodgers and the Yankees. When the Dodgers left Brooklyn and crossed the continent to settle at Chavez Ravine, Alex was infuriated, like his American-born classmates. 'They betrayed us,' he said to Nina that night, his eyes burning with fury. 'They betrayed Brooklyn!'

He started dressing like the other children and using the same language; he asked Nina for eggs and cornflakes, Hershey bars and chewing gum, hamburgers and hot dogs, that he found irresistible. He brought home children's magazines and comics, followed with bated breath Superman's adventures, enjoyed the cartoon adventures of Mickey Mouse, Pluto and Donald Duck. And after school he often went with Joey to the Hollywood Soda Fountain that had a real television set.

But the event that alarmed Nina most happened the day Alex came home and told her he had learned the American anthem at school. He stood before her, an earnest, bright-eyed child of seven, placed his right hand over his heart, and in a sweet, melodious voice, solemnly sang the national anthem. When he concluded, he stared at her, his face transformed with emotion.

She suddenly realized he was expecting her to say something.

'Wonderful, *golubchek*,' she managed. 'Very good, *ochen khorosho*.'

The telephone seldom rang in the Kramer apartment. It was mostly Mr Spiegel who called Nina on business. Sometimes it was one of her friends from the Peace Movement. But that autumn evening Nina handed the receiver to Alex. 'It's for you,' she said.

He had spoken on the telephone only twice. He pressed the receiver tightly against his ear. 'Hello,' he said tensely.

It was Joey. 'Did you hear the news?' He sounded jubilant.

'What news?' It had to be something quite extraordinary to make Joey sound so elated.

'Wait. I asked my father to write it down,' Joey said and quoted solemnly: 'The Soviet news agency TASS announces that the Soviet Union has put a satellite into orbit around the earth.'

'Wow!'

'The satellite,' Joey went on, 'is called Sputnik . . . hey, what does Sputnik mean?'

'Companion. Go on,' Alex said urgently.

'. . . and has been put into orbit by one of the Soviet Union's missiles, which are used for peaceful purposes. Sputnik continuously sends radio signals to earth, and they can be captured all around the globe. The Soviet Union,' Joey triumphantly concluded, 'has launched the first artificial satellite in the history of man and started the conquest of space.'

Alex was so excited, he could hardly find words to express his feelings. 'Wonderful, Joey, wonderful,' he shouted into the mouthpiece. 'We won!'

'Well, you did!' Joey conceded. 'Congratulations.'

Beside himself with joy, Alex grabbed Nina by the waist and led her in a wild dance round the room. 'We won!' he shouted. 'We won the space race!' Between shouts, and leaps and bits of singing, he told her the great news. His enthusiasm infected her. She finally burst out laughing, and obediently spun with him in the living room. He had never before seen her laugh like that. 'Really, *golubchek*? Sputnik? What a beautiful name. Yes, my sweet, it's a great day indeed!'

'The Americans bragged they were about to launch a satellite, but did nothing,' he babbled excitedly, holding tight to her waist. His head was turning and he almost slipped and fell. 'While the Russians . . . They didn't say a word and – paff! We're in space!'

Nina nodded, smiling. Alex suddenly had an idea. He left Nina in the middle of the dance and ran downstairs. At Louey's stall he bought an evening newspaper, which already heralded on its front page: 'Red satellite in space'. Under the banner headline was printed the photograph released by the Soviet news agency – a shining round sphere from which several thin antennae emerged.

Back home, under the benign gaze of Nina, Alex cut out the front page of the newspaper, then pasted it on cardboard and tacked it to the wall over his desk. Sputnik looked great on the wall beside a colour print of Red Square and a black-and-white photograph of Soviet soldiers hoisting the red flag over Berlin, at the end of the Second World War. On the wall also hung pictures of Marx, Stalin, and the famous cruiser *Potemkin*, which had fired a shot on the Winter Palace in Petrograd in 1917, starting the October Revolution. A tiny bronze bust of Lenin, completing Alex's private collection, reigned over his desk.

Over the following years, other photographs, paintings and press cuttings were to join Alex's picture gallery. A portrait of Yuri Gagarin, the first astronaut whom the Russians called 'cosmonaut'; a brightly coloured poster of the Bolshoi Ballet; the Dinamo soccer team, clad in red shirts, in their Moscow stadium. Every year, Alex would select his 'picture of the year' and hang it on the wall, diligently inscribing the date in its bottom right corner. In 1960, it was the wreck of Gary Powers's U-2 spy plane, downed over the Soviet Union by a SAM missile; in 1961 a picture of bearded, cigar-smoking Fidel Castro, inspecting the Bay of Pigs where the CIA imperialist operation had ended in dismal failure.

Actually, Alex had also wanted to hang on the wall a couple of pennants, a poster of the Beatles in concert, a funny print of Bugs Bunny that Joey had given him, and a photograph of Johnny Weissmuller as Tarzan. But Nina had been furious. 'I shall not allow such trash in my living room,' she had said.

She had also refused to let him display his favourite picture of John Kennedy. The young president was wearing a sports shirt and walking up a field, against a background of ominous black clouds. But Nina had said no again, even though it was before the Bay of Pigs invasion. Alex felt she was being unfair. Actually, Kennedy had boldly criticized President Eisenhower for having lied to the Russians about the U-2 plane. Eisenhower had said to the Soviet leader Khrushchev that he had no knowledge of the U-2 missions over Russia. That had been a lie, and Kennedy had said so although the American people could turn against him for saying such unpleasant things about their beloved Ike.

But Nina didn't want to hear any of that. She angrily tore Kennedy's picture off Alex's wall. 'No friends of mine will find an American president in my living room,' she snapped, and he complied, although he failed to understand what could be so wrong with an American president.

Besides, friends of hers almost never came to see her, now that he was sleeping in the living room. He understood that before his arrival they were holding some of their meetings there. There was the Brooklyn chapter of the Peace movement, and the League for the Rosenbergs (who had been executed meanwhile) and other organizations manned mostly by elderly people, shabbily dressed, with strong foreign accents. 'That's why those men in the cars are watching me,' Nina had told him. Alex didn't know who the men in the cars were, but he understood that Nina was being watched by American agents because she supported the Soviet Union.

Still, the people in the cars came very rarely now, once every few months. They came mostly in the evenings, sat for a couple of hours in their car, watching their house, then drove away. Sometimes they came on foot, and lingered close to their building for hours, or followed Alex in the streets. They thought they were clever, but he had learned to spot them; they couldn't fool him.

He was quite observant, had sharp instincts, and developed his own methods for finding out if he was being shadowed. As he grew up, it turned into a game he enjoyed playing: he would always look out for strangers in their street, check up if the mailman, the milkman, the laundry and the grocery delivery boys who passed by their house were people he knew. He would inspect closely the commercial automobiles stationed in their street, and memorize the names of the companies that owned them, looking for cars that didn't belong in their part of the city.

On his way to school he would continually change his route, cross and recross the street several times, use shop windows as mirrors to find out if he was being followed, stop suddenly and go back, watching the other passers-by for any unusual reaction; he would also memorize the faces of people he saw in the street. Alex's sharp memory was his best asset. A couple of times he noticed that two men, whom he had seen outside their house, followed him on his way back from school. Shaking them off was easy. He was amused by the strangers' clumsiness.

He was in seventh grade now, a student at Jefferson Junior High. His friend Joey was still in his class, but so were his enemies Ralph and Stacy. He was doing quite well in school, except for mathematics, which was his weak spot. He was thirteen years old and growing up fast. He started looking at girls, although he wasn't interested in anyone in particular. Joey was madly in love with a girl from their class who already had breasts, Laura Hendel, but Alex found her too fat for his taste.

He was becoming a tall, athletic boy. Since his fights with Ralph he had become obsessed with the ability to hit back and defend himself. He ran around their block every morning, in the summer swam in the ocean, and doggedly exercised at home. In his free afternoons, he would go to Big Jack Macmillan's boxing school and help clean the rings, collect the towels, and sort out the soiled garments of the trainees. He watched the training sessions, trying to memorize the fighters' moves. Big Jack, a huge florid-faced man with a fighter's broken nose, would let him be; once in a while he would give Alex a pair of gloves and make him punch the ball, or even teach him a couple of boxer's passes.

'When you fight,' Big Jack would say, chewing on his cigar, 'remember rule number one. Left foot forward, bent at the knee, right foot backward, your weight is on the right foot, then throw all your body forward, shift your weight to the left foot, your force to your right arm, and – bang!' Alex did it time after time, but Big Jack would dejectedly shake his head. 'No way, lad, you're never going to be a fighter. There's no fire in you, no killing instinct. That's the most important, see? The killer streak.'

Still, the training at Macmillan's was bearing fruit; Alex's biceps became tougher, and he enjoyed the feel of his hardening muscles when he clenched his fists. His shirts became too tight at the shoulders. Nina was constantly busy repairing his clothes, or buying him longer trousers and larger shirts to keep up with his growth. This year, at Marshall's summer sale, she bought him a beautiful flyer's jacket, made of genuine leather. It carried that wonderful leather smell, and had a soft fur collar which felt so good against his skin when he raised it! And the jacket was brand new, not like most of the clothes she bought him at Polack's used garments store. Alex was very excited with his jacket, and couldn't wait for the weather to cool so he could put it on.

But on the first cold day of the autumn, when he went to school proudly clad in his flyer's jacket, he saw a small group of boys waiting for him outside the gate. Ralph was there, and Stacy, and two other boys named Brad and Tommy. Burt, who had called him names back in first grade, had left the neighbourhood because his father had got rich and they had moved to Manhattan. Alex looked at the four boys, noticed that they abruptly stopped talking as they saw him, and realized he was headed for trouble.

He knew what the trouble was. The previous night, President Kennedy had dramatically announced that Russian missiles had been positioned in Cuba, and threatened the United States. American reconnaissance planes, overflying Cuba, had taken photographs of the missiles. Alex had watched the evening news on television with Joey, at the Hollywood Soda Fountain, and seen the photographs.

Kennedy also said that the missile bases were manned by Red Army crews. Joey had said America must invade Cuba and kill Castro.

The discovery of the missiles in Cuba had shocked the world. Alex too had been surprised. The Soviet Union was a peace-loving nation, why should she threaten America with missiles? But Nina explained to him that it was the other way around. America had missiles all over the globe pointed at the Soviet Union; American bombers were constantly in the skies, ready to drop atomic bombs over the Soviet Union if the President gave the order. America was the aggressor, plotting to destroy Russia. The Soviet Prime Minister, Nikita Khrushchev, had to defend his country!

Alex didn't like Khrushchev. A couple of years before he had visited America. At a meeting of the United Nations' general assembly, he had been involved in an unpleasant incident. Infuriated by an anti-Soviet speech, Khrushchev had taken off his shoe and pounded with it on his desk, shouting angrily. Alex thought that was gross, it didn't become the proud leader of the Soviets, but Nina said there was nothing wrong with it.

'The United Nations,' she said, 'has been turned by the Americans into a propaganda machine against the Soviet Union. Russia should show them she will not tolerate this anymore.'

Alex didn't argue with Nina. But last night, during Kennedy's speech about Cuba, he recalled Khrushchev pounding his shoe on the desk, waving his fist and yelling.

As Alex approached the school gate now, Ralph barred his way. 'We don't want you in our school,' he said spitefully. 'This is an American school. We don't want Russian spies in it.' Saying that, he caught Alex by the sleeve.

'Let me go,' he muttered. 'I don't want to fight.' He hadn't fought with Ralph since that day in first grade. They disliked each other and almost never spoke.

'Chicken,' Ralph taunted him. 'Yellow chicken.'

Easy, Alex said to himself, you're one and they are four. You must be very careful.

'Are you going to shoot your missiles now?' Tommy threw at him. Tommy was a very handsome boy with bleached hair and clear but hard blue eyes.

'You're a spy!' Stacy accused, taking a step toward him.

'No, I'm not,' Alex said angrily. He shook off Ralph's hand.

'We saw on TV how you spied on our ambassador in Moscow. What a shame, to use our seal,' Tommy said. 'Aren't you ashamed?'

On the television news last night, a silver-haired man named Cabot Lodge had displayed the seal of the United States that had hung in the office of the American ambassador in Moscow. The seal was engraved on a round piece of wood. The Russians had sliced it off then glued it back after planting a listening device in the hollowed out interior. The Russians had placed the bug in the very beak of the American eagle carved upon the seal. This way they could listen to all the ambassador's conversations.

Alex had asked Nina about it, and she had said that the Soviet Union had to protect itself; everybody knew that the American embassy collected intelligence about the Soviet military forces.

'You're spies, all of you,' Brad intervened. He was a squat boy with pockmarked cheeks. His black eyes were small and suspicious. 'All your family are spies, we know.'

'That's a lie,' Alex protested. Other children had gathered around them, their angry stares converging upon him. 'Go back to Russia!' a thin voice called behind his back.

'Your parents are in jail for spying,' Brad insisted.

'They're not,' Alex flared. 'They were killed in an accident.'

'You're lying,' Ralph said venomously. 'Your sweet aunt is a spy too! My father told me that her name is Nina Kramer, and she was tried for spying. He saw her picture in the paper.'

'That's not true!'

'We saw your Aunt Nina when she came to pick you up at school,' Ralph went on. Nina had come two or three times, and waited for him by the gate. 'She came to spy on our school, so you could fire your missiles on us. She'll go to jail too, like all the other spies.' The crowd of children cheered him.

'Alex! Aliosha!' Stacy called theatrically, holding out his arms to him. He started walking in circles round Alex, mimicking Nina's gait and her heavy accent. 'Come, Aliosha, my little dove.' He had apparently overheard her talking. The children now bellowed with laughter.

'She'll hang as a spy,' Ralph said, encouraged by the cheering audience, 'or perhaps we'll fry her in the electric chair.'

'You jerk!' Alex exploded. He couldn't let the repulsive Ralph insult his aunt. He lunged forward but Ralph saw the blow coming and stepped back. Alex's fist barely touched his cheek. Ralph kicked Alex in the groin. The pain was excruciating. He moaned and doubled up. He heard some of the students clapping hands and shouting, cheering Ralph. His three friends hesitated for a moment, then joined the mêlée.

This saved Alex from being defeated in the very first minute, when he was still dizzy and in great pain. His assailants stepped in each other's way and most of their blows were ineffective. While repelling their punches he searched for a weak spot in their attack. Brad tried to seize him by the waist, and Alex kicked his ankle, making him lose balance. As he fell, he got hold of Alex's arm and pulled him down. He heard a ripping noise. Brad had torn the sleeve of his jacket. Mad with fury, he shook Brad off, and drove his right elbow into Stacy's belly. He recoiled, gasping for air. Tommy bent to help Brad to his feet.

Suddenly Ralph was standing before Alex, looking confident, his face unprotected. Now! With crystal clarity Big Jack's instructions surfaced in Alex's mind. Weight on the right foot, left foot forward, slightly bent, then a shift of the weight to the left foot, all your force in the fist – go! He hit Ralph's exposed chin with all his concentrated power; the angry blow came from beneath in an upward arc. Ralph was flung backwards, then collapsed on the pavement, his eyes glassy.

But Alex's triumph was brief. Brad and Stacy, back on their feet, grabbed his arms from both sides. Tommy emerged before him, his face set in ugly determination. He drove his fists into Alex's belly, four or five times, and when he jacknifed in agony, struck him in the face. Alex squirmed, trying to kick his enemies, but they held him tight as Tommy mercilessly punched him again. 'You damn spy!' he kept repeating. A blow landed on Alex's eyebrow, and blood trickled into his left eye, blurring his vision. A burning sensation spread along his cheek, that Tommy had scratched.

'Stop that at once! What are you doing?' An adult voice rose from behind, and Alex's assailants let go of him and fled. 'I saw you!' the man shouted. Alex recognized the voice of Mr Lieblich, the maths teacher.

Alex saw the teacher, in his perpetual blue suit and wide-brimmed black hat, chasing the children into the schoolyard. He swayed, then squatted on the dirty pavement, holding his stomach. He was going to be sick. His new jacket was a mess; beside the torn sleeve, there were ugly cuts and scratches on the brown leather. What would Nina say? he thought. But he forgot his troubles as he saw Ralph lying groaning, then dazedly trying to straighten up. He was shaking his head like a dog coming out of water. Macmillan should have seen me, Alex thought proudly. It was the perfect knock out, worthy of a killer.

The next morning, Nina and Alex were summoned to see the school's principal. Mr Holloway was standing behind his desk, nervously tapping with his pen on an open file. A large portrait of Thomas Jefferson hung on the wall behind him, beside the American flag. On his right, in a cupboard with glass doors, stood scores of gleaming trophies the school had won in sport tournaments. A stale odour of tobacco hung inside the small office.

Mr Holloway was a thin middle-aged man with sparse greying hair, tired eyes and prominent cheekbones. His worn-out suit hung loosely from his skeletal frame, and the collar of his grey shirt seemed a couple of sizes too large for his scrawny neck. He had bony hands with long gnarled fingers. Alex knew him as a soft-spoken man, who never raised his voice. But today, his eyes had a cold, mean look, and angry spots of colour flared in his cheeks.

He didn't ask Nina to sit down. 'I'll be brief,' he said. His voice was thick with anger. 'Yesterday's events brought shame on the Jefferson Junior High. Your conduct, Alex Gordon, has no excuse. I shall not tolerate any violence between my students.'

'There were four of them against me,' he protested.

'The school hasn't overcome yesterday's scandal yet,' the principal said. He reached for the pipe that lay in an ashtray, then changed his mind. 'Many students saw the fight. Some were scared, a few hurt.' He glanced at Alex's bruised face. 'Ralph Barr has two broken teeth, and needs medical attention.'

Good, Alex rejoiced, but kept his thoughts to himself. 'My new jacket was torn,' he said, not looking at Nina.

Mr Holloway raised his hand. 'I shall not tolerate my school being turned into an anti-American institution.'

'What did he say?' Nina asked Alex, but he motioned to her to wait. It was clear that Mr Holloway regarded him as totally responsible for yesterday's fight.

'You, young man,' Mr Holloway went on, 'can hardly be suspected of giving your fellow students an example of American patriotism.'

'But I didn't . . .' Alex started, stung at the unfair accusation.

'Since you've become a student in this school, you haven't ceased voicing opinions hostile to this country and favourable to our greatest enemy, Soviet Russia. I am well aware of the views that you express in class. You speak as if you don't belong in this country. Perhaps it's not your fault, but that of your family.' Holloway looked at Nina.

'What you say?' she managed in her limping English.

'Since yesterday morning the telephone hasn't stopped ringing,' Mr Holloway said to her. 'I have had complaints from many parents. They demand that your nephew be expelled from the school.'

'Who are this parents?' Nina said belligerently. Last night, when Alex had narrated the incident to her, she had kissed him warmly. 'You did right, *golubchek*.'

'There's Mr Barr for one, and Mr Warzsawski, Stacy's father. And also Mr John Simpson, who is a teacher.'

'Mr Simpson?' Alex was stunned. It couldn't be. Mr Simpson was Joey's father.

'Yes,' the principal said. 'He claims that you are a very bad influence on his son.'

Joey's father didn't want them to be friends anymore. Alex felt afraid for the first time. In spite of everything he liked the school, some of the teachers, and quite a few of the children. If he were thrown out, he wouldn't be able to see Joey anymore; that would certainly mean an end to their friendship.

'No, please, Mister . . .' Nina started, guessing Mr Holloway's threat.

'I decided not to expel you, though,' the principal said sternly, watching Alex. 'You're a good student and this time you'll get away with a warning. You should be grateful that your adoptive country is a democracy where you can express the most revolting opinions. That is certainly not the case in the Soviet Union.' He wiped his brow with a grey handkerchief. 'But I'll transfer you to another class. You'll be separated from Ralph Barr and his friends.'

And from Joey, Alex thought.

'And I am also officially advising you that the next time any complaint about you reaches me, I'll expel you from our school without further warning. Is that clear?'

'Yes,' Alex whispered. His throat was constricted. This is unfair, he wanted to protest. It wasn't my fault! But he was afraid he would be thrown out of school, so he remained silent. He had never felt so humiliated.

But it wasn't Mr Holloway's warning, nor the prospect of another fight, not even the fear of losing Joey's friendship that made Alex stop voicing his opinions. It was the turn of political events.

That afternoon, a few days after the Cuba crisis started, he was again at the soda fountain with Joey. His father had forbidden him to see Alex again, but Joey didn't care. The skinny boy didn't scare easily, and had a lot of backbone. He was now happily blabbering about Laura's answer to a note he had sent to her, but Alex wasn't listening. He expected war to break out at any moment between the United States and the Soviet Union, especially after Kennedy had imposed a naval blockade on Cuba. On the television screen harried speakers kept announcing that a special news bulletin was due any minute.

'So she came to me,' Joey narrated in ecstasy, 'and said: "Was that you who wrote that sweet note to me, Joey?" And I said . . .'

'Not now, Joey,' Alex said, and he clammed up, visibly hurt. But the words 'Special Report' flashed onto the screen, and a newscaster's face appeared. 'The Soviet Prime Minister,' he solemnly started, 'Mr Nikita Khrushchev, declared that he would pull out all his missiles from Cuba in the interests of peace.'

'What?' Alex gasped.

Joey was shaking his head. 'I don't believe it.'

'The Soviet Union will put at the disposal of the international community all the necessary proofs and guarantees that her intentions are serious,' the newscaster went on. On the screen, his face was replaced by film sequences taken from low-flying aircraft in which Soviet ships could be seen sailing away from Cuba. On the ships' decks were stacked long cylindrical shapes covered with tarpaulin. At the sight of the approaching American craft, the Russian crews removed the tarpaulin, uncovering the missiles. They waved to the Americans; one of the shots had been taken from a very short distance, and the Russians could be clearly seen, grinning and cheering.

'I must be dreaming,' Joey murmured. Alex was too dismayed to speak. He felt as if somebody had sandbagged him, dealing him a stunning blow. Why did they do it? What was going on?

He slowly came to his senses. The Russians had capitulated before the Americans, they were unconditionally retreating and they were pulling out of Cuba 'in the interests of peace'. Which meant that by bringing the missiles to Cuba in the first place, they had acted against peace. Had Russia made a mistake? Was Kennedy right when he called the Russians aggressors?

He jumped up from his seat and darted toward the exit. 'Where are you going?' Joey called after him, but Alex didn't answer. He ran all the way home and burst like a hurricane into the apartment. Nina was standing in the kitchen, cooking. 'Khrushchev announced that he's pulling out the missiles from Cuba,' he announced breathlessly. 'He gave in.' He watched Nina intently as he spoke.

For a moment she was at a loss. She blinked several times, frowning, then said half-heartedly: 'What is this, Alex, a joke?'

'No, not a joke. I saw the Russian ships carrying the missiles back. They showed them on TV!'

She stared back at him for a while, then slowly settled into a chair, pursing her lips as she always did when she was thinking. '*Nu*,' she said, 'that proves once again, that the Soviet Union is ready to do anything for peace, even . . .'

He couldn't take it. 'How can you say that!' he exploded. 'How can you still defend them? Now it's clear that they acted recklessly, and almost caused a world war.'

'Now, Alex . . .'

'But you always defend them, don't you? You always find an excuse for what they're doing. You'll never admit they could be wrong, even once!' He ran into the living room and furiously tore off his wall Castro's smiling picture. 'He has nothing to smile about,' he muttered furiously.

But the hardest blow came right after the Festival of Shavuot.

Lately Alex was getting mildly interested in his religion. Last year he had turned thirteen, but Nina had refused to celebrate his Bar-Mitzvah, which she regarded as a barbaric custom. Alex was unhappy with her decision; he wanted to learn more about his Jewish origins, and fathom the secret of Jewish survival throughout the ages. There must be something in our religion, he thought, that made us overcome all the disasters, persecutions and massacres along our history. He hoped that the religious studies held in preparation for the Bar-Mitzvah might unlock for him the door to Judaism, but didn't want to confront Nina on this question. One day, he thought, when I grow older, I'll look into this myself.

On the day of Shavuot, the Jewish Pentecost, he visited their neighbourhood synagogue. He hadn't told Nina about it. But he left the service disappointed. People in skullcaps and prayer shawls were reciting and chanting in Hebrew. He understood nothing, didn't know the meaning of the prayers, didn't know when to get up and when to sit down; he was a stranger among his own people.

The following morning he saw Ralph Barr coming out of his classroom. They had bumped into each other in the past but didn't talk. They were afraid to get into another fight that could cause their expulsion from school. But this morning Alex noticed an evil, malicious grin on Ralph's face. There was pure hatred mixed with triumph in his eyes. Alex was startled and walked to his desk wondering what the reason was for Ralph's elation.

On his desk was a plain white envelope, unsealed.

He opened it. A press cutting fell out. It was an article from the *Daily News*, dated last Thursday. The headline said: 'Soviets secretly massacred eminent Jewish writers'. The article was illustrated with several portraits: a bespectacled man named Mikhoels, a man with a gaunt face and large forehead named Fefer. But his attention was drawn to two names circled in vivid red.

Victor Wolf and Tonya Gordon-Wolf.

His knees buckled and he slumped into his chair. His heart was suddenly pounding in his chest. Somebody called his name and said something, but he couldn't hear. He swallowed hard, and tried to concentrate on reading. The words were dancing before his eyes. He had to read every sentence three or four times to understand it.

In the years 1949 and 1953, the article said, the KGB had secretly executed some of the greatest Jewish writers and philosophers in Russia. In a mock trial, they had been accused of spying for the United States and Great Britain. Most of the writers had been shot, the rest had perished in the concentration camps. They were all victims of Stalin's persecution mania.

The massacre had been kept secret, the article continued, until the defection of a Soviet diplomat last month. His revelations explained at last the disappearance of so many famous writers from the Soviet literary scene in the early fifties.

There followed a list of the writers murdered by Stalin. And the names of his mother and father.

He got up from his seat and walked out of the class. The maths teacher was saying something, looking at him strangely, but Alex didn't hear. It was raining outside, a warm, early-summer rain. Heavy drops splashed on his face as he crossed the schoolyard. Ralph was behind all this, he knew, but he didn't care about Ralph. The jerk had only cut out the article and put it on his desk.

Alex walked into the street, the rain soaking his hair and clothes and streaming down his face. As he crossed Flatbush Avenue, he was almost run over by a car. The driver, a round-faced man smoking a huge cigar, angrily waved his fist and yelled at him.

Alex entered Spiegel's Furs and went straight to the back of the store. Two salesgirls came toward him, alarmed, and one said: 'It's Nina's nephew, he looks a mess.' His water-soaked shoes left muddy prints on the carpet. Mr Spiegel, a fat bald man with golden-rimmed spectacles and a blue suit, got up from his seat, furiously glaring at him.

Finally he saw Nina. She hurried towards him, her face a mixture of puzzlement and concern. She had told him never to come to the store, Mr Spiegel might get upset.

Nina asked something, but he didn't hear. He delved into his shirt pocket and his hand came out clutching the press cutting, now wet and dripping.

'Did you . . .' he started, but his voice was oddly thin, almost inaudible, '. . . did you know about this? Did you know that Stalin murdered my parents? Did you?'

Nina was staring at him, her trembling hand rising to her mouth, her eyes filled with anguish.

'Dimitri, my beloved brother,' he wrote in Russian, 'for many years I tried to write to you, but I didn't find you. I sent you greetings for the

New Year and your birthday (Aunt Nina, Mother's sister, said you were born on July 6, 1950), but the letters were returned by the Moscow Post Office. Perhaps I have the wrong address. I am therefore writing on the envelope that they should forward the letter to your new address. This time I hope it will reach you. This is important because I've got terrible news.

'An American newspaper published an article saying that our mother and my father were executed for treason by the Soviet security services. Did you know that? I don't believe my parents were traitors. You know that our mother wasn't a traitor, she was a great Soviet poetess. Your father wouldn't have married her if she or her former husband had done anything wrong. This must have been a terrible mistake. Perhaps your father can help us find the truth? I know he is an officer in your security services, can you ask him? I often read Mother's poems and I can't believe that she has been shot for treason, she was so devoted to the Soviet Union. I often dream at night about her death, and I wake up crying.

'Please write to me when you receive this letter. I so much want to meet you. I think I remember you. Do you have brown hair and black eyes? That's how I remember you. And how are you doing at school? I am doing fine, except for maths, which I hate, or perhaps it is because of our teacher. I love reading books, I like movies, rock music, mostly the Beatles, and colour television. How is the television in Moscow? Aunt Nina says it's the best in the world. Do you like the Beatles? I am also boxing a little and play softball. No soccer in America, could you imagine?

'Please write to me. Your loving older brother,

Alex.'

Three months later, the letter was returned to Alex. The envelope was stamped with a large purple inscription, saying: 'Unknown at this address'.

Chapter Five

At five minutes to eight Nikita stuck his egglike head in at the door and beckoned. 'Get ready,' he rasped, revealing his tobacco-stained teeth, 'they're here. Good luck.'

'Thank you, Nikita,' he said affectionately. Nikita was one of the few men in the institution who had ever been kind to him. The old janitor waved a gnarled hand at him and was gone.

He stood up, pulled tight his uniform jacket, buckled up his heavy belt, and rubbed the toes of his shoes against his ankles, polishing the leather with the back crease of his trousers. From the dented mirror by the door, a slim youth stared angrily back at him. He critically examined his reflection: the cropped brown hair, the pale forehead, the gaunt, saturnine face. There was smouldering hostility in the black almond-shaped eyes, sheltered under thick eyebrows. His stubborn mouth, clamped with bitterness, was a thin line under the straight nose; a brown mole lay, a stranded punctuation mark, over his upper lip. The jawline was sharp and the square chin jutted defiantly forward. It could have been a handsome, passionate face, were it not so fierce and accusing; his black stare made people ill at ease.

Relax, he thought, calm down, don't show your bitterness. And keep your chin down, don't look too aggressive, they want you tame and subdued. That's the secret of climbing the ladder in Mother Russia: only the tame and subdued are allowed to become fierce and brutal. And you, Dimka, you already bare your fangs like a wolf, while you're still expected to bleat as a baby lamb.

The far door of the deserted dormitory opened, and Vanya barged in. He was short of breath, he must have been running. Vanya waved at him with both hands. 'I wanted to catch you before you left,' he called. 'Good luck, Dimka!'

He waved back and went out. The corridor was cold, but his forehead and palms were sweating profusely. His knees were shaky and a sensation of emptiness lingered at the pit of his stomach. His footsteps echoed loudly in the long passage. Along his way, the portraits of legendary Russian generals stared at him from their frames on the peeling light green walls: Suvorov, the eighteenth-century master; Kutuzov, who drove Napoleon out of Moscow; Budienny, the revolutionary commander of the Red Cavalry; Zhukov, the conqueror of Berlin in the Second World War. From the spaces between the portraits, slogans painted on thick cardboard praised the glorious Red Army and its heroes. The largest slogan, fixed above the refectory door, proclaimed: 'The Panfilov Institution for Orphans of Soviet Heroes salutes the Motherland on the Anniversary of the October Revolution'. Some joker had erased the H of the word Heroes and painted a Z instead.

He entered the office of Lev Brudny, the new administrator. By the window he could see the vegetable garden, still buried in deep snow. 'You can go right in,' Brudny said to him, half rising from his chair, a greasy smile on his stupid face. He knocked on the heavy door made of thick oak. 'The Panfilov Institution', the chipped enamel sign read. 'Colonel Pavel Borodin, Principal'.

He stepped into the principal's office. Colonel Borodin wasn't there. Behind his large desk three chairs had been placed. Two men and a woman were seated close together, smoking and quietly talking. On the desk were steaming glasses of tea and a bowl of sugar cubes. When they saw him enter, they fell silent. From the far wall a portrait of Lenin observed them with a benign smile. When Dimitri had first entered this room, as a little child, it had been Stalin who had scornfully surveyed him from the same spot.

'Good morning, Comrades,' he said, and stood to attention.

'Good morning,' answered the man in the middle, apparently the Commission Chairman. Before him lay Dimitri's application forms. The Chairman was a corpulent man of about fifty, dressed in a grey suit, with greying blond hair and a sallow face. His watery eyes had a guarded expression, and his mouth was large and rubbery. He was wearing a crimson silk tie. A small pin, representing a red flag crossed with a bayonetted rifle, was stuck in the lapel of his suit jacket. It indicated he was a Red Army veteran.

'I am Genadi Bodrov,' he said, 'from the Committee of State Security.' The Committee was better known by its initials, the KGB. 'This is Comrade Helena Kraiova, Deputy Director of the Higher School of State Security.' The woman, dressed in a conservative blue suit and white blouse, had a stout torso; her forehead was mottled with tiny spots over sharp, alert eyes. She held her cigarette like a pencil, between her thumb and forefinger. 'And Colonel Oleg Kalinin from the GRU.' The GRU was Military Intelligence. The tall, handsome colonel was wearing an elegant dark-blue suit and a dazzling white shirt. He nodded at Dimitri, a quick smile flashing over his face. A friend perhaps, Dimitri thought. A groove of scarred white tissue ran across Kalini's left cheek, below the cheekbone.

'You may stand at ease,' Bodrov said briskly, pretending to study Dimitri's application forms. He suddenly raised his head. 'I see that your mother and father have been shot for treason, and that your half-brother lives in America.'

A chill ran up his spine and he nodded woodenly.

'That makes you a security risk, don't you think?' the woman said coldly, exhaling a puff of smoke.

'If you were in our place,' Bodrov followed, 'would you admit somebody with such a record into the KGB?'

'Now, now, Comrades,' Colonel Kalinin said pleasantly. 'We know that both Tonya Gordon and Boris Morozov have been fully rehabilitated.' He picked up Dimitri's application forms and glanced at them for a moment, then put them back on the desk. 'Dimitri Morozov is a fine young man, and his record is commendable. We don't want him to pay for what Stalin did – wrongly – to his parents.'

Dimitri felt a surge of relief. Thank God for Colonel Kalinin, he thought, he was openly siding with him.

Bodrov, forehead thoughtfully puckered, slowly nodded, then looked at Dimitri. 'Tell the Commission why you wish to study at the Higher School of State Security.'

He cleared his throat. Kalinin smiled at him encouragingly. He was much more confident now. 'If they intend to reject you,' General Takachenko had told him the day before, 'the interview will be over in thirty seconds. That's the ritual.'

So let's proceed according to the ritual, he thought. 'My name is Dimitri Morozov,' he started. He had learned the trite formula by heart. 'I want to participate in the building of socialism. I am a member of the Soviet communist youth, the Komsomol. I want to serve the Soviet Union and protect our just society against its enemies from within and without. I want to join the KGB and follow the footsteps of my father, Colonel Boris Morozov.'

Do you really want to know why I am joining you? he bitterly reflected while declaiming the banal answers they expected. Do you want me to describe the life of a helpless child, abandoned to his fate in this accursed orphanage? Do you want to hear about a childhood of privation and abuse? Do you want to know how I learned to cheat, and lie, and steal, in order to survive? And how my despair made me swear I'd escape from this place, and erase this ugly chapter from my life?

He didn't remember the day this black chapter had started. When he had arrived at the Panfilov Orphanage, he was barely two and a half years old. He had lived here practically all his life; although, at times, a succession of blurred images would surface in his mind, like an enigmatic message from a former existence. And he would perceive short, fragmentary glimpses of a stocky, black-haired man with severe features, a faceless woman with long golden hair and a sweet smell, and another child, a merry blond boy. He recalled riding in an automobile with a driver through large, snow-covered avenues, the blond child jumping and giggling beside him.

He never mentioned these memories to his classmates at Panfilov; he was a quiet, lonely child, and kept mostly to himself. He often longed painfully for a mother, for a hug, a loving touch; sometimes he would dream about the woman with the golden hair. But he didn't know if she was his mother. She was probably dead, she couldn't have knowingly abandoned him to his fate. And the blond child? Was he his brother? What had happened to him?

Dimitri felt that there was something unclear about his origins. He had asked his teachers about his father, but his questions had been met with cold, silent stares. To his friends' questions he answered that his father had been a colonel and had perished fighting for the motherland. 'Where did he fight?' his classmates would ask. 'How come he was killed fighting? There was no war when you were born.'

'And what about you?' he countered. 'We are the same age.'

Their own fathers, they replied, had been heroes of the Soviet Union, but had died years after the war. He bowed his head, confused. He didn't know what to say.

Only at the age of thirteen had he heard about his parents' execution. Panic-stricken, he had retreated even further into himself, raising the ramparts and pulling up bridges, determined to preserve his shameful secret. Nobody at Panfilov, he decided, should ever find out what fate had befallen Boris and Tonya Morozov.

The Panfilov Orphanage was located in an old barracks of the Tzar's 17th Cavalry Regiment outside the Leningrad suburb of Pushkin. The barracks consisted of drab, dun-coloured structures stuck in the middle of an exercise area that was frozen solid in the winter, and turned into a muddy mire in the spring and fall. The soldiers' dormitories and most of the stables had been hastily rebuilt to lodge three hundred boys, aged from two to eighteen. The orphanage was named after a war hero, General Panfilov, who had been killed defending Moscow. It was run by a retired colonel, and organized as a regular military unit.

Dimitri and the other children were issued uniforms – a dark woollen set for winter and two light khaki outfits for summertime. Each boy was also given a cap and an overcoat, a pair of high shoes and a pair of felt boots. Their hair was cropped short; their beds and lockers subject to constant inspections. The dorms were often fumigated, but the lice and ticks of Panfilov didn't seem to mind and kept sucking the children's blood, together with all the other parasites living on their backs.

Each dormitory corresponded to an age group and a school class. Older boys, attached to the dormitories, served as 'duty sergeants' and ran the classes as military platoons. There were roll calls, drills on the parade grounds, physical exercises, paramilitary training. The teachers and instructors, most of them former officers, lived in the compound with their families.

No student was allowed to leave the orphanage without special permission, which was almost never given; the only way Dimitri and his friends could catch a glimpse of Leningrad was during the class trips to various museums and stadia in the city. Girls were not allowed in the Panfilov compound, except for the families of the staff. The staff quarters were several tidy cottages, separated from the orphanage by the parade grounds. A shady chestnut grove stretched behind the cottages.

At Panfilov Dimitri learned to live in constant, degrading poverty. He never received a new garment, or a new pair of shoes. The uniforms issued to him were threadbare hand-me-downs, repaired and patched countless times, as were the shoes. Private property wasn't allowed. Any clothes, underwear, money, pocket knives or food discovered in the students' lockers was immediately confiscated. The school was in a state of constant disrepair; in the winter, icy gusts of wind swept the decrepit buildings, howling through the broken windows. The children almost froze to death in their poorly heated dormitories, shivering under thin blankets.

Hunger became Dimitri's most faithful companion. Black bread and gluey porridge for breakfast, black bread and potatoes for lunch, black bread and watery soup for dinner: this was the invariable menu in the refectory. On national holidays the students also received meat, fish or sausage. The vegetables they grew in the backyard never reached their plates. 'Rotten,' the chief cook would invariably answer their timid inquiries, 'everything was rotten this year.' He was a burly man with huge arms and a malevolent face. Nobody dared to contradict him; that was considered insubordination. The punishment for insubordination could be expulsion from the school, and they had nowhere to go.

But there was a priceless subject that Dimitri mastered at Panfilov: the art of survival.

As long as he lived in the small children's wing, Dimitri had been protected. But on the first night he spent in the third grade dormitory, somebody stole his shoes. In the morning he trudged barefoot to the duty sergeant and reported the theft. The older boy, a sturdy youth with tallow-coloured hair, a round face and small porcine eyes, coldly shrugged. 'That's your problem,' he drawled. His front teeth were rotten. 'You must be more careful next time.'

Dimitri didn't know what to do. He was only nine. Classes were about to start. He ran to the administrator's office, to complain, but on the way bumped into the janitor, Nikita. 'Lost your shoes, little one?' the man asked kindly. He was bald, frail, always wearing a worn-out *rubashka* and walking with a funny, gooselike gait. But he had a warm voice and kind soft eyes.

'Yes, and I'm going to report it to the administrator.'

Nikita sadly shook his head. 'Don't,' he said, gently touching the boy's cheek. 'You'll be punished, they won't help you. Do you have any money?'

'No,' he said, surprised. 'Why?'

'That's what I thought,' said Nikita. 'If you had money, or anything of value, you could have asked your duty sergeant to help. He would have found your shoes.'

'I have some books,' Dimitri said hopefully. He was devouring travel and adventure books, and had won *Gulliver's Travels*, *Treasure Island* and *Oliver Twist* in school contests.

Nikita shook his head. 'Books are no good. Money, that's what you need. If not . . .' He stared fixedly at Dimitri. 'You can wear your boots to class today, nobody will mind. But if your shoes are missing at the inspection on Saturday, you'll be in big trouble. You'll be punished, and they'll enter a warning in your file.'

'But why would anybody steal my shoes?' Dimitri asked, his eyes welling with tears.

The janitor took a tin box full of black tobacco out of his pocket, and rolled a cigarette in a piece of grey wrapping paper. 'To sell them, of course,' he said. Noticing Dimitri's puzzlement, Nikita added: 'Back to you, or at the market in Pushkin. People would pay a good price for a pair of shoes, even second-hand.'

'But,' Dimitri stammered, 'we aren't allowed out of school.'

Nikita lit his cigarette, and let out a murky puff of smoke. 'There are ways, little one, there are always ways.'

Only when Nikita had gone did Dimitri understand. He was expected to buy back his shoes, and if he didn't have money or valuables – to steal a pair of shoes from another child.

He went to class in his felt boots. During the day he kept thinking about Oliver Twist, the hero of the Dickens novel. How helpless he had been, all alone in the orphanage! At nightfall, he lay awake in his cot, listening to the regular snoring of his roommates. Long after everybody had fallen asleep, he slipped down from his bed and crawled to the far end of the dorm. His arms and legs were trembling with fear. Stealing was wrong, he knew, he had never stolen before. If he were caught, he would be thrown out of the orphanage. But if he didn't get another pair of shoes, he would be punished. He had to succeed.

One of the children stirred in his sleep, and Dimitri froze, holding his breath. But the boy turned the other way and Dimitri continued to crawl. Shoes were nowhere to be seen; apparently the other boys, smarter than he, had safely hidden them in their lockers or under their pillows before going to bed. He was too naive, that's why his shoes had been stolen.

By the last bed he saw a pair of shoes. He approached, and crouched in the dark. Nobody moved. His heart was thumping wildly. Twice he reached for the shoes, but withdrew his hand. He couldn't do it, he didn't want to become a thief. But he didn't want to be punished either, this coming Saturday. He didn't want a warning in his file. He hadn't done anything wrong, why should he suffer? Oliver Twist had also been forced to steal when he escaped to London, he'd had no choice.

Finally he grabbed the shoes and lunged back. But the shoes wouldn't come! They clanged against the iron bedpost, the sharp noise making his heart leap with dread. The shoes had been tied to the bed! He dropped them and darted in panic towards his bed. On both sides of the passage, heads were rising from the pillows.

'Catch him,' somebody yelled. 'He tried to steal my shoes!'

'Catch the thief!' a few other voices shouted. He kept running, but one of the boys stretched his leg across the passage between the beds. He stumbled and fell on his face. Several pairs of hands grasped his arms and feet and pinned him to the ground. He wildly fought, kicking and striving to yank his arms free. 'Let me go!' he groaned, tears choking his throat. 'Let me go!'

'A blanket,' somebody called urgently, in a low voice. The duty sergeant! 'A blanket, and keep quiet!'

Somebody threw a blanket on him, and a strong hand clamped over his mouth. Then they fell on him, perhaps five or six boys, hitting and kicking him with all their force. The pain was terrible; he was suffocating, gasping for air, and tears were streaming down his face. The boys beat him silently, viciously, and he could hear their rasping breath as they threw their punches at him. He couldn't protect his face, his arms were held behind his back. A blow smashed his nose, another landed on the side of his mouth, and he felt the salty taste of blood. Somebody kicked him in the spine, and he jerked in pain. But he didn't moan and didn't shout, biting his lips.

The blows suddenly stopped, and somebody removed the blanket. At first he didn't open his eyes, he felt so humiliated. Finally he looked up. In the darkness he made out a group of boys, surrounding him, staring down at him. 'Dirty thief!' one of them said, and spat at him. A child standing behind the others tried to kick him. A dazzling beam of light shone in his face, somebody had switched on an electric torch. He blinked in the light, and looked away.

'Look at him,' the duty sergeant said. He was the one with the torch. 'That's the thief, one of your own. Remember him, and don't let him come near your belongings. And not a word to the teachers. We settle these matters between ourselves.'

He lay on his bed, aching, humiliated, and silently cried. Once or twice he sank into fitful sleep that lasted only a few minutes. When he woke up he couldn't believe that he had been caught stealing, and the other children had beaten him up. It hadn't happened, he thought, he'd only had a nightmare. But as he turned on his bed, he felt the raw pain from the beating. It hadn't been a dream after all; his nightmare had just begun.

As morning came, he experienced the ignominy of being an outcast. Nobody spoke to him. Children grimaced at him, spat on the floor, or called him names. At breakfast, when he sat down, his classmates moved to another table. In class, he heard the boys around him whispering: 'thief'. When he came back to the classroom after lunch break he found that somebody had chalked a skull and cross bones on his desk.

'What happened to your face?' the arithmetic teacher asked him. In the mirror his face had glowed with all the colours of the rainbow. His upper lip was swollen, and a crust of coagulated blood had formed under his nose. Two long scratches ran across his left cheek. 'I fell,' he said. His classmates giggled.

The teacher, an old man with wise eyes, peered at him closely. 'Be more careful,' he suggested. He probably understood what had happened, but obeying the orphanage code, didn't investigate further.

Dimitri knew that the following days were going to be terrible; he had been branded an outcast by his class. Still, his problem remained unsolved. He needed new shoes before the Saturday inspection. Tonight, or tomorrow at the latest, he had to try again. He had no choice, he had to do it.

This time, though, he prepared his operation carefully. He wouldn't attempt to steal the shoes of one of his room mates, but try another class. He should also choose the right time. After spending another sleepless night he thought he had a plan. In the morning he studied the school schedule posted on a board beside the administrator's door. During lunch, he stole a knife at the refectory, and concealed it in his blouse. In the middle of geography class, at two-thirty, he suddenly doubled up in his seat, feigning stomach ache, and raised his hand. 'I must have eaten something bad,' he moaned, 'may I go to the toilet?'

The teacher, Comrade Lydia Raznukhina, stared at him severely, then reluctantly nodded agreement. As soon as he was out of her sight, he dashed to the calisthenics hall where the fifth grade was exercising in dark blue shorts and undershirts. Their clothes hung in the adjacent locker room; their shoes were neatly lined up on the floor, each pair tied together by the laces.

Dimitri selected two pairs of shoes which looked roughly his size, then took the knife out of his blouse and cut the laces. He took the right shoe from one pair and the left from the other, and stuck them in his blouse. Then he collected all the other shoes, cutting the laces that tied the pairs together, and piled them in one corner. When the students came back, they would think somebody had played a practical joke on them. Everybody would try to retrieve his own shoes; by the time two of the students realized they were left with one shoe each, he would be safe.

Five minutes later, he walked back into his class. His face was flushed and his breathing shallow, but he was elated. The knife was securely hidden in his mattress; the felt boots were back in his locker. He was wearing the stolen shoes. He went back to his desk and sat down. Nobody had seen the change in his footwear. Nobody but a Georgian boy named Vanya, who sat across the aisle. Vanya looked down at Dimitri's shoes, then slowly raised his head, and smiled, the cunning, knowing smile of an accomplice. Last night, Dimitri recalled, Vanya had participated in the beating. But today he wanted to make up.

Dimitri smiled wanly back.

On Saturday the inspection went smoothly. A half hour later, in a ceremony on the parade grounds, Dimitri and his classmates received the pioneers' red scarves, becoming members of the Lenin Pioneer Organization. Soviet tradition required that every child of the age of nine joined the pioneers, the communist children's movement. As they were awarded the neckerchiefs and the badges, the boys solemnly chanted the Laws of the Soviet Pioneers:

'The Pioneer adheres to the motherland, the party, communism.

'The Pioneer emulates the heroes of struggle and labour.

'The Pioneer is persistent in studies, work and sports.

'The Pioneer is an honest and true comrade and always stands for the truth.'

Vanya turned back and winked at him.

A ruthless determination was born in him the night of his beating. The memory of his humiliation by the entire class never left him; he carried the pain and the shame of that night imprinted in his flesh. And he swore that never again would he let somebody hurt him without hurting back, without making his enemy pay tenfold. Never again would he lie under a stinking blanket, his arms and legs pinned down, and let a horde of damned cowards beat him up.

He threw himself into physical training like one possessed. He got up in the morning earlier than the other boys and ran for an hour around the fence surrounding the institution, then did push-ups and exercises. He joined the courses on boxing and karate that were held in the students' free evenings. He would spend hours at the gymnasium, venting his hatred and frustration on the punching bag, or splitting wooden boards with the hardened edges of his hands till the skin broke and started bleeding.

'*Molodetz,* Dimka, great fellow,' his sports teacher would smile, feeling his bulging muscles. The teacher was a bow-legged Don Kossack, with a balding head, a half-crescent moustache and huge shoulders. 'I wouldn't like to be on the other side of that fist.'

He'd show them one day, he thought. He'd pay them back. He often dreamt of revenge, although against whom he didn't know.

He expected the shoes' theft to be his first and his last. He had stolen because he had been forced to. He wasn't a thief, he was a student. He wanted to become an important man. He did well in his studies. He excelled in geography and in the history of the Soviet Union. He devoured more books by Dickens, the works of Jules Verne, Alexander Beck's war trilogy and *The Young Guard* by Ostrovski. Some of the children in his dormitory started speaking to him, and he curtly answered, smothering his hatred. The shameful episode of the theft was slowly fading away.

But winter came, the most murderous winter since 1937, and the terrible Leningrad cold settled upon the earth. The Gulf of Finland and the River Neva froze solid; the orphanage and its grounds disappeared under a deep layer of snow. The water pipes inside the orphanage building froze as well, and the washroom taps grew sparkling beards of icicles. Each morning the staff had to work for hours to make the water pipes yield a trickle of ice-cold water. The frost glazed the windows, crept into the poorly heated rooms and settled in the corners, like some living, alien presence, blowing its icy breath on the children.

The weaker boys couldn't fight the cold; six Panfilov students, two of them from Dimitri's dormitory, were rushed to the Chapayev Hospital with acute pneumonia; two died. At the funeral of the second boy, Vanya approached Dimitri. 'We might be next, you know,' he said. He cocked his head towards the group of teachers. 'They wouldn't care if anything happened to us.'

Dimitri nodded. 'What should we do?'

'We'll need warmer clothes and more blankets,' Vanya whispered, his eyes conveying an unspoken question.

'And better food, too,' Dimitri added.

That night, he and Vanya broke into the workshop and stole several saws, hammers and screwdrivers that they concealed in the coal cellar. They started stealing whatever they could – money and personal objects from the boys' lockers, bags of potatoes and flour from the kitchen, jars of alcohol from the biology lab. One of the cook's helpers, an Uzbek named Kolya, sold the stolen goods at the free market outside the church. He brought them in return woollen sweaters that they wore under their uniforms, extra blankets, canned meat and vegetables that they would heat late at night in the deserted kitchen. Some nights they smoked Prima cigarettes in the backyard. Their duty sergeant, Kuzma Bunin, cooperated at the cost of a cut from the proceedings. He told them that a network of students from the higher classes was smuggling stolen goods over the school fence. They had never been caught.

When he lay in his cot at night, Dimitri was assailed with guilt. What had happened to him? He, the son of a colonel in the Red Army, had become a thief, robbing his friends and his school. He despised himself for what he was doing. But he didn't want to die! Besides, he didn't owe them anything. During the remaining months of that terrible winter three more children were taken to the hospital. One of them died, one was found unfit to return to the orphanage; they never saw him again.

Dimitri and Vanya, on the other hand, started the eleventh year of their lives in excellent physical shape. Dimitri emerged as a brilliant student. In an essay he read out in class, Dimitri explained why life in the Soviet Union was so much better than life in America. 'The decay of American society,' his paper started, 'can be seen in the high crime rate and the narcotics addiction encouraged by the capitalist regime. People in America become swindlers, robbers and thieves because their families are hungry.'

'Excellent,' exclaimed the teacher, Karmiya Tolbukhina. She came from an old communist family and her unusual name had a patriotic meaning. It had been composed of the words *Krasnaya Armiya* – Red Army. 'Proceed, Dimitri,' Karmiya said warmly.

Dimitri went on to describe the suffering of the American workers, exploited by the capitalists; the armaments industry used by American imperialists to foment wars in South America and in Asia; the social injustice; the persecution of intellectuals. 'America is an imperialist country that sucks the blood of smaller states, robbing them of their wheat, their steel and their oil.' The Soviet Union, by contrast, helped small countries, protected its workers, and struggled for world peace and fraternity.

'I am lucky I was born in the Soviet Union,' Dimitri's paper concluded, 'because in America children are starving.'

Karmiya Tolbukhina, deeply moved, stepped towards him and kissed him on the forehead. At the end of the term, Dimitri was awarded a prize: a small bust of Lenin.

'Dimitri! Dimitri, wake up!'

He tried to push away the hand that shook him. He was immersed in a dream about some faraway place. A girl was holding his arm and looking into his eyes. She loved him. All his dreams lately were about girls, and all had the same wet ending. But not this one. 'Dimka, wake up!' the voice in his ear kept whispering urgently, and the hand continued shaking his shoulder.

He opened his eyes. 'What . . .'

The hand swiftly covered his mouth. 'Keep quiet.' He recognized Vanya's voice. 'Come with me. Something is going on.'

He grabbed his clothes – it was late spring and the weather was warming up – and tiptoed after Vanya. Kuzma Bunin, the duty sergeant, snored loudly in his bed by the door. They sneaked into the dimly lit corridor. 'What happened?' Dimitri asked while dressing. His mouth had a foul, bitter taste. 'What time is it?'

'Two-thirty. Don't put your shoes on, they'll hear us.'

'Who?'

But Vanya was already dashing ahead. 'Come, I want you to see something.'

Vanya led him to the kitchen, then through the dark backyard to the kitchen store. They crouched behind the backyard fence. A truck was parked beside the store. Two men were loading heavy bags on the truck.

'That's the cook,' Vanya said, 'and the driver.'

'What's in the bags?'

'Flour,' Vanya said, 'and potatoes. They already loaded several crates of vegetables, all what we grew this year. And blankets from the other store.'

A third man came out and joined the two others. 'That's the administrator,' Vanya said.

Dimitri gasped. 'The administrator? I don't believe it.' He thought of the friendly, elderly clerk who used to lecture them about hard times and the shortages of food and fuel in the Soviet Union. 'We all have to make sacrifices for the sake of our country,' the administrator would say. Now he was stealing from the school, together with the cook.

'How did you find out?' he whispered.

'I was hungry, I came to heat a can of vegetables in the kitchen. I heard a noise.'

Dimitri thought of his own guilty feelings. His thefts were nothing compared to those of the cook and the administrator. They robbed the school by truckloads!

'Did you take down the truck number?' he whispered.

'Yes,' Vanya said. 'I also heard them talking to the driver. His name is Rodion.'

'Let's go,' Dimitri said.

The following morning they asked to see the principal. They were wearing their red pioneer scarves. Dimitri was the one who spoke. 'We believe, Comrade Colonel, that we have to stick to the glorious tradition set by Pavlik Morozov.'

'What's that?' the colonel smiled. 'Dimitri Morozov follows Pavlik Morozov?'

Dimitri smiled back nervously. 'It's only a coincidence that we have the same last name, Comrade Colonel.'

'Of course.' Colonel Borodin nodded. 'I was only joking.'

Only a week before, Dimitri and Vanya had learned about Pavlik Morozov in class. Pavlik was a hero to Soviet children. He was a twelve-year-old pioneer who lived in the Urals. During the famine of 1932, he overhead his father and his uncle plotting to conceal a part of their grain and not deliver it to the government as required. As a good pioneer, Pavlik reported his parent's crime to the authorities. His father went to trial, and Pavlik testified against him. Pavlik's uncle mercilessly murdered the boy. The police arrested Pavlik's uncle and he was hanged.

Pavlik emerged as a martyr of the revolution and became the subject of countless stories and poems. The Soviet pioneers sang songs and performed in plays dealing with Pavlik's heroism. His deed was taught in schools as an example of the Soviet citizen's duty towards the state. A good pioneer had to report even his parents to the KGB, if they caused harm to Soviet Russia.

'We asked to see you because we want to follow Pavlik Morozov's example,' Dimitri said. 'Last night, Vanya felt dizzy. He thought he was going to be sick. He woke me up, and I helped him get outside for some fresh air. We didn't want to wake up the duty sergeant. And then, by the kitchen store, we saw . . .'

Half an hour later, a militia automobile arrived at Panfilov. The chief cook and the administrator were arrested; the truck with the stolen goods was found the same afternoon. Dimitri and Vanya were honoured at the weekly pioneer meeting, and a reporter and photographer for the *Red Pioneer* magazine came to interview them about their noble feat. Colonel Borodin himself pinned the Pioneer medal of honour on their chests.

In a special ceremony on the parade grounds, the two little heroes raised the red flag on top of the mast, while all the students and teachers stood to attention, the officers saluting. The Pioneer choir sang the Youth Anthem. Dimitri watched the faces of his roommates, who had beaten him four years ago. They're singing in my honour, he thought. I am the pride of the school. Let them dare call me a thief again.

Shortly after Dimitri's thirteenth birthday, the principal entered his class. 'Excuse me, Yakim Efremovitch,' he said to the geometry teacher. 'Dimitri Morozov, come out, please.'

He exchanged alarmed looks with Vanya, then got up and left the class. 'Did anything happen, Comrade Colonel?' he inquired, trying to keep his voice casual.

'You have a visitor,' Colonel Borodin replied, and led the way to his office. He opened the door and let Dimitri in. 'I'll leave you now, Comrade General,' he said in a respectful tone. 'You can use my office for as long as you need.'

A general? Dimitri stared in apprehension at the old man who stood behind the principal's desk. 'Thank you, Comrade Colonel,' he said, and was seized by a spasm of dry coughing that seemed to tear his lungs apart. His face grew ashen, and he grabbed the edge of the desk for support. 'Sorry,' he muttered as his cough subsided, wiping his mouth with a crumpled handkerchief.

'My office . . .' Borodin repeated.

'No, no, Comrade Colonel, I won't bother you anymore.' The general kindly patted Dimitri's back. 'I'll talk to Dimitri in his dormitory. I'd like to see how he lives.' Puzzled, he led the man Borodin called 'General' to his dormitory. The large room was deserted, except for the duty sergeant, who was asleep on his cot after night duty at the infirmary. A bleak October sun cast a fuzzy light inside the room, and dust particles, caught in its beams, briefly turned into specks of gold.

'My name is Takachenko,' the general said. 'I am a KGB officer, an old-fashioned Chekist. I was your father's friend.'

Dimitri felt tremendous relief. When Borodin had called his name, he had feared that his thefts had been discovered. Thank God, it was a false alarm. He examined the general. He was tall, skeletal, with a caved-in chest and a scrawny neck. His hair and eyebrows were snow white, but the edges of his drooping moustache had turned yellow, apparently from too much smoking. He had several gold teeth in his mouth. He was dressed in a plain brown suit and his outmoded red tie was carelessly knotted.

But his look was alert, penetrating, and he spoke in concise phrases. 'Your father asked me to look after you. I couldn't do it until now for reasons that I shall explain later. Your father was my deputy at the Second Chief Directorate of the KGB. He was an excellent man, a patriot and a good communist. You have to remember that, Dimitri, always.'

He took a cigarette out of a blue package of foreign manufacture, apparently French. He went into another bout of coughing. The cigarette had a pungent smell. 'Do you kids smoke over here?' Takachenko asked.

'We aren't allowed, Tovaritch General.'

'I didn't ask if you were allowed, I asked if you smoked,' Takachenko said sternly, then threw him the package. 'If you don't smoke, trade it for something else. I know how things are in these places. Don't worry about me, I've got another package. I never go out without my poison.' He patted his other pocket. 'And don't call me General. My name is Anatoli Sergeyevitch. Understood?'

'Understood,' Dimitri said, grinning.

'Are they treating you all right here?' the general asked through a cloud of smoke. 'Is the food adequate?'

Dimitri frowned. Was the general trying to deviate from the subject they were talking about, his father? 'You said my father had asked you to look after me. When was that – before he died?'

Takachenko nodded gravely.

'How did my father die?'

Takachenko stared at him closely. 'Nobody told you,' he said softly. It was a statement, not a question.

'How did he die?' Dimitri repeated, sudden anxiety seeping into his mind.

Takachenko bowed his head for a moment, then looked straight into his eyes. 'Your father was shot by an execution squad at the prison camp of Vorkuta, in April of 1954.'

An execution squad. Dimitri stared speechless at the old general, unable to digest the shattering news.

'He was condemned to death because of his wife – your mother – a Jewish writer named Tonya Gordon. Your mother and her former husband, Victor Wolf, had been found guilty of anti-Soviet activities. Your father married Tonya Gordon after her divorce from her first husband. Your mother was later executed. You have a half-brother, Alexander, living in America. He's your mother's son from her previous marriage.'

He had a brother! 'Is he blond?' Dimitri asked inconsequentially. He thought he noticed the duty sergeant stirring on his bed.

'What?' Takachenko looked at him oddly. 'Oh, your brother. As a matter of fact he is, yes. But if I were you, I wouldn't mention his existence. People who have relatives abroad are not trusted, you know.'

'And you say both my parents were shot?' Dimitri said slowly, as if awakening from a dream.

'Your mother was shot first, and your father a year later.'

'But why? What did he do?'

'Your father will be posthumously rehabilitated,' Takachenko said forcefully. 'Two months ago, a special court was appointed by Chairman Khrushchev to review the verdicts issued before his time. I have no doubt that your father's verdict will be annulled, and his rank restored. He did nothing wrong, and died only because he had married this woman. Morozov is a hero of the Soviet Union. They will rehabilitate him, mark my words.'

'And who will rehabilitate me?' Dimitri shouted angrily. All the shock and the pain caused by the general's revelations, all the frustration and suffering accumulated in eleven years at Panfilov, exploded in one furious outburst. 'Me! Who will rehabilitate me? Who'll get me out of here?' He stared at Takachenko. 'You?'

The general didn't flinch. 'No,' he said. 'I won't rehabilitate you, and I won't get you out of here. I wanted you to know the truth about your father.'

'That he was shot as a traitor?' Dimitri threw back at him.

'That he was a good man, and an excellent officer. I wanted to come and tell you the truth years ago but . . .' Takachenko sadly smiled, '. . . I wasn't in a very good position myself. I was forced to retire soon after the arrest of your father. They brought me back last year.'

'Why?'

Takachenko shrugged. 'I guess I can tell you, it's not a secret anymore. Have you heard the name of Colonel Oleg Penkovski?'

He shook his head.

'Penkovski was a colonel in military intelligence who committed treason and disclosed military secrets to the American espionage. He caused terrible damage to the GRU and the KGB.'

'What's the GRU?' Dimitri asked.

'Military Intelligence.' Takachenko cleared his throat, then wiped his mouth with his handkerchief. 'We must now rebuild the service. The Politburo decided to recall some of the old Chekists who hadn't been involved with Penkovski in any way, like myself, to clean up the services. And here I am. I had to visit one of our facilities in Leningrad this week, so I dropped in to see you.' He doubled up under another spasm of shrill coughing.

For a long moment Dimitri sat huddled and silent. 'General Takachenko,' he said finally, looking up.

'Anatoli Sergeyevitch.'

'Anatoli Sergeyevitch.' His voice was different now, dropping almost to a murmur. 'Could you please tell me about my father?'

And for more than an hour, between bouts of ugly coughing, enveloped in the smoke of his pestilential cigarettes, sitting in the dormitory or walking back and forth on the deserted parade grounds, his bony hand on the youth's shoulder, Takachenko described the life and times of Boris Morozov.

'Why did he marry Tonya?' Dimitri forlornly asked at the gate, before Takachenko got into his chauffeur-driven Chaika. This car could have been my father's today, he thought morosely.

The general spread his arms. 'We all warned him, Dimitri. This woman was not for him. A Jewess, and involved in that organization besides . . . But he was obsessed with her. He married her although she was already marked for death. When she sank, she pulled him down with her.'

Alone at the gate, shivering in the afternoon breeze, Dimitri watched the departing car. And felt, rising from the depths of his miserable life, a wave of hatred for Tonya Gordon.

Jews, he thought on his way back. Damned, hateful, disgusting Jews. They were everywhere: ministers, officers, party aparatchiks, professors, speculators, profiteers. Like the Jew Fagin from *Oliver*

Twist, all of them a curse to society. His father had been a fine officer, he might have become a general by now, perhaps even the KGB director! Why did he marry that Jewess? Why did he let himself be bewitched by her cheap tricks? It was clear why she had lured him into marriage. She had lost her husband, she had a baby, she needed protection; so she cunningly spread her net at the feet of an unsuspecting Soviet officer. And he had fallen into her trap.

His mother was responsible for all the disasters that had befallen him. If his father had married a Russian woman, Dimitri would be living now in a spacious apartment in Moscow, studying at the best schools, eating the best food, vacationing on the Black Sea or abroad in East Germany and Czechoslovakia. It was all the fault of the Jews. When he rose in the Soviet hierarchy one day, he would purge the government of Jews. Let them go to Palestine, where they belonged, or to Birobidjan, their autonomous territory in Armenia. Let them simmer in their own juice, let them cheat and swindle and betray each other.

Vanya had told him that several students of the higher grades had formed a nationalist cell. They wanted Russia to be Russian again, he said, and to clean the country from the foreign parasites that thrived on the people's back. They were inspired by the memory of the old Russia that for centuries had been kept pure of the alien scum. *Pamyat* – Memory – the cell was called. Perhaps he'd ask Vanya to take him to one of their meetings.

Still, one of those Jews was his half-brother. It didn't make him better than the others, of course, but he was Dimitri's only living relative. It could be nice to meet somebody who was family. They might even like each other. But that could never happen. Alexander must have grown like the other Jewish children in America. An American and a Jew, that was the worst combination. Yet what if one day he just met him at a place where nobody knew them? His blond brother would be standing in the middle of the street, or sitting in a restaurant, and Dimitri would suddenly appear before him and say: 'Alexander, I'm your brother!'

The thread of his thoughts was broken by the sight of his duty sergeant, Kuzma Bunin, who stood by the side entrance of the school, arms folded on his chest, lazily leaning against the wall. Dimitri hated him wholeheartedly, although Kuzma worked with him and Vanya in smuggling stolen goods. He could never forget that Kuzma had ordered him beaten under the blanket that night.

'You're in a hurry, I see,' Kuzma said in a mellifluous voice.

Dimitri nodded, and hastened his pace.

Kuzma barred his way. 'What's the rush?' he said, his lazy smile revealing his bad teeth. 'You have news for your class?'

Dimitri pushed him aside. 'Kuzma, let me go, I'm late.'

'You'll tell them about Tonya Gordon?' the sergeant called after him.

He stopped dead in his tracks. A sudden chill made him shudder. 'What do you know about Tonya Gordon?'

'I know all about your mother,' Kuzma scoffed. 'I heard everything the old goat told you, back in the dorm.'

Dimitri recalled Kuzma moving on his bed while Takachenko spoke about Morozov and Tonya. The swine, he thought, he must have been feigning sleep, listening to all we said.

'I heard the touching story about your father too,' Kuzma was saying mockingly. 'The great hero, shot at Vorkuta for treason. Your friends will be delighted to hear about that. Our Dimitri is not only a thief and a black marketeer, but also a traitor's son. I don't want to detain you. Why not go and tell them?'

'Wait,' Dimitri said, pulling Kuzma into the nearby porch. Frantic thoughts rushed through his mind. If the truth about his father was exposed, it would be the end for him here. He would become the laughing stock of Panfilov; the Pamyat association wouldn't accept a half-Jewish boy. But much worse, he certainly would be thrown out of school. Sons of traitors couldn't study at Panfilov. He didn't know how he had been admitted to the orphanage eleven years ago.

But if it now became known that his father was officially a traitor, he would be kicked out of the school and branded an 'enemy of the people'. People were labelled this even if they were only relatives of someone suspected of anti-Soviet activities. An enemy of the people could never become a member of the communist party, or reach an important position. He was condemned to the most miserable existence; banned from the upper circles of Soviet society. And for Dimitri, that meant the end of all his dreams.

'Wait,' he said, clutching Kuzma's sleeve. 'Tell me, what do you want?'

'What do you offer?' Kuzma asked, studying him through half-closed eyelids.

'I'll give you five bottles of vodka,' Dimitri said quickly.

Kuzma burst out laughing. 'You must try harder, brother.'

'I'll give you a uniform, brand new,' Dimitri said. 'I have one, honest. It's yours.'

Kuzma shook his head. 'No. You've got to do much more than that.'

'What do you want?' Dimitri asked in desperation.

'I want everything you have,' Kuzma said softly, a sly cunning flame lighting up in his pale eyes. 'And I want a double cut in the operation you're running with Vanya.'

Dimitri could have strangled the pig, right there. Kuzma left him no way out. How could he convince Vanya to double the sergeant's cut? And even if he succeeded in buying Kuzma's silence, the dirty bastard would keep blackmailing him forever. With him his secret would never be safe. Not as long as he lived.

'I agree,' Dimitri mumbled. His throat was dry. 'I'll give you all I have.' Think, he told himself. Think quickly, you must find a solution. 'I'll take you to my cache, all right? You can take whatever you want.'

And then he realized, in a surge of boundless horror, that there was a way out after all. The only way. He shivered. No, he couldn't do it. But Kuzma was looking at him with a confident smile, his eyes gleaming with malice. The stinking oaf. He held Dimitri in the palm of his hand. What shall I do? he thought in despair. It is the worst of all crimes! All this can't be real, it's a nightmare, I am only a child after all. And yet a plan was already starting to take shape in his mind. He looked around. There was nobody in the corridor but them.

'What do you have in your cache?' Kuzma asked suspiciously, disengaging from his grip.

'Everything. I have all you could dream of.' That was true. In the last year Vanya and Dimitri, instead of stealing, had become middlemen in the black market that flourished in the school. With the complicity of Kuzma Bunin, they kept selling and buying stolen goods, skimming a fat profit.

'I have canned food, beef, chicken, fish. I have a uniform, brand new. I have six bottles of vodka. I have cigarettes, and money, even a watch. German. I'll give you everything.' I must make him come tonight, he thought, before he starts blabbering.

'Where is all that treasure?' Kuzma asked with forced indifference. 'I don't believe you.'

Oh yes you do, Dimitri thought, you know I'm telling the truth, you were part of all our deals. 'I have a cache in the old quarry. I dug it myself, at the very bottom. Nobody ever looks there.' The abandoned quarry was cut in the flank of a sloping hill, about two hundred yards east of the orphanage fence.

Kuzma cocked his head. 'So that's where you keep your goods. No wonder your locker was always clean. But I thought there was no access to the bottom of the quarry.'

'There's no access for those who don't know the place,' Dimitri said. 'I know my way around.' The old quarry was sixty feet deep, a rectangular pit dug in the limestone. In the nineteenth century it had been used as a water cistern for the fields that stretched south-east of St Petersburg. There were still black water marks on the vertical walls of white stone.

Kuzma gave him a long look. Finally he shrugged. 'Let's go and see what you've got there,' he said non-committally.

'Not now. Tonight, after curfew. I'll go first, and you come five minutes after me. Be careful that nobody sees you.' He paused. 'And bring your torch with you, it's dark down there.'

Kuzma nodded. 'Go now,' he said, again cocking his head and squinting warily at him. 'And no foul play, Dimka. Remember.'

He crouched behind a boulder, waiting. A crescent moon lay low over the land, but the quarry was plunged in shadow, illuminated only by the eerie incandescence of the naked limestone. Perhaps he won't come, Dimitri secretly prayed. Perhaps he'll have second thoughts. We'll find a solution tomorrow. The very idea of what he intended to do was overwhelming. There were about ten yards between the place where he cowered, and the edge of the pit; even if he pushed Kuzma hard, he couldn't shove him over the edge. He had to stun him first. He had no weapon but must rely on his hands alone.

He saw Kuzma's furtive shadow and heard his cautious, catlike steps, then the old door in the quarry fence creaked on its hinges. 'Dimka, are you there?' Kuzma called softly.

He didn't move. Don't come in, he thought. Go away.

'Dimka?' The beam of Kuzma's torch pierced the darkness, and the duty sergeant stepped into the quarry. 'Fuck your mother, Dimka. I know you're there, you little piece of shit!'

Dimitri hesitated another moment, then clenched his fists and lunged sideways towards the hand holding the torch. But he had underestimated his enemy. As his clothes rustled, Kuzma swiftly turned the torch towards him and Dimitri was briefly dazzled. At that moment something moved swiftly and a tremendous blow landed on his right forearm. Dimitri cried in agony. The bloody bastard. He had brought a weapon. He hadn't trusted Dimitri in the first place.

Kuzma hit him again, and sharp pain exploded in his thigh. He slipped and fell. And that probably saved his life, as for a split second he disappeared from Kuzma's field of vision and felt the long, heavy club swishing over his head. He threw himself at Kuzma's feet, and pulled him down. Kuzma lost his balance and collapsed, his torch clanging on the ground and rolling towards the pit's edge. The duty sergeant still held on to his club, but he was now crawling on the ground, struggling to get up, and Dimitri didn't fear him anymore. He tried to get hold of Kuzma's neck, groping in the dark with outstretched hands. He caught him by the waist, and the club struck his exposed back, but with less force. Kuzma succeeded in shaking him off, and scrambled to his feet.

'Help!' the duty sergeant shrilly screamed.

You can yell until tomorrow, Dimitri furiously thought, nobody will hear you. He grabbed Kuzma's waist again, from behind. The duty sergeant's silhouette was clearly outlined against a heap of chalky limestone. Releasing him, Dimitri brought down his clasped hand on Kuzma's right wrist. He cried out in pain and his club – a length of lead pipe – clattered to the ground.

Dimitri seized Kuzma's neck in a vice-like grip with his left arm, locking with his right. He was smaller, but more vigorous than his opponent. He could have strangled him now, but something made him stop. No marks, he thought, it must look like an accident. Kuzma was moaning and groaning, trying to tear himself from Dimitri's hold. He let go, then with legs spread and torso stretched, hatred doubling his strength, raised both arms and hit Kuzma's exposed neck with the stone-hard edges of his hands. The duty sergeant slumped down like a bag of rags.

He didn't waste time finding out if his enemy was dead or only dazed but dragged him over the ground. Kuzma's torch, that had rolled towards the pit, spread fuzzy light over its opposite wall. Dimitri stopped a couple of feet from the edge, and swept the stone floor with his hand. His fingers felt the jagged rim of the pit. He stared down into the smoky abyss and shivered.

Beside him, Kuzma stirred.

He turned back in terror, his hands raised to strike. But the duty sergeant was shuddering and shifting, a gurgling sound erupting from his chest.

'Die!' Dimitri mouthed. 'Die, you swine!' He grabbed the limp, twitching body and rolled it over the edge. He heard the echo as it hit the vertical side of the quarry, then the sickening thud as it crashed to the bottom.

He got up, swaying. The torch lay to the right, its light weakening. He kicked it into the pit, then did the same with the piece of pipe. He could leave now. There was no danger of his cache being exposed; it had never been near the quarry. He had said that just to lure Kuzma over. He stepped outside, leaving the door in the fence open. He wanted somebody to find Kuzma.

They found him the next afternoon, after his absence had been reported at roll call. Several teachers searched the school first, then the orphanage grounds, and finally the surrounding fields. The history teacher, Karmiya Tolbukhina, discovered the body and staggered back to the school in a state of shock. The news of Kuzma's death spread throughout the school, and set it buzzing with excitement, like a bee swarm. Colonel Borodin called the militia, and four investigators interrogated the boys. When his turn came, Dimitri calmly reported that he had seen Kuzma asleep in his cot, while he spoke with General Takachenko, then he had strolled with the general on the parade grounds and escorted him to his car. In the evening he hadn't spoken with Kuzma Bunin. No, he hadn't seen him leaving the dormitory after curfew.

The general's name produced the desired effect, and nobody asked Dimitri to testify again. The investigators reached the inevitable conclusion: Kuzma had wandered for some reason to the old quarry, stumbled, and fallen to his death. The only puzzling discovery was the length of pipe that lay at the bottom of the quarry, close to the body. But it could have been lying there for quite a while, with no connection to Bunin's death.

The next morning, Dimitri and Vanya were getting ready for Kuzma's funeral. He had no known relatives, so there was no use delaying the interment. Dimitri, wearing only an undershirt, was fumbling with the buttons of his trousers.

'Hey, what's that?' Vanya asked, pointing at Dimitri's forearm. It was swollen, and the skin above the elbow had turned a sickening purple colour.

Dimitri shrugged. 'I fell.'

For a moment Vanya stared at him, frowning. Then he nodded in understanding. 'I see,' he said. After a moment, he asked casually: 'You didn't get up the night before last, did you?'

'Me?' Dimitri said. 'I slept like an angel.'

Dimitri put on his blouse. There was something new in Vanya's eyes, he realized. Something he had never seen before. Fear. Vanya was afraid of him.

And he decided that he rather liked that.

On Christmas Eve he was exercising in the gymnasium when Vanya popped up beside him, a conspiratorial look on his face. Since Kuzma's death Dimitri had spent every evening in the gymnasium, ferociously hitting the punching bag, groaning under the weights, torturing his body into complete exhaustion. He hoped that his physical fatigue would induce him to sleep.

Still, night after night, as he closed his eyes, the tormenting memories of that day in October would overwhelm him. There was Takachenko again, describing his father's infamous death and his mother's revolting game: there was Kuzma again, threatening to expose him, then gurgling and kicking before he died. Dimitri knew that Bunin was a swine, a poisonous snake who deserved to be crushed. Besides, the duty sergeant had left him no other choice. But this didn't make him feel better. The infernal experience at the quarry haunted his sleep and instilled horror into dreams from which he would waken with a start, shivering and gasping for air.

But another feeling had been born in him the night of Kuzma's murder. Sometimes he enjoyed it; at times he feared it. It was a strange sensation of power; an awareness that he was able to gain his own way by breaking the rules of ordinary people. He knew that he could kill without flinching if necessary. He also knew that he was going to make it in life, and if somebody dared to stand in his way, he might well end up like Kuzma Bunin.

Vanya never spoke to him about that night again. But Dimitri felt the shrewd Georgian had guessed much more than he cared to admit. Since Kuzma's death their relationship had changed. Vanya now totally submitted to Dimitri's authority, and did his best to please him. Dimitri couldn't tell if Vanya acted so out of friendship or fear. Vanya brought him presents – good food, vodka, found somewhere two American cigarettes, and even swapped Dimitri's old German watch for his own, a heavy steel beauty with a black dial and green phosphorescent digits.

Vanya also introduced him to the Pamyat circle, but Dimitri was disappointed in it. They met in the grove behind the staff cottages and performed an oath-swearing ceremony at candlelight, over a rusty revolver. It was ridiculous. There was a lot of bombastic talk about Mother Russia, and empty slogans against the Jews, but no apparent will to act. He didn't care about slogans; he wanted to do something, purge Russia of Jews and liberals. One day, he thought, when I get out of here.

Tonight Vanya looked different. His face was flushed, and his eyes burned with a mischievous flame. He stood in front of Dimitri and pulled the punching bag aside. 'Don't you think it's time for you to fuck a girl?' he asked loudly.

'What?' Dimitri stared at him, baffled.

'Come,' Vanya said. 'I've got it all set up.'

Dimitri was confused. 'But the curfew . . .'

'It's arranged,' Vanya threw over his shoulder as he led the way across the parade grounds. 'I gave a can to chicken to Aram.' He was their new duty sergeant, a timid Armenian boy of seventeen who quickly understood that Dimitri and Vanya were calling the shots in their dorm.

'Where are we going?' he asked.

Vanya pointed at the staff cottages, lined against the shadow of the chestnut grove. Their lights were on. 'Remember Zoya?'

Zoya! The voluptuous daughter of the biology teacher was the embodiment of all his fantasies. He saw her every morning at the gate when she took the bus to her school in Leningrad. She was stunning. Her short hair was light brown, her eyes too; her skin was milky but her large, swelling mouth bestowed upon her face a hungry sexuality. How many nights he had lain on his bed craving her full breasts, firm buttocks and boyish hips.

He swallowed hard. 'Zoya will let me screw her? I don't believe you.'

Vanya softly chuckled. 'She'll let both of us screw her tonight.' He pointed to the right. 'We'll enter the cottage from the back. We shouldn't be seen around here.'

'Vanya, wait, what are you talking about? She's only fifteen, her parents would kill her.'

'Exactly,' Vanya said. He caught Dimitri by the arm and they stopped. 'You don't know, but she's been fucking a guy from the eleventh grade, Misha Pugachev. Know him?'

He nodded. Misha was a gentle boy with a fragile body and a beautiful face, illuminated by innocent blue eyes.

'I saw them in the grove,' Vanya whispered. 'Fucking like mad. Then I went to see Zoya yesterday. Her parents have gone to visit relatives in Odessa for Christmas. She didn't want to go. I guess she wanted to spend her holiday fucking Misha.'

'What did you say to her?' Dimitri asked.

'I said that if she let us fuck her, we wouldn't reveal what she did with Misha. If she refused, all Panfilov would know. Her father would be fired, and she would never fuck her Misha again.' He paused. 'Yesterday she refused, but I saw her again this afternoon, and she said yes. She's waiting for us now.'

'She spoke to Misha?'

Vanya shrugged. 'I don't think so.'

Dimitri followed him, feeling strangely lightheaded. God, it couldn't be, he was dreaming. He was going to fuck a girl at last. And not just *a* girl, the best, the sexiest, the most exciting. Zoya, he was about to fuck Zoya!

She opened the door of the cottage. She was wearing a long skirt and a sweater that stretched tight over her heavenly breasts. Her face was puffy, she had probably been crying. Her lips were trembling. She led them across the kitchen and a living room furnished with rustic chairs and tables. There was an old radio set by the wall. A standard lamp, covered with a shade of oilpaper, was surrounded by a circle of light. A pearl grey Persian cat perched on a couch staring at them suspiciously. Zoya opened a door. 'Here,' she said.

'You go first,' Dimitri said, turning his back to Vanya. 'I'll wait here.'

'Don't you want to watch?' Vanya asked with a lascivious smile.

'No,' he said. I don't want to watch you, he thought, and I don't want you to watch me. On entering Zoya's room, Vanya flipped the light switch and Dimitri heard the muted protest of the girl. He stepped towards the door and closed it. He sat on a chair, then got up, the cat's eyes followed each of his moves, He picked up the *Ogonyok* weekly that lay on the table, flipped through it and threw it back. He idly turned the radio buttons, then moved away. His palms were sweating and he wiped them on his trousers.

He heard Vanya's rising moans and a final groan of ecstasy. Then there was silence. A moment later Vanya came out. His hair was dishevelled, and his eyes sparkled. He looked ecstatic. He was fumbling with his trousers. 'Brother,' he grunted, 'that was something. Go on, you'll see what paradise is all about.'

Dimitri entered the room, closing the door behind him, Zoya's bedroom was lit by a lamp hanging from the ceiling. There were some stuffed toys in one corner, and three shelves of books by the window. An old cupboard, a desk and a chair were lined against the near wall. A print of a ballerina graciously bowing was pinned to the wall, above the desk.

He looked at the bed and held his breath. Zoya was lying on the crumpled sheet, completely naked. Her arms lay limp by her sides, she didn't even try to cover her nudity. He felt his penis harden. He had never seen a naked woman before. His head swayed as he stared at Zoya's round breasts with the pink nipples. Her crotch was covered with a thick mass of pubic hair and that excited him even more. He approached the bed, unbuttoning his trousers. Her eyes were closed and she was silently weeping, the tears trickling through her eyelashes. He wanted to kiss her, he had so often dreamt of her full lips parting under his. He bent over her, but when she felt his breath she jerked her head to the other side. She couldn't restrain herself any more and burst out crying, desperate spasms shaking her body. She covered her face with her hands.

He stared at her, bewildered. He hadn't imagined it this way. He wanted Zoya's mouth, her abandon, her fire. He wanted her wildly making love to him. But before him lay a wretched girl, crying in shame and humiliation. She didn't want him to touch her. For a second, anger surged in his chest, the same black anger he had felt before killing Kuzma. His blood was pounding wildly in his temples. Instinctively he clenched his fists and his body tensed. But Zoya looked so defenceless, so desperate, his fury faded away. He felt disgusted, and didn't know what to do.

He turned away and stared at the sylphlike ballerina on Zoya's poster, spreading her long white arms. His hardness dissolved and he shivered. Timidly he reached for Zoya and touched her hair with his fingertips. Then he ran from the room.

'What happened?' Vanya was staring at him, puzzled, his stupid smile slowly fading away.

'Let's go!' Dimitri fiercely mouthed, and rushed toward the back door. On his way he stumbled over a chair, that fell to the floor with a crash. 'Fuck your mother!' he muttered. The cat arched its back and angrily hissed at him.

He lost his virginity only a year later to Valya, the younger daughter of the new chief cook. Valya was a large, big-breasted and round-hipped girl of seventeen, with long bleached hair, a broad face, merry brown eyes and rolling laughter. It took her barely a couple of months in Panfilov to gain the reputation of an easy lay. 'Give her something, anything,' Aram told him knowingly, 'and she'll show you the seventh heaven.'

Dimitri sent Vanya to her and they struck a deal immediately. Valya was ready to service Dimitri for two one-litre bottles of vodka 'with the original seal, not a drop of water inside.' She met him behind the kitchen, and carefully inspected the bottles. 'Let's go inside,' she said then, taking his hand. Her skin was soft and dry.

She led him to the kitchen store where she had improvised a bed with a heap of bags. When Dimitri told her that he had never slept with a woman, her enthusiasm soared. The squat, sullen girl turned into a hot-blooded woman with an insatiable appetite. She pulled him to her, apparently delighted to initiate him in the joys of sex. 'Come, my little one,' she murmured, her tongue darting in and out of his mouth, probing his ear, then licking its way down his throat. 'Let me take care of you. Let Valya show you why we don't need storks and cabbage patches anymore.'

On the soft flour bags, in the dark kitchen store, she hugged and kissed him, undressed him like a little child, made him fondle her breasts and rub her swelling nipples, enveloped him in her long, strong arms and legs, and rode him astride, caressed him with her expert hands, excited him with her plump breasts, her wet, pulsating vagina and gentle mouth.

She lay on him, kissed him, bit him, sucked him, drank him, coming over and over again, moaning, whining and groaning in ecstasy. She feasted on him with such abandon and such uninhibited pleasure, interspersed by delighted screams and explosions of laughter, that Dimitri decided she was having the best part of the deal. She was the one who should have paid him two bottles of vodka for her pleasure. Still, he had never believed sex could be such fun. And the hours he spent with that simple peasant's daughter, smelling of ripe wheat, fresh soap and women's musk, were to remain one of the sweetest memories of his tormented youth.

General Takachenko came to see him again a few months before his seventeenth birthday. Dimitri had just traded his pioneer scarf for full membership in the Komsomol, the organization of Soviet communist youth. Takachenko had barely changed since they had met three years before. His clothes were as sloppy, his voice as alert, only the pouches under his eyes had grown more flaccid, and his cough acquired a more grating edge.

Khrushchev's demise two years ago, Takachenko said, and his replacement by Leonid Brezhnev, had somewhat delayed the work of the special tribunal that was to review his father's case. But the tribunal had finally ruled, last month, and Boris Morozov had been completely rehabilitated. His military rank and medals had been posthumously restored.

Dimitri listened, dumbstruck. He had grown used to misfortunes, didn't know how to accept good news.

'It's time for you to get out of here, my boy,' Takachenko said, taking a sheaf of papers from his pocket. 'I want you to fill in those forms. They are application papers for the KGB Academy, or as we officially call it – the Higher School of State Security. In a couple of months a Commission will come to interview you. I want you beside me, like your father. I think you have a great future.'

Three months after the Commission interviewed him, Borodin handed Dimitri an official government envelope. The Commission Chairman, Bodrov, informed Dimitri Morozov that he had been admitted to the KGB Academy.

On October 1, he was to report to the Academy compound, in Moscow.

Chapter Six

Alex Gordon came out of the subway station on Flatbush Avenue and dejectedly paced in the direction of home. Damn the bloody assistant! he thought, clenching his teeth. Damn the sonafabitch! He recalled the stupid stare of the Russian he had just met. Had all his efforts of the last four years been for nothing? All those letters, and phone calls, and months of waiting – for what? For being almost slapped in the face by a stupid Russian clerk.

Four years ago he had been devastated by the newspaper item describing his parents' deaths. His first reaction had been to find his brother and share the shattering news with him. Perhaps Dimitri knew about their parents' fate? He had written a long letter and sent it to their former Moscow address, but the letter had been returned with a stamp saying there was no such a person at that address. That setback didn't stop him. On the contrary. Finding his brother became an obsession with him. He wrote to Dimitri again, with the same result. He wrote to his Uncle Valery in Leningrad. There was no reply. He wrote to the American embassy in Moscow, to the Soviet embassy in Washington, to their mission to the UN. He besieged the Soviet consulate in New York with phone calls, asking for an appointment with the consul. They always told him to call next week, or next month, the consul wasn't there, he was in a meeting, on a lecture tour, on home leave.

Finally, last week, they told him that his request had been granted. And today he had rung at the consulate door at four pm exactly, dressed in his Sunday best. He had been screened, searched and inspected by two big, silent men in the consulate lobby. Then an aging woman, her square shoulders draped in a black woollen shawl despite the early summer heat, had appeared from nowhere, and grudgingly led him to a small cubicle on the ground floor.

'This is the consul's office?' he asked.

'The consul is busy,' she said, 'and you'll be received by one of his assistants.'

The assistant was a portly middle-aged man with cropped brown hair and a moon-shaped face, wearing an ill-fitting grey suit. He had formally shaken Alex's hand and squeezed behind the cheap desk. The room was bare except for a faded poster of Red Square, hanging behind the assistant. There were no filing cabinets along the walls, and no files on the desk; the office was apparently used for interviews only. Alex spoke for ten minutes, in Russian. He had diligently rehearsed his discourse at home until he knew it by heart. He described his efforts to get in touch with his brother, the inscriptions on the letters he had sent him, his appeals to the Soviet foreign ministry, the ambassador and the consul-general.

The Russian listened, his face sealed, his pudgy hand tapping on the desk with a ball-pen. He didn't react throughout Alex's exposition, even when he stressed that Dimitri's father was a high-ranking KGB officer. When Alex finished, the assistant asked for his brother's name and address and wrote them down in a small notebook. 'Very well,' he said, and got up. 'We'll check that and let you know.'

'I can give you some more details about the family,' Alex said. 'Dimitri's grandmother lives in a Ukrainian township . . .'

The man in grey raised his hand. 'No need for that,' he said and repeated his magic formula: 'We'll check and let you know.'

The sour-faced woman suddenly materialized by the door, and escorted Alex out of the building. And he found himself on the pavement, boiling with anger and frustration. In spite of their promises, they hadn't let him see the consul. The man in the grey suit was just a junior employee. He didn't care about Alex's request, hadn't even bothered asking him any questions that might help in locating his brother.

All his efforts during the last four years had been flushed down the drain. How could people like this assistant be employed by the Soviet foreign service? The Soviet diplomats, entrusted with representing the USSR abroad, were supposed to be the very best people; but he had found himself facing a fat, dyspeptic bureaucrat who wanted only to get rid of him. The bastard! he thought. He could at least have pretended he wanted to help me.

He threw an absent look at the kids playing softball across the street. Two of them were shirtless and their naked backs glistened with sweat. It was only the beginning of June but the heat was oppressive. He took off the jeans jacket that Nina had washed and pressed for his interview with the consul. What shall I do now? he wondered. Today's visit might have been his last chance. He ground his teeth, recalling the bovine stare of the assistant and the scowl on the woman's face. He furiously kicked an empty garbage can and sent it rolling along, then turned to corner into their street.

It was blocked by a huge removal van, parked in front of his house. The van belonged to the world famous Tramontana Movers, according to the huge sign stencilled in flaming red letters on its white side. A group of people were unloading pieces of furniture and crates of possessions from the van and carrying them into the old two-storey house that stood across the street from his own. As he approached the van, he realized that beside the employees of the world famous Tramontana company, dressed in blue coveralls, an entire clan was participating in the operation: older men, women, some younger boys and girls. They argued, shouted, laughed, conversed, mostly in English but also in melodious Italian. 'Adriano!' an old man was calling. 'Adriano!' And every time he shouted, a woman's head popped out of the open window of the Italians' new house and she shouted back: 'Adriano has gone home, you fool!'

The Italians yelled at each other, joked with each other, warmly patted each other's shoulders, panted, cursed, stopped once in a while to circulate a bottle of dark red wine or a tray of overstuffed sandwiches. The entire street echoed with their laughter, shouting and quarrels. One of the movers, a black-haired man with a double chin, sang a melodramatic Italian song at the top of his lungs. Some of his friends joined him for the refrain; others, including an old woman with a mobile face, mimicked his theatrical gestures and erupted in laughter every time he embarked upon a new verse.

Alex stopped by the van, staring in wonder at the cheerful crowd. An Italian family was moving in and their relatives – apparently the whole tribe – had come to help. He wanted to go home, but the bubbling exuberance of the merry newcomers fascinated him, and he stayed planted in the middle of the pavement, grinning foolishly. His bad mood had faded away.

Somebody bent under a huge bale of clothes blindly advanced towards him and he stepped aside. It was a girl. She slowly lowered her load by the house door, then straightened up and turned towards him. He stood still, staring.

'Hi, I'm Claudia,' she said. 'What's your name?'

Restlessly stirring and turning on his narrow bed that night, his face on fire and a new, sharp pain throbbing deep in his chest, he remembered Claudia. She haunted his sleeplessness, as enticing as when he first saw her yesterday: black eyes, full lips, high breasts and rounded, sensuous hips. He craved her swelling mouth; wanted to bury his face in the silken mass of hair that fell over her left shoulder in a dark cascade, revealing the gracious line of her neck, the delicate contour of her chin. The thought of her naked body drove him mad. A strange fever had awakened inside him for the first time, and his imagination, suddenly unleashed, galloped drunkenly towards unknown horizons.

First love is a love of torment, Joey had gravely quoted to him from a book he was reading. That was a few years ago, when he had fallen head over heels for his fat, pimpled Laura. (She was gone now, replaced by fat, pimpled Frida.) But only today did Alex realize how right the book was, how painful and agonizing love could be. He had never loved before. No girl had stirred such desire in his body, such physical pain. He hadn't suspected that such emotions existed and a casual meeting in the street could turn into obsession. As the morning light seeped into his room, the first rays of sunshine caressing his body, he solemnly decided he could never love again. Not the way he loved Claudia Benevento.

Yesterday evening he had helped her carry her load into the old house, where heavy, big-breasted women in dark dresses had already taken control and were unceremoniously ordering the men around. The younger men had welcomed Claudia's entrance with whistles and catcalls, which she accepted with unmitigated delight. As Alex stepped in behind her, carrying a bale of colourful blouses and dresses, a wave of good-natured laughter had swept the living room. 'Caught one already, Claudia?' a skinny youth called from the top of a ladder. His athletic partner, who was handing him a heavy chandelier, ominously added: 'Wait till I tell Stevie!'

'My brothers,' Claudia groaned, then burst out laughing. She moved about like the princess of the household, obviously enjoying her role. 'This is my friend Alex,' she solemnly proclaimed. To the old white-haired woman who trudged in, leaning on her walking stick and gazing at him in puzzlement, she repeated in a louder voice: 'Alex, Grandmother.'

'Who?' the old lady squeaked.

'Alex – Alexander, Alessandro.'

After dumping his bale in the middle of the living room, Alessandro asked her to the Hollywood Ice Cream Parlour.

'What?' she said belligerently, planting her fists on her hips. 'You mean I should let my poor family sweat and slave, while I lick ice cream with you at a soda fountain?'

'Well . . . yes,' he stammered.

'Great,' she exclaimed, mischievous flames lighting up her eyes. 'Wonderful! Let's go.' She merrily linked her arm through his, her firm breast brushing against his elbow. He was panic-stricken. No girl had touched him like that before. 'I'm going away with Alex,' Claudia shouted, and regally departed, dragging him behind her.

At the Hollywood Parlour she gobbled down two orders of Our Special Double Banana Sundae, her carefree laughter infecting everybody present. Their waiter, fat Louey who had a wooden leg, and sparse silver hair plastered over his skull, whispered in Alex's ear: 'This girl of yours, she's something!'

His girl. Gathering all his courage, he turned to her and blurted: 'Who's Stevie?'

'Oh, you heard,' she laughed, then shrugged. 'My boyfriend,' she said. His heart sank, but she looked at him without laughing this time. And he had the fleeting impression that there was a message for him in those dark, ardent eyes.

But the look dissolved and she was her bubbly self again, animatedly telling him the story of her life. She was a natural story teller, and had the gift of making every detail, even the most trivial, sound exciting. Her family had moved over from New Jersey where her father, after fighting corrupt politicians, local muscle and organized crime, had become a respected entrepreneur. They were second generation Americans; her grandparents had been born in Calabria: 'The tip of the Italian boot, if you know geography.' She had inherited the blood of notorious Calabrese bandits, she revealed darkly, lowering her voice.

She had one sister, nurturing a secret, desperate love, and three brothers, one of them married and the father of twins. She was sixteen and two months, the youngest of the five children: 'And the most spoiled, of course.' She liked to sketch and paint, had won a couple of awards at school, and for a long time had wanted to study art. A famous artist had asked her to become his student; but if she told her brothers what he had wanted in return, it might start the bloodiest vendetta on this side of the Atlantic.

Fortunately, she also loved clothes, she said, stressing the word 'loved', and closing her eyes in rapture. 'Do you like my sweater?' she asked coquettishly, turning around to make him admire it, but he had eyes only for her young breasts. Her family, she added, unanimously agreed she had very original taste in clothes, and all believed she was going to become a great fashion designer. Wasn't that wonderful? Clothes and art together. And he said, Oh, yes, great. Absolutely.

Then she assailed him with questions about himself and he readily complied, describing to that strange girl feelings, thoughts, frustrations and hopes he hadn't revealed even to Joey. He told her about his parents' death, his lost brother, his efforts to discover the truth concerning his family. She seemed captivated by his story. When he described his mother's execution, he saw to his surprise tears streaming down her cheeks. 'I'm sorry,' she said, embarrassed, and looked away. It occurred to him that she was the first person apart from himself to shed a tear for his dead mother.

To change the subject, he told her of his ill-fated visit to the Soviet consulate this afternoon. Claudia laughed as he humorously described the assistant consul and his black-shawled dragon; later she put her hand on his arm and let it lie there for a while. And he suddenly realized that he had never been as happy as right now, perched on a high stool beside this lovely girl, at the Hollywood Ice Cream Parlour.

When he finally delivered her to the Italian tribe across the street, it occurred to him that the incident at the Soviet consulate had lost its importance. His disappointment with the assistant consul seemed to belong to the distant past. Dimitri could wait. All he wanted now was to see Claudia again.

He came back from school the next afternoon and immediately took up position by the living room window, overlooking Claudia's house. He had to speak to her again. He wouldn't budge from his observation post, he decided, until he saw her. Then it would be a matter of seconds; out of the apartment, down the steps, into the street. He would run to the corner, cross the street, come back and bump into her, so that their meeting would look accidental. 'You shouldn't show a girl that you're interested,' little Joey had sternly lectured him today when Alex told him about his great love. 'A woman is never attracted to someone who is too readily available. And remember, if she asks you – you'll say that you've had lots of girls before. If she knew you were a virgin, she'd leave you right away.' The little Casanova looked at him severely, and explained: 'At this age, they're only attracted to guys with experience, see?'

And so he lurked in ambush by the window, watching the Italians' house. To avoid an interrogation by Nina, from whose sharp eyes nothing escaped, he pretended to read a book on the Battle of Moscow in 1941. He answered her occasional questions with monosyllables, unwilling to enter into a discussion that might divert him from his task.

His relationship with Nina had switched back to normal after their painful dispute of four years ago. On that rainy day, when he had found out she had lied to him about his parents' fate, his first impulse had been to run away from home. Seething with bitterness and frustration, he didn't want to see Nina again. But after he had confronted her at Spiegel's, she had followed him to the apartment, and they'd had a long agonizing discussion, during which he had cried his heart out, and Nina too had shed a few tears. She had tried, she said, to spare him the terrible shock of learning how his parents had died. That was why she had invented the story about the car accident.

'I knew that you would finally get to know the truth, Aliosha,' she sadly admitted. 'I wanted to tell you myself, but not yet. I knew it would be a terrible shock to you. I didn't want you to go through hell while you were still a child.' How could she ever imagine that the story would be published in the newspaper, and some evil little boy would put the cutting on Alex's desk, to hurt him? Watching her distraught face, with the tears streaming down her cheeks, Alex finally embraced her. She was right, he admitted, she had lied to him for his own good.

They knew that the accusations against Tonya and Victor Wolf were phoney, of course, a fiendish intrigue fabricated by deranged minds, and that the Soviet government had made a terrible mistake. Nina hesitated for a while, then showed him a copy of a secret speech Krushchev had made in 1956, before the Twentieth Congress of the communist party. The speech, smuggled to the West, had been published a few months later. Krushchev had denounced Stalin as a murderer and a criminal, who had been responsible for show trials, torture and terrible massacres.

'It is hard to believe, *golubchek*,' Nina sighed. 'Our little Father Stalin, the man we used to call the Sun of the nations, the Prophet of communism – a murderer!'

'I read that Lenin, before his death, warned the party against him,' Alex said.

'Lenin would have turned in his grave if he had only known what Stalin did,' Nina stated firmly. 'This explains all that happened to Tonya and Victor. There's no fault with communism. It was Stalin who ordered his henchmen to commit those terrible crimes, and that's how your parents paid with their lives.' Their deaths were a warning that the march toward communism might be deviated by enemies of the working class or by megalomaniac dictators. Therefore his mother and father hadn't died in vain.

Besides, she added, perhaps his father was still alive. Nobody had seen him die in the camps. But Alex just looked at her and she fell silent. They both knew his father was dead. No prisoner could have survived more than a year or two beyond the Arctic Circle.

He was torn from his memories when he suddenly saw the door of the Benevento house open and Claudia come out, munching an apple. A couple of window-cleaners, working at the neighbouring house, stuck their fingers in their mouths and whistled shrilly. She didn't look up. Alex stared hungrily at her, and a pang stabbed him, deep inside. She was dressed in jeans, flat ballerina shoes and a white shirt embroidered with large green flowers. Green was apparently her favourite colour. He was already on his feet, about to dart for the door, when to his immense surprise Claudia casually crossed the street and walked straight to his house. She was coming in!

He panicked. He rushed to the door, then scurried back to his desk, frantically tidying books and writing pads, scooping up pens and pencils. He didn't know what to do, he had never received a girl in his house! But the doorbell was already ringing, and Nina's brisk steps echoed in the vestibule. He heard the door open, and in floated the sunny, warm voice of Claudia. 'Hi, you must be Nina. I am Claudia Benevento, a friend of Alex's. Is he home?'

'Yes, he is home.' There was surprise and reserve in Nina's voice. She could be more friendly, dammit! He stepped towards the door, but Claudia was in the room already, grinning at him. 'Hi, Alex,' she called. God, how pretty she was! In the dusk reigning in the vestibule, he could make out the stern expression on Nina's face, looking at him over Claudia's shoulder.

'I came to see your picture gallery,' she went on. 'May I?' He had told her last night about the photographs and posters he had hung over his desk.

'On one condition,' he said.

'What?' She was already by his desk, staring at the wall. 'This must be the Sputnik. And who is this – Lenin?' she asked. As he didn't answer, she turned back to him, the mischievous sparks dancing in her eyes again. 'What condition?'

'That you give me one of your paintings, for my collection.'

'Done!' she readily announced. 'But on one condition.'

He crossed his arms, amused, and bowed his head in solemn agreement.

'Will you have dinner with us tonight? We're celebrating our move to Brooklyn. My mother's been cooking since morning, and my grandmother thinks you're very cute. Bring Alessandro, she said, bring the blond ragazzo. Will you come?'

He smiled. 'I'm in love with your grandmother. For her, and for her only, I'd love to come.' Then he realized that it meant leaving his aunt alone. 'Nina, my friend, Claudia . . .'

But Nina had vanished from the vestibule, and her quick steps retreating towards her small room, carried a ring of loneliness and mute, sullen reproach.

Nina faded out of his mind the moment he entered Claudia's home. Crossing the threshold of the Benevento house was like discovering

112

another world, aeons away from his own. He was used to the sepulchral silence of Nina Kramer's apartment, interrupted only rarely by the ringing of the telephone, or by the playing of a Russian record. Claudia's house echoed with a fascinating melange of sounds. Everybody was calling everybody at the top of their lungs, there was always somebody singing, and there was always somebody quarrelling; the radio was blasting in the living room. Mrs Benevento was shouting orders to the tribe from her kitchen, and the telephone was always in use, transmitting business discussions, young girls' chatter, boys' bragging, recipes exchanged by the women of the house, young voices mutilating the English language with the barbaric accents of New York and New Jersey, older voices flowing in rich, musical Italian.

Tantalizing smells of cooking, garlic and spices, grilled fish and meat, frying butter and pungent sauces, wafted from the large kitchen at the back of the house. There was always movement: some distant cousin coming or going, the twin children of Claudia's brother crying or laughing or just embarking on a spree of destruction, throughout the rooms, her mother trudging about carrying bags bursting with foods, the grandmother diligently tap-tapping with her walking stick, associates of Mr Benevento coming to discuss their affairs.

Even the decor was alive. In sharp contrast to the austere furnishings of Nina's apartment, the Benevento house was densely populated with colourful rugs, heavy Italian sofas dressed in faded velvet and laden with soft cushions, carved wooden cupboards ornamented with lace mats, big lamps with shades made of tasselled fabric or coloured glass, china statuettes, massive tables, ramshackle armchairs, bright paintings of Italian landscapes and scenes of rural life, beside pictures of saints, angels, apostles, madonnas and the Lord Almighty himself in various costumes.

The Beneventos were a happy, earthy bunch of people, thriving in delightful disorder, brimming with infectious vitality. Claudia's father was a stout man with a big belly who liked to wear collarless striped shirts. Her mother, whose cameo face still carried traces of beauty, controlled the household with an iron hand, scolding her flock from her kitchen, loudly complaining of her misery, sharing her troubles with the Almighty in loud, poignant monologues. Claudia, her brothers and her sister, treated their parents with amused reverence. Alex was soon to discover that the shouting and fighting were not even half as serious as they could seem, and beneath the thunderous vocal exchanges, the family ties were close and warm.

But the most disturbing truth he discovered in the Benevento house was that life could be exciting, even if not devoted to the fanatical pursuit of an idea. Fiercely individualistic, these people didn't want to blend in faceless masses, marching towards glorious achievements; they were happy with their lot, living for the present, and not for future generations. They wanted to make the best of life, today. If Karl Marx had known the Beneventos, Alex suspected, he might have written a different book.

These heretical thoughts invaded his mind that first evening when he walked into the house with Claudia, ceremoniously shook everybody's hand, and was invited to the living room where the huge dining table, covered with a checkered cloth and napkins, an array of glasses, trays, bowls, and old, massive silver, seemed ready for an extraordinary feast.

And a feast it was indeed, with the slices of red carpaccio in its piquant sauce followed by prosciutto and melon, delicious pastas and lasagnas, sun-dried tomatoes swimming in olive oil, grilled jumbo shrimp, breaded veal, hot Italian sausages and sharp cheeses, all served in gargantuan quantities, while the Chianti and Soave flowed into their wine glasses in clouds of merry bouquet. Meals in Nina's apartment were consumed quickly, mostly in silence. Here there was not a moment of quiet. Everybody cheered and clapped their hands at the appearance of every new dish, talked, laughed, and shouted their compliments at the lady of the house, who shouted back, her face flushed with contentment, enjoining her guests to clean their plates.

Dinner was almost over when a newcomer walked in and was greeted by a merry chorus. 'Hi, Stevie,' Claudia's brother Ricky called, 'how was the game?'

'Okay,' he answered. His voice was tired. 'We won.'

Claudia's sister Maria ran to him and hugged him warmly. She was wearing a tight wine red blouse. 'Claudia, come over!' her middle brother Michael yelled, and threw an odd look at Alex. Her second brother, the wiry, agile Ricky, bent across the table and explained to Alex: 'Stevie is a basketball player. Great athlete.' Claudia's boyfriend seemed to be the hero of the Benevento household.

Claudia, who had sat during the meal beside Alex, had just gone to the kitchen to help her mother. Now she came out and briefly hugged Stevie, who kissed her on the cheek. She turned to Alex, looking ill at ease. 'This is Stevie, my boyfriend,' she said. 'Stevie – Alex.' He looked up at Stevie whom he already considered his rival. He was Alex's own age, very tall, with dark hair and eyes, a straight nose and an angular jaw. He was dressed in a white jeans outfit, which was fashionable this year, with a white sports bag hanging on his shoulder. He looked very handsome. 'Hi, Alex,' he said and smiled.

Alex smiled back. 'Hi,' he said. He hated the guy.

He felt utterly humiliated. He had no business here. Why did Claudia ask him over? To meet her boyfriend? Evading Stevie's stare he looked up at a painting of St Sebastian that hung over a Livorno chest. The saint, painted in gloomy dark colours, was tied to a pole, his body pierced by arrows. Alex got up. His face was burning. Maria was looking at him sideways, her plump hand smoothing her red blouse. Don't blush, he said to himself. His palms were sticky. Don't blush. 'I've got to go,' he said. 'I left my aunt alone at home. Thank you very much. Thank you, Mrs Benevento, it was the greatest meal of my life.'

'Wait, Alex,' Claudia's mother called, wiping her hands on a kitchen towel. 'The dessert is coming. Wait!'

'Alessandro,' Grandmother Benevento rasped.

'I'm sorry,' he said. 'Excuse me, I've got to go.' He made a vague gesture with his hand. ' 'Bye everybody, thanks.' Claudia was staring at him, her face distressed.

'Bye, Claudia,' he said. 'Thank you.'

He all but ran out of the house. The street was dark and the night air cool against his flushed face. He started crossing the street then changed his mind. He couldn't go home yet, Nina would still be awake, and he couldn't face her critical stare. He decided to walk a little, to put some order in his thoughts. But Claudia had taken control of his mind, her face chasing him through the dark streets, her voice whispering in his ears. Why the hell did she invite him? he asked himself. Did she want to tease him, or to make her boyfriend jealous when he found Alex at the table, eating her bloody lasagna? Women were like that, Joey had told him, they loved using men for their sordid little games.

He saw the neon sign of the Hollywood Ice Cream Parlour and turned the other way. Damn Claudia, he thought. And yet she didn't seem that sort of girl. Last night she had cried when he had told her about his mother. And today, in his apartment, he had shown her Tonya Gordon's book of poems and had recited to her his own translation of 'My Magic Kingdom' and 'A Soldier's Letter'. Afterwards Claudia had reached over and squeezed his hand. He could swear she had been deeply moved. She had said that 'A Soldier's Letter' was one of the most beautiful poems she had ever heard, and also that she had never met someone as romantic as him. She had looked at him, and there was something in her eyes which wasn't just friendship.

That's nonsense, an inner voice immediately countered. A girl wouldn't fall for you the first time she met you. It can happen only to you, stupid, because of that romantic streak you inherited from your parents. What did you think, that she had been waiting all her life just for you? Of course she has a boyfriend, she even told you that yesterday. Why didn't you ask her if she loved him? If he didn't mind her seeing other guys? Perhaps they're even sleeping together, it happens a lot nowadays. He clenched his fists. The very thought of somebody touching Claudia's naked body drove him crazy. And he had met her only yesterday!

Could she really be sleeping with Stevie? Wasn't she too young? But many girls started young. Joey had told him and Frida were very close to 'this' already. Joey thought he would do her in a couple of weeks. They want it as much as we do, he had said knowingly, but we must play the tough guys. Play it cool, you see, detached, don't show them you care, and then, at the right moment, just help them come across. Alex wondered where Joey had got all this carnal knowledge. After all they were the same age, and he'd had only a couple of ugly girl friends, Laura and Frida.

He must find something that would keep him busy. He had neglected his swimming lately, and hadn't been to Jack Macmillan's boxing school for years. Tomorrow he'd start again. In a year at the most he could become a great athlete, much better than her Stevie. He must also devote more time to his studies. He was not just muscle like Stevie, he had brains. He visualized himself graduating from Brooklyn High, the best in his class, and Claudia hearing about it from the neighbours. Just you wait and see, Claudia, he thought, one day you'll be sorry for letting me go.

It was almost midnight when he came back home. As he stepped into the entrance of his house, a shadow detached itself from the darkness and moved towards him.

'Claudia,' he gasped. 'What are you doing here?'

'You weren't home,' she said. 'I called your house. Your aunt said you hadn't come back.'

'I went for a walk,' he said uneasily. 'Where's Stevie?'

'Why did you go away?' she asked. 'I wanted you to stay, you were my guest. Why did you leave?' The entrance hall was dark, but he could see her face was pale and troubled.

'You know why,' he said.

'No, I don't.'

'You have a boyfriend,' he said. 'Why did you ask me over for dinner?'

'Because we had lots of fun, yesterday evening,' she said, 'so I wanted you to come to my house. We're friends, aren't we?'

'And Stevie doesn't mind?'

'I didn't know he was coming,' she said defensively. 'But why should he mind? We did nothing bad, did we?'

'We might.' Cool, he recalled Joey's advice, play it cool, detached. Well, the hell with Joey. 'Let me tell you something, Claudia. I don't know you, I don't own you . . .'

'Of course not,' she said.

'. . . and I have no claim whatsoever on you. But I don't want to be the kid next door to you, okay? I met you last night, and I liked you very much. I don't have a girlfriend and I've never had one. I thought of you all night, and I thought of you all day. I don't want us to be "good friends". And I don't want to be a replacement for Stevie when he isn't there.'

'Things between me and Stevie are not what you think,' she said.

'Oh, yes? I've heard that one before, believe me, it's a great line from the movies. My husband doesn't understand me. Things between us are not what you think.'

'Don't make fun of me,' she said. 'He's not my husband.'

'I don't know how things are between you and Stevie, but . . .' he hesitated, and finally blurted out '. . . it so happens that I want you all to myself. No Stevie, no good friends, just you and me. Now I've said it. Do you understand? Do you?'

She stared at him for a long moment. 'You're really something, you know?' she said in wonder. 'I've never met a boy like you before. You speak as if you've come here from another planet. You say what you feel and you don't play tricks. You make me think of something your mother wrote: "A dream for pures at heart". You know what? I think you're a pure at heart, Alex Gordon.'

She ran away before he could answer.

He slowly climbed the stairs, puzzled by her words. Did she really like him? Would he see her again?

The door to their apartment wasn't locked. All the lights were on. Nina was sitting in the living room, her hands on her lap. She looked up at him, but there was no rebuke in her eyes, just tired resignation. 'Alex,' she took a deep breath, 'it's your Uncle Samuel. He died tonight.'

There were very few people at Samuel Kramer's funeral: Alex and Nina, two distant cousins of Samuel who came all the way from Buffalo, a couple of salesgirls from Spiegel's Furs – Mr Spiegel himself couldn't come to the cemetery, he sent a wreath and a telegram – and three elderly women with unhappy faces and burning eyes, Nina's friends from the Peace Movement. An old man who lived in their building was the first to arrive; he could hardly walk, and had to lean on a tree, to catch his breath. He said to Nina that perhaps it was for the best, dear Mr Kramer was released from his suffering at last. The poor man, Alex thought. He was talking about Samuel Kramer but thinking about himself.

There was also a strange car, a Chevrolet, parked at a distance, with two men in the front seat. Alex briefly saw the glint of a camera lens. He recalled the strange men who used to follow him, once in a while, in the streets of Brooklyn.

Joey was the last to arrive, short of breath. He warmly hugged Alex, signalling with his eyes to the left. 'That's her?' he whispered. There, to Alex's great surprise, stood Claudia in a severe dark blue dress, and two of her brothers, Michael and Ricky, looking very solemn. 'Thank you,' Alex said, shaking Ricky's hand. 'Thank you very much for coming. You didn't even know him.'

'But we know you,' Ricky said. 'You are our best friend in the neighbourhood. You helped us move, you came to our celebration. If you need anything, just open your window and yell. Okay?'

Claudia didn't say anything, she just held his hand and looked at him searchingly, as if expecting an answer to some unspoken question. Yes, he wanted to say, I love you. As she moved to shake Nina's hand, he saw his aunt's back stiffen. Nina regarded Claudia as a rival, he thought, as somebody who might steal his love. Well, he had to admit, Nina's instincts were pointing her in the right direction. Claudia's appearance on their street had completely confused his feelings. For him, nothing would be the same again. He thought that his love for his aunt and his infatuation with Claudia were two different things, but perhaps Nina knew better.

Back at home, they prepared the living room for the seven days of mourning, which Nina, after much hesitation, had agreed to observe. They covered the mirrors with pieces of cloth, and arranged the sofa and the chairs in a half-circle for their guests. Nina made him sit on the sofa. She sat upright in one of her straight-backed chairs, facing him.

'There are some things we should discuss, Alex,' she said. 'First, the apartment. Tomorrow some workers will come, and a cleaning woman. We'll take your uncle's things out of the apartment. His room is going to be yours now. It's time for you to have your own room.'

'But, Nina, you need a room too,' he protested. Yet deep in his heart he felt a surge of exultation. He was going to have his own room at last! He wasn't going to sleep and work in a corner of the living room any more. And his uncle's room was the largest in the apartment. He only prayed that the sour repulsive smell would vanish together with his old furniture.

'I am very well where I am now,' Nina was saying. 'I've already ordered a new bed for you, a nightstand, and a couple of chairs. We'll transfer your desk to your room, and of course' – she faintly smiled – 'your picture gallery.'

He was about to thank her, but she raised her hand. 'There's something else, Alex. Your uncle had life insurance, I've been taking care of the payments for years. I don't need the money. We'll use it to pay for your studies. You can pick the college you like. Have you thought about it?'

It couldn't be! He was dreaming. He had never dared to hope he might pursue his studies. 'Brown University in Providence, Rhode Island,' he blurted. 'Sovietology.'

Nina nodded contentedly. 'I hoped you'd choose Soviet studies,' she said. 'Why Brown?'

'They have a student exchange programme with the Soviet Union and East Germany,' he said.

'And you want to find Dimitri,' she completed his thought.

'I must find him,' he said forcefully. He leaned towards her. 'What about you? Don't you want to find him?'

'Of course,' she said. 'He's my nephew, exactly like you.' But after a moment she laid her hand on his arm. 'No,' she said, 'not exactly. This is not true. I raised you, Alex, you're like a son to me. I'd never care about anybody else as I care for you, even if I wanted to.'

The same day he called Brown, long distance, and ordered the application forms and the curriculum brochures. If he were admitted, he could combine his college and university studies at Brown. He still had ample time to apply but was burning with impatience to know where he was heading.

Yet even in these moments of exhilaration, Claudia was on his mind. Going to Brown meant he wouldn't be able to see her so often, he would be away for most of the time. Perhaps it was for the best. He couldn't bear the thought of living close to her, seeing her daily from his window, while forbidden to reach for her. If he stayed in town his obsession with Claudia wouldn't leave him for a single moment; he could go mad, imagining her in the arms of that vain, dandyish boyfriend of hers.

Nina was watching him closely with sharp, clever eyes. It occurred to him that she had probably figured out what he was thinking, and wasn't displeased to see him go away, for the same reason.

The brochures arrived on a balmy afternoon a week later. As the day drifted to its end, he sat in his new room, cleaned, sprayed and newly furnished, reading the application forms for the umpteenth time. The windows were wide open, letting in the fusty smell of early summer; darkness was already settling in. There was a knock on his door. Nina appeared on the threshold, her face dour. 'You have a visitor,' she said.

She moved aside, and before him stood Claudia. She was very pale, and looked thinner. She was wearing a tight, sleeveless blouse made of thin blue fabric and a knee-long zippered skirt. Her face was drawn. Her breathing was shallow, as if she had ran up the steps.

'Claudia, come in,' he said. 'Something's wrong?'

She stepped inside and closed the door behind her, leaning back, her hand clutching the handle. 'I came to tell you,' she started, then paused and took a deep breath. Her eyes carried an uncertain look. 'I came to tell you that Stevie and I broke up.'

He stood facing her, unable to speak. His heart was thumping and a strange tremor rose inside him. He didn't know what to say. 'What happened?' he finally managed. She didn't answer. Her mouth was trembling.

Suddenly nothing else mattered. In a dream, he stepped towards Claudia, and awkwardly leaned over her, feeling her breath on his face, staring into her eyes. Her lips were hot and dry, and as they parted under his he forgot everything else, sinking into an abyss of feelings: triumph and elation, passion and boundless love. And a slight twinge of fear.

For a long moment they couldn't speak, and the only sound in the room was the soft whisper of their skin, the rustling of their clothes. His feverish hands roamed Claudia's body, removing her clothes, cupping her breasts, caressing her silken thighs. His impatient mouth closed on her nipples, and his heart, a wild sledgehammer, madly pounded inside his chest. He carried her to the bed, dismayed by the beauty of her nude body that the moonlight had painted the colour of ivory. He had never undressed a woman before, had never felt such an explosion of passion in his heart. She gasped as she opened herself to him and suddenly he was inside her, his mouth drinking hers.

'I love you, Claudia,' he murmured, 'I love you.' Pressing her against him, feeling her breasts against his chest. 'Tell me you love me, tell me you feel me deep inside, tell me you want me, only me, my love.'

And only later, when he propped himself on his elbow and leaned over her in a surge of tenderness, did he notice the stain spreading on the white bedsheets.

'I thought . . . I didn't know you were a virgin,' he whispered.

She didn't answer, holding him tight, softly kissing him, softly crying.

Part Two
LOVE
1967–1977

Chapter Seven

It was raining hard, grey slanting sheets of rain, as the Lear jet shakily landed on the deserted runway. Grimaldi wistfully gazed out of the plane window at the dark mass of trees that bent low, beaten by the wind. He didn't recognize the airfield. His guess was that they had landed in Virginia, possibly at the Farm, the CIA training facility; or perhaps somewhere along the east coast, between New York and Washington. Judging by the heavy air traffic they had encountered before landing, they couldn't be far from the main gateway airfields of JFK and Dulles.

The aircraft was private, unmarked, and Grimaldi was the only passenger on board. The steward handed him his overcoat and bulging bag, flashing him a quick smile. He was a slim, graceful boy, with matte skin and slightly slanted eyes, and Grimaldi felt a sharp pang as a bittersweet memory surfaced in his mind then slowly dissolved. He placed the neatly folded coat beside him, checked the knot of his vivid blue silk tie and smoothed his moustache. The plane slowly taxied on the runway and Grimaldi sunk back in thought. For the last two days, and during the long journey from London, he had tried to figure out the purpose of his sudden recall, and of the cloak-and-dagger procedures that had surrounded his precipitate flight.

For some nebulous reason, CIA headquarters had organized his return as an emergency rescue operation, as if he were in mortal danger. First there was the cable to his London apartment: Top Secret – immediate – for your eyes only – decode by own hand. Then, the explicit instructions not to reveal anything to his colleagues at the CIA liaison office. The convoluted scheme of establishing contact, the phone calls from public booths, the meeting at crowded Charing Cross station, and finally the night trip in the black Rover, with a driver he had never met. Using a tortuous route, designed to avoid surveillance, they had made it to the Basingstoke Air Force base where his plane was waiting on the runway, engines turning. He hadn't played those games since Berlin, and that was more than fifteen years ago.

Not that he didn't like games. On the contrary. Since he had shed the naivete of his younger years, Grimaldi regarded life as a never ending, fascinating game. It was a charade, he believed, a perpetual contest of wits. He had boldly stepped into the charade himself at the age of eighteen, when he had adopted his Corsican stepfather's name and country of origin and metamorphosed from Frankie Flanagan into Franco Grimaldi.

This mutation had crowned a strange and painful process young Frankie had gone through in his teens. He had always been different from the other boys. Effeminate, artistic, attracted by flashy colours and flamboyant clothes, he was a smart but weak youth. The neighbourhood boys hounded him, calling him a sissy; he often returned home beaten and bruised. He was seventeen when he met a soft-spoken saxophone player at a jazz concert. Frankie returned home the next morning, horrified yet thrilled by the discovery of his homosexuality. Now he understood why he was not attracted to women. But he also realized he had to conceal his sexual urges, if he wanted to succeed in life. New Orleans, in 1937, didn't tolerate homosexuals; neither did any other city, as far as he knew.

Frankie was driven by a burning ambition to make it in life. But how could he? He was weak, ridiculed and disliked by his classmates. There was nothing special about him. He was half-Italian, half-Irish. His mother had been born in a small village near Ancona, on Italy's Adriatic coast. She had met Colin Flanagan in Louisiana, where she had immigrated with her family. His father had died when Frankie was a baby. He had seen him only in some old photographs: a light, ferret-faced Irishman. Frankie had been raised and taught French by his mother's second husband, a warm-hearted man with a booming laugh, born in the island of Corsica.

Corsica, the birthplace of Napoleon, was famous for its fierce brigands. And Frank, thrilled by their romantic aura, desperately searching for something that would make him intriguing, took his stepfather's name and usurped his roots. He also converted his Christian name to Franco. Since the age of eighteen, when he left school and moved to the East Coast, Franco Grimaldi had claimed to be the descendant of a long line of Corsican bandits. The truth was that his family operated two restaurants in New Orleans, where the only acts of banditry were valiantly performed at the cash registers.

The deception had been working for years. Grimaldi was known to all his friends as a Corsican. His colleagues at the CIA had nicknamed him 'Napoleone'. They also made fun of his flowery waistcoats, colourful bow ties, silk scarves and heavy golden jewellery, but that was sheer envy and their jabs left him unconcerned.

He had been drawn to espionage because he liked adventure and was ready to take risks, as long as he didn't have to fight with his fists. And in spite of the Corsican legend he had spun around himself, it had been his Italian-sounding name and his knowledge of the language that had got him his first assignment. It was 1943, the war was at its peak, and he had landed in Sicily with a group of Italian-born agents. Their mission was to reach the Mafia strongholds, on General Patton's behalf, and negotiate an alliance with the local dons against Mussolini.

He was just a kid then, barely twenty-three, the youngest man on the team. He would never forget the smoke-filled huts in the Palermo hills where he faced the tough gun-toting Mafia dons. He knew that each of those men could be a fascist in disguise or a German-paid assassin. But he had survived, and the agreement had been concluded; the Mafiosi had launched a rebellion against Mussolini and the Germans. Since Sicily Grimaldi had started believing in his lucky star.

He had continued teasing danger in Berlin, after VE Day, where Russian and American agents were already dying, the first casualties of the Cold War. He had struck up a unique relationship with a Russian officer and embarked with him on many an adventure. But their last joint operation had ended sourly. Alone again, he engaged upon his most ambitious initiative: the Gehlen gambit.

These were the days when the American wartime intelligence organization, the Office of Strategic Services, was drawing its last breaths: and the OSS's founding fathers, a team of endearingly clumsy blue-eyed and blue-blooded Americans, were striving to build an organization capable of confronting the Soviet spying machine. To Grimaldi they looked like boy scouts declaring war on the Chicago mob, gullible crusaders waving the cross in front of Saladin's ruthless hordes. The KGB had infiltrated the vital centres of the west with thousands of agents. The newborn Central Intelligence Agency had nothing similar in Russia: no resident agents, no networks, no high-placed moles. And then Grimaldi, still a young man but already a cold-blooded cynic, had stepped on the stage and offered a solution called Gehlen.

Strangely enough, he had learned about Gehlen from the Russians, in one of the rare instances when he had joined forces with them, hunting escaped Nazi criminals. General Reinhard Gehlen was the Russians' nightmare, he learned, a man they had sworn to annihilate. Gehlen, the German wartime chief of espionage against the Soviet Union, had spun a web of excellent networks all over Russia. At the end of the war most of Gehlen's networks were still intact, his spies under cover. That drove the Russians mad with frustration. Among them, in their army headquarters and their government offices, thrived treacherous Nazi spies. The KGB officers wanted Gehlen's files, the list of the traitors who worked for him; most of all they wanted his head. And Grimaldi suddenly had an idea.

He used every trick of his trade. He bought information from former German officers for food, liquor, and cigarettes scavenged in the US Army stores. He sweet-talked some of the secretaries working for his bosses and typing their reports. But mostly he shamelessly traded in secrets with two British intelligence experts, baiting them with the minutes of the Russian-American negotiations about the future of the dismembered German empire.

After months of groundwork, he succeeded in locating Gehlen's hideout in the Taubenstein Mountains. He secretly travelled to Lake Schliersee, where he got hold of the gaunt spymaster and whisked him to safety. Gehlen could be the jewel in Grimaldi's crown. If he succeeded, it would mean rapid promotion, high position, a substantial salary. And a lot more power to play his games. They hadn't nicknamed him Napoleone for nothing.

In his talks with Gehlen, Grimaldi displayed cold logic and a cynical attitude. He offered the spymaster a deal: his personal safety in exchange for the German networks in Russia. He pointed out that Gehlen's networks were not worth much to the general, if his own life were not protected. Besides, Gehlen couldn't turn to the Russians for help, therefore he didn't have a choice. Thus General Reinhard Gehlen, once Hitler's master spy, became America's prime asset in the secret war against Russia.

In the following years Gehlen revived his legendary networks in Russia and put Hitler's former spies at the service of his new masters. And Grimaldi took up residence at the dreary compound in Pullach where Gehlen had established his headquarters. He was the CIA watchdog, peering over Gehlen's shoulder, supervising his operations, perusing his lists.

He knew that he was now a target for the KGB that would have paid dearly for the secrets passing through his hands. But it was not the KGB that caused his downfall. It was Willie Schiller, a beautiful Pullach youngster he had met in January 1952, a lithe boy with graceful limbs, a soft mouth and dark eyelashes.

Grimaldi had been very careful since joining the CIA. Except for that one secret adventure in Berlin, he had suppressed his sexual urges. If his superiors found out he was a homosexual, he could be thrown out of the Company. Homosexuals were regarded as high security risks, who could become blackmail targets for the enemy.

He couldn't say what made him lose his head. Perhaps his excessive confidence, perhaps Willy's enticing sensuality. Grimaldi fell desperately in love with him, and spent a few unforgettable nights feasting on his soft, docile body. When the boy finally broke up with him, he lost all self-control. He started following Willie in Pullach's streets, phoned him at all hours, pounded on his house door, begging him to return. Finally Willie's parents – the boy was only seventeen – complained to the local police.

The following morning Grimaldi was summoned to a suite at the Vier Jahreszeiten Hotel in Munich, where his superior officer, Colonel James Macpherson Jr, confronted him. Macpherson was seething with rage. 'You're a piece of shit, Grimaldi,' he hissed at him. 'You got the top slot in Europe, with the best promotion chances, and you blew it. You fucked this kid and you fucked up your future. I want you on the next flight home. You'll probably be kicked out of the service as soon as you get to Langley.'

Grimaldi was listening dejectedly, his head bowed. He didn't know what to say. 'Can't you help me, Jim?' he finally managed. 'The Company is my whole life, you know.'

Macpherson shook his head. 'I tried my best to save you, but nobody would listen.' He looked away, shaking his head. 'You fool,' he rasped, 'you bloody fool.'

Macpherson interceded on Grimaldi's behalf, though, and finally saved his hide. They didn't kick him out. He was one of the Company's best Soviet experts. But his operational career was over and he was exiled to a desk job in Washington. In 1957 they sent him to France, five years later to England. Everywhere he held positions of high responsibility; but the closest he came to field operations was in his dreams. The Pullach scandal barred him from the job he coveted: control of the Russian networks.

Now, in the autumn of 1967, fifteen years after the German scandal, he had no chance of taking part in field operations again. Time had blunted his lust for action and his frustration had simmered down. He had grown used to the comfort of a less precarious existence. He liked grooming his Clark Gable moustache, and let his wavy brown hair grow longer. His catlike green eyes stood out in startling contrast to his swarthy gypsy's face. The only vestige of his swashbuckling years was his flamboyant taste in clothes, jewellery, gourmet foods and fine wines. It suited the role he had chosen, that of the daredevil, pleasure-loving adventurer.

Tonight, during the long transatlantic flight, he had slept fitfully, alone in the cabin. A tiny blue light shone at the far end of the aisle, where the flight attendant dozed in his seat. Even in his sleep, Grimaldi was haunted by the secrecy veiling the goal of his journey. Why had they summoned him? Why all the precautions? An important assignment probably waited for him at the end of this voyage. But what? He had gone through some turns in his career; not always for the better.

The plane slowly taxied to a stop. The steward opened the cabin door and beckoned to Grimaldi. He threw his coat cape-style around his shoulders and stepped outside. It was a nasty morning, with a low, dark sky, and a cold gusty wind. The folding stairs were slippery from the rain and the wind sharply slapped his exposed face. The heavy raindrops were cold against his skin.

A black Chevrolet waited on the tarmac, close to the aircraft. Grimaldi opened the rear door. A gust of warm air enveloped him and he smelled the aroma of sandalwood-scented tobacco.

'Come in, Napoleone,' said a husky voice with a New England accent, and he looked up, startled.

'Good morning, Jim,' he managed. 'Well, this is a surprise.'

Jim Macpherson, his former boss in Germany, had made it to the top and was now Deputy Director for Plans. Macpherson held the number three position in the Company hierarchy, after the Director and his Deputy for Operations. Grimaldi hadn't expected the DDP to come in person to meet him. He stepped into the car and settled uneasily on the back seat beside Macpherson.

'How was your flight?' the DDP casually inquired, without expecting an answer, and puffed on his pipe. 'And how's London these days?' His rebellious shock of hair had grown white, but still bestowed a boyish air on his handsome features.

The second man in the car, who sat behind the wheel, turned around, his skull-like face cracking into a lopsided grin. His pallid eyes had the cold, calculating look that Grimaldi recalled only too well. '*Bonjour, cher ami,*' he drawled in heavily accented French.

'Hello, Walt,' Grimaldi said, hardly disguising his displeasure. 'Driving the boss now, I see. I always believed you'd climb the ladder one day.' Walt Reiner's smile vanished. Grimaldi couldn't stand the DDP's assistant, who was nothing but a pompous ass. Years ago, Walt had acquired the habit of scattering his conversations with Grimaldi with high school French, and believed this to be very funny.

'We didn't want to take a driver along,' Macpherson explained. 'We want to keep our meetings with you as discreet as possible.'

'Why?' he asked. If they had come in a car, the landing strip must be close to Langley Woods. 'Why all this secrecy?'

Macpherson took his pipe from his mouth and glanced out of the car window. 'I'd rather talk about this over breakfast somewhere.'

'I'd rather talk about this now,' Grimaldi said, his voice quiet but firm. 'I'm fed up with being ordered around, Jim. I'm a big boy now. I don't like being instructed to leave my job in the middle of the night, then fly five thousand miles without knowing what it's all about. So let's skip the breakfast and talk now.'

Macpherson didn't answer right away. Morosely he studied the moist stem of his pipe, then threw a look at Walt Reiner who shrugged. In the silence that ensued, the drumming of the rain on the car roof rose to an angry staccato. Finally the DDP turned to face Grimaldi. 'All right,' he agreed. His finely lined face was suddenly very earnest. 'We want you to go to Moscow.'

For a second, Grimaldi was speechless. He felt a surge of disbelief, mixed with nascent joy. 'Moscow? What for?'

'We want you to run an agent,' Macpherson said, his brown eyes studying Grimaldi closely.

Grimaldi returned the stare. The entire situation didn't make sense. 'I've been in mothballs for fifteen years, Jim. I thought you had better qualified men in Moscow.'

'I certainly do,' the DDP agreed. 'But this one needs special attention. He's an extraordinary man.'

'Now, wait . . . wait . . .' Grimaldi stammered, then blurted out the question that burned on the tip of his tongue, 'Why me?'

Macpherson and Reiner exchanged sour smiles. 'We wouldn't have ever done this of our free will, *bien sûr*,' Reiner breezily said, enjoying his own wit. 'We had quite a few other candidates. But the man asked for you. *Comprenez-vous*?'

Macpherson's narrative started in the car, then continued in the vinyl-padded booth of a Denny's roadside restaurant, where Grimaldi had finally agreed to have breakfast, softened by the good news; it ended in a small apartment in downtown Washington, which has been prepared for him by the Company.

'We'll call our Russian comrade Top Hat for the time being,' Macpherson suggested, and Grimaldi nodded agreement.

The Russian had been recruited in Vienna three weeks before, Macpherson's story went. He had established contact with Bob Collier, the CIA man at the embassy, which proved he was well informed. He sent Collier's wife a dozen roses. Stapled to the bunch was the florist's envelope, but inside it the Russian had slipped a note for Bob with directions for a meeting. When he met Collier, in a car parked outside the Museum of Fine Arts, he identified himself as a colonel in Soviet military intelligence. His office was in the Kremlin complex, and he had access to highly classified documents. He was in Vienna for the debriefing of an agent who worked in the entourage of a European leader.

'We think it's either Herr Ehrhardt or the *cher* General de Gaulle,' Reiner interjected, then raised his eyebrows when his revelation failed to provoke any response.

The Russian said to Collier that he wanted to defect, Macpherson continued; he had been a communist all his life, but his dream had crumbled.

And how did that happen? Collier asked. After some hesitation Top Hat revealed his motive. His sister, a scientist at the Michurin Institute in Volgograd, had discovered that the famous heredity theory of the Soviet geneticist Lysenko was nothing but a fraud. She reported her findings to the institute director. As a result, she was arrested and taken to a mental hospital, where she was still imprisoned. 'My sister is not mad,' the furious Russian said to Collier, 'and a regime that throws scientists into asylums doesn't deserve to exist.'

Collier, Macpherson went on, immediately perceived the tremendous potential of the Russian. The man was a treasure; he moved in the highest circles of Soviet intelligence. Collier didn't want him to defect; he wanted him back in the Kremlin, working for the CIA. The Russian's lust for revenge could make him the greatest spy the CIA ever had in Moscow.

At the second meeting, Top Hat was more relaxed, and revealed his name to Collier. The CIA carried out some discreet inquiries, and found that the man was speaking the truth. Collier then suggested that he return to Moscow as a CIA agent. He offered him a tempting salary and the rank of colonel in the US Army. In ten years' time, maybe less, he would be brought over to the United States, given a new identity and helped to live happily ever after. The Russian had agreed, under certain conditions. Now he was back in his Kremlin lair, waiting to be contacted.

'I met Top Hat,' the DDP said. 'Jim Nolan – you know, the Chief of the Soviet Division – suggested I looked into the matter myself. So I flew to Vienna. There was not even a breach of security involved,' he smiled wanly. 'The Russian knew all about me. He even showed my picture to Collier.'

'Didn't it occur to you it might be a set-up?' Grimaldi suggested. 'Double agents are the KGB house speciality. They've been planting double agents in the west since 1945 and we've been swallowing all their baits. If we buy this guy now, he might feed us red herrings for the next ten years.'

'It's a possibility,' Macpherson admitted, 'but my feeling is the man is honest.' He sank into a long silence. 'Anyway,' he finally said, 'that's why we want you to go over there and hold his hand. You've got enough experience to spot a double, if he is one.'

'Did he bring any samples?' Grimaldi asked.

Macpherson nodded again. A couple of reports. One was a memo to the Politburo, signed by Major-General Pugachev.'

'The Deputy Defence Minister?'

'Yes. It deals with the missile programme. It says that testing has been stopped since an SS-20 exploded on the launching pad at Baikonur last May. More than a hundred people were killed.'

Grimaldi took a sleek gold-plated cigarette case out of his pocket and chose a thin black cigar. 'That's true?'

'We sent an SR-71 to verify,' Reiner said. 'They almost shot it down, but the pilot made it, with half a dozen photos. The ground is scorched for a radius of two hundred yards around the launching pad. Lots of debris over the place. *Voilà.*'

The telephone beside Reiner buzzed, and he picked it up.

'We had two long meetings and I liked him,' Macpherson frankly confessed, then suddenly smiled. 'You wouldn't guess what the first thing he asked for was.'

Grimaldi looked at him sideways. 'I give up. You tell me.' Reiner was whispering into the telephone, glaring at Grimaldi.

'He asked to see his colonel's uniform,' Macpherson scoffed. '"If you make me American colonel"' – he mimicked the Russian's accent – '"I want to see my uniform."' He resumed in his normal voice: 'I had to send Collier to the Ramstein airbase, to find a colonel's uniform. You should have seen our Russian trying it on in front of the mirror. He was the happiest man on earth.'

Macpherson had asked the Russian how he would pass over the information he collected, and had been amazed by the answer. 'He asked for you,' the DDP said. 'He met you in Berlin, after the war. He said he knew you were in the intelligence business, and he would work with nobody but you. His name is Kalinin.'

Grimaldi stared at him, stunned. 'I'll be damned,' he finally mumbled. 'Oleg Kalinin. I'll be damned.' He frowned, staring at Macpherson suspiciously. 'You're not kidding, are you?'

Macpherson shook his head.

'I don't believe it.' Grimaldi's memory took him back to the black ruins of post-war Berlin. 'He made it,' he murmured, shaking his head in wonder. 'He made it, he's alive!'

Perturbed by a surge of recollections, he didn't immediately realize that Macpherson was speaking to him. 'What I want to know,' Macpherson was saying, 'is why? Why does he want you, of all people, after all these years?'

'We were involved in several operations together,' Grimaldi said cautiously. 'They had to do with Nazi criminals.'

Oleg's face sailed from the dark niches of his memory as he had seen him first, that evening at the Berlin Kommandatura Bureau. Those were the days of the Nuremberg trials, when Russians and Americans had briefly joined forces in the hunt for Nazi criminals. Many wanted Nazis had assumed false identities and gone to ground. Some had escaped to village and forest hideouts. Most had blended in with the hordes of famished Wehrmacht soldiers roaming the ruins of the defunct Reich, looking for homes and families that no longer existed. Grimaldi had been instructed to report to the Kommandatura, to meet a Russian officer, Captain Kalinin.

Tall and handsome, broad-faced and sandy-haired, with a child's curiosity, a dimpled chin, and eyes sparkling with life, Oleg Kalinin had shattered his image of a Soviet officer. Grimaldi had expected the run-of-the-mill Russian, stiff, stolid, suspicious and hostile. The young officer with the infectious laugh stunned him. Kalinin was outspoken, irreverent and quick-tempered; they ended their evening in a glorious brawl with British military police at the notorious Fett Madchen bar. Grimaldi couldn't help succumbing to his new friend's charm. In many ways the Russian was his mirror image: he was a gambler, he was ambitious, and he nurtured a sublime disregard for military hierarchy. And there was something in his look, his smile, the furtive touch of his hand, that conveyed to Grimaldi a message only he could understand.

Two nights later they became lovers. Never since had Grimaldi felt such profound love for another human being; such a blend of physical satisfaction, intellectual challenge, emotional harmony. His affair with Oleg lasted only a few months, but it was the love of his life. He still dreamt about him at night, still woke up longing for the touch of his skin, the warmth of his body.

'He was an adventurer,' Grimaldi said loudly, looking at Macpherson searchingly. Did he know? he anxiously asked himself. Did he suspect? 'A communist, a KGB officer, but a bandit all the same.' On the sofa in front of him, Macpherson was sipping black coffee, watching him over the rim of his cup.

Grimaldi accepted more coffee, just for the pleasure of having Reiner serve it to him. Kalinin was the man who had stirred his interest in Russia, that enigmatic empire sworn to destroy his own world, while still desperately trying to imitate it; a nation of men who could be warm, sentimental people, devoted friends – and yet ruthless, scheming enemies.

'We were very excited about the Nazi project,' he said. 'Kalinin spoke good English, and understood a few words of German. We also had with us a British expert named Tony Whitcombe. He had been born in Berlin and spoke German fluently. We succeeded in unravelling some of the escape routes the Nazis were using to get out of Germany.' He smiled, despite himself. 'You should have seen us. Excited as schoolboys when we found out about the Spider.'

Macpherson raised his eyebrows.

'*Die Spinne* in German,' Grimaldi explained. The organization was a spider indeed, spinning its web over several countries, smuggling wanted criminals from Southern Germany and Austria to Spain or the ports of Italy. 'There was another network, *Die Schleuse* – the Lock-gate – that had established a route that went through Germany, Austria, Italy, ending at Genoa or Naples.' In the Italian ports the Nazis embarked for Peron's Argentina.

'The most dangerous criminals, however, escaped with the help of Odessa,' he quickly explained. '*Organisation der Ehemaligen SS Angehorigen* – Association of ex-SS members.'

The three of them, Grimaldi went on, were willing to take risks. Dressed in civilian clothes, Whitcombe posing as a Bavarian sergeant, Grimaldi claiming he was a former French collaborater, they succeeded in sneaking into former-SS circles. Kalinin was less fortunate. He carried the papers of a Russian officer in General Vlassov's pro-Nazi army, but they were of little use. Nobody wanted to mess with the Russians.

Whitcombe and Grimaldi participated in several Odessa meetings in Berlin. 'Twice we succeeded in locating Odessa headquarters. The first time in a wing of a hospital, housing the contagious diseases wards, then in a farm off the road to Dresden.' Frustration surfaced as if it had happened yesterday. 'We were so proud when we submitted our reports. But they were drowned in red tape. The liaison office was leaking like a bloody sieve. Finally, when our special units arrived at the Odessa hideouts, they found that the villains had flown.

'That was too much for Kalinin and myself,' he went on. 'We couldn't bear the mediocrity of our superiors. They were unable to carry out an operation – so we decided to do it on our own.'

'Same old Grimaldi,' Reiner quipped. Macpherson didn't say a word, his eyes narrowed intently.

'I had a plan,' Grimaldi said.

He suggested to his friends they should 'roll up' the Odessa network, from the inside. The three of them, posing as fugitives, would ask for Odessa's assistance in their escape. They should follow the Odessa trail, ascertaining names and places; after reaching one of the ports of Italy – the final destination of their journey – they would report to Berlin and lead the raid on Odessa's entire network.

At the beginning the plan had worked. The Odessa escape committee in Berlin had submitted them to a gruelling interrogation, but they had passed the test with flying colours. 'At least, we thought so at the time.'

'Same cover stories?'

'Yes,' Grimaldi said. 'They sounded genuine. This time we had no problem with Kalinin. The Odessa people had objected to a Russian participating in their meetings, but they didn't object to his joining us in our escape. The Vlassov officers had been even more cruel than the Nazis during the Russian campaign.' He paused to light another small cigar. 'So we were on our way.'

It took them twelve days to reach the Italian border, after travelling across Germany and Austria, sleeping in mountain lodges, farms, a monastery, and once even in a policeman's house. They then embarked on the last stage of their trip – the crossing into Italy. They spent the night in a gamekeeper's home outside Obergurgl, and in the early morning sneaked to the Italian border where the guide from Merano would pick them up.

Grimaldi well remembered the last time he had seen Oleg, that early dawn by the Brenner pass: tense yet thrilled, dark eyes burning with anticipation under the visor of his cap, hand stuck deep in the pockets of a thick brown jacket. Tony Whitcombe crouched beside him behind a low stone wall, shabbily dressed in a cracked leather coat, baggy breeches and scuffed shoes. Two tiny figures, barely noticeable against the backdrop of the Tyrolean Alps, their peaks hidden in the clouds, slopes plunging into the narrow valleys, buried in the morning mist.

'I had stayed behind to pack some food in my rucksack. I hurried to catch up with them before the guide from Merano came to the forest. It covered the slope of the Tyrolean ridge.'

All of a sudden Grimaldi saw Tony throw up his arms grotesquely, then heard the shots and realized that his friend's contortions were the convulsions of a dying man. Oleg also rolled onto the ground, kicking, then disappeared behind the stone wall. Shots echoed throughout the gorge, reverberating against the cliffs. There was no man from Merano waiting for them, Grimaldi realized, just a murderous ambuscade.

He darted towards a jagged outcrop stretching from a hill on his right. Bullets buzzed by his ears, one of them ricocheting between the boulders. In the shelter of the stone rampart he stopped to catch his breath. His face was on fire and his shirt was soaked with sweat. He should go back, he thought, he must save Oleg! But he was unarmed, he couldn't fight the gunmen, and he was trembling with fear. He ran all the way to the village and alerted the burgmeister, who telephoned Allied Army headquarters.

'We found Tony's body by the stone wall. He had been bit in the back by several bullets and had died instantaneously. Kalinin had disappeared. We found traces of blood and followed them for about three hundred yards.' The traces led into a ravine flanked by muddy slopes. One of the mountaineers, whose dog panted at the end of a short leash, found the footprints of three other men; they had either followed the wounded man or carried him away. All the footprints, though, disappeared at the stream that gushed through the gully. 'I never saw Oleg Kalinin again,' he concluded. And I longed for him all those years, he thought.

'So you blew it,' Reiner concluded. A police car's siren wailed in the street, summoning them back to the present.

'I did,' he admitted. That had been the bloody ending of Grimaldi's scheme to defeat Odessa. Months of planning, intelligence gathering and personal risk had produced the Brenner pass massacre; and the taste of panic, his running away in terror, the trembling of his hands, the cold sweat breaking out on his forehead, had haunted Grimaldi for years.

'And nobody blamed you when you came back?' Macpherson asked. 'I would have court-martialled you on the spot.'

Grimaldi crushed out his cigar in a chipped ashtray shaped like a maple leaf. 'A month later, I brought them Reinhard Gehlen. So they chose to ignore the Brenner pass incident.'

'What about the killers? They were never found?'

'No,' Grimaldi said. 'Our men raided the relays where we had stopped on our way, I gave them a detailed list.' He took a deep breath. 'They found nothing. All the Odessa agents had vanished. Odessa designed new routes and stayed in business for a few more years.' He walked to the window and looked down. Two Hispanics in brightly coloured jackets were loading bales and suitcases into an old blue Chevrolet. He turned back. 'Perhaps Kalinin will tell us how he managed to escape.'

'He was your friend, wasn't he?' Macpherson asked coldly. 'Didn't you try to find out what had happened to him?'

Grimaldi's throat was dry. The phantoms were rising from his past. 'How could I? I thought he was dead. Either murdered by the Nazis, or, in the unlikely case that he had escaped, shot by the Russians for insubordination. The Soviet comissars shot people for much less than that. If by any chance he had survived, I would only have complicated matters for him by asking questions.'

'You still think of him as your friend?' Macpherson continued, probing, while poking into his pipe with an ugly silver instrument. 'You didn't act very gallantly by abandoning him there, wounded. Perhaps he hates your guts for that.'

Grimaldi didn't answer, his eyes focused on an Andy Warhol print hanging on the wall.

'But you'll take the job, won't you? You'll go to Moscow.'

'I don't know,' he said. 'Let me think about it.'

Macpherson slowly shook his head. 'Walt, would you leave us alone for a moment?' he said softly.

Reiner shrugged, and left the room. Macpherson turned to Grimaldi. His face was distorted with anger. 'You bloody old queen,' he muttered. 'I saved your ass, back in Pullach, remember? I protected you all these years, and turned a blind eye to all your sordid adventures with the scum you've been picking up in New York and in London. You want me to give you a list of all the queers who've passed through your bed?'

'My private life . . .' Grimaldi started.

'I don't give a damn about your private life. One phone call from me will be more than enough to have you kicked out, and this time for good.' He paused. 'Do you want me to make that call? Or would you rather take the Moscow job and say thank you, sir?'

Grimaldi swallowed but kept quiet, staring blankly at Macpherson.

'That's better. Someone will drive you to the office later.' Macpherson's voice had changed. It was brisk now, matter-of-fact, ringing with command. 'You'll spend a few weeks with us, for briefing procedures and so on. Then a short stay at the Farm, and you'll be on your way. I want you there before Christmas.'

The door opened and Reiner walked in, his sly eyes darting from Macpherson to Grimaldi.

'Cover?' he asked, ignoring Reiner.

Macpherson examined his pipe and put it in the pocket of his corduroy jacket. 'French-Canadian,' he said. 'Representative of the Delices du Nord company of Montreal. They import caviar and fish from Russia. Their man in Moscow is going back home in six weeks.'

'Canadian Immigration is all screwed-up,' Reiner pointed out. 'Lousy filing system, no records of passport numbers. You'll be absolutely safe.'

Grimaldi leaned back against the window, feeling its chill like a cold breath down his neck. 'You had it all sewn up, didn't you, Jim? You knew I was going to accept.'

Macpherson shrugged. 'You bet,' he said bluntly. 'Very few people get a second chance, Napoleone.'

He was on his feet, preceded by Reiner who rushed to the door.

'I asked you before but you didn't answer me, Jim,' Grimaldi said. 'Why all the secrecy? What was all the rush?'

Macpherson turned back towards him, looking annoyed. 'We wanted you out of England at once. We feared a leak.'

'What kind of leak?'

Faced with Grimaldi's righteous puzzlement, the DDP reluctantly explained: 'I told you Kalinin had brought us two documents. The first was the memo of the missile mishap. The second was a GRU analysis of Soviet espionage in England. It seems British Intelligence is still riddled with Russian agents.' He paused. 'I didn't want the British, or our liaison office, to hear the news about your going undercover. That would have been reported to Moscow Centre in twenty-four hours.'

'But . . .'

'Any regular transfer would have raised questions, and people would have asked where you were going next,' Macpherson went on. 'This morning' – he consulted his watch – 'London was informed by cable that you had to fly home urgently because your father was terminally ill. In a couple of weeks we'll inform them that you're resigning from the service, and going to take care of the family business. It's a restaurant chain, isn't it?'

He turned to the door, without waiting for an answer. Reiner hurried after him.

Grimaldi didn't ask if they had told his stepfather about his ghastly malady.

Grimaldi stepped out of the elevator on the fourth floor of the main Langley building, amiably nodding at the employees he saw on his way. He popped a mint in his mouth; a faint touch of garlic still lingered on his breath. It had been an excellent lunch, Fernand was as good as ever. He had recognized him immediately. 'Monsieur Grimaldi, I can't believe it.' The stout Parisian chef was exaggerating his French accent, as usual. It worked wonders with his Washington clientèle. 'How long since you were here last?'

'I've been away for years,' Grimaldi had said. 'In Europe, mostly in Paris. You're still the best, *mon ami*.' Fernand retreated, beaming, and sent Grimaldi's party a Mirabelle on the house. It was a great ending to an excellent meal, Grimaldi decided. And productive, too. He had been extensively briefed by Jim Nolan, the Director of the Clandestine Services – Soviet division (S/D), and Steve Pershing, of the GRU desk. They had chosen to meet at a Washington restaurant rather than the Executive dining room at Headquarters. That way their lunch looked like another of the many farewell meals offered to Grimaldi by his colleagues; while the same meeting, held at Langley Woods, might have raised quite a few eyebrows. His superiors were religiously clinging to the cover story concocted by Macpherson – broken with grief, Grimaldi was resigning from the Agency and going back to Louisiana. As far as his colleagues were concerned, his future from now on lay in Cajun chicken wings and Bahamanian conch chowder. Only Macpherson's staff and six people at Clandestine Services knew that he was bound for a more sinister destination.

It was his last visit to Langley, before starting his journey to Moscow. On Monday he had returned from a refresher course at the Farm which included, according to the local dialect, Mass, Wheel of Torture, and Gunsmoke – respectively low-level briefings, physical training, shooting practice. And Sunday school, of course, an utterly irrelevant initiation to invisible inks, microdots and James Bond gadgets, which Grimaldi knew, and S/D knew, that he was never going to use.

The following morning he flew to Buffalo. In a small motel by Niagara Falls he handed his American papers to a man he had never seen before. The stranger gave him the keys to a car with Quebec plates, and a Canadian passport. The same night Mr Charles Saint-Clair, from Montreal, crossed the Canadian border on his way home.

Six weeks later, an hour after sunset, Grimaldi left a Moscow taxi on Chkalova Street and entered the low dreary building that housed the Kursk railway station, the gateway to southern USSR. The place was bustling with people: peasants from the Ukraine, swarthy Kossacks from the Don, squat Georgians, their dark eyes bleary after the long train journey.

First he had to make sure that he would reach his destination without a KGB goon on his tail. Mixing with a group of Volgograd engineers, Grimaldi donned a cheap rabbit-fur hat and removed his coat, then plunged into a delegation of Tula teachers, carrying red banners and signs proclaiming their support for the teachers of revolutionary Cuba.

He walked into the crowded cafeteria, cautiously navigating between families, children, old people, dogs, and heaps of bales, packages and cracked suitcases. He had memorized his instructions.

He entered the corridor leading to the rest rooms, but instead of going to the back, he pushed a door on his left, crossed a dark room full of cases of bottled water and jars of pickles, almost tripped on a couple of brooms, and went out by another door.

He emerged on the gloomy Kostomarovsky Prospect, crossed the street and casually sauntered into the parking lot, facing the station. A bitter wind was blowing from the east and he draped his coat over his shoulders. The instructions had been very clear: second row from the left, then to the left again. A black Moskvitch with a broken radio antenna, and toy teddy bear on the dashboard. He tried the handle, and it gave in smoothly. He bent down.

'Come in, Franco.' He'd recognize that warm, deep voice with its clipped accent anywhere. 'Long time no see.'

He slipped inside the car and sat upright in the front seat beside Oleg. He took off his hat. His mouth was dry and his heart was pounding. His mission here, perhaps even his life, depended on the next few minutes. Twenty years ago, Oleg Kalinin had been his lover. Today he could be his enemy. Perhaps he had walked straight into a KGB ambush. He imagined Kalinin raising his hand, or lighting a cigarette, and swarm of KGB goons emerging out of the dark, dragging him to the Lubyanka cellars.

Grimaldi had dreaded this meeting since the moment he had accepted Macpherson's offer. Time after time he had raised, from the far recesses of his memory, the ghosts that haunted him: the nightmare in the Austrian ravine, when Tony Whitcombe had died and Oleg had disappeared. He had desperately tried to find an excuse for his behaviour that day. He wondered what Oleg felt about him, after he had abandoned him under fire, wounded. Was Oleg still his friend? Or did he hate him for running away? Perhaps he had concocted some devious plan to make Grimaldi pay for his betrayal, and wanted him here, in his power. The idea seemed farfetched, but Grimaldi was a sceptical, suspicious man.

But as soon as he closed the car door, Kalinin leaned over and hugged him. 'So good to see you, Franco, I am so happy we meet again.' He warmly patted Grimaldi's arm. 'When did you arrive?'

'Yesterday.' He tried to sound natural. 'I am staying at the Ukraina Hotel until I find an apartment. My cover name is Charles Saint-Clair, from Montreal.'

'Monsieur Saint-Clair,' Kalinin chuckled. 'Welcome to Moscow.'

In the faint light emanating from the Kursk station's windows, Grimaldi glanced at his friend. Kalinin was still handsome, although he was losing his hair and deep wrinkles surrounded his eyes. A pale scar ran below his left eye but didn't disfigure his face; on the contrary, it bestowed upon it a kind of roguish charm.

'Your scar . . .' Grimaldi started. He felt awkward.

'Yes.' The Russian nodded. 'From that day in the Alps.'

'I never found out what had happened to you,' Grimaldi mumbled. 'I tried, but you had vanished.'

'I got hit in the face and in the ass.' Kalinin grinned boyishly. 'Remember the ambush? You were behind, I was beside Tony. He got hit first. They were firing at us from behind, so I had no choice but to run forward. I was bleeding, and my wounds hurt like hell. I limped down to the creek, heard them running after me. Thank God for that stream. They lost me there. I spent the night on top of a tree. I heard people, and dogs . . .'

'That was us,' Grimaldi said, 'we were searching for you.'

A man and woman passed by the car, leaning forward against the wind, and Grimaldi slid down in his seat then straightened up again. Kalinin's voice dropped to a murmur.

'I was too exhausted to call for help. Besides, I wasn't sure the same bastards hadn't come back for me.' He turned towards Grimaldi. 'You know, the funniest thing is that they never saw through our cover. Odessa didn't order our killing.'

'What are you talking about?'

'I checked. It was a local initiative.'

'I don't understand. The killers were not from Odessa?'

'They were, but they acted on their own. They belonged to the local Odessa network. They had no idea who we really were, they thought we were genuine Nazi fugitives. We were not their first victims. Their game was knocking off fugitives whom they presumed to be rich. They killed for the money and valuables, and hid the bodies. Nobody ever lived to complain, and even if somebody survived, he could hardly report them to the authorities.'

'But after the attack on us, the Odessa network vanished.'

Kalinin shrugged. 'Of course. The Odessa bosses heard of the incident, and ordered everybody into hiding until an alternative route was established. By the way' – he lightly touched his scar – 'the Odessa people themselves bumped off the guys who attacked us. That was bad publicity for Odessa Travel.'

'And your superiors didn't blame you for disobeying orders?'

Another man passed by. 'It's crowded here,' Grimaldi muttered.

'I had a few unpleasant moments. There was a colonel who wanted me court-martialled for insubordination. But I had barely survived, I had been wounded by the Nazis, and my colonel realized he would have trouble explaining why he was court-martialling me. He finally agreed that I had been punished enough.' He laughed softly. 'Oh, enough of that. We haven't seen each other for about twenty years, we are about to start the most risky adventure of our lives, but all we can talk about is that day at the Brenner pass.'

'What happened since?' Grimaldi said. 'You got married?'

'Married to the GRU and to a fine woman. And father of three beautiful daughters,' Kalinin proudly added, then cast a sideways look at Grimaldi. 'You haven't, I know.'

He nodded silently. They would never be lovers again, he realized. Oleg was married, he liked it, and wanted Grimaldi to know it.

A shadow passed over Oleg's face and he slapped his hand on the dashboard. 'That's enough small talk for today. We have a lot of ground to cover.' He paused. 'We must be very careful, Franco, this is a deadly business. Two weeks ago they shot somebody in the Lubyanka, for treason. We don't know yet who he was.'

Grimaldi kept silent, and Kalinin glanced at his watch. 'Let's start with drops and crash meeting procedures.'

'Good,' Grimaldi said. He ignored Kalinin's warning. He was still thinking about their conversation. They were not lovers any more, but they were friends, close friends. Everything was going to be all right, he could count on Oleg. He was pervaded by a blissful sensation of relief. It had started snowing, and large flakes gracefully fluttered down, melting on the warm windshield.

'Good,' Grimaldi repeated.

Chapter Eight

'Comrades!' the short general pompously declared. 'I welcome you to the Higher School of State Security.'

The general was sitting behind a table, on a raised podium, that overlooked the austere conference room. His thick eyebrows fused into a straight grey line that surmounted black beady eyes and a sharp nose hovering over a cupid's-bow mouth. The general's uniform was neatly pressed, and his chest covered with four rows of glinting medals, hanging from multi-coloured ribbons. The narrow windows on his right, giving upon an inner court, cast a morose greyness upon the assembly. On the wall behind him, a colour poster of Lenin in a three-piece suit, haranguing the working masses, hung next to a charcoal sketch of Marx and Engels, who stared grimly at the artist.

'You are being entrusted with a great responsibility,' the general went on. 'To defend the achievements of the October Revolution. After you graduate you will be dispatched to the front where a bitter battle is being fought against a crafty enemy. The Western intelligence services are out to undermine the foundations of socialism, using the most despicable means. International capitalism is the enemy. And in order to overcome this enemy you must know all about him.'

'What's the general's name?' Dimitri whispered to his neighbour, a bulky young man with curly blond hair and hard brown eyes.

'General Lubelski, the school commander.' The blond boy chuckled. 'They say he never stands up in public, doesn't want people to see how short he is. That's why he's called the Bloody Dwarf. He always delivers his lectures sitting on his fat ass.'

'Your success,' the general was saying, 'will depend on how well you master the methods used by intelligence agents; how well you study the fundamentals of Marxism-Leninism and the mentality of Western nations, and how well you can use your weapons and your hands which might save your life in a desperate situation.'

The small general surveyed his sixty-two students. 'Remember,' he said, jutting his chin forward, 'an officer in State Security is more than a mere party member or government official. He is a Chekist, meaning that he is a communist first, last and always. Every act of his daily life must be bound to this premise: he eats, reads, loves, thinks, acts and sleeps – as a Chekist. He must remember, always, that the world is divided into two classes of people: communists and others.'

Dimitri couldn't concentrate, he was still overwhelmed by the new world that was unfolding before him. He had arrived in Moscow yesterday afternoon, after a twelve-hour journey in a crowded train. He had taken the Metro, then walked to the four-storey house at 19 Stanislavskaya Street. He had never travelled on an underground train before, never seen such large crowds and such bustling streets. Huge edifices from the Stalin era towered over the city; they were massive conglomerates of concrete, from which pointed spires emerged, crowned with red stars.

Shortly after sunset Dimitri reached his destination – a redbrick building facing the drab East German embassy. This was the Visshaya Shkola, the School of State Security, where he was going to live for the next four years.

On presenting his papers to the armed guards at the gate, Dimitri was sent to the school secretariat. A sour-faced officer took him for a medical inspection, then to the quartermaster who issued him three new sets of uniforms, a new overcoat, new shoes, new shirts, a leather belt, two khaki-coloured ties, sneakers and new underwear. Dimitri couldn't believe they were giving him all this. God, he thought, at Panfilov I could trade these goodies for a year's supply of food, vodka and cigarettes! The quartermaster also gave him a smart military cap, adorned with a shiny emblem. It represented a red star embossed with the Soviet sickle and hammer on the background of a sword and a shield. Dimitri was excited as never before in his life. He felt a surge of gratitude to General Takachenko, who had helped him get out of Panfilov; and to that handsome colonel, Kalinin, the member of the State Security Commission who had stood by him when his loyalty had been questioned. Here he was now, a KGB cadet, on his way to the top.

The school administrator, a bald major named Nekrasov, escorted him to his dormitory, where sixteen beds awaited the new students. Beside each there was a nightstand, a lamp, and a big locker. 'You'll be sixty-two students,' the major droned, 'divided into four dormitories and two classes. Classes start at nine am and end at ten pm. The period from five to seven pm is set aside for individual studies. Sundays are free for rest and amusement, and only then are you allowed to leave the building. Your salary, during your studies, will be 200 roubles a month.'

Two hundred roubles! Dimitri gaped at him, amazed. He had never seen so much money. Two hundred roubles was a judge's salary. As a mere KGB trainee he was going to earn the same salary as a judge, and more money than a teacher. At Panfilov, the teachers made barely one hundred and twenty roubles! 'Reveille at six-thirty am,' the major was declaiming. 'At seven, physical exercise in the courtyard – shorts, undershirt, sneakers. Breakfast at eight.' He consulted his watch. 'You can have dinner now, the mess is still open. That's all.'

At the door, he stopped. 'By the way, you are our youngest student. Most are twenty-two or older, and usually army officers or university graduates. You're either very bright or you know somebody very high up.' His face briefly contorted in a lopsided grin.

'Comrade Major!' Dimitri jumped to attention. 'I request permission to go out tonight. It's my first night in Moscow. I know this is highly unusual, but I was born here and have been away for more than fifteen years.'

To his surprise, the administrator smiled. 'No, it's not unusual. Every new student has the same request on his first night in Moscow.' He shrugged, then nodded. 'All right, you can go. Stop on your way out at the secretariat for a written authorization. By the way, you can dress in civilian clothes. That's one of our privileges here.' He nodded again and was gone.

Civilian clothes! There was nothing in the world that would prevent him from putting on his dashing new uniform. He would have paid dearly for his schoolmates from Panfilov to see him now, a smart young trainee walking the streets of Moscow, the KGB insignia shining on his cap. But what he really wanted – he felt a pang in his chest as the thought struck him – was that his father could see him; that Boris Morozov could know he was alive, had overcome all the obstacles, and was going to be a KGB officer, like him.

His father's memory haunted him all through a chilly October evening, when he explored Moscow. He thought of his father when he stood in Red Square, watching the government buildings that rose behind the sturdy Kremlin wall. He could imagine KGB Colonel Boris Morozov arriving on a night like this into the supreme centre of Soviet power to brief Beria, Kaganovitch, perhaps even Stalin! His shiny ZIL limousine probably passed through the Spasskaya Gate, alongside the colourful onion domes of St Basil's, then hours later would dart on its way out, like the luxurious automobiles he now saw speeding out of the Kremlin into the Moscow streets, respectfully saluted by KGB guards and militiamen. One day I too will enter the Kremlin in my black limousine, thought Dimitri.

But the place he had most wanted to visit tonight, even more than Red Square, even more than the Kremlin, was Dzerzhinski Square. The famous Moscow square, named after the ascetic Polish aristocrat who had founded the Cheka, the precursor of the KGB; the square where the KGB had established its formidable stronghold, and its most notorious prison.

The square was deserted. A timid rain was dropping from a dull sky and a sharp autumn wind swept the desolate pavements. Dimitri stood under the sinister statue of Felix Dzerzhinski, bearded and hollow-eyed, dressed in his black executioner's robes, and watched the massive bulk of the Lubyanka, looming over the north side of the square, exuding an air of brutal menace, like the awesome, evil-looking fortresses of the dark ages.

His mother had died there, in one of the execution yards, but he didn't really care about her. It was his father he again thought of, visualizing that terrible moment when several officers, perhaps young like him, perhaps wearing the same uniforms and insignia, had walked into Boris Morozov's office and ordered him to surrender his revolver and come with them. There had followed the humiliating scene of the stripping of his epaulettes and medals, the insults, the dark cell, the branding as traitor. And finally the camps, the freezing cold, the hunger, the beatings and the firing squad.

You, he vowed in a surge of black hatred, you who've taken part in the killing of my father, whoever you are, I'll find you one day and I'll crush you. But I shall not act like a fool. I shall not go for you in a suicidal outburst that will cost me my head too. Revenge is a dish that one should eat cold. First I'll climb to the top floor of the Lubyanka, I'll become a KGB baron, your chief. And as your chief I'll use my power to get your hide.

The merry laughter of children jolted him out of his reverie. He looked across the square to where a group of little boys and girls, accompanied by their parents, were screaming in delight, watching the illuminated windows of *Detsky Mir* – Children's World – the largest toy store in the Soviet Union. What an absurdity, he thought, to erect that toy palace, the symbol of innocence and children's joy, across the street from the torture cellars and execution chambers of the Lubyanka.

He stared for a long time at Dzerzhinski's black statue. Even Khrushchev, who had denounced Stalin's and Beria's crimes, accusing them of murdering scores of thousands of people, couldn't remove Dzerzhinski's statue from this place, and had to leave that black thorn stuck in the heart of Moscow.

What a strange nation we Russians are, he thought, in our present and our distant past. Hating power and yet admiring it; praising democracy yet yearning for a strong hand; loathing the secret police but crawling on our bellies before them; speaking against torture and violation of human rights, and still making torturers and executioners the princes of our society. What other nation would have raised a statue to the man who founded the bloodiest secret service in the world? What other people would have given that man's name to one of their capital's main squares, then turned one of their capital's main buildings into a prison and an execution site?

I will be a Chekist, he thought ruefully on his way back, and certainly one of the most reliable, the most dedicated. But I'll never be a believer. For whatever faith I had, whatever innocence I was born with, I lost it at Panfilov long ago, long before I lost my virginity to the cook's daughter.

'The sluggards in the artillery!' the burly drill sergeant roared, and sixty-two voices yelled back, their running steps marking the measure:

'Braggarts in the cavalry –
Drunkards in the fleet –
Idiots in the infantry!'

The sergeant bellowed again: 'And who are we?'

They yelled in unison: 'All the smart ones KGB! KGB! KGB!'

They had been running for fifteen minutes already in the inner court of the school, their weary feet pounding the uneven flagstones. It was a freezing, brittle morning in February, the low winter sky blowing its frozen breath upon their sweating bodies. Dimitri felt good. He enjoyed the early morning exercises. His training at Panfilov was bearing its fruit; he was in excellent shape, not like some of his classmates who were panting, flushed and bleary-eyed, at his sides.

The drill sergeant, a huge, bald Latvian, raised his voice again. He is more interested in us yelling his stupid slogans, Dimitri thought, than doing our exercises. This time the sergeant chose the popular joke on the initials of the OGPU, one of the secret services that had preceded the KGB.

'*O Gospodi Pomogi Ubezhat!*' the Latvian shouted, quoting the popular interpretation of the OGPU initials: Oh God, help me escape!

Dimitri and the other students shouted the answer, which was based on the reversal of the initials: '*Ubēzhish, Psymayem, Golovu Otorvem!*' You'll escape, we'll catch you and cut off your head.

The drill sergeant brayed his laughter. Very funny indeed, Dimitri thought.

Still, he enjoyed the physical training as much as the intensive studies. Early this morning, after a sleepless night in the library, he had completed an essay on the history of the Soviet secret services. It was a fascinating story, that reminded him of a medieval succession war between fierce warlords, each coveting the throne, every new chief murdering his predecessor. The cycle started with Felix Dzerzhinski founding the Cheka – the All-Russian Extraordinary Commission for Combatting Counterrevolution and Sabotage – in December 1917. It continued with the Red Terror, the necessary liquidation of thousands of dissidents that was ordered by Lenin in September 1918.

Dimitri liked the romantic aura of the Cheka. It soon metamorphosed into the OGPU, that pursued Lenin's war by unmasking and annihilating the surviving enemies of the revolution: the Whites, the aristocrats, the rich kulaks, the treacherous foreign agents. The OGPU was replaced by the NKVD, an excellent organization that unfortunately became Stalin's instrument for the purges of the thirties, in which countless innocent communists perished. In 1936, NKVD chief Heinrich Yagoda was shot on Stalin's orders, to be replaced by Stalin's bloodthirsty hangman, Nikolai Yezhov. Ironically, Dimitri noted, Yezhob met the exact fate of Yagoda; he was shot in the same Lubyanka cellar where he had executed his predecessor.

These were the dark years. Dimitri wrote, when Stalin used the Soviet security services for his criminal enterprises. In 1938, Stalin's henchman Beria stepped on the scene, taking over the organization, already known as the NKGB. Beria incorporated it into the Ministry of Internal Affairs, the MVD. Beria was the man who had ordered Boris Morozov's arrest, but he didn't live to send him to the hangman. In 1953, soon after Stalin's death, it was Beria's turn to follow Yagoda and Yezhov's footsteps into the execution chamber. At the end of Beria's rule, the new KGB was born. It was detached from the MVD, and became its sworn enemy.

'By the creation of the KGB a circle was closed,' Dimitri wrote in conclusion, 'the new organization acquiring the same political status and powers as the revolutionary Cheka. That was how the Cheka rose from its ashes.' This year, shortly before Dimitri arrived in Moscow, a new chairman had taken over the KGB command: a scholarly-looking man with sallow skin, greying blond hair and pale eyes magnified by steel-rimmed glasses: Yuri Andropov.

Beside mastering KGB history, Dimitri penetrated the convoluted labyrinths of the KGB internal structure. The KGB Chairman, he learned, was under the direct orders of the Politburo. KGB headquarters, entrenched in the Dzerzhinski Square compound, was a cluster of separate branches: four Chief Directorates, seven independent Directorates, and six Departments. Those, in turn, were subdivided into an intricate web of directorates, departments, directions and services.

Most of the KGB power was concentrated in three Chief Directorates and one Directorate. These were the First (KGB operations abroad), the Second (counterintelligence and surveillance of Soviet citizens), the Fifth (struggle against dissidence) and the Armed Forces Directorate that was responsible for the loyalty of all Soviet officers, from Red Army headquarters down to company level.

Dimitri was amazed by the incredible scope of KGB powers. Its branches, he discovered, dealt with numerous activities, from espionage, subversion and assassination abroad to surveillance of foreign tourists, students, and businessmen; from planting spies in the West, and sexually blackmailing foreign dignitaries – to controlling the East European satellites, operating against China, watching Soviet leaders and sending the KGB special troops to fight border wars. KGB guards managed labour camps beyond the Arctic Circle, and protected the Kremlin. KGB operatives granted travel visas, manned the telephone and radio systems and carried out necessary disinformation campaigns. KGB sleuths shadowed potential enemies: dissidents, priests, Jews, ethnic minorities, emigré organizations, foreign right-wing movements. KGB officers investigated economic crimes, and protected industrial secrets; KGB scientists manufactured deadly, untraceable poisons.

Dimitri was amazed by the incredible number of people employed in the gigantic machine of the KGB: 90,000 staff officers in the Soviet Union and around the world, another 400,000 special troops, border guards, clerks and employees, and hundreds of thousands of informants and agents, most of them on the government payroll.

The KGB, Dimitri realized, had grown into a secret world, an invisible web that covered the entire Soviet Union, and reached to the most remote corners of the globe. From the Lubyanka headquarters, known as Moscow Centre, the KGB could reach to every village in the Soviet Union, to foreign capitals, army headquarters, scientific installations. For their own security the Soviet citizens were watched, surveyed, vetted and appraised; the foreign nations couldn't imagine that a secret army was protecting the Soviet Union while striving to penetrate their secrets.

Inside the Soviet Union, the KGB had become a parallel nation, a closed caste that lived off the fat of the land. 'Take Moscow, for example,' Misha Ponomarev said to Dimitri one evening when they were alone in the library. 'You think you know Moscow?'

Ponomarev, tall and clumsy, narrow-faced and round-eyed, was a twenty-seven-year-old White Russian whose parents had been hanged by the Germans in Borisov. He had been raised in orphanages and youth institutions, and had grown fond of Dimitri, perhaps because of their similar background. A fourth-year student, he expected to graduate in May. In his last year at the Visshaya Shkola, he was assistant lecturer on the structure and organization of the KGB.

'There are two cities in Moscow,' he eagerly said. He was the happiest KGB student Dimitri had ever met. 'One is the city that every tourist discovers: Red Square, St Basil's, Novodevichny Monastery, Gorky Park, the Bolshoi, the Economic Achievements Exhibition.

'And there is the second city, *our* city.'

Dimitri raised his eyebrows.

'The secret city of government and KGB,' Misha triumphantly announced. He paused, apparently waiting for his words to sink in. 'Imagine a street map of Moscow,' he said, his long hands floating in the air, drawing an imaginary circle. 'No, wait.'

He disappeared between the book shelves, and was back a moment later, eagerly unfolding a large map before Dimitri. 'Let's take the portion delimited by the Garden ring, and start with the Kremlin.' His bony finger landed on Red Square. 'A few hundred metres from the Kremlin you have the KGB official and secret compounds: Moscow Centre at Dzerzhinsky Square, our offices at Dzerzhinsky Street, Malaya Lubyanka Street, Kuznetsky Most – see? Take Gorky Street and go by the special KGB living quarters at Mozhayskoye Road. First Meshchanskaya Street, the Arbat.' Ponomarev's hands were dancing, shaping concentric circles on the map. 'All this within the Garden ring, see? Oh, yes, and behind the Bolshoi Conservatory we have the MVD headquarters.'

Dimitri nodded. The MVD was in charge of the militia and the special interior troops.

'Further down,' Ponomarev's enthusiasm soared to new heights, 'at Kaluzhskoye Chaussée, we have a special unit of the KGB guard protecting the Academy of Sciences; and at Pokrovsky Boulevard, the compounds of two MVD and KGB divisions, kept in constant readiness.'

Ponomarev shot a satisfied look at Dimitri, like a magician who had just conjured up a string of colourful kerchiefs. 'We control the city, see? And I didn't mention the KGB club, nor the clusters of buildings

– like Kutuzovsky Prospect – where the Politburo members live, the Kremlin top brass and our own chiefs.'

'Where does Andropov live?' Dimitri asked.

'Kutuzovsky Prospect, the same building where Brezhnev has his apartment.' Misha briefly paused. 'I didn't mention our secret safe-houses, like . . . here, on 62 Novokuznetzkaya Street, 32 Bolotnaya, 11 Sirotzky, 17 Taganskaya, and the villa on Zubovskaya Square . . .' His finger punched the map at different points. 'Now, besides all this, we have scores of operational flats in town; we have our own farms outside the city, where we grow our food; our own slaughterhouses, for our meat; our own doctors, cooks, electricians, and handymen.'

'Our own, you say?'

'Let me show you something,' Misha chuckled. 'Take your coat and let's go.'

'Where?' Dimitri asked.

'You'll see.'

Half an hour later they were seated at the elegant KGB restaurant, on the eighth floor of the Lubyanka, where Misha had the right to entertain visitors. It was the first time Dimitri visited Moscow Centre, and he was so awed he barely dared to breathe. His heart thumped wildly when he showed his credentials to the KGB guards at the entrance, and cast a quick look at the hammer and sickle emblems engraved upon the massive gates. In the elevator he stood silent, imagining the devious coups being concocted at this very moment in some locked rooms, barely a few yards away.

At the restaurant he stared wide-eyed at the officers and civilians who moved about. He was sure some of them were daredevil secret agents, back from dangerous assignments abroad.

'Aren't you eating?' Misha said.

He ordered salted salmon, real sour cream, and the delicacy he craved most – chocolate. The waitress brought him a bar of real Swiss chocolate, not the cheap substitutes one could buy in Moscow's stores.

'As you can see,' Misha was blabbering, 'we have our own restaurants, our own stores and our own schools.'

'The ordinary citizens don't know about this?' Dimitri asked.

'Most of them do, but they wouldn't dare talk about it,' Pomomarev chortled. He was marked with the cynicism and the obsession for food of the orphan child. He made a sweeping gesture around him, as if he owned the place. 'Here you can get a royal breakfast for almost nothing. They serve you milk, eggs, bacon, sausages and fresh fruit. At the KGB club, across the square, we've got a gym, a sauna and a swimming pool, a restaurant and a delicatessen. You can buy everything there – caviar, sturgeon, smoked salmon, apples and oranges. A bottle of Scotch whisky costs you less than in America – the equivalent of one dollar! That, brother, is what they call living!'

Misha loaded two thick slices of pink salmon on his buttered toast and bent forward. 'But there is something much more exciting than food or drink in the KGB. Have you ever heard of Department Thirteen?' He cast a wary glance about him, and lowered his voice. 'Let me tell you about it.'

Colonel Igor Guzenko, tall, cool, looking very English with his trim reddish moustache and cold blue eyes, cleared his throat and surveyed the class. 'Today we'll deal with the First Chief Directorate,' he said, and pointed with his stick at a chart he had pinned to the blackboard. A storm was raging outside, and gusts of wind moaned through the cracked window frames, billowing Guzenko's chart like a ship's sail.

'The First,' he announced, 'is the KGB branch charged with clandestine activities abroad. As you can see' – his stick pointed at the middle of the chart – 'it is subdivided into three Sub-Directorates, three Services, and twelve Departments.'

Dimitri frowned. There was another department he knew about, but it didn't figure on the diagram.

'We'll start,' Guzenko was saying, 'with the Illegals Directorate. It infiltrates into foreign countries KGB agents who operate under false identities. Each agent is trained individually, for security reasons.'

Dimitri listened to Guzenko concisely describing the Information and Counterintelligence services, the ten geographic departments, the Disinformation department and, finally the Cover Organs department.

'Cover Organs,' the colonel pointed out, 'places KGB personnel in cover jobs abroad with other government agencies, like TASS, Aeroflot, Sovtorg, Intourist, Sovfilm, and various newspapers. We also use foreign organizations, like the World Bank, the United Nations, the Red Cross and international sports associations.'

Guzenko examined his audience and laid down his stick. 'And that, Comrades, wraps up the First Chief Directorate,' he said contentedly, puffing on his pipe. 'Any questions?'

Dimitri stood up. 'What about Department Thirteen?'

Guzenko stiffened. 'What? What was your question?'

'Department Thirteen,' Dimitri repeated, 'Executive Action.'

Guzenko stared at him sharply. 'What is your name, Student?'

'Dimitri Morozov, Comrade Colonel.'

'Dimitri Morozov,' Guzenko repeated. 'There is no Department Thirteen in the First Chief Directorate. You may sit down.'

'It is also known as Department V, Comrade Colonel,' Dimitri insisted, then reluctantly released the last item of information he possessed: 'It's nicknamed *Mokrie Dela* – Wet Affairs.'

'I told you,' Guzenko said tersely, anger exploding in his eyes, 'there is no such department. Now sit down!'

Dimitri complied, feeling the stares of his classmates converging upon him. His cheeks were flushed. Fuck your mother, Guzenko, he thought, you lying carcass. There is no such department? The Thirteenth is the most important department in the entire KGB!

He morosely picked at his steak at dinner, his mind still on the afternoon's incident, when Major Nekrasov, the school administrator, appeared beside him. 'General Lubelski wants to see you,' he said. 'Right away.'

The dwarfish school commander was sitting behind the desk in his austere office. He was going through a file, pursing his lips, and raised his eyes with a frown when Dimitri entered and saluted. 'Student Morozov reporting, Comrade General.'

Lubelski seemed angry, very angry. The deep frown made the straight line of his eyebrows plunge downward, bestowing a malevolent expression upon the broad face. He didn't waste time in niceties. 'Who told you about Department Thirteen?'

Dimitri swallowed. 'I heard about it from friends.'

'Who? What are their names?'

Dimitri didn't answer.

'I want to know,' Lubelski repeated. 'How did you hear about Department Thirteen?'

I can't tell him it was Ponomarev, Dimitri thought. They'll kick him out a few weeks before his graduation. 'You know the school grapevine, Comrade General. We hear all kinds of rumours.'

Lubelski picked up a sheet of paper, covered with handwriting. 'And all you said today – Mokrie Dela, Department V, Thirteen – was rumours? What other rumours did you hear, Student Morozov?'

He didn't reply. The Bloody Dwarf is going to kick me out, he thought in panic.

Lubelski was seething with contained anger. 'I want you to know, Morozov, that behaving as you did today is an adequate reason for expulsion from our school.' He scowled, his jaw clamped, until Dimitri lowered his eyes. 'However, I found in your file that you were recommended by General Takachenko.'

A sensation of relief slowly descended upon him. He tried not to show it, penitently bowing his head. 'I spoke to General Takachenko who assured me that I shall have no more reasons to complain until the completion of your studies. Understand?'

'Yes, Comrade General.'

'Good.' The general angrily closed the file, and it dawned upon Dimitri that Lubelski wasn't so angry at him as frustrated at having to bend to Takachenko.

'Morozov!' Lubelski's voice caught him at the door, still irritated but now tinged with a shade of curiosity. 'Why this interest in Department Thirteen?'

'That's where I would like to serve, Comrade General.' Dimitri saluted and left the office.

He wasn't interested in internal surveillance, in persecuting terrified Soviet citizens or harassing long-haired intellectuals and big-mouthed dissidents. He wanted to take part in dangerous operations in foreign capitals, cross swords with the aces of the British MI5 and the American CIA, travel to exotic countries, conquer mysterious women.

Still, Dimitri didn't dream of becoming a Soviet spy abroad, nor even a *rezident* – commander of a KGB station in a foreign capital. He wanted something more challenging; something he could do by himself. He was a loner, and his childhood had taught him not to trust anybody. He remembered the sensation of power that had swept him the night he killed Kuzma Bunin. He recalled Vanya's fear and respect. And he felt he could kill again, but this time win a medal for it. He had set his sights on the ultra-secret Thirteen, nicknamed 'Wet Affairs' because of the bloody trail its agents left behind them. And he had chosen it because of the meteoric rise of its officers in the KGB hierarchy, once they came back from field duty.

Thirteen, whose very existence was so vigorously denied, was in charge of violent operations abroad – kidnappings, sabotage, assaults on enemy safehouses. And murder.

Student Morozov wanted to become a killer.

But before that, he had to learn how to become a secret agent.

Two slant-eyed Tartars, officers of the Soviet commandos, instructed the students in hand-to-hand combat, and in the use of small firearms. An elderly civilian with a disfigured face and a glass eye, Sergei Grozny, taught Dimitri and his classmates to use plastic and conventional explosives, build a bomb, concoct incendiary devices from components they could buy at any pharmacy. The students joked that one of Grozny's home-made bombs had apparently blown his eye away. But Misha Pnomarev told Dimitri another story about Grozny.

'He was teaching a class in this very building,' Misha said, 'when news came that Stalin was dead. Grozny started crying but his tears streamed from only one eye, as the other one was made of glass. Two students in the first row burst out laughing. Their timing was bad. They were never seen again.'

The legendary Colonel Rudolf Abel, who had spent many years as an illegal in New York and had been exchanged for the U-2 pilot Gary Powers, taught the trainees the basic rules of operating in an American city. Abel looked a broken man. After his lecture, Dimitri saw the gaunt colonel sitting all alone at the officers' mess, but nobody approached him. 'Since his return from America,' Misha revealed, 'he is not fully trusted any more.'

A comely employee of Communications, Vera Shevchenko, trained them to code, cypher and transmit with miniaturized devices. 'Many messages to our agents abroad,' she disclosed, 'are conveyed by means of Radio Moscow musical programmes.'

'You mean that you tell Radio Moscow what music to broadcast?' Dimitri asked.

She nodded. A British agent who had been unfortunately captured – she gravely disclosed – used to receive his orders by a code based on four popular tunes: 'Kalinka', 'The Nutcracker', 'The Sabre Dance' and 'Swan Lake'. Shevchenko also instructed the students to manufacture invisible inks, and reduce photographed documents to the size of microdots.

Other retired KGB officers taught the rules of running field agents, servicing dead-letter drops, street shadowing and dodging surveillance. The students practised the techniques acquired in full-day exercises on the streets of Moscow.

The most sensational lecture was delivered by Kim Philby, the KGB spy who almost became chief of British Intelligence before escaping to Moscow. Dimitri drank in Philby's appearance. He saw an ageing, handsome man, with greying blond hair and a mischievous twinkle in his eyes. In spite of his swollen beer gut, and his baggy suit, he still looked distinguished. Or perhaps Dimitri felt so because of Philby's irreverent style, that survived even translation from English into Russian performed by a fat civilian with a stony face.

Strangely enough, Philby used his lecture to launch a violent diatribe against the clumsiness and shortcomings of the KGB foreign operations. He accused KGB agents abroad of always repeating the same outmoded procedures. He criticized the political interference in analysis and evaluation. 'Many brilliant researchers,' he said, 'write wrong assessments of a situation not because they believe them but to please their superiors.'

Moscow Centre, Philby said, was being defeated by Soviet bureaucracy. Instead of an aggressive, sophisticated organization, the KGB had become 'a huge dinosaur', whose efficiency was in decline. 'Soviet agents,' Philby warned, 'are easily recognized by their ill-fitting suits, their heavy accents, their archaic methods, their lack of imagination. If the KGB doesn't change soon, it will be routed by the Western services.'

Philby's words were received with uneasy laughter and confused stares. Dimitri was surprised that Philby had been allowed to give such a lecture. He was impressed by the courage of the Englishman, who had dared to revolt against KGB routine. Dimitri believed every word he said. One day, he thought, I'll remodel the First, the way Philby suggests.

'A Soviet Intelligence officer must be *kulturny*,' Colonel Helena Kraiova announced as she started her first lecture. Dimitri remembered her from Panfilov, where she had come to interview him with the KGB Commission. She was Deputy Director of the school and theoretical studies were her domain. She made the students devote two hours daily to the study of English or French. She invited to the school former residents in Western capitals who described the structure and modus operandi of foreign services like the SIS, the CIA, the Mossad and the French SDECE.

But that was not what Kraiova meant by the word *kulturny*. Her ambition was to instil in her pupils fine Western manners – for the good of the cause, of course. She taught the students etiquette, table manners, proper social behaviour. Once a week she brought a busload of young ballet dancers from the Bolshoi to teach the students dancing. Only years later was Dimitri to find out that he had perhaps become *kulturny,* but hadn't learned to dance. The ballerinas' classical upbringing didn't exactly accord with modern dancing; in the *kultura* lessons he learned mostly mazurkas, Viennese waltzes, boleros and schottisches, which were not exactly the hottest items in the discos of the swinging West.

One evening in May, he cornered his dancing partner, an elfin girl with flaven hair and very white skin. Her name was Ludmila and she reminded him of the dancer in Zoya's poster, back in Panfilov. 'Can I see you on Sunday?' he asked.

'Why?' She stared at him with her enormous blue eyes.

'I think you're very cute,' he said. She didn't respond, so he added: 'I can bring some good food if you like. Hungarian salami and caviar, some salmon. We can have a picnic at Sokolniki.'

'Could you also get us a jar of French marmalade?' she asked in a little girl's voice.

'Sure.' He wondered if she was a virgin, she looked so young.

On Sunday they had their picnic in Sokolniki Park. Ludmila was very sassy, gaily chattering about the Bolshoi, her girlfriends, her two sisters that she had left behind in Smolensk. They ate the food and drank a bottle of sparkling Georgian wine. He kissed her rosy mouth, and she returned his kiss with unexpected fire. Then she deftly packed the leftovers of their meal, gravely inspecting the volume of French marmalade left in the jar. She got up, brushing the crumbs from her skirt. Let's go, her eyes said.

Ludmila behaved as if everything had been agreed between them beforehand. She led him to her room in the apartment she shared with three other girls. The moment she closed the door behind her he kissed her again, and she responded at once, rubbing herself against his hardness, offering her breasts to his kisses. He didn't wonder about her virginity any more.

Ludmila undressed quickly and lay naked on her bed, waiting for him. She had small breasts with bulging pink nipples and a flat stomach culminating with a rise of thick dark blond hair. That excited him. As he crawled into bed, she pulled him inside her, letting out short, contented screams. She made love eagerly, yet Dimitri felt there was something mechanical in her behaviour, as if sex was the obvious dessert after their picnic lunch.

He returned to Stanislavskaya Street strangely dissatisfied. He knew he wasn't bad-looking, and there were women who found him attractive; he had seen some inviting looks in the streets of Moscow. Still, he had the feeling that he had bought an afternoon of sex for a jar of French marmalade.

The same sensation kept returning, time after time, during the following months. After Ludmila, there were other ballet dancers, or girls from the Foreign Language classes who took the English course with the students. They lit up at the prospect of a good meal, fancy foreign food, a tin of coffee, even a bottle of expensive vodka they could exchange for a bar of soap. 'When you graduate it will become much easier, brother,' Misha knowingly whispered. He had graduated three days before. 'Very few girls refuse to date a KGB officer. We can get the choice pieces, see?'

How could he tell him, Dimitri wondered, that it was not sex alone he was after? That sometimes he felt a sea of love boil and churn inside him, but had nobody to share it with? His loneliness was suffocating him. He had never experienced motherly love, and the dreams he'd had as a child about his mother had been shattered by Takachenko's revelations. He hadn't experienced brotherly love either; his half-brother had vanished, somewhere in America. He would have paid dearly to meet him, but didn't even know how to get in touch with him. Anyway, Dimitri doubted if they had anything in common, if love could still exist between them.

He had never been loved by a woman. The women who had slept with him had done so out of routine or for a present; it was sheer whoring, even if disguised. He had never experienced true love.

He longed for a woman who would love him, make him feel the burning passion and total devotion he had read about in books. Sometimes he couldn't sleep for imagining how wonderful life could be if he had just one person, his girl, beside him, to share with him everything he achieved. But he always reached the same black conclusion, dictated by his morbid streak: he was condemned to live and die alone, and never experience the taste of real love.

He knew he could discuss his painful yearning with nobody, even with Misha. His friend would shoot at him a conspiratorial wink and announce: 'I know the medicine for your trouble, brother. I'll get you a pair of silk stockings, and for that price you can screw Miss Komsomol herself, see?'

At the beginning of his second winter in Moscow, four days before the Revolution Day parade, he was summoned to Lubelski's office. Only a week before, Dimitri had become a member of the communist party, and Lubelsky had firmly shaken his hand at the end of the short ceremony. This morning the Bloody Dwarf was seated behind his desk, buried in his files. He was smoking a fat Cuban cigar. 'Morozov,' he said. He didn't look angry this time. 'You have an hour to pack your belongings. You're leaving us.'

Dimitri missed a heartbeat. What had happened? He hadn't done anything wrong. His marks were good, he was one of the best students in his class, and an excellent shot as well. 'May I ask where I'm going, Comrade General?'

'You may,' Lubelski said. 'Remember our conversation a few months ago?'

'Yes, Comrade General.' He recalled the general's fury after he had mentioned the Thirteenth in class.

'You are transferred to the Foreign Intelligence School,' the Bloody Dwarf said, spewing grey smoke, 'the private school of the First Chief Directorate. That's where we train our officers for operational assignments abroad.'

It took Dimitri a moment to digest the general's words. An operational assignment abroad. God, this could be a first step towards the Thirteenth! He was transported, but didn't let it show. 'Yes, Comrade General.'

Lubelski spoke out of a cloud of smoke. 'I think you'll like the place. It's three years of hard work, but it's worthwhile. Not everybody makes it, Morozov, remember that.'

He saluted. 'Thank you, Comrade General.'

He packed hastily and ran down the stairs; he didn't even have time to break the news to Misha. A car was waiting for him outside, a battered Zhiguli, but a car all the same. The driver was a Red Army soldier. He didn't speak to Dimitri. It was already snowing, the first snow of the year. The tiny snowflakes melted as they landed on the pavements. The car drove past Red Square, and Dimitri glimpsed the grandstands rising along the Kremlin wall. Hundreds of people had worked around the clock for the last three weeks, to have them ready for the Revolution Day parade. The streets adjoining Red Square had been freshly tarred, yellow lines and arrows indicating the parade itinerary.

The car left Moscow by the Volokolamskoye highway. About a kilometre after passing by the monument to the Defence of Moscow, it took a narrow road that plunged into the forest. The snow had turned into drizzle, and raindrops beat on the car's roof. They entered a village.

'What is this place?' Dimitri asked.

'Yurlovo,' the driver said, revealing two steel front teeth. His breath carried an odour of onions. The Zhiguli passed through the village, scaring a flock of meagre chicken. A turkey ballooned in anger and ran after the car, clucking menacingly. They drove through an open field, then entered the forest again. On the left side of the road appeared a yellow masonry fence, about eight feet high, topped with broken glass and barbed wire. The car stopped by a gate where two soldiers stood guard, armed with rifles.

'This is the place,' the driver said, and Dimitri got out, dragging his knapsack. From a booth, its windows thick with condensation, came two civilians huddled in padded jackets. They wore leather belts and Makarov automatics in holsters over their coats.

'Papers,' the smaller one said. Dimitri gave him his documents. The civilian went to the booth, apparently to use the telephone. He was back in a minute. 'You can go in,' he said, 'across the parade ground, second door to your right. There's a sign saying "Secretariat". Welcome to Yurlovo.' He stood by the gate, glowering suspiciously at Dimitri, his breath escaping from his mouth in short white puffs.

Colonel Yakovlev was a heavy man in his late forties with a red beefy neck, wrestler's arms and feet, and a bulging belly. But the oblong eyes peering through layers of fat were keen and alert. The small mouth, contrasting with the meaty nose, smiled often.

'I'll be your personal tutor, Morozov. Your father, your confessor, and your most ferocious critic.' They were walking around the compound, Yakovlev showing Dimitri the main facilities. 'You may make friends in your class, but no serious friendships. No disclosure of personal information. You may visit the village in pairs, but no partying or dinners together. There will be a bus leaving for Moscow every Saturday night and Sunday morning, back from Sverdlov Square every Sunday night.'

'How should I dress in Moscow?'

'No uniforms outside the school buildings. You'll be issued civilian clothes. For all practical purposes, you're a student of International Relations, Moscow university, class of Professor Rudin. I'll give you a telephone number in case of emergency. You'll have to memorize it.'

Dimitri nodded. A flock of geese flew low over their heads.

'In the school we have one hundred and twenty-two students, divided into five sections. In yours there are only fifteen students. You're not supposed to say to anybody what you're doing and what subjects you're studying.'

Dimitri raised his head. It had started snowing again, large soft flakes falling from a bleak sky.

Two civilians armed with Makarovs crossed their path. They held German shepherds on long leaches. Yakovlev followed them with his eyes. 'They patrol the grounds twenty-four hours a day. Besides that the place is riddled with infra-red sensors, triggered by body heat.'

They came in view of the main cluster of buildings. 'On the right,' Yakovlev pointed at a three-storey concrete house, 'we have the classrooms, two separate libraries, for classified and unclassified material, laboratories, mess, and offices.'

'The dorms?' Dimitri asked.

'No dorms. Our students live three men to a room.' A room. For the first time in my life, Dimitri thought, I'll live in a real room, not a stable for humans.

Yakovlev pointed to a new building across the yard. 'Gymnasium and heated swimming pool. Firing range in the basement.' He stopped by the door, straightening his uniform with an air of finality. 'Your status as of today is Junior Lieutenant. There is going to be a small raise in your salary. That's all, I believe.' He paused. 'I think you'll enjoy tomorrow's lecture, Morozov.'

Dimitri looked at him searchingly. 'Why, Comrade Colonel?'

'I read your file,' Yakovlev said.

'If Hitler had been assassinated in 1939, there would have been no world war,' said the gaunt civilian who had introduced himself by the pseudonym of Oktober. 'Remember that. Execution of criminal elements can be, at times, not only forgivable but vital for the protection of society and the survival of democracy.'

The man, Dimitri felt, believed every word he said. He had an ascetic, tormented face. Sad, intense eyes, hollow cheeks, an aquiline nose, two grim furrows ploughing the skin all the way down to the sharp jawline and framing a large, bitter mouth. His white hair was long, drawn back, descending to the black collar of his rollneck pullover. A strange fire illuminated his face from within, bestowing upon it a sort of sinister magnetism. It made Dimitri think of a religious martyr, about to be burned at the stake; or perhaps the very opposite, a Spanish inquisitor, his face exuding pain and compassion, but also the willingness to inflict horrible suffering in the name of Christ. The torturers during the great purges must have been people like this, he thought.

'You know him?' Dimitri whispered to his neighbour, a lanky Bielorussian named Tabenkin.

'I was told he is General Sudoplatov, who was deputy chief of Department V until 1953,' Tabenkin whispered back.

Dimitri had heard the name. 'It can't be, I know Sudoplatov was shot, shortly after Beria.'

Oktober was looking at him. 'As students training for executive action, you'll discuss and analyse operations performed by chekists in the line of duty. But these discussions shouldn't turn into an academic seminar' – Oktober wanly smiled – 'therefore I'll start by telling you how I killed the Ukrainian reactionary Konovalenko in Rotterdam, in 1938.'

Thus, with the concise description of a rigged box of Swiss chocolates that had blown Konovalenko to bits, commenced Oktober's lectures on the bloody history of Department Thirteen.

Dimitri followed with bated breath these chronicles of violence: the liquidation of scores of White emigrés in Paris, Hamburg, New York and Macao in the thirties. The establishment, in 1936, of the Wet Affairs department, whose men murdered Leon Trotzky in Mexico. The transformation of the Wet Affairs into the Spetz-buro that assassinated notorious emigrés in Germany and Austria.

After Beria's death, the Spetz-buro changed names again, becoming Department Thirteen. Its most efficient killer was a twenty-five-year old Ukrainian, Bogdan Stashinsky. He had been recruited at the age of nineteen, Oktober said. Dimitri had the impression that Oktober was looking hard at him as he gave Stashinsky's age.

In the late fifties, Oktober continued, Stashinsky killed two Ukrainian emigrés in Munich, Lev Rebet and Stefan Bandera. In both cases the assassin used a hellish device: an electric pistol, loaded with poison bullets – ampules of prussic acid that blew up on contact with the victim's face.

At his next lecture, Oktober displayed before his students the electric pistols. For a couple of hours they practised the loading and unloading of the weapons. Oktober then led them to a clearing in the forest, where fifteen dogs had been tied to trees. Two KGB guards stood beside the dogs, but Oktober dismissed them with a nod. He opened a combination-locked attaché case and handed each student a gun, an ampoule of prussic acid, and an ampoule containing antidotes. No explanation was needed.

'Who is going to be the first?' Oktober asked, his dark eyes surveying the young men.

Dimitri stepped forward, and approached one of the dogs. The animal, a friendly Great Dane, playfully wagged his tail. Dimitri bent towards it and fired. There was no discharge, just a soft click. The big dog staggered, awkwardly kicking, fell, and died in frenzied convulsions. Dimitri inhaled the antidote from a second ampoule, lit a Prima and sat on a log to wait for the others.

The other students followed, killing their dogs in silence. Oktober wants us to get the feel, Dimitri thought, to see how efficient this is – and how easy. When Tabenkin's turn came, he stood still, as if nailed to the spot. His face was deathly pale, and his eyes acquired a dull glint. He suddenly swayed and threw up. Dimitri yanked the gun from his hand and shot his dog, a German Shepherd with a mangy hide. When he turned back, he caught Oktober watching him thoughtfully.

Tabenkin was expelled from the school the same day. Only fourteen remained in the class.

A week later, Oktober took the Untouchables – they adopted that name after watching the American series on the school television – to an isolated villa in Vnukovo where the Kamara was based, the KGB institute for developing untraceable poisons. Oktober led them through a succession of laboratories where silent researchers in white smocks subjected guinea pigs to various experiments. 'The substances must satisfy two requirements,' Oktober said. 'First, they must kill, quickly and efficiently. Second, the target's death must appear to be the result of natural causes.' One of the students stumbled and leaned on a table laden with vials. Oktober sharply turned back. 'Don't touch anything!' he snapped. 'You may die in a matter of hours.' They exchanged stares, wondering if they were supposed to laugh.

The visit to the poison chamber concluded the training of the Untouchables in the use of exotic devices. The new chapter in Oktober's course was purely physical – the use of one's bare hands as a weapon. An old, heavily built Chekist with huge arms, named Sanakoyev, came to describe the assassination of the defector Agabekov in Bucarest. When he narrated in detail the killing of Agabekov, Dimitri raised his hand.

'How do you know all these details?' he asked. 'Agabekov and his killer were alone that day.'

'I was the killer,' Sanakoyev said.

Winter was drawing to its close when Dimitri was summoned to Colonel Yakovlev. 'Have you had any practice in surveillance?' Yakovlev asked pleasantly.

Dimitri shrugged. 'The routine Visshaya Shkola exercises.'

'Tomorrow we'll have a full day exercise in Moscow. All the students will participate. Each will be given the name of a foreign resident in Moscow, picked at random. You'll have to follow him for one day and report every detail of his movements. We start at six, so you'd better get to bed early.'

It was a bleak dawn, with smoky fog rising from the frozen Moskva River and stealthily invading the neighbouring streets. The streetlamps were smouldering globes of yellow light. The first cars out drove cautiously along the snow-lined streets, sometimes skidding on the black ice that had formed during the night.

An old ZIL sedan slid on the slippery road and nearly hit Dimitri as he crossed the Leningradski Prospect; he tripped and almost fell, then regained his balance and unsteadily covered the last few metres before the entrance to number 74. He had chosen the dark porch of a nineteenth-century townhouse as an observation post. His target was number 78, an apartment building mostly occupied by foreigners. The man he was supposed to follow was a Canadian businessman, Charles Saint-Clair. He had been assigned to somebody else, actually, an Italian visiting professor of Renaissance art; but one of the Untouchables, Youri Savonov, fell sick toward midnight, developing a high fever. In the reshuffle that ensued, his assignment was transferred to Dimitri.

He was disappointed. He was fascinated by Italians, and it would have been a pleasure shadowing an art professor in a cosy promenade through Moscow's museums. But he found himself stuck with the Canadian, an importer of fish and caviar. He represented a Montreal company called Delices du Nord, whose offices were on Gorky Street. The photographs in the file showed a dapper man in his fifties, with wavy brown hair which Dimitri suspected was dyed. His face was well-groomed, with a dandyish moustache and bright eyes. The photostat of his Canadian passport said the eyes of Saint-Clair were green.

Saint-Clair's file had been established by the seventh department of the Second Chief Directorate. The seventh watched foreign residents. Its report also said that Charles Saint-Clair was a bachelor with expensive tastes. He liked stylish clothes, jewellery, and wore heavy gold rings. Saint-Clair spent a fortune at the Moscow foreign currency restaurants. He was also a ballet lover, and went to the Bolshoi at least once every fortnight.

Dimitri raised the collar of the heavy brown coat he had been issued. The sky over the Lenin hills glowed with a faint orange hue and the street was awakening. He could make out the huge sign fixed on top of the building across the street. 'Lenin lived, lives and will live forever', it revealed. The spire of Moscow university emerged from the fog, the glint of its red star dulled by the frost. More cars passed by, and people started coming out of the houses. A couple of babushkas, huddled in thick clothes, were sweeping the sidewalks, calling to each other across the street.

A militiaman suddenly emerged beside him. He was young, with fair skin and red cheeks. 'Waiting for somebody, Comrade?'

Dimitri proudly flashed the red KGB card he had been given the night before. The young officer sullenly glanced at it, and was gone. The militia didn't like the KGB. Their officers were better paid, better dressed, better lodged and fed, and had much more clout.

At seven forty five Saint-Clair came out of the house and walked to a chauffeur-driven Mercedes with foreign plates. He was dressed in a tan camel hair coat with a fur collar, and an expensive mink hat. Dimitri crossed the street and entered the battered Zhaporozhetz he had been given for today's assignment. Saint-Clair was on his way to his office; Dimitri didn't have to hurry. Fifteen minutes later he parked on Gorky Street, just in time to see Saint-Clair enter his office building. He noted the departure and arrival times, then slumped in his seat. What a bore, he thought. He had nothing to do but wait until lunchtime, when Saint-Clair took his break.

The Canadian came out at twelve-thirty, on foot, and turned south. He behaved as if he had read the seventh department report, Dimitri thought; exactly the same routine as described. He followed Saint-Clair through the revolving doors of the National Hotel, and was admitted inside by the armed guards on presentation of his KGB card. In the Russalka Restaurant Dimitri ordered a salami sandwich, watching Saint-Clair who was devouring a steaming chunk of meat at the opposite side of the dining-room. When Saint-Clair was finished, Dimitri followed him back to the street.

It was after crossing the bustling Stanislavski Street that Dimitri realized Saint-Clair had spotted him.

It was nothing tangible at first. Just a change in Saint-Clair's pace, then two unnecessary crossings of the street, and afterwards a stop, then another, before some shop windows. Dimitri knew the routine of crossing streets and using shop windows as mirrors to check if one was being followed. But that was KGB routine, it certainly wasn't an art the Delices du Nord company taught its employees! Vaguely alarmed, he kept following Saint-Clair. And Saint-Clair kept expertly employing all the tricks of Dimitri's trade. He walked into a large government store for 'meat, fish and fowl' on Gorky Street and came out by the second exit on Ogarev; he repeated the trick again in the Krimskaya cafeteria. Soon after that he suddenly turned back, retracing his steps, and Dimitri had to dive into the entrance to a bookstore. Saint-Clair wasn't trying to shake him off; he was on his way back to the office. But he wanted to make sure that he was indeed being followed.

Saint-Clair entered a phone booth and picked up the receiver. That was odd. Why should he call from a phone booth when his office was barely two hundred metres away? Unless he wanted to use a line that wasn't tapped by the KGB?

Dimitri watched Saint-Clair hang up and walk straight back to his office. He didn't cross the street any more or stop before shop windows. Dimitri thought of calling Yakovlev with an interim report; Saint-Clair's behaviour was certainly very unusual. But after second thoughts he decided to wait. Saint-Clair might have felt that he was being followed, and perhaps had tried to make sure of it, using techniques he had learned from espionage novels.

Shortly before sunset, Dimitri called the phone-tapping service of Second. After identifying himself, he asked if Saint-Clair had made any unusual calls from his office in the afternoon.

No, answered the officer on duty, a woman with a low, grating voice. He had made no unusual calls . . . except for booking a seat for tonight's performance of *Gisele* at the Bolshoi.

And what was so unusual about that? he asked.

'Well, he always books tickets a week in advance,' the weary voice answered. 'Besides, the telephone log shows that Charles Saint-Clair already saw *Gisele* last week.'

When the curtain rose on the first act of *Gisele,* Dimitri stood in the shadow of an unoccupied box, watching Saint-Clair. The Canadian had a seat on the sixth row, beside a group of noisy Americans in raincoats and sneakers. Getting here had been child's play. Dimitri had come to the Bolshoi a half hour before the performance, shown the assistant manager his card, and got what he wanted. Power made things so easy. It could be intoxicating.

At the interval, Saint-Clair casually stepped into the aisle and walked out. Dimitri rushed after him, elbowing his way through the crowd, but when he finally reached the brightly lit lobby, Saint-Clair had vanished. Dimitri scrambled to the men's rest room, but Saint-Clair wasn't there. Neither was he at the lobby bar nor at the mezzanine small buffet.

Dimitri felt a surge of panic. Could Saint-Clair have used the crowd as cover to leave the theatre? Dimitri knew he would become the laughing stock of Yurlovo tomorrow if he had to explain how an amateur had easily given him the slip.

But the bell for the second act was ringing, and from a side passage Saint-Clair emerged, calm and relaxed, and strutted back to his seat, extinguishing his cigar in a standing ashtray. Dimitri stared at the passage by which other people were appearing, mostly couples. And then, when the flow of people ceased almost completely and the last bell rang, another man appeared at the passage entrance.

Dimitri stood still. He knew that man. He had met him before. He remembered the handsome face, the dimpled chin, the scar below the cheekbone. This man had helped him, and he had thought him a friend. He was Colonel Oleg Kalinin, the GRU colonel and friendly member of the State Security Commission who had interviewed Dimitri back at Panfilov. Following Kalinin's remarks, the two other commission members had agreed that Dimitri's loyalty was beyond reproach.

He stared insistently at the CRU colonel. Kalinin apparently recognized Dimitri, too, because he smiled at him as he passed by, nodded in a friendly fashion and entered the theatre.

Dimitri remained alone in the deserted lobby. What was Kalinin doing here? Had he met Saint-Clair in the passage? But he had seen at least another twenty people come out of that shady place. He entered the passage. It led to a flight of stairs descending to a lower gallery, where an exhibition of Bolshoi posters was on display. At the far end of the gallery there were two doors. Dimitri tried them. They were both locked. Perhaps Kalinin had a key? Perhaps he had met Saint-Clair in one of those rooms? But that idea was farfetched. He hadn't witnessed any contact between the two men. Saint-Clair could have met any of the twenty-odd men and women who had visited the gallery.

When the ballet was over and Gisele was finally laid to rest, Dimitri followed Saint-Clair to his apartment house and started his drive back to Yurlovo. He couldn't make up his mind about Kalinin. Should he mention him in his report? Casting unjustified suspicion on a Military Intelligence colonel could be risky; it could cost him his career. he finally decided to wait until the next morning, when he was supposed to prepare his report.

But his report was never to be written.

'Morozov! Wake up!'

The sharp, sinister face of Oktober appeared from the dark, framed by wispy white hair. A nightmare, Dimitri thought, turning away, seeking refuge from the dull glint of the smouldering eyes; but the rasping voice insisted, commanded, and a bony hand kept shaking his shoulder. 'Get up. Get dressed. Parade uniform. Down at the gate in ten minutes. Repeat.'

He sat upright, staring into the blackness. 'Yes, Oktober.' He repeated the orders but Oktober was already bending over his roommate, Victor Seletzin. In his loose black coat, with the rippling white halo of hair floating around his skull-like face, Oktober looked like a harbinger of death. Dimitri's third roommate, a Finn named Arno Tuuomi, was already dressing with quick, spare movements.

Dimitri threw back the covers. The room was freezing. His watch showed four fifteen. Oktober had disappeared and Victor was waking up in a crescendo of curses. Fuck your mother, it's four in the morning, fuck this bloody school, fuck the KGB, and a final fuck you, addressed at Arno and Dimitri, who stared at him forgivingly.

Dimitri's first thought was that World War Three had started; but when he reached the gate, and found there only the Untouchables, he discarded the idea. Perhaps a government crisis had broken out, or somebody had died. At Stalin's death, KGB troops had been deployed all over Moscow. But why only the Untouchables? Where were the other Yurlovo inmates? It didn't make sense.

An army ZIL truck was parked outside, its engine hoarsely coughing, the exhaust spewing pale smoke. He climbed in the back, huddled in a corner and lit a cigarette. 'I bet it's another exercise,' grunted Victor Seletzin, slumping heavily beside him. 'Fuck the day I met Oktober.'

Once everybody was on board, the truck rumbled, squeaked, and was on its way. They were too tired to talk, only a few cigarette tips glowed in the dark. As they crossed Yurlovo, a dog barked, joined immediately by others. Dimitri killed his cigarette on the floor, wrapped himself in his topcoat and dozed for the rest of the way.

He awoke with a start as the truck abruptly braked. The beam of an electric torch swept the interior, dazzling him momentarily, and he recalled Kuzma Bunin, that night at the quarry. They were being checked at some kind of roadblock. He could hear voices, truck engines, running steps. The truck moved, then stopped again. Strong light seeped in from every crack in the tarpaulin cover. A voice rasped: 'Everybody out.' It was Oktober.

He jumped out of the truck. The place was brightly lit with floodlights, and batteries of white, green and blue lights along two straight lines on the ground. They were standing at the edge of a runway. Behind them hovered a huge building, all glass and steel; most of its windows were brightly lit. Across the runway, in a long open garage, he could make out the contours of fire engines, two trucks and pale-coloured ambulances. On the right loomed the rectangular shadows of hangars. In a parking area, on the left, stood several passenger aircraft. One of them, a PanAm airliner, was being serviced by men in white coveralls. 'Fuck your mother,' Victor muttered behind him, 'this is Vnukovo.'

The international airport was in turmoil. Military trucks kept arriving and discharging KGB border troops who took up position around and inside the terminal. Harried civilians and militia officers scurried around, barking orders. Airport tractors started towing aircraft away from the VIP lounge, whose elegant interior they could see by the bay windows.

'Look at these flags,' Arno murmured. Huge banners, their colours orange, white and green, were floating in the wind beside the Soviet flags. 'What are those?' Dimitri asked.

'Indian,' somebody said. 'Indira Gandhi is arriving on a state visit.' Dimitri and Arno turned to Victor, and he didn't disappoint them.

'Fuck Indira,' he groaned.

'This way,' Oktober ordered. The man had a spooky ability to emerge from the dark without anybody noticing his approach. He led them, long coat floating behind him, into a dark room, apparently a departure lounge. They gathered around him.

'Moscow Centre has been struck by disaster,' he said. 'A Department Thirteen officer, Colonel Lyalin, has turned traitor.' His eyes glowed strangely in the dark. 'He gave to the British Intelligence Service the names of one hundred and five of our agents. They've all been expelled.'

He paused. 'There's worse. Lyalin revealed to the British the existence of Department Thirteen. We've been denying for years that we have a unit specializing in violent activities. Lyalin disclosed the names of our men serving abroad, and now they're running for their lives. Since the early evening they have been fleeing from the main cities of Europe and America. I hope they all arrive home safely.'

'What will happen to the department?' Arno asked.

Somebody struck a match and Dimitri glimpsed in the flare tense, perplexed faces.

'The department,' Oktober said, 'is dead.'

'It can be rebuilt, though,' Dimitri suggested.

'That's you, Morozov?' Oktober cackled. 'You're right. But to rebuilt it we need new men, totally unknown, who don't figure on any list Lyalin could have furnished. An entirely new team.'

'You want us to become the core of the new department,' Dimitri said. The darkness and the atmosphere of crisis allowed a certain familiarity.

'I have to convince the political level it's feasible.'

'And the political level . . ' Dimitri started.

'Comrade Brezhnev has cut short a visit to Czechoslovakia. He will be landing in a few minutes. The KGB chairman and most Politburo members are already here. I hope we'll convince them.'

Why is the meeting being held here, Dimitri wondered, and not in Moscow? He could guess the answer. Oktober wanted a decision from Brezhnev before he met the other KGB chiefs, who might advise him otherwise. With sudden clarity, Dimitri grasped Oktober's ploy. The man was using Lyalin's betrayal as a lever to carry out his own coup and take over Department Thirteen.

He had probably approached the KGB chairman, Andropov, to suggest to the Politburo a new operational unit that could replace Department Thirteen. Andropov had good reasons to accept Oktober's offer. It could take the heat off him, and spare him some embarrassing questions about Lyalin. Oktober had brought the Untouchables to Vnukovo, to prove to the Politburo that he had good men, ready for action. If he succeeded, their training would be over, and the Untouchables would become the new 'Wet Affairs' team. Oktober's exile would be over as well.

'What about Indira Gandhi's visit?' Bosjanov asked. He was a Kazakh, from Alma Ata.

'She's arriving today,' Oktober said. 'The control tower will order her plane to keep circling the airport till the Politburo meeting is over.' He surveyed his small army. 'I have to go. Stay here, and keep quiet.'

At the break of dawn Brezhnev's Tupolev landed and taxied to the VIP lounge. Dimitri and his friends watched the bulky Secretary General heavily descend from the aircraft, hug and kiss his Politburo colleagues. Large snowflakes were swirling and dancing over the

Soviet leaders, then softly landing on their shoulders. Andropov himself was at the end of the receiving line. Brezhnev only stared at him and coldly shook his hand. The small crowd entered the VIP lounge. Oktober was nowhere to be seen.

They settled in the standard plastic chairs and waited. Arno and the resourceful Bosjanov started a card game, and several others joined in. A moon-faced matron in a white apron brought them tasteless coffee and biscuits. Dimitri didn't eat, neither did he play cards with his friends. He stood by the window, watching the snow-covered fields, the grey runway and the line of graceful aircraft. This was the gate to another world, to another life.

'On your feet, Comrades!'

Oktober stood at the door. His face was sealed. 'Leave your overcoats here. I want you lined up outside in one minute.' Dimitri threw a look over his shoulder. A convoy of Chaikas was slowly moving towards the VIP lounge to pick up the Politburo members.

'Chairman Andropov would like to shake your hands,' Oktober was saying, a note of triumph finally sneaking into his voice. He paused, a cunning smile slowly cracking his face.

'Welcome,' he rasped. 'Welcome to Department Thirteen.'

Chapter Nine

Nina was rushed to Mount Sinai hospital with a bleeding ulcer on the very day Alex left for Brown. It was a beautiful, crisp day in October. In the morning she had stood by the window, watching him load his bags in his first car, a bright red convertible Mustang. He had bought it second hand after working the whole summer at a car-wash in Brooklyn. Nina felt the first burning pains in her stomach when she saw Alex exchange a long goodbye kiss with Claudia. She was revolted. The girl was clinging to him with all her body, holding him as if he were her property. She had no shame, acting like this in the middle of the street, behaving as a slut in front of everybody.

Nina was happy that Alex was leaving town. In Brown, she was sure, her boy would meet some other girls and forget the little Italian. She watched them by the window, her lips tightly clamped, till finally they parted and Alex drove away. She then went to the kitchen, to make herself a cup of tea, and collapsed on the chequered floor tiles.

She woke up at the hospital three hours later. She had been found by Myra, the cleaning woman. Thank God Myra hadn't called an ambulance but had asked their neighbour to help her carry Nina into a taxi. Nina would rather die than let herself be carted into an ambulance, sirens screaming, red lights flashing, and the entire neighbourhood watching. She made Myra swear not to breathe a word to anybody, but Myra of course was unable to keep her big mouth shut and the news spread like bush fire along Elm Street.

Alex arrived during the night, alerted by Claudia. Nina later learned that he had just arrived at the campus and hadn't even started unpacking when the message had reached him. He had caught a plane back to New York, leaving his car at the airport. When Nina woke up, he was sitting beside her bed. His face was unshaven. 'Ninochka, *lyubimaya*,' he said in his soft, caressing Russian, 'How could you do this to me, *dushenka maya*, my little soul?'

Despite Nina's protests Alex stayed with her the entire six days until Dr Sapirstein decided not to operate. He took her home and made her swear to take her medication regularly, watch her diet and not get upset. He left on the seventh day. As the door closed behind him, a heavy silence settled upon the apartment. And a feeling of desperate loneliness stole into her heart.

Thus started Nina's bleak years of solitude. The death of Samuel had put an end to an existence she hated, but to which she had grown accustomed. Then Alex had spread his wings and left her alone. Because of her illness she had to stop working. Her friends from the Peace Movement were either dead or disillusioned: the only beam of light in her grim existence was Alex.

Throughout the four following years, she lived for his letters, his telephone calls, his short visits home; she read his books, his university papers, questioned him about his professors. She knew all about Brown without being there. In the summers, when he returned for his long vacation, she was the happiest person in the world. He was growing into a handsome, confident young man, and she had no doubt he was going to be a famous scholar.

But often, when she sat by the window, letting her mind wander, she was pervaded by a sense of failure. Alex was slipping through her fingers, inexorably moving away from her. Alex, the boy she had shaped and raised in her ideas, the man she had wanted to make worthy of his parents, had taken a different road, and the gap between them was growing wider every day.

She recalled the first signs when he was still a child, and had been swept by the temptations only America could offer – games, movies, sports . . . He had grown to love America more than Russia. Alex had admired John Kennedy, in spite of his reactionary policy in Cuba and Vietnam; Kennedy's assassination had devastated the boy. The next shock had been caused by the newspaper clipping revealing the truth about his parents' deaths. The child wasn't ready to cope with such appalling facts. His admiration for the Soviet Union was shattered; on top of that, he was deeply offended by the way the Russian bureaucrats had treated his letters.

Then this girl came and turned his head. Claudia was the worst disaster that had ever befallen Alex. Nina didn't object, of course, to Alex having a girl friend. But this one tore him away from her. At this age sexual attraction was everything. She remembered her infatuation with Sasha Kolodny, back in Kiev, when she was only sixteen. Still, she hadn't considered Alex capable of such passion. Once, at the very beginning of the romance, she had hinted that he should spend more time studying. 'Don't worry about Claudia,' Nina had observed. 'She won't run away.'

'What's this, Nina, are you jealous?' he retorted jokingly.

'Stop that nonsense!' she snapped.

Perhaps she was jealous: she had every right to be. After all, Alex was her life, she had dedicated her existence to him. She so loved their evenings together, when they would listen to classical music or discuss Russian literature and history. And all of a sudden he had no more time for her, and his evenings were monopolized by a girl with a pretty face and young breasts.

Claudia was very nice to her and Nina really tried her best to reciprocate. Only she couldn't help it. Whenever she saw the girl she would feel a surge of anger in her insides. Bitterness would grip her throat, the blood would drain from her face and her voice would become cold and remote, that of an insecure woman confronting her rival.

Besides Alex had fallen in love not only with the girl but with her entire clan. He spent more time in the Benevento house than he did in his own home. The Beneventos simply swallowed him, treating him as one of their own. They had given him something he'd never had: a family.

Shortly before Alex left for Brown, there had been an ugly quarrel between him and Nina. She had seen it coming for a long time, but wasn't ready when it erupted, in the hectic summer of 1967. War broke out between Israel and her neighbours, and Alex came home from school cursing the Russians, ready to strangle Brezhnev with his bare hands. He admired Moshe Dayan, the handsome Israeli general who looked like a pirate with his black eyepatch. She tried to explain the Soviet point of view to the boy, but he yelled at her and left the house.

A year later, Russian tanks invaded Czechoslovakia and Alex organized a student rally on the campus. It was even reported on television. They showed Alex speaking, condemning 'Red imperialism' and haranguing the crowd against 'Soviet brutality'. She was so ashamed, she had terrible pains that night, but she didn't alert the doctor and didn't answer the telephone for several days, lest somebody called about Alex's speech.

After calming down, she decided to adopt a new strategy. She should avoid confrontation, should rather use logic and common sense. When Alex came back for a weekend, she made him a cup of coffee and served it on the kitchen table. Israel was an imperialist state, she said, everybody knew that: Moshe Dayan had fought with the British Army. The Czech revolt was a Western ploy, and the Red Army had entered Prague at the people's request.

Alex was beside himself with frustration. How can you say this, Nina? The Russians only have to whistle and you click your heels. Don't you ever try to make up your own mind?'

She felt the familiar pain in her stomach, and put down her coffee cup. Her fingers were trembling and some coffee spilled on the table cloth. 'Is this what Claudia says of me?'

She regretted her words immediately. She had spoken without thinking, and saw the fury kindle in his eyes.

'Leave her out of his, Nina. This is between you and me.'

She didn't know what to say, so she got up and left the table. He ran after her and hugged her. 'I love you very much, Nina,' he said, 'I shall always love you. But I can't stand your fanatical devotion to your Kremlin idols.'

Since this conversation he came home very rarely. But Nina refused to humiliate herself; not once, during Alex's studies, did she call Claudia Benevento to inquire after her nephew.

In January 1971 somebody discreetly knocked on the door. She was having her afternoon tea by the living room window, watching the dance of the snowflakes over the city. The snowfalls of January always made her think of Tonya's last hours, and she sank into a morose brooding mood. When she heard the rapping, she got up and briskly walked to the door. Even when she was alone at home she was properly attired. Today she was wearing her polka-dot dress with the starched white collar and her patent leather black shoes.

On the landing stood a young man, no more than thirty years of age. He was rather sloppily dressed in a beige duffle coat, frayed at the cuffs, a thick woollen scarf, brown corduroy trousers and thick-soled yellow shoes. His big nose stuck out of a pale face, he wore thick glasses and his untidy hair was covered with melting snowflakes. 'Mrs Kramer?'

'Yes?'

'I hope I am not disturbing you,' the man said, and before she even realized, he was inside the vestibule, dripping water all over her carpet. 'My name is David Hughes, I am a writer.'

He had a distinct English accent, which could also account for the old-fashioned clothes. 'May I have a word with you?'

'About what?' she said. What has Alex done? she thought.

'About Sasha Kolodny.'

It took her a moment to digest the name. Sasha Kolodny. Her Sasha. She hadn't heard his name in thirty years. She swayed and leaned on a chair for support. 'Sasha? You know Sasha?'

'He was your husband, wasn't he?' Hughes's eyes were darting incessantly, sweeping the apartment.

'No, no my husband.' When she was disturbed her English became even worse. 'Sasha he dead?' she managed, her heart pounding.

'No, I don't think so,' the Englishman said, and entered the living room. 'May I sit down?'

'Where is Sasha?'

He settled in one of her armchairs. 'As a matter of fact, I hoped you could tell me that.' He glanced around and grimaced in disappointment. He had probably expected to see Sasha's picture on the wall. 'I was told he was your first husband.'

She shook her head. 'No, no husband, just my friend.'

'Of course,' Hughes said, unbuttoning his coat. 'I am writing a book about him, you see, and I hope you can help me.'

She sat up, very tense, then stood. 'A book? On Sasha? Why you write a book?' That was very suspicious, and so was the Englishman. She hadn't heard of Sasha since the beginning of the war when Emily Mayer had seen him in Paris.

He smiled, revealing huge buck teeth. 'Come on, you know why. Your Sasha is a big hero. Do you have any pictures of him? Or of you two together?'

'A hero?' Her hand darted to her chest, her knees buckled and she sat down again, very stiff, facing him. 'What hero?'

The Englishman shook his head. 'You really don't know, do you? Well, you haven't been reading European papers, I suppose.' He fumbled inside his pocket and produced a photograph. She hastily adjusted her glasses., It was a portrait of a man taken from a low, unusual angle. He was staring at the camera over his shoulder. His face was totally expressionless, his eyes sharp, cold, with a hint of condescending contempt. He looked very elegant, wearing a jacket over a white shirt and a tie. His fair hair was cropped very short; gone was the unruly shock of honey blond hair. The jowls and neck had thickened with the years. The mouth was powerful, almost brutal. But this was, unmistakeably, her Sasha.

'This picture,' the Englishman said, 'was taken by the Gestapo, in Paris, when Sasha Kolodny was under arrest. He was known as Theodor Shroeder, but his friends in the Resistance called him the Chief.' He handed her the picture. 'Take it, this is a copy. I have another one at home.'

She took the photograph and her fingers, as if acting on their own, gently caressed the beloved face. 'The Chief,' she repeated. Her Sasha was the Chief. She leaned towards the Englishman. 'Please tell me what happened with Sasha.' She was forgetting her manners. 'Please excuse me. You want coffee? Tea?'

Sasha had reached Paris in 1929, the Englishman's story went, and had worked for a few years as a bricklayer, dish-washer, and carpenter. In 1936 he had crossed the border into Spain, where he had fought with the Republicans against Franco: he had been wounded at the battle of the Ebro. Back in France, Kolodny had been appointed chief of Soviet espionage in Western Europe. Actually, that was why he had left Russia in the first place; he was sent to Palestine, then to France, to create his networks and recruit agents years in advance.

Nina was astonished. She recalled the night when Sasha had woken her up, saying: 'Let's go to Palestine.' She had refused, they were not Zionist. Only now she understood that he had been assigned a special mission, but couldn't tell her, of course. And she was afraid to tell him she was with child. It had been such a stupid misunderstanding, yet it had shattered her life. God, how different things could have been!

'Kolodny,' the Englishman was saying, 'now changed his name to Shroeder. He emerged in the posh sixteenth *arrondissement* of Paris, posing as a wealthy businessman. He had lots of money, a large office on Avenue Victor Hugo, and influential connections. And women,' Hughes added, briefly avoiding her eyes, 'young and attractive women.'

She shook her head. Sasha was such a handsome man, of course he had many women.

After the German Army conquered France, Shroeder had been among the first Parisian businessmen to deal with the Germans. But in secret, his network was transmitting to Moscow vital information about the German military machine. His greatest achievement was a message to Stalin announcing Hitler's imminent attack on the Soviet Union. The Chief reported the code-name of the assault; Operation Barbarossa. And the date: June 22, 1941.

'But . . . this is impossible,' Nina stammered. 'The Red Army didn't expect attack.'

Hughes was nodding his head. 'Exactly,' he said. 'Stalin didn't believe the Chief.'

Shortly after, the Gestapo had captured the Chief, but he had managed to escape. He had gained the Gestapo's trust by promising to cooperate and feeding them with second-rate information about his networks. Then, one day, while crossing Paris, he had asked permission to buy some aspirin. The Gestapo car had stopped by the Lyons railway station. Sasha had entered the large corner pharmacy, then calmly walked out by the back exit and vanished into thin air.

Nina was listening, enthralled.

'And at the end of the war,' the Englishman said, 'the most painful chapter in Sasha's life began.'

Outside night was falling and wind whined in the kitchen window.

'A special Red Army plane came to Paris to take the Chief back to Moscow. Stalin wanted to see him, the Russians said to Kolodny. He wanted to thank him and decorate him.'

'Decorate?' she asked, puzzled. 'What is decorate?'

'A medal. They said Stalin would give him a medal.'

'And what Stalin say to Sasha?' Nina bent forward, sensing a forthcoming blow.

'Sasha never saw Stalin. From the airport he was taken directly to the Lubyanka. He spent eleven years in jail, and was released only in 1956.'

Nina was on her feet. 'I don't believe you. Why . . . why can Stalin do this?'

The Englishman looked at her over the rim of his tea cup. 'Actually, Stalin should have given your Sasha a medal. But by doing so he would be admitting that Sasha had been right, and he, the generalissimo, had been wrong. He hadn't listened to Sasha's warnings, he had preferred to trust Hitler. This blindness had cost millions of Russian dead . . .'

'I don't believe,' Nina said stubbornly. 'I don't believe.'

'. . . so rather than admit his own failure, Stalin threw Sasha Kolodny in the Lubyanka.'

It suddenly occurred to Nina that Tonya and Sasha had been imprisoned at the Lubyanka at the same time, perhaps their cells had been in the same wing. They might even have met, without knowing each other. Stalin, she thought, hadn't been responsible for Tonya's death only; Sasha, too, had been his victim.

'Where is Sasha now?' she asked.

The Englishman shrugged. 'I hoped you knew. There were rumours that he was reincorporated in the KGB, then he disappeared from view. Now. let's go back to the time when you met him. Can you tell me about him?'

'No,' said Nina, panicking. 'Is nothing to tell.'

'Why? Because of the other women he had?'

'No, no, I not care about other women.' She took off her glasses, then put them on again. She didn't know how to cope with such emotions.

'Don't you ever want to see Sasha again?'

'Why you ask this?'

'Because my book will be published all over the world. I believe it will also reach the Soviet Union. And if Sasha Kolodny is still alive, he'll know where his Nina is, and how to find her.'

'No,' she said. 'He will not want to find his Nina. Is nothing to tell.'

But he insisted, argued, explained, and finally she gave in. Not to the ugly Englishman, of course, but to her own, long-suppressed desire to tell aloud the story of her love for Sasha Kolodny. She let herself go, and told the Englishman about Sasha, and their life together, as a married couple. 'As man and wife, but no rabbi.' She even brought from her room some yellow-edged letters and photographs, which she showed him but refused to entrust to his hands. As she spoke, she felt a wonderful sensation of deliverance, as if another woman, who had been jailed inside her for many years, had suddenly blazed her way to freedom and recognition.

It was late at night before the Englishman left. She washed the tea cups and the glass in which she had served sherry to him, then turned off the lights and went to her room. Angry winds howled outside as she lay awake in her bed. She cried a lot for her lost youth, and that tremendous mistake she had made when she had refused to follow her man. But she also smiled to herself, thinking that the timid teenager she had been in those far-off days in Kiev had made the right choice after all. Sasha was a great man. She had known it since the first time she laid eyes on him.

Her life wasn't over, not yet. She now had new hope to light up her old age. Perhaps one day they'd find Sasha, perhaps the Englishman's book would help. And she might live long enough to see him again. A pang of delightful anticipation shot through her body. She had so much to tell him, they could speak for days.

What a pity that their child had died. Sasha would have been thrilled to find out he had a son. but the boy was gone, and this was the only part of her story she didn't tell the Englishman. Neither would she tell it to Sasha, if she ever saw him again.

Dimitri didn't know the real identity of the old man who trained him in 'Modus operandi/deep cover in a Western city'. The man was impressive; broad-shouldered, with a leonine head, a white mane that had been blond once, a big, straight nose and a wilful mouth. He wore a tired tweed jacket over a black woollen shirt, buttoned up to his chin; his gait was clumsy, deceptively slow. Oktober spoke of him with unusual respect, calling him 'the Chief', although nobody knew the origin of that war name. The rumour had it that the Chief was a Lubyanka graduate. He had spent a long prison term there after a nebulous wartime mission. A morose, sardonic man, he didn't belong to the department's inner circle, and had no access to operational files. He had spent many years in the West, and now trained the Wet Affairs' agents for their missions abroad.

'Your base and your headquarters will be a cafe, always a cafe,' the Chief told Dimitri. He had met him at the gate of the black mansion on Balaklavskaya Street where Oktober had established the Wet Affairs' new headquarters. Dimitri was about to leave on his first assignment abroad, and the Chief had been charged with his personal training.

'In Paris,' he went on, 'there's a cafe on every street corner. In Rome and Brussels as well.' He had a grating, cavernous voice. 'In England, Germany and the United States rather fewer, but you'll find bars and cafes in every big hotel. You can carry out all your meetings in a cafe. Remember, the best protection is a crowd. Wherever there are lots of people, you're safe.'

He drove Dimitri to a KGB operational model at Gavrikovo, out of Moscow. The complex was spread over a vast area, surrounded by a pine forest, protected by fences and guard towers. The Chief headed for the eastern wing of the sprawling structure, and trod past the guards to the lower level. The room they entered was built like a Parisian cafe, with mirrors on the wall, formica-topped tables, electric pinball machines and a zinc-topped counter. The place was empty, but Dimitri could easily imagine it full of men and women, sitting by the tables, and waiters with long white aprons passing between the patrons.

'You always sit with your back against the wall, close to the service exit,' the Chief said, and nodded as Dimitri chose a convenient table. 'Never raise your voice to call a waiter, never pull him by the sleeve, never order something that isn't on the menu. Never draw attention to yourself.'

He spoke in a monotonous voice, and Dimitri realized he didn't care about his job. The old man's eyes had an inner, listless look. The Chief was long dead, Dimitri thought, his body functioning more by habit than by the will to live. He kept on with his routine duties probably because espionage was the only trade he knew.

'For all practical purposes, you're a Canadian,' the Chief was saying. 'We use their passports because they don't have computerized records of their citizens. We use their identities, because there isn't such a thing as a Canadian.'

'How's that?' Dimitri asked.

The Chief lit a Bulgarian Sobranie cigarette. It was black and gold-tipped. The fingers holding the cigarette were yellow around the joints; the Chief's teeth were stained by nicotine. He saw Dimitri watching him and smiled wryly, offering him a cigarette. 'Never do that when on a mission. Never smoke an unusual brand of cigarette. It might lead you to trouble. People and ashtrays remember such things.'

He slowly exhaled. 'Where were we? Oh, yes, the Canadians. Canada is a mosaic of immigrants, from all the corners of the earth.

The country is full of Italians, East Europeans, Portuguese, French, Greeks. Nobody would be surprised if a Canadian didn't speak English or spoke it with a heavy accent. Get it?'

Dimitri nodded. The Sobranie had a rich, sharp flavour.

'Now,' said the Chief, 'let me take you to the lavatory.'

Dimitri followed him, puzzled. The Chief went through a door, stepped into one of the cubicles, and pointed at the water cistern. It was a European model, fixed to the wall above their heads and connected to the seat with a long pipe; the water flow was activated by a chain, hanging from the cistern.

'This is your dead-letter drop,' the Chief said. 'If you want to survive, stay away from the KGB nonsense. Don't ever establish your drops in woods or fields, beneath shrubs or in holes in trees. Our people in America do it, and are regularly caught by the FBI with their pants down. Their American agents too. Good for them, the poor SOBs don't deserve anything better.'

Dimitri chuckled. The old boy didn't mince his words.

The Chief's rasping voice was charged with utter contempt. 'A man who sneaks alone into the woods is always suspect. A man who drives his car from his office to the woods, or to a deserted field, is always suspect. The same for a man who parks his car by the road, in the middle of nowhere. But a man who goes to pee in a cafe lavatory is not, see? So here's what you do.'

He fished a small box from his pocket, took a condom out of it and unrolled it. 'You place your message or microfilm or whatever inside the rubber, tie it up, twice for security, and drown it.' He climbed on the lavatory stool and deftly plunged the condom into the water cistern. 'Nobody will look there, and if they do, they can never trace it to you or your contact.'

He led the way back to the cafe. 'The first thing you need whenever you get into a big city, is a map of all the stores, shopping centres, train stations and hotels with multiple exits. Your case officer should have one ready for you before you set out on your mission. You memorize it and destroy it. We call these places sanctuaries. If you're shadowed, you head for the closest sanctuary, move in by one entrance, out by another.' He paused, searchingly looking at Dimitri. 'It may save your life. I can tell you of a pharmacy in Paris . . .' He smiled to himself, his eyes suddenly lighting up, and let his voice fade away.

As they left the place, he turned back to Dimitri and the cavernous voice doomed again. 'And remember: you enter a cafe, a restaurant, a hotel – as if they belong to you. Don't linger by the door, don't look uncertain. In the West, there is no police guard on hotels. Everyone can walk in and out, and the more confident you look, the less they'll suspect you.'

Dimitri recalled the Chief's advice three weeks later, as he confidently walked into the brass-and-leather lobby of the Hotel Universal in Frankfurt. The soft Western clothes, made to measure, caressed his skin. He smiled absently at the concierge, paused by the souvenir shop, lighting a cigarette with deliberately slow gestures, then casually walked towards the elevators, swinging his leather briefcase.

He had arrived the night before on a direct Lufthansa flight, carrying a Finnish passport in the name of Timo Kuusinen. At the airport's lower level, he boarded the direct train to the Hauptbahnhof, the main railway station. The station buffet was a poorly-lit restaurant with solid wooden furniture and hefty waitresses in white aprons. Dimitri ordered a couple of grilled sausages and two strong cold beers – his first meal in the West, which he found excellent, especially when he plunged his spoon into the dessert, a cup of creamy, unctuous chocolate mousse. He gulped down his coffee, then stepped into the men's lavatory.

Locking behind him the door of the third cubicle from the left, he climbed on the seat, rolled up his sleeve, and plunged his hand inside the water cistern. The condom he took out of the water contained an unmarked key, which he used to open the third upper locker from the left in the waiting hall of the station. Inside he found a bag containing an entire new set of clothes, purchased in Hamilton, Ontario, and a Canadian passport in the name of Stefan Nagi. There was no photograph on the passport. This was done as a security measure, in case someone accidentally opened the locker and found the bag. Under the clothes, packed in a leather pouch, were an electric-powered gun, three ampoules of prussic acid and three of antidote.

A sign in German at the other side of the hall offered showers to travellers for 4.5 Deutschemarks. He changed in the dressing room; five minutes later he stashed his Finnish clothes and passport in the same locker. That way, no one could establish a connection between the Finn who flew in from Moscow, and the Canadian who now left the train station and walked into the city of Frankfurt. If anything went wrong, and Stefan Nagi's role in the forthcoming operation was exposed, his trail would grow cold at the entrance to the Hauptbahnhof.

It was early evening when Stefan Nagi checked in at the Globe, a tacky fleabag hotel in the red-light district which was within walking distance from the station. On his way he saw huge signs announcing the Buchmesse – the annual Frankfurt Book Fair. Enormous posters praised the latest bestsellers and their authors. Once inside his room, he ordered a couple of ham and salami sandwiches and two more beers. From a plain envelope he had brought with him, he took his own photograph which he carefully glued to his Canadian passport. He spent the evening and most of the next day in his room, valiantly struggling with a decrepit black-and-white television set. He kept furiously turning the chipped button, as he didn't understand the German programmes. He finally tuned to the US armed forces television, and watched some old sitcoms which he found boring and utterly stupid.

He had lunch in a crowded bar down the street where he was apparently the only patron who wasn't either pimping or whoring. Back in his room, he reluctantly switched on the TV set again and wolfed down two huge bars of milk and hazelnut chocolate. Once in a while he would hear steps in the corridor outside, men's voices and women's forced giggles. The Globe was apparently doing good business.

As the afternoon neared its end he donned his Canadian clothes, picked up an elegant leather case, then hailed a taxi outside the hotel. Through the cab window, he hungrily stared at the opulent shops, the luxurious cars, the well-dressed people. The food stores were crammed with a variety of products. You could just walk in and buy all you wanted, without having to stand in line. It was an overcast afternoon and the colourful neon signs were merrily blazing all along the Kaiserstrasse. A cascade of lights, shaped like women's bodies, invited him to a sex-show. So that's the West, he thought. Fat, rich and decadent. And that's Germany. We won the war, we raised our flag in Berlin, and the bastards are thriving on the fat of the land.

As he walked into the Universal, a blonde woman in an expensive fur coat came out and flashed him an inviting smile. It jolted him. For a second he fantasized that he was alone in a hotel bed with such a ravishing woman, away from everything.

But as he entered the hotel lobby, he pushed all other thoughts from his mind and concentrated on the mission ahead. His target was an American staying in room 1218, Lawrence Tierney. He was American by name only; his real name was Genadi Lyubimov, a former deputy head of the Soviet mission to the United Nations, Lyubimov had defected to the West six months before, and delivered to the CIA a devastatingly accurate report of Soviet infiltration into American government agencies.

Lyubimov was a greedy man, Oktober had said. Braving the danger, he had emerged from hiding and come to the Frankfurt Book

Fair. He had flown all the way to Germany to meet a Berlin publisher and convince him of the authenticity of his memoirs. And collect a fat cheque, of course.

But as far as Dimitri knew, there was no German publisher interested in Lyubimov's memoirs. Just Oktober. Dimitri's wily chief must have been the one who had smoked Lyubimov out into the open, by dangling the bait before his eyes.

'I want him dead,' Oktober had said to Dimitri at Sheremetyevo airport, before he boarded his flight. It was shortly before dawn, and they stood on the tarmac in the freezing cold. That's the way Death probably looks, Dimitri mused, gazing at the emaciated features, the cruel mouth, the implacable resolve burning in the dark eyes.

'I want him dead,' Oktober repeated. 'For what he did, and for what others might do if they believe they'd get away with it.'

'You're trying to resuscitate Smersh,' Dimitri observed.

Oktober's bony hands grabbed him by the shoulders. 'Your father was a Smersh officer, never forget that.'

I'll never forget, Dimitri thought now as he stepped into the lift of the Univeral Hotel. A bearded Jew with sidelocks and a large black hat got in after him. Dimitri had seen Orthodox Jews only once before. Bloody bastards, he though, they're everywhere. They too won the war, beside the Germans and the Japanese.

He got out on the tenth floor, and climbed two flights up on the service stairs. Before stepping into the corridor, he stuffed his raincoat and jacket into his case and put on a white tunic embossed with the Universal logo. He had found it in the bag he had collected at the station. He left his briefcase in the cupboard where the fire equipment was stored.

He entered the corridor. Its walls, decorated in beige and brown, were discreetly lit and the thick carpet muffled his footsteps. Two men, softly laughing at something one of them had said, passed by him, and he politely bowed. On his right was room 1216, on his left 1215. His heart was beating faster and he felt the familiar hollow sensation in the pit of his stomach.

1218. He rapped on the door.

'Yes?' The voice was reserved, suspicious.

'Minibar check.'

'No need, I didn't use it.'

'Sorry sir,' he said in English, assuming a German accent. 'I must check, these are hotel regulations.'

There was a long silence. 'Okay, wait.' He stood facing the brown door, his right hand gripping the electric gun inside his pocket. The ampoule containing the antidote was in his left hand. Lyubimov will now open the door, he thought, I'll step in, fire the poison ampoule in his face, and it will all be over. He remembered the sharp odour of the antidote gas and the convulsions of the dogs he had shot in the Yurlovo Forest.

The door opened. A middle-aged man wearing a silk robe stared sullenly at Dimitri. He was heavily built, with a broad face, a shock of dyed brown hair over white sideburns, and a cupid's bow mouth. A cigarette was dangling from his fingers.

'Mr Tierney?' Dimitri managed.

The man nodded, glancing suspiciously at Dimitri's right hand still stuck in his pocket.

'Sorry to disturb you,' Dimitri started. The target moved aside, letting him pass. 'Get on with it,' he said impatiently. 'I'm busy.'

Dimitri bowed subserviently and closed the door behind him. On the right wall, over the mini-bar, he glimpsed a print of two men wrestling, their muscles bulging with the strain.

And all of a sudden he remembered that black night at the quarry outside the Panfilov Orphanage, the crushing grip of Kuzma Bunin, the stunning blows of his iron bar. And the brief surge of ecstasy, sweeter than orgasm, that had swept him when he had squeezed the life from his enemy's body with his hands.

He let go of the gun, and dropped the antidote ampoule. He turned back and hurled himself on Lyubimov, his clawed hands reaching for the defector's throat. For an instant, Lyubimov was stunned, staring at him in dismay. But he swiftly recovered and dived sideways. Dimitri crashed onto one of the sleek Danish chairs and landed on the floor, amidst broken pieces of wood.

Lyubimov grabbed the phone. Dimitri rolled on the carpet, yanking the telephone cord from its socket, then sprang again. This time he managed to seize his victim by the waist. Lyubimov screamed in terror, wildly kicking and punching Dimitri in the face. He tasted the metallic flavour of blood trickling into his mouth. His jaw ached, and his enemy's screams rang in his ears. But all this didn't matter. While the defector squealed like a slaughtered pig, Dimitri's hands tightened on his beefy throat. And in one quick move, that transported him with rapture, he snapped the traitor's neck. He heard the crack of Lyubimov's upper vertebrae, and his heavy body went limp in his arms.

The following morning, after another night spent in the Globe with a teenage prostitute, blonde, slight and freckled, the man named Timo Kuusinen boarded a flight to Berlin, and connected with Finnair flight 118 to Helsinki, with stops at Prague and Moscow.

The electric gun and Nagi's clothes were returned to a Frankfurt locker, whose key, tied in a condom of reinforced latex, splashed into a water cistern at the Hauptbahnhof's lavatory.

During his journey back Dimitri kept worrying about Oktober's reaction when he told him he hadn't shot Lyubimov but liquidated him with his bare hands. Oktober, however, didn't seem upset by the transgression of the rules. He received Dimitri in his dark lair, made him sit in the single visitor's chair, then paced in circles around him, listening to his account. His questions weren't hostile; on the contrary, Dimitri had the impression that his chief was far from shocked by his brutal impulse.

'What did you feel when you killed him?' he asked, studying Dimitri intently. Dimitri stared back without answering, and a sardonic smile briefly lit Oktober's wan face. 'You loved it,' he said. 'That's good. That's really good.'

But the real surprise for Dimitri was the truth about Lyubimov that he heard from Oktober's mouth.

Lyubimov had never been a defector, Oktober disclosed in a conspiratorial tone, his dark eyes twinkling oddly. His defection had been staged by Moscow Centre. Lyubimov had been planted in the West as a double agent, and the intelligence he had provided to the CIA was, of course, a well-concocted blend of *disinformatzia*.

'Then we had a hitch,' Oktober said. He was again pacing around, restless, long-limbed, a spider weaving his deadly web. 'The Americans smelled a rat. Somebody at Langley said Lyubimov was a phoney, and labelled his defection "a Chekist plot".'

'They had proof against him?' Dimitri asked.

'None, but they started doubting his word, and wanted to run a check on all the reports he provided. The Lyubimov affair was one of our most difficult and costly operations. We had been preparing the ground for his defection for years. And then all our efforts were about to go down the drain.'

He paused. 'To save the project, we had to convince Langley that Lyubimov was genuine, that everything he had told them was God's gospel. And what better proof that he was a genuine defector than having him assassinated by KGB agents?'

A sudden chill spread through Dimitri's body. 'You mean to tell me,' he started, stunned, 'you mean to tell me I killed one of our men? A fellow Chekist?'

Oktober stared back, motionless. 'Yes, and now they believe every word he said.' His crooked grin was blood-chilling. 'Why, do you feel sorry for him?'

Not for him, Dimitri wanted to say, for me, for all the others you might use in your game. 'Oktober,' he said slowly, 'you deliberately ordered one of our best men killed?'

The older man nodded.

'How would I know,' Dimitri continued, 'that tomorrow, or in a year, you wouldn't sacrifice me as well, in one of your games?'

Oktober chuckled, a sly look pervading his black eyes. 'That's exactly the point, my boy. You'll never know.'

When Dimitri was already at the door, Oktober called after him: 'I was joking, of course.'

'Of course,' Dimitri said. Oktober's hoarse cackle rang in his ears as he went out and closed the door behind him.

In the following years Dimitri assassinated four more people, two in Munich, one in New York, and one in Madrid. Three of them were well-known dissidents; one, an American agent about to infiltrate the Soviet Union posing as a Spanish communist, a hero of the civil war.

Dimitri quickly became familiar with the Western way of life. No member of the widely publicized jet set crowd flew about Europe and North America as much as Dimitri Morozov. But he always observed an austere, almost monastic way of life. Europe oozed pleasures and temptations that could easily turn the head of a Russian burdened with the memories of hunger and cold, like himself. But he couldn't afford any deviation from his strict routine. He was risking his life daily, and knew that the smallest mistake could cost him his life. It might start with returning twice to the same gourmet restaurant, the same night club or the same hotel suite in a European capital; it might end with him rolling bullet-ridden into a side-street gutter. Any breach of Department rules could be fatal.

He learned from his Lisbon experience in April 1972. He had been sent to the Portuguese capital to liquidate a Latvian refugee leader, who intended to establish a government in exile. But as he sneaked into the Latvian's room he found himself facing his target's bodyguard, who wasn't supposed to be at the scene. He barely escaped with a bullet wound in his shoulder. On his return to Moscow Oktober told him he could never travel to Lisbon again. It had been an unfortunate accident, Oktober said.

But Dimitri knew better. If he had more thoroughly investigated his target's habits, instead of enjoying a lobster dinner at Cascais on the night of his arrival, he wouldn't still be carrying a 7.65 slug embedded in his left shoulder, six inches from the heart.

His other operations were successful. He always used his bare hands; he never felt any pity for his targets. Nobody had ever felt pity for him, he recalled. Dimitri's most recent victim, a statuesque Estonian woman, had briefly stirred his desire, and he had held her firm body against him just a second longer before he snapped her neck.

Dimitri also carried out the kidnapping of Dr Ernst Muller, the Deputy Director of West Germany's secret service, and his transfer to East Germany. Muller turned to be a treasure trove for the East German Stasi. Before he was liquidated, he delivered priceless information about the joint Pullach and Langley operations in the Warsaw Pact countries.

Following the success of Muller's abduction, Oktober promoted Dimitri to the key position of Chief Operations Officer in Western Europe. He was posted to Paris under the cover of a senior Sovtorg representative.

And it was in his Paris office late one evening, that, hearing a knock on his door and raising his eyes from the report he was reading, he saw before him the tall, handsome man he remembered so well: GRU Colonel Oleg Kalinin.

Chapter Ten

La Guardia airport was buried in snow, but the runways had been swept clean and the landing was smooth. 'The captain, the crew, and the 33,000 shareholders of Transamerica Airways thank you for flying with us,' a flight attendant giggled into the loudspeaker system. Alex slipped a bookmark between the pages of Dylan Thomas's *Collected Poems* and dropped the fiery Welshman's book in his bag. Lately, after so many years of studying Russian poetry, he had discovered the English and American romantic masters. He was mesmerized by Thomas's talent, that had come to such a tragic end. One of the verses made him think of his mother: 'Though lovers be lost love shall not; and death shall have no dominion.'

Claudia was waiting for him at the arrival gate, waving happily. 'Some guys get all the fun,' the man walking behind him muttered. Claudia was wearing an embroidered white sheepskin over a flimsy blouse of blue silk, white jeans and high-heeled boots. There was hardly anybody in the arrival lounge who didn't stare at her, men with hungry eyes, women with a cold mean look that missed nothing. 'God, I always forget how gorgeous you are,' he murmured as she slipped into his arms.

'How can you remember,' she quipped, 'with all those sexy little things crawling over you in Providence?' She kissed him passionately, then took his hand. 'Come,' she said, a tiny dimple budding on her left cheek. She brushed a few strands of hair from her face. It was snowing outside, heavy, soft flakes that briefly blossomed like daisies on the wavy blackness of her hair.

'We'll take a taxi. I'm picking up the tab,' she announced. In the cab, he wanted to ask why this sudden generosity, but she assailed him with questions. Was he going to stay in Providence after he got his doctor's degree? Perhaps he could teach at Brown? What about Columbia or Boston? And the offer from Stanford, was it still valid?

No, I don't want to teach at Brown, he said. No, Columbia neither. Yes, Stanford is still open, but it depended.

On what? she asked.

On you, he replied. What about you?

This was the question she had apparently been waiting for. Sitting on the edge of the seat, draping her sheepskin like ermine around her shoulders, she plunged into a breathless account of her adventures. She had called everybody, absolutely everybody in the fashion business during these last three weeks. Nobody had agreed even to set up an appointment with her, nobody cared for her sketches or her resumé or her arts degree. We're not hiring, everybody said. We're overstaffed. Actually we're firing. No, thank you, Miss Benevento, we don't need new fashion designers. Our old fashion designers are very good. Don't call us, and we won't call you.

On the front seat, the bearded cab driver was shaking his head dejectedly; he seemed distressed by Claudia's ordeal.

Alex couldn't take his eyes off her. She was totally immersed in her story, illustrating it with spontaneous hand gestures and facial expressions. Her bursting vitality was irresistible. While talking she imitated the different voices on the phone, the French accents, the Italian intonation, the Southern drawls. When quoting the negative answers her face assumed a mask of contempt and her eyes shot deadly lightning.

So, she dramatically resumed, nobody, absolutely nobody wanted her. But – and there was of course a but, in every Claudia story told with such gusto there always was a but – at the end she had said to herself: Basta! Enough! You're young, Claudia, you're talented, what am I saying, you're unique, and you're not so bad-looking on top of that (my damn modesty, Alex, you know), so don't just stand in your Brooklyn kitchen holding your mama's hand and begging those sharks over the phone. This is something any fat, ugly, and dumb broad can do. Go for them, show them who you are and what you are and what you can do.

He looked at her sideways, half amused, and half intrigued. Her style fitted too closely the Italian girl portrayed in any second-rate Hollywood movie. He had the feeling that she was talking like that just to amuse him. She was much too clever to think the way she talked. But with Claudia one could never tell.

This decided, she was saying, she had set out on the conquest of Manhattan, armed with her resumé and her sketches – the summer collection I showed you in New Haven, remember, Alex? And he said yes, he remembered, but now he was really worried, because the cab driver was getting too interested in Claudia, nodding his head to her story, sighing in compassion for her vicissitudes, clicking his tongue sympathetically, and too busy throwing longing glances at her to watch the snowbound road ahead.

To cut a long story short, Claudia said, she had been shamefully thrown out of Sergio Valenti's and Giorgio Romano's and Nina Laurent's by a few ageing dragons who had stared at her hatefully and announced she wouldn't get even one step past them without an appointment. But finally she had landed at Havermeyer's, and walked out of the elevator at the very moment old Mr Havermeyer was trying to get in. Such a nice old gentleman, Alex, exactly the opposite of what those poison pens are writing in the papers. 'So I got hold of his sleeve and didn't let go till he heard my little speech. And guess what, Alex?'

'He hired you,' he ventured.

'How did you guess?'

Alex leaned forward, to ask Claudia's new friend to keep his eyes on the road. The sights unfolding before the car were unfamiliar. They whizzed past a sign saying 49th Street. 'Hey, what the hell is this?' he said to the driver. 'This isn't Brooklyn. Where are you going?'

But Claudia's soft laughter made him turn back. Her eyes were sparkling. 'Easy, Professor, easy.'

'I should have guessed it was you,' he sighed. 'What did you tell the driver?'

But the cab had already turned into Park Avenue, and sailed to a stop. A generalissimo in parade uniform opened the cab door. 'Welcome to the Waldorf Astoria, Sir. Welcome, Miss.'

Smiling mysteriously, Claudia walked up the marble staircase of the sumptuous hotel and through the blue-and-white Art Deco lobby. People were turning their heads at her passage, and she didn't seem to dislike it. An old gentleman in a velvet smoking jacket, sitting under the ornate clock, rose and smiled hopefully at Claudia. Alex followed her, carrying his overnight bag, puzzled but enchanted at the same time. Every moment with Claudia was an adventure, he thought, a new lesson in the pleasures life can offer to a young person. She was unique, indeed. 'Thirty-one,' Claudia whispered with a conspiratorial wink at the liveried operator of the carpeted elevator, and the poor man nervously fidgeted with his buttons all the way up, apparently debating if he should call the house detective.

When they arrived at their floor Claudia took Alex by the hand, dragged him to a double door, and unlocked it. 'Welcome to my place,' she said. Then, stepping aside, she let him walk in first.

Alex was dismayed by the elegance of the suite. It was softly lit, furnished in light grey and vivid plum colours. The walls, covered with beige-shaded wallpaper were decorated with colourful sketches of Paris scenes – the Sacré-Coeur, the Arc de Triomphe, a crowd on the Champs Elysées. The living room was furnished with exquisite chests and cupboards in turn-of-the century style. The desk by the window, lit by a brass table-lamp, was covered with green Italian marble. Alex liked the sketch of a barge on the Seine that hung over it. It sailed under one of Paris's bridges, with the Notre-Dame Cathedral looming in the background. The beige carpet was deep and soft under his feet. Two Oriental vases stood by the door. On a round table, set between two old-fashioned chairs with padded armrests, was spread an artful assortment of canapes. A golden box of Godiva, his favourite chocolates, stood beside the hors d'oeuvres, tied with a golden ribbon. A bottle of champagne peeked out of a silver ice bucket.

'Right on time,' Claudia quipped, carelessly throwing her coat on a sofa and scooping up a smoked salmon sandwich.

'Claud,' he said, still holding his bag, 'I must call Nina.'

'I called her myself,' she said, planting a languorous kiss on his cheek. 'She knows you won't be home before tomorrow.'

She nibbled on her sandwich. 'Divine!' she gasped, fluttering her eyelids. 'Darling, will you pour the champagne?'

'I'd be delighted,' Alex said, struggling with the cork. 'Now you just tell me what all this is about.' The cork popped out of the bottle, hit the ceiling and landed on a plum-coloured armchair. Alex gauchely wiped the foam from his sleeve and reached for the slender champagne glasses.

Claudia sank contentedly into a deep armchair, stretching her legs. 'This is a celebration, Alex. I got an advance today. We're celebrating my first salary. And the forthcoming graduation of Alex Gordon, PhD.'

'Good Lord, Claud, you spent your entire salary on one night at the Waldorf!'

She frowned, plunging into a mental calculation. 'Yes, that's about it,' She brightened up and the delicious dimple bloomed in her cheek again. 'So what? It's my money, and it's how I want to spend it. I bought us a memory. A night of outrageous decadence. Will you make love to me, big boy?'

She fell silent, and when she spoke again her voice was lower, softer. 'Can you think of anything better to spend our money on, Alessandro?'

He watched her sleep, her long body stretched across the double bed, her head cradled on one curved arm, the soft contours of her face barely visible under the heavy mass of black hair. Her other arm was extended behind her, resting on the pillows.

The bedroom was very still, very peaceful. He turned off the lights. In the window, the contours of the New York skyline were enhanced, the Chrysler building cutting its jagged profile against the dark background. A few brightly-lit windows forlornly glowed in the night. His eyes shifted back to Claudia's nude body and he listened to her quiet breathing.

His life, he thought, had been moulded by three women. Tonya, whose intense romantic streak had flown into his blood; Nina, who had instilled in him the love of Russia; and Claudia, who had quenched his teenage yearnings and dispelled his solitude, but who had also taught him that life could be fun, not just an endless procession of slogans, red flags and faceless crowds, docilely treading towards the future.

He knew that Nina resented Claudia and thought she had stolen his love from her. She probably blamed the girl for the change in his political opinions as well.

He loved Nina dearly. But her fanatical devotion to her communist gods had turned into a formidable wall between them. Every time he came home, he would fight with her over the Kremlin policy. His former admiration for the Soviet Union had shattered; he now regarded Brezhnev as a cynical dictator, who oppressed with an iron fist a beautiful country and a great nation.

He wasn't the little Russian boy any more, lost in a faraway country. He considered himself American. He was intensely involved in the major issues: the Vietnam War and the struggle for equal rights that revived his dreams of social justice. He took part in a few political rallies on the Watergate scandal. But his main interest was in his studies. His deep knowledge of Russia, its society and history, gave him an advantage over his fellow students: he was by far the best Sovietology student in Brown, easily scooping scholarships and awards. His disappointment with communism had turned him from an unconditional admirer of Soviet Russia into a sober and unbiased critic. An article on the power struggle at the Kremlin that he wrote for the students' magazine was quoted in several national newspapers, and he was described as 'a Brown scholar'.

Still he failed in his efforts to obtain a visa to the Soviet Union. A few months ago, twenty-two post-graduate students had applied for a Russian visa to participate in a student exchange programme. Twenty-one were approved, Alex Gordon stayed home.

Beside him, Claudia stirred, and her hand came to rest on his thigh. Thank God for Claudia, he thought. She lit up his life. The peppy teenager had turned into a smart young woman before his eyes. A year after they met she graduated, and a prettier homecoming queen there never was in Brooklyn High. Her proud parents sent her to the University of New Haven, in Connecticut. Since then Claudia spent every second weekend with him at Providence or in some little country inn. They explored the forgotten forests and mountains of New England, driving along country roads, discovering quaint inns and lodges. When in town, they would go to a movie and then to a disco; late at night Claudia adored dancing. Her family, after a few half-hearted protests – her brothers were very close to her former boyfriend – had finally accepted Alex. Mrs Benevento desperately tried to tame her rebellious daughter, but finally capitulated and let her be. Claudia was too independent to be curbed by a family that spoiled her for eighteen years. There was nothing they could do to keep her away from Alex.

But this beautiful period in their lives was coming to an end. Claudia had majored in arts, and returned home. He was about to get the doctor's degree and start a new chapter in his life. And he wanted her to be part of it.

In a surge of tenderness, he leaned over the sleeping girl and kissed her exposed neck, breathing her perfume. He gently shook her shoulder. 'Claud. Claud, wake up.'

She stretched lazily and rolled on her back, her eyes slowly opening. He thought again of a Dylan Thomas verse: '. . . The opening of her nightlong eyes.' That line had been written for Claudia.

'What is it?' she murmured. 'What time is it?'

'Claud,' he said again. 'Are you awake? Do you hear me?'

'Yes,' she groaned. 'What happened, Alex?'

'Marry me,' he said.

'What?'

'Marry me. Please.'

She was wide awake now, staring at him in astonishment. 'What are you talking about? Go to sleep, you need some rest.'

'Claud, I'm serious. We love each other, we're great together, let's get married.'

'You are serious,' she decided. She moved closer and stared at him gravely, a look in her eyes he'd never seen before.

'What?' he said, vaguely troubled.

She got up, put on a white bathrobe embroidered with the hotel logo, and carried her bag to the window. She took out her cigarettes and lit one with unsteady, nervous gestures. 'No,' she said finally, 'I don't want to get married.'

'You don't want to get married?' he repeated stupidly. He had been sure she would be thrilled by his proposal. 'Why, don't you love me?' He felt uncomfortable, standing naked in front of her, so he stepped into the bathroom and wrapped a towel around his waist.

'I love you more than anything in the world,' Claudia was saying, 'but I don't want to get married. Not now.'

'Why, Claud, what's the matter?'

'Why? Because I want to become a fashion designer,' she said. 'It's a tremendous challenge, Alex. I want to give it my best shot.'

'But nobody asked you to give it up.'

'Oh yes you did.' She sat beside him on the bed, softly caressing his shoulder. 'If we get married now, I'll have to live with you all the time, perhaps at Brown, perhaps at Stanford. But I can't. Alex, don't you see? I must be in New York most of the time. It's the fashion capital of this country. But even New York isn't available to me for the moment. Havermeyer wants me, for the next year or so, to travel around the country and organize his fashion shows. He said that if I'm good at that, he might take a couple of my designs for his collection. This is going to be an exhausting year, I can't just get married and stay home.'

'You're going to travel with him?' Alex asked suspiciously.

'With a team that he is putting together now. His son is going to be in charge.'

'Oh, him,' Alex muttered angrily. Ronnie Havermeyer was a frequent name in the newspapers' gossip columns. A handsome man, he had the reputation of being a hedonist and a womanizer. Alex suddenly had the feeling that he might lose Claudia. 'We can get married and you can travel wherever you want,' he half-heartedly suggested.

She shook her head. 'You know, while I was looking for work I even thought of modelling for a while. I went to this agency on Fifty-ninth and Sixth . . . Cosmopolitan models, that's its name. I met a middle-aged guy who sat in an office with his feet on his desk, smoking a big cigar. He just glanced at me and shook his head. "Lady," this guy says to me, looking at my hips, "you're made to be a mother, not a model."'

'Don't you want to be a mother?'

'Of course I do. And that will happen if we get married now.' She saw him shaking his head. 'Yes, yes, believe me. In two years I'll have two kids, and all my travels will be between the kitchen and the nursery, with a hop to the supermarket once in a while. I want to have children, but in my own time. I'll get married, but not right now.' Trying to soften him, she adopted an exaggerated Italian accent. 'I'll make you a lot of *bambinos*, okay, Alessandro? But in a couple of years, *capisce*?'

'No, *non capisco*,' he said testily. He was annoyed by her cool-headed attitude, and her resolve that her career came first. What the hell? he thought. If she was really in love, she would have agreed to marry him right away. He had always thought she was as romantic and impulsive as he. Three years ago it was Claudia who had raised the subject of marriage. She had wanted to get married then, but he had cooled her enthusiasm, saying that he had to get his PhD first.

She had been deeply disappointed, and had said so. Since then he'd assumed she had been counting the days until his graduation, eager to get married. But tonight she was behaving differently. If she started travelling, and with Havermeyer's son on top of that, they might drift apart. A year was a long time.

'So what is this?' he challenged her, making a sweeping gesture with his hand. 'A farewell night?'

'Alex, I love you,' she said. 'Nothing has changed.' Her hand slipped under his towel. 'Let's go to bed, let's make love.'

'No,' he said, seething. 'I don't want to make love now.' He pulled away and went out the bedroom. She called after him, but he didn't answer. He groped his way in the dark sitting room, hurting his knee against the table where the food had been served. He pulled the curtains aside. The window glass was ice-cold against his burning forehead. He glanced at the empty street below. A lonely figure was scurrying in the snow. What am I going to do if I lose her? Alex thought. How can I live without Claudia?

The insistent ringing of the telephone tore Grimaldi out of a bad dream. He recalled only darkness and piercing screams, or perhaps they had been the strident summons of the telephone. He was bathed in sweat, and gasped for air as he picked up the receiver. 'Yes,' he mumbled, 'hello.' The first spring rain furiously rapped on the windows that were tinged in an eerie grey light.

'Is this the Evdokiev hospital?' a deep voice asked in Russian. 'My wife is about to have a baby and . . .'

'Wrong number,' he muttered. 'Always the same mistake.' He slammed down the phone and wiped his moist forehead. The modular red figures on his digital clock spelled 6.50 a.m. In the greyness outside, skeletal boughs were swaying before his window, whipped by the Moscow wind.

Grimaldi got up, showered and dressed quickly. He cut himself shaving, and his skin burned as he splashed some Missoni aftershave on his face. His fingers were trembling, slipping over his shirt buttons.

What happened? he thought. What's the emergency? If it were something really serious, Kalinin would have given him the code signal to leave the country, but he hadn't. His voice sounded confident. Calm down, he said to himself, don't panic. Kalinin had been away for two weeks, on some assignment to Paris and Amsterdam. He was supposed to be back at the end of this week. He had returned earlier, perhaps he had something urgent to report.

He made himself a cup of black coffee, with no sugar, and slowly sipped it by the kitchen window. It gave onto a drab courtyard, flooded by the rain; the carcass of an ancient motorcycle with sidecar was rotting by a rusty iron gate adorned with broken spikes. Nobody could suspect that the phone call was an emergency signal. The Evdokiev hospital's number was almost identical with his own, only the last digit was different. Kalinin had worked hard to find a number close to his own for the 'wrong number' routine: the hospital was ideal, because it allowed emergency calls around the clock without raising the suspicions of the KGB who doubtlessly tapped his telephone.

He picked up his coat and went out. There was nobody outside the apartment, and the staircase was dark; somebody – probably the janitor – had again stolen the light bulbs. The lobby was deserted. The rain was pouring furiously, its drops ricocheting from the pavement. The militiaman who watched the building had found refuge in the porch next door. The streetlamps were still on, looming behind the wavering curtain of water like smoky globes of pale fire. He opened his umbrella. There was a public phone on the corner of Chapayevski, but he didn't use it. With all the foreigners living in his building, Grimaldi had no doubt that the bloody booth was more heavily bugged than his own apartment.

Scurrying toward Balteiskaya, he stepped into a puddle and felt cold water trickle into his shoe. He threw a look over his shoulder, but didn't notice anything suspicious. At the corner of Balteiskaya there was a small workers' buffet that opened at six am. Twice a week he came over and ate their disgusting breakfast, only to justify the occasional use of the phone booth outside.

As he opened the door, warm air breathed into his face, thick with the smells of stale tobacco, sweat and frying oil. *'Dobroye Utro,'* he said, squeezing in among the construction workers, Metro employees and police officers who crowded the narrow buffet. Wisps of cigarette smoke hovered in the air, and crushed butts littered the floor. The woman behind the counter, a middle-aged Siberian wearing a soiled white apron on her fat body and an angry scowl on her lined face, knew him well. 'Good morning, Mister Saint-Clair,' she said formally, a steel tooth gleaming in her mouth.

Several glances converged upon him, focusing on his expensive coat and tailored suit. He had grown used to the envious stares of the Muscovites, could understand the poor devils. He ordered some black bread, a cube of butter, a piece of salted herring and a cup of tea, and carried his chipped tray to a table at the back.

After a moment, the Russians stopped staring at him, and resumed their conversations. He carefully studied the people clustered by the counter. He vaguely knew most of them, and their behaviour seemed normal. His fears subsided; he could tell he wasn't being watched. He took his time munching the tasteless food, then at 7.45 went back to the counter. There were only a few people left; the morning crowd had already dispersed. The Siberian woman was washing dishes in a sink half-full of greasy, soapy water. 'I'll be late for the office,' he said in stilted Russian. 'Would you have ten kopecks for the telephone?'

The woman wiped her red hands on her apron and handed him a coin, then slid two red and one yellow beads on her abacus that stood beside the cash register. Russians could live without computers and calculators, he thought, but dare to deprive them of their abacus and they would be lost.

He stepped into the phone booth. His first call was to his driver, Nikita, to come and pick him up at the buffet and not at home as usual. The second, at exactly seven fifty, was to another call box, a couple of miles away. The numbers of public phones he could call changed every week, according to a prearranged schedule.

On the other end of the line the receiver was picked up; Grimaldi didn't say a word. 'Tomorrow at seven am, at the Gastronom entrance on Tchaikovskaya,' a voice said calmly.

Grimaldi knew the code by heart. Tomorrow was today, seven am was eight pm, the Gastronom was the parking lot of the Ukraina Hotel. He felt reassured by Kalinin's serene voice. He was pleased he would see him tonight.

He went back to the buffet and paid his bill, ignoring the change the Siberian handed him. Tipping was forbidden in Russia but nobody really cared. His Mercedes stopped outside and he hurried out, wondering why Kalinin had requested a crash meeting.

At the end of the day, as Nikita steered the Mercedes through the evening traffic, Grimaldi sank back in his seat. Lately he was getting restless. His seventh year in Moscow was drawing to its close and he wasn't thrilled any more by the secret knowledge that he was running the top CIA agent in the Kremlin. His days at the office, buying caviar and salmon for his bogus Canadian company, were boring, his meetings with the stolid bureaucrats of the ministries of Fisheries and

Foreign Trade were maddening. He barely mixed with the foreign community, had no friends, found little interest in the limited pleasures Moscow could offer.

He never approached a man, although he had run into some very attractive boys, and by their looks and gestures had understood they belonged to his own breed. But accosting one of them would be equivalent to suicide. Oleg, too, was out of bounds, of course; besides, the man was married and had children now.

From lack of choice Grimaldi tried, once in a while, to satisfy his sexual fantasies with a female, and picked up a woman who was probably a KGB swallow anyway, instructed to sleep with him as part of the routine surveillance of foreigners. In the morning she would leave thrilled by his presents – a tin of Nescafe, some sticks of chewing gum and a couple of bath soaps. He was tired of this ritual too. Russian women had no imagination, he decided; they were no partners for kinky sex, brutal as he liked it. Poor things. With the lives they led, all they could think about was survival, not pleasure.

Even his mission in Moscow had slipped into a routine pattern – communications with Kalinin, servicing of dead-letter drops, coding the information, then dispatching the innocuous-looking letters to a cover address in Montreal. During his first months in Moscow he would read with bated breath the top-secret documents Kalinin supplied: minutes of the Politburo, military production reports, position papers for the disarmament talks, intelligence assessments. But after a while he had grown used to handling the top-notch product; now he coded the reports mechanically, like a robot, and dispatched them to Langley via Montreal.

He didn't even enjoy his yearly home leave, the flight to Montreal, the sneaking to Buffalo, the switch of identities from Saint-Clair to Grimaldi, then his trip to New York for debriefing and some decent food and games. Washington was out of bounds, the risk of exposure was too high. All this had become routine, and he knew how dangerous routine could be for a secret agent.

He had panicked only once, in 1970, when a young Russian had tailed him from his office to the National Hotel. If it had happened today he might not have noticed the bastard, he wasn't as alert any more. But this was almost four years ago; he had rushed to a phone, and called Kalinin for help. His fear had soared when the young man had popped up at the Bolshoi, minutes before his crash meeting with Oleg. He had barely overcome his impulse to run away during the interval. He had good reason to worry. As a Canadian businessman he didn't have diplomatic status. If he were caught he was bound to rot in the Lubyanka for the rest of his life.

Thank God, it turned out to be a false alert. The young man was just a KGB trainee who had been assigned to tail a foreigner about Moscow, like a couple of hundred other students. Kalinin had brought him the good news a couple of days later; it appeared that the young man hadn't even filed a report, as he had been transferred to another department. Perhaps Oleg had something to do with that, he never gave a full explanation.

When accepting the Moscow job, he had hoped it would catapult him to a top position in the Company. His prospects still looked promising; he knew that at Langley they spoke of him with awe, regarding him as the perfect spy, the CIA Scarlet Pimpernel. But even a legend couldn't last forever. He should quit while he was still on top, unbeaten, and return to headquarters to reap all the glory. The CIA was changing, a younger generation was taking over. He should have packed and left already, gone back to Langley and claimed his part in the spoils.

But he didn't want to leave without taking Kalinin with him: this would give the operation a dazzling panache. The greatest American spy since World War Two, and his master, returning unscathed from the lion's den! Oleg wasn't ready yet, though. Grimaldi suspected he enjoyed his cosy position at the Kremlin and his personal privileges. His friend seemed to fear the challenge of resettling in an alien country, under a false identity.

Grimaldi didn't have to wait forever; he could ask to be relieved, and his demand would be granted. But his relationship with Kalinin kept him in Moscow. They met very rarely, for brief, factual conversations. Still, he felt he was Oleg's only support, and that pleased him; their intimacy was something far beyond their common endeavour. One day, when they were back at the States, they might become lovers again, like in those glorious days in Berlin.

'Here we are,' Nikita said. The car stopped by the brightly lit entrance to the Ukraina. Two tourist buses waited outside, one carrying the sign 'Moscow Circus', the other 'Folklore'. The Western tourists were about to start their night of fun, Russian-style. He glanced at his watch. It was seven fifty. He guessed that the meeting with Kalinin would last five or ten minutes, then he would dine at the Ukraina to justify his visit to the hotel. 'Pick me up at nine thirty,' he said to Nikita. 'And be good.'

'*Khorosho.*' The driver grinned. In ten minutes, Grimaldi thought, Nikita would be screwing his little girlfriend who lived off Kropotkinskaya. She wanted to leave him, but Nikita was always tempting her with American cigarettes he stole from Grimaldi's office. Well, at least he had something to think about other than his boss's nightly outings.

He entered the Ukraina, nervously looking for something unusual, somebody waiting by the entrance, reading a newspaper, a couple hanging by the phone booths or strolling by the duty-free shops. He didn't spot anybody except the two uniformed officers who checked the foreigners' papers, and kept local swindlers, whores and black marketeers out of the hotel. The front desk looked normal too, with a couple of girls bent over large ledgers and a squat concierge suppressing a bored yawn. When the KGB laid a trap, the front desk was the first place where they planted a couple of agents, in hotel uniforms.

Grimaldi had a couple of vodkas at the foreign currency bar. He was getting jumpy again. Perhaps he wasn't so brave after all, he thought. Perhaps he had been ashamed of his behaviour back there in the Alps because he refused to admit that he was a coward. Clever, cunning, smart, but a coward all the same. It was time for him to settle down in a cosy office back home and let somebody else play cops and robbers with the KGB.

At two minutes past eight he left the hotel by the lower entrance and casually strolled to the parking lot.

Kalinin's car wasn't there.

He stood shivering on the dark Kutuzovsky Prospect, and it wasn't from the cold. Cabs were rare in Moscow at this hour, but he raised his hand, holding a pack of Marlboro cigarettes, and three taxis stopped in a screech of brakes. He took the second. On the way to Gorky Park he slumped down on the back seat, wiping his perspiring face with a linen handkerchief. Emergency rules, he thought. God, I never expected to use them. Never wait for me if I'm late, Kalinin had said, never come to the parking lot again. Call me at the current pay phone number three times, at five-minutes intervals. If there's no answer, check our dead drop. Twelve hours after the missed appointment call me at the pay phone again. If there's no answer, take a cab to Sheremetyevo and leave the bloody country before they get you too.

He had called from the Ukraina. The first time the number had been busy, but the second and third there had been no answer. That left him with the dead letter drop at Gorky Park. His thoughts were confused. He had an open Air France ticket to Montreal, via Paris, but it was too late to make a reservation tonight. His papers were in order, he had nothing to fear from this side. But he couldn't just walk into the airport tomorrow and catch the plane, that would seem too suspicious. He might have to use the emergency procedure, reserved only for cases of extreme danger.

What could have happened to Kalinin? He had spoken to him twice this morning, which meant he was free. Unless he was under arrest already, and had been forced by the KGB to establish contact. They had some quite persuasive methods, at the Lubyanka. But if he had been forced to call Grimaldi, why didn't the Russkies arrest him now, at the Ukraina parking lot?

'Gorky Park.' The driver smiled happily when Grimaldi handed him the cigarettes and gunned his Zhiguli like a racing car. It was raining again, a fine, steady drizzle. He stood for a moment at the park entrance, then doubled back toward the Moskva River. The riverfront was deserted; the nasty weather had chased away even the occasional pair of lovers. He stopped several times, looking back. But there were no shadows sneaking behind him, no sound of footsteps but his own, He raised his eyes. Ahead of him loomed the massive shape of Krimsky Bridge.

As he reached the near pillar of the bridge, sunk deep in the soaked ground, he knelt as if to tie his shoelaces. His fingers were trembling, and a hollow feeling pervaded his stomach. If they were after him, now was the time. He cursed under his breath. This cloak and dagger stuff wasn't for him any more. There should be a chain of agents serving Kalinin, and collecting his product. But Oleg had been adamant; no other agents, he had said, no cutouts, no intermediaries. Just you and me.

In the concrete support of the pillar, gaped a deep fissure. He delved into it a feet from the ground level. He removed the chunk of concrete blocking the opening, then probed deeper. His fingers almost missed the single sheet of thick paper, folded several times. He picked it up and stuck it in his shoe, then got up. His knees were shaking.

The drizzle enveloped him. He crossed the bridge, and caught another cab outside the golden-domed church of St Nicholas. He was back at the Ukraina long before Nikita had completed his amorous exploit.

The message was blunt and stunning as a death sentence. Brief and concise, it was printed in block letters and numerals on a thick sheet of paper. He decoded it in the locked privacy of his home, checking the groups of numbers against his 1965 edition of *Anna Karenina*. His astonishment grew with every new word he jotted on the notepad lying on his desk, beside Kalinin's message.

> *1720 hours. Can't contact you, too late. Am leaving this message in case something happens to me and our meeting is aborted. Incidentally met at Paris Sovtorg office young officer KGB Department Thirteen violent operations. Turned out to be the one*

who tailed you to the National and the Bolshoi four years ago. Knew me, remembered seeing me in theatre, asked if I knew you. I denied, he didn't believe me. I flew home earlier to warn you. Border police advised me at 1705 hours he had just landed. I believe he flew in to investigate our ties. If you don't meet me tonight get out, please get out. Your devoted friend.

Your devoted friend. Grimaldi rubbed his eyes. The room was plunged in darkness, except for the yellow circle the desk lamp cast on the papers before him. A lump was choking his throat. His devoted friend hadn't come. His devoted friend was certainly under arrest, probably tortured, possibly dead.

Perhaps they were watching the apartment now, perhaps they had planted microphones while he wasn't there? It was too late to start looking for them, though. His devoted friend might have told them everything by now. Very few people could withstand torture.

He looked at Kalinin's letter again. There was another phrase, hastily scribbled at the bottom of the page, and he decoded it, already considering it a message from the grave.

'Officer's name Dimitri Morozov' were Kalinin's last words.

Dimitri Morozov. Did he know that name? He tried to concentrate but was too agitated by Kalinin's message. Relax, he said to himself, calm down, try to think, try to remember. Every detail might be crucial. Who is Dimitri Morozov? He probed backwards into his memory. Where had he stumbled upon that name? It wasn't in Moscow, he was certain of that. It must have been years ago, back in Washington or New York, when he worked in the Soviet Division. Who the hell was Morozov?

A memory slowly surfaced. There had been a Morozov in Stalin's time. But it wasn't Dimitri, it was Nikolai . . . no, Boris. Colonel Boris Morozov, KGB, Second Chief Directorate. The fog started to clear. There was something odd connected with him. Of course, his wife! Tonya Gordon, the Jewish poetess. She had been shot in 1953. She had two children: Alexander who was her first husband's son and the second Morozov's little boy.

He sat still, his eyes glued to Oleg's message. Dimitri Morozov. He had to be the son of Boris Morozov, The father had disappeared twenty years ago, but not before whisking his stepson, Alexander Gordon, to the United States. He remembered seeing an FBI report about the child who lived with relatives in Brooklyn.

Two brothers, he thought, the son and the stepson of a KGB spymaster, one in Moscow, one in New York. One of them was a spy already. He wondered what had happened to the other. He went to the window and looked outside. The militiaman was walking back and forth before the house. A light blue car passed by, an old Zis, its exhaust growling, and turned the corner at Chapayevski. Grimaldi pulled down the blind. He tore Kalinin's message and the top page of his pad to pieces, piled them in the ashtray and lit them with his golden lighter. He watched them burn, stirring the ashes.

So Dimitri had become a KGB officer, and a dangerous one. Moscow Centre placed in Western Europe only trustworthy personnel. Department Thirteen sent to the West only accomplished killers. Morozov had trapped, perhaps murdered, Kalinin. The only friend Grimaldi had ever had. He felt a sudden surge of hatred. Perhaps at this very moment Dimitri Morozov was torturing Oleg; perhaps he was laying a trap for Grimaldi too. But if he succeeded in getting out of here, he would hit back. He would crush the motherfucker!

Grimaldi took a deep breath, feeling energy and resolve course into his blood. He'd make the young sonofabitch pay. He went to the kitchen and took an ice-cold bottle of vodka from the freezer. He broke the seal and poured himself a generous drink, then returned to his desk. He lit a thin black cigar and exhaled the smoke.

First, he had to get out of here. He must give the Russians a plausible reason for his sudden departure, and therefore had to revert to the emergency procedure.

He leafed through the foreign diplomats' directory until he found the home number of Oscar Housman, the economic attaché at the Canadian Embassy. He knew the man very superficially, had met him only a couple of times before. They had never exchanged anything but banalities. Housman was the only one who knew of Grimaldi's existence, but his knowledge was limited. He had been told there was an undercover agent in Moscow, who might contact him in case of emergency; he hadn't been told under what name Grimaldi operated.

He lit a new cigar and dialled the number. His fingers were trembling slightly. A woman's voice, low and reserved, answered.

'Good evening,' he said, 'this is Charles Saint-Clair. We met at the ambassador's New Year reception.'

'Oh, yes,' she lied. 'Of course. How are you?'

'I hope I am not calling too late. May I speak to Oscar?'

'Just a moment.'

He took a sip of his vodka and spilled a couple of drops on his sleeve. Oscar Housman picked up the phone immediately; he must have been standing beside his wife. He had a tired, gravelly voice. 'Good evening,' he said.

'Charles Saint-Clair here.' He carefully planted the code words into his question, the way he had been instructed back home. 'Excuse me for disturbing you at this late hour, but perhaps you have the last commercial agreement between Canada and the Soviet Union?' He waited for a moment for the first codeword to sink in.

'Yes?' Housman said cautiously.

'I heard a rumour,' Grimaldi went on, 'that the Russians might sign a new contract for fish exports with France, and that might allow them to dump Canada and the US via the Common Market.'

There was a short silence at the other end of the line. Housman had understood his message, now he had to acknowledge. 'I have no information about such a contract,' he said calmly. 'But if you wish I can check for you. As for the agreement. I have it in my office.'

'I'll be very grateful if . . .'

'I'll look it up first thing in the morning. But I'm almost sure we benefit from the most favoured nation clause, which means that if they lower their prices for the Europeans, they must do it for us too. I'll check that and call you tomorrow.'

Grimaldi hung off, relieved. Housman had used the 'most favoured nation' and 'Europeans' key words, meaning he had got the message. There was nothing to do now but pack and await the telegram. He gulped down his drink, thinking of Morozov again. Then, pulling the ashtray towards him, he viciously killed his cigar.

The telegram was delivered at his flat at seven fifteen am by a young mailman with red hair and black nails. 'Come back at once. Mother very ill' his alleged sister had cabled from Montreal.

Two hours later he arrived at Sheremetyevo in a fierce rain. His flight was already boarding. He had called earlier, and his boarding pass was waiting at the Air France counter. He went through customs without a hitch, carrying only one bag. He was tieless and wore dark glasses, in spite of the deluge outside. He kept waving his telegram at everybody and it helped; the custom officers and the KGB representative at the Air France counter mournfully shook their heads, spoke to him in low voices and looked at him with compassion. The telegram had suddenly quelled any doubts they might have about his sudden departure.

At the immigration booth, he handed his papers to the uniformed officer, a heavy grey-haired man with a permanent frown lingering over round, suspicious eyes. The officer unhurriedly studied his documents, wetting his sturdy thumb on his tongue. He diligently compared the passport with the Russian visa form, casting long speculative looks at Grimaldi. A shadow fell on his open passport, and he turned round.

Mean black eyes, shaded by thick eyebrows, stared at him from a lean bloodless face. There was ruthless, almost savage power in the sharp jaw and aggressive chin. Yet it was a handsome young face, crowned by wavy brown hair, the nose and lips delicately carved in the waxen skin; the lined forehead and the sensitive mouth suggested inner torment. The odd contrast in the young man's features made Grimaldi think of a Robespierre or a Dzerzhinsky, a fanatic revolutionary so utterly dedicated to the freedom of men that he would readily chop off their heads for it.

Dimitri Morozov hadn't changed much, except for the hair – that had been cropped short when Grimaldi had seen him four years ago. He recalled his shabby clothes at the Bolshoi. Today Morozov was wearing a foreign-made suit of charcoal woollen fabric that fitted him well, a smart blue shirt and striped tie. He shifted his eyes to the immigration officer.

'Charles Saint-Clair,' the KGB officer said to the young civilian. 'Canadian.'

A chill ran up Grimaldi's spine. Morozov picked up the passport. Grimaldi turned back, looking for Morozov's team. They never came alone. He focused on four men in raincoats and hats, clustered by the customs' main counter. They were smoking and conversing in low voices. Stinging sweat prickled his skin and soaked his underclothes. Morozov was playing with him a cat and mouse game. In a moment he would ask him, very politely, to step into the next room, a mere formality, and there they would arrest him, far from the crowd. A closed van with blackened windows would rush him to the Lubyanka where the investigators would be waiting in their underground domain. They might have already done their job on Kalinin.

Morozov thoughtfully leafed through the passport, then raised his eyes, studying Grimaldi's face. His expression didn't change, but there was stark fury burning in the deep-set eyes. He leaned towards the booth and handed the passport, with a nod, to the immigration officer. He was letting him go! Grimaldi stared in disbelief at the uniformed clerk, who laboriously stamped his papers then turned to the next passenger.

Grimaldi felt Morozov's eyes boring into his neck but didn't turn around. He feared another trick. He stepped into the departure hall, looking straight ahead, and stiffly walked to the gate. The place was full of uniformed officers, armed with handguns. Everybody seemed to watch him. He mentally assessed the distance between him and the gate. Twenty yards, ten, five. The ground hostess was nervously smiling at him, he was the last passenger.

'Monsieur Saint-Clair!'

He winced and turned back. Morozov faced him, his arms crossed. His face was impassive. 'I wish your mother a prompt recovery,' he said.

Only after gulping down the third double vodka served by a skinny Air France hostess, did Grimaldi start to recover his senses. From the window he could see the carpet of murky clouds they had pierced, soaring higher into the blue, sunny sky. He was safe now, out of Morozov's reach.

He felt a surge of tremendous hatred for the black-eyed devil who had debased him a few minutes ago, just for fun; he could swear that Morozov had enjoyed scaring the living daylights out of him. Grimaldi had never felt more humiliated. The Russian motherfucker had almost made him shit in his pants, deliberately ridiculing him. Just you wait, Morozov, he thought. We'll meet again, and it will be you biting the dust before me.

Last night, reading Oleg's last message, he had dreamt of revenge. Now it was turning into an obsession, he could feel it in his bones. Not only revenge for what Morozov did to him and Kalinin, but for the damage caused to Grimaldi's career. He ground his teeth, thinking of the debriefing in Langley that would probably start tomorrow. The Company experts would be cruel, merciless, suspicious, and he would have to endure all their insinuations. 'Did you have to escape in such a hurry?' someone would ask. 'Wasn't there any way to rescue Top Hat?' And someone else would pick up from there, 'Perhaps if you had waited another twenty-four hours he would have established contact? Did you seriously consider a different solution? How come you escaped so easily, with Morozov breathing down your neck?'

Even if he emerged from the debriefing unscathed, his hasty escape would tarnish his reputation. The story would trail in his wake, like the rumour of an incurable malady. Why did he stay in Moscow so long? prissy officials would ask in conference rooms. If he had left a year ago, he might have saved the operation and Top Hat as well. Now the Russkies would be able to assess the damage – knowing what subjects Top Hat had dealt with – and in a year or two all the material he'd given would become obsolete.

Grimaldi had to prove he was still valuable. If he wanted to survive, he had to offer his superiors something new, that wouldn't depend on the Top Hat fiasco. And he could think of nothing else but Morozov. He was with Department Thirteen, the most secret unit of Moscow Centre. He was stationed in Paris, under the cover of a Sovtorg employee. If Grimaldi presented the Company with the means to destroy him, he could kill two birds with one stone: defeat Department Thirteen, and settle his personal account with Morozov.

For that, he could use Alexander Gordon. He would serve one brother to the other on a platter, and watch from behind the scenes, lending a helpful hand if needed.

Yes, that could be done. He smiled back at the hostess who brought him a plate of food. The planning of revenge had made him feel definitely better.

It was like hunting the wolverine, Dimitri thought, when you spend hours painstakingly trying to outwit the cunning furry predator. And when you finally succeed in cornering the animal, bring it within your power and start squeezing the trigger, you wait just a split second too long, and the little beast suddenly darts between your feet and makes it to safety. He had hunted the wolverine in Siberia during a two-week endurance exercise with the Untouchables. He remembered the trapped look in the animal's mean eyes. It trembled before him, crouching, waiting for its death. Dimitri felt the intoxicating sensation of power as he stood in the snow, tasting the pleasure of the kill. The trigger had slowly yielded to his steady pressure. He didn't want to fire yet, he enjoyed the moment, he didn't want the chase to end. But the shot had been too late coming, and the wolverine had suddenly darted beside him, into the low bushes and out of view.

Saint-Clair had made it this time, he thought, as he stood on the tarmac, hatless in the furious rain, watching the Air France Boeing head for the low sky. He had escaped because Dimitri had waited, that night at the Bolshoi, and last night at the Ukraina. There was nothing he could do now to prevent the spy from leaving. 'Do you have any evidence against him?' Oktober had asked him yesterday. 'Without evidence, you cannot arrest an eminent Canadian businessman.'

Damn you, Oktober, he thought. Evidence or no evidence, he should have whisked Saint-Clair away last night; he knew how to wrench a confession from the perfumed playboy in no time. He had missed his moment. To arrest the Canadian at the airport, Oktober said, he needed evidence. But the only man who could incriminate Saint-Clair was Colonel Oleg Kalinin. And Kalinin had vanished.

Fuck your mother, Kalinin, Dimitri inwardly cursed. As soon as he had confronted him in Paris, he had realized the GRU colonel was guilty. He hadn't expected Kalinin's visit, and Kalinin hadn't expected to find him there. They had met late at night, at the Sovtorg office on Boulevard Pereire, and while they were discussing operational matters – the kidnapping of a NATO courier on his way to Brussels – Dimitri had suddenly asked about that night at the Bolshoi, four years ago. Kalinin had been caught off guard, and denied everything. They both knew he was lying.

Dimitri had picked up the phone as soon as Kalinin left. He was sure the colonel was going to defect, to save his neck; therefore he had blocked all his escape routes. Kalinin was a damned traitor, he was dead meat, he would run for his life, Dimitri assumed. But Kalinin hadn't tried to escape but had chosen the one destination Dimitri hadn't thought of – back to Russia. By the time Dimitri had landed in Moscow, Kalinin had gone to ground.

He stepped back under the gate marquee, and lit a cigarette, watching the black wake of smoke left by the Boeing. He'd had no choice actually. If he had phoned Moscow Centre from Paris and accused Kalinin of treason, nobody would have believed him. He would have been brought back sedated and tied to a stretcher. From the airport they would have taken him straight to an asylum. Kalinin, after all, was the GRU man at the Kremlin, and no Moscow Centre official would dare touch him without an ironclad case.

There was one man, though, whom Dimitri had trusted: Oktober. On his arrival in Moscow he had rushed to headquarters. But Oktober had shaken his head. 'You can't even approach Kalinin without proof, my boy,' he had croaked. 'And you don't have a case against Saint-Clair.'

Dimitri could guess what had happened. Back in Moscow, Kalinin had probably established contact with Saint-Clair by a crash meeting or a dead letter drop. Dimitri had followed Saint-Clair last night, but had lost him for an hour at the Ukraina. Saint-Clair had vanished from the hotel lobby at two minutes past eight and returned at ten past nine. Soon after, his driver had taken him home. During the unaccountable hour he must have received Kalinin's message.

He wryly mused on the irony of the situation. Saint-Clair's hurried departure was the very proof against Kalinin he so badly needed. He shrugged. He would find Kalinin, sooner or later; and if he handled the traitor wisely, he might even use him as a bait to trap Saint-Clair.

It took his men three months to capture Kalinin, when, wearing an elaborate disguise and carrying a Czech passport, he tried to cross the Czech-Austrian frontier. By then, Dimitri was already back in France, and the Saint-Clair affair had been taken out of his hands. In different circumstances, he would have flown to Moscow and asked to resume the investigation. But the hunt for Kalinin had meanwhile become of limited interest for him – because that same week, Dimitri had come across an amazing revelation that made other matters pale in comparison.

One of Dimitri's major functions was to keep an eye on the various emigré associations that swarmed in Paris like bees on a honeycomb. He had informers in some of the groups, consisting mostly of elderly Ukrainians, Balts and Armenians, meeting in drab unheated halls, saluting dead flags, singing forgotten anthems and reciting pathetic speeches; at times they dressed in ludicrous uniforms, weighted with rusty medals, and solemnly announced the forthcoming liberation of their motherland.

Among all those lunatics, there were a few dangerous leaders, capable of organizing a serious resistance movement. But Department Thirteen was efficiently disposing of those enemies of the Soviet nation, gladly testing on them its latest weapons: electric pistols, poison bullets and untraceable chemical potions.

Dimitri's most amusing occupation was reading the brochures and magazines the emigrés published, scraping together the meagre revenues required to keep them going. One of them, cheerfully christened *Victory is Near*, had a section called 'Soviet Crimes'. It always carried the same stories – the gulags, the great purges, the massacre of the kulaks. The dodos who wrote the articles raised the numbers of communism's victims from one issue to the next, as if another couple of zeroes in the dead toll could send the world on a crusade against Russia. Dimitri's colleagues joked that at this inflation rate, the entire Soviet population would be dead on paper in a couple of years. Perhaps that was the reason the old nutcases called their magazine *Victory is Near*.

In the June issue of the magazine Dimitri found an article about Stalin's massacre of the Jewish writers. He absently perused the paragraph about his mother's execution at the Lubyanka; it was a rehash of old newspaper reports, and said nothing new.

But in a box on the article's second page was an interview with Tanya Gordon's son.

Dr Alexander Gordon, the article said, was one of the brilliant dons of Brown University, at Providence, Rhode Island.

Dr Alexander Gordon, whose face was smiling from a grainy photograph, spoke of his deep love for his mother, and his unsuccessful search, during the last twelve years, for his brother, Dimitri.

He read every word in the article several times, then turned to the picture of the smiling blond man. He picked up a magnifying glass and meticulously studied the photograph of the blond guy, who looked confidently into the camera. He was wearing a shirt with an open collar. A heavy Star of David hung on a chain around his brother's neck and Dimitri clenched his teeth. Another Jew. Still, Jew or no Jew, he was his brother.

He didn't budge from his seat for a long moment, perhaps an hour, mesmerized by his brother's face. Alexander was alive and well. Alexander had been looking for him since he was a child. His brother cared about him.

It was a strange feeling. For the first time in his life, he discovered he was important to somebody. Alexander was his family, they had the same blood. He wondered what kind of man his brother was. Another big-mouthed Jewish activist? An American reactionary? In the interview he didn't express an opinion about the Soviet regime, only spoke of his deep love for Russia.

Keep away from him, his instincts screamed. A Jewish-American brother is the last thing you need. Lesser connections have put an end to many promising careers. You killed a man, back at Panfilov, because you feared he would expose you. Forget about Alexander Gordon, don't meet him, don't call him, don't write to him. Burn this magazine.

Dimitri slowly emerged from his stupor and reached for the phone. His voice was unsteady, strangely muffled; he had to repeat his orders twice, to make himself understood.

Chapter Eleven

The letter from Paris reached Alex on a Friday in August, in the middle of a violent summer storm. Nina wasn't home, and he trod to the door still unshaven, wearing an old bathrobe. Angry thunder roared outside, and white lightning seared the sky.

'Sign here, please, it's registered,' the mailman said, studying him critically, and handed him an airmail envelope. He was wearing yellow oilskins, and his cap dripped water on the foreign stamps. Alex scribbled his name, glancing at the letter; it had been sent to Brown and forwarded to his home address. 'Institut de l'Europe de l'Est – Centre de Récherches', said the heading on the envelope. Alex took the letter to the kitchen, where he was having his morning coffee, although it was almost noon.

The howling winds and the greyness of the pouring rain reflected his morose mood. For the first time in his life, he was idle and listless; his future uncertain. He had graduated in June; Nina had proudly framed his Doctor of Philosophy diploma and hung it over his desk. But his satisfaction had soon degenerated into apathy. Teaching at a prestigious university suddenly seemed to him dull and unexciting. The clash with Claudia, that night at the Waldorf-Astoria, had affected him deeply. Their life together had been the cornerstone of his plans for the future. Without her, he didn't want to go to Stanford; he didn't want to teach at Brown either. And if he took a job at Columbia or in Boston, his life would turn into endless waiting for the occasional weekend she would throw his way, like a bone to a starving dog.

Perhaps the best thing for him was to take a break, go away for a while. But where could he go? His renewed demands for a Soviet visa weren't even answered. He had written to several French and English universities, but the replies had been disappointing. In the middle of the dog days he had left Brown and come home, hoping to see

Claudia. But she was on the road, calling from faraway places like Gainesville, Florida, or Great Falls, Montana. She kept excitedly reporting how successful she was, what superb collections she presented, what she said to Ronnie Havermeyer and what Ronnie Havermeyer said to her. She didn't seem to care about Alex's plans. Anyway, she was due back today; they were going away for the weekend. Perhaps a trip to one of their old haunts in New England might be good for them?

He ripped open the envelope. It contained a letter and a glossy colour brochure. The cover represented a beautiful eighteenth-century mansion with a steep slate roof and sturdy chimneys, a cobbled courtyard before it. Inside there were photographs of libraries, seminars in spacious classrooms, a small lecture hall, and a garden with big shady trees. The caption on the front page was in French, the same as on the envelope. It was easy to understand: Institute of Eastern Europe – Research Centre. An address in the fourth district of Paris was printed underneath.

The letter was written in English.

Dear Dr Gordon,
Allow me to congratulate you on your brilliant graduation from the prestigious Brown University. I hope you are familiar with our Research Centre, which is reputed to be one of the most prominent institutions specializing in Eastern Europe and the Soviet Union.

We maintain constant contact with Brown University, and it came to our attention that you had written a PhD. thesis on 'Stalin's Obsession – the Writers' and Doctors' Trials'. This is a fascinating subject and we have asked the Dean of Brown University to send us a copy of your work for our library.

Besides our 25,000-volume library, we are very proud of our archives which contain a vast array of documents, many of them unique. I believe that you may find a great deal of original material in our archives, if you're interested in some additional research. We have succeeded in obtaining many unpublished documents on Stalin's secret projects for deporting and resettling the Soviet Jews, following the Writers' Trials. As you know, these projects were scuttled by his death in 1953.

Currently we have 12 scholars in residence, most of them from European countries, and one from Canada. I have great pleasure in offering you a one-year scholarship in our Centre, starting October 1, 1974. We cannot, unfortunately, offer you an American salary, but our visiting scholars claim that our scholarship of 7.500 Francs (roughly 1,500 US dollars) a month, plus a subsidy of 75% of housing expenses incurred, is quite adequate. The airfare will also be covered by the Centre. You will have no obligations except to hold a weekly seminar of two hours and give a monthly lecture.

If you accept our offer, please let us know by the end of August. I do hope your answer will be affirmative.
Yours sincerely,
Rene Martineau, Director General.

Alex put down the letter, then picked it up and read it again. He couldn't believe it. He reached for the phone, but there was nobody he could call. Nina had gone to see her doctor; Joey was in Washington, striving to become a reporter; Claudia was on her way back from Georgia. Besides, she wouldn't be very happy to hear about this letter. The wind was wailing outside, fiercely casting a hail of heavy raindrops that clattered on the windows like volleys of buckshot. He peeled the wrapper off a bar of chocolate and, chewing slowly, reread the brochure about the Paris Centre.

It was not a dream, it was for real! Written down, black on white, a wonderful scholarship offer addressed to Dr Gordon. Its timing couldn't be better. A wave of elation gradually peaked inside him, and he leaned back, clasping his hands behind his neck. A year in Paris! He caught his reflection in the window that overlooked the dark wall of the neighbouring house. He was grinning. Life wasn't so bad after all. His luck was turning. A year in Paris was the best thing that could happen to him now. This letter was a godsend, exactly what he had prayed for.

'This letter is exactly what I prayed for,' Grimaldi said, glancing again at the photocopy of the Paris letter before passing it to the Chief of the Soviet Division.

'Really?' Grimaldi's lunch companion at Fernand's wasn't very talkative. Vince Morton was a bearlike man with a fair-skinned wrestler's face, framed by some vestiges of limp blond hair pasted over his bald skull. A big-boned Texan, he had been a defector hunter in Vienna in his younger years, and regarded the KGB as the bad guys in a corpse-strewn Western movie. He had liked Grimaldi's plan of using Alexander Gordon to ensnare Morozov. Now he studied the letter, and finally raised his head. 'That's good, Napoloeone.'

'You know that the Research Centre is a KGB front organization,' Grimaldi pointed out, relishing his baked escargots and dipping a crust of bread in the garlic butter. He sighed with delight. 'You know, Vince, all those years in Moscow I had this dream of eating at Fernand's again.'

Vince raised his head from his T-bone steak. 'What do they need the Centre for?'

Grimaldi shrugged. 'To provide cover for people they want to bring to Paris, maintain a permanent safehouse for their agents, funnel funds into Europe. It's an important operation. The director, Martineau, is an old-timer. Fought in Spain, spent two years in the First Department School at Sverdlovsk.'

How did you hook Morozov?'

'I planted an article about the Jewish writers in the *Victory is Near* magazine, which is financed by us anyway.' A black-haired young man with a sleek, graceful body slipped into a booth across the room and Grimaldi followed him with his eyes.

'Most emigré publications are,' Vince said, laboriously chewing his steak. 'You also planted the Gordon interview?' His voice dropped as an elderly couple passed by their table.

'More or less. The guy who interviewed him is a freelance journalist, paid by us.'

'How did you know that Morozov would read the article?'

'He was bound to read it.' A dapper old man joined the black-haired beauty. Why him and not me? Grimaldi thought. He stared at the boy who responded by a brief, demure grin. He went on: 'The Thirteenth keeps an eye on emigré organizations. Morozov is their representative in Paris, he had to read the article. And if he hadn't' – Grimaldi refilled his glass of Muscadet – 'I would have found some other way to make him meet his brother.'

You're sure he is behind this scholarship offer?'

'Positive,' Grimaldi said, looking up. 'Oh, my main course.'

'A sole meunière for Monsieur,' Fernand announced, placing the dish before Grimaldi. He had aged considerably since Grimaldi had seen him last, but looked as phoney as ever. He fussed around Grimaldi and tried to pour some Muscadet in Morton's glass. Vince grabbed his arm, shaking his head. 'Another beer,' he muttered, and Fernand retreated, his face a mixture of disdain and despair.

Grimaldi picked up his knife and attacked the golden sole with gusto. He was in an ebullient mood. The black premonitions that had tormented him during his flight from Moscow had turned out to be unfounded. On arrival in Washington he had received a hero's welcome; nobody had blamed him for the Moscow mishap, and there was talk of a promotion to a key position in the Soviet Division. In the meantime he had rented an elegant apartment in Watergate. A car

216

and driver from the Langley pool were put at his disposal, and his expense account was liberal.

The very night of his arrival, he had requested Alex Gordon's file from the Company archives. Page by page, he read the material that had accumulated since the boy arrived in New York, more than twenty years before. He leafed through old FBI surveillance reports and memos on Nina's communist activities. Some press cuttings described the deaths of Tonya and Victor Wolf. They were dated 1962. The boy must have been about thirteen then.

This was with a photocopy of a letter the child had written shortly afterwards, to his brother Dimitri in Russia. The letter had been returned by the Russian authorities, and intercepted by the FBI. Another envelope contained a few glossy photographs of Alex Gordon taken at different periods. The first was of a meagre boy of seven or eight; the last of a handsome young man, tall and broad-shouldered, with fair hair, clear eyes and a serious mouth. He was wearing a open-necked shirt and looked very American.

The file also contained records of Gordon's studies at Brown, the rallies he had organized against the Soviet invasion of Czechoslovakia, his excellent grades. Grimaldi was particularly impressed with a paper Gordon had written, in his senior year, about 'the KGB mentality'.

'Americans don't always understand,' Alex Gordon wrote, 'that the Russians, the party leaders in particular, have a different way of thinking. They are haunted by a paranoid fear of conspiracy. They see conspiracy everywhere – among enemies of the regime, ethnic minorities, Balts, Muslims, Armenians, Georgians. They fear dissidents, intellectuals, writers, emigrés. They attribute tremendous powers to those tiny groups. That's why they fill their gulags with intellectuals and dispatch assassination teams all over the globe, to murder old, toothless emigrés who print ridiculous brochures and swear allegiance to phoney Anastasias.

'Most of all, the Russians dread a Western conspiracy. They see a diabolical plot behind every newspaper article or political declaration; they believe Western intelligence might poison the food exported to Russia, or dissolve hallucinatory drugs in their water. They don't trust the free press and employ armies of spies to check and double check any trivial item of information published in the Western newspapers. A press release about a new bridge over the Rhine, for instance, would send every KGB agent running.

'They still suspect Germany, fearing it would attack them again, on America's orders. Their resident agents in London, Paris and Bonn, have standing orders to check the reserves in the hospital blood banks. If the reserves rise, it would be an indication the West is about to launch World War Three. They fear Israel, and believe American policy is conducted by a secret Zionist-capitalist conspiracy . . .'

Grimaldi lit a cigar and puffed the smoke to the ceiling. Alex Gordon was the man he needed. Morozov probably wanted to meet his brother as intensely as Alex yearned to find him. Dimitri must feel affection or at least a blood bond to Alexander. Feeling was a weakness, of course. It clouded one's judgment. Family ties could be a deadly weapon if properly used. If Grimaldi succeeded in turning Gordon into his tool, he would destroy Morozov and avenge Oleg.

But where as Oleg? Since his disappearance, he hadn't established contact. He hadn't used the tiny radio transceiver Grimaldi had given him, or any other means to signal if he was alive and free. Grimaldi spent long nights at the Operations room in Langley, alerting the East European stations, listening to Soviet security forces' transmissions, perusing intelligence reports from the Soviet Bloc. He doggedly explored any avenue that could lead to Top Hat.

Oleg Kalinin had taken a tremendous risk by coming back to Moscow to warn him and save his life. The least Grimaldi could do was try to reciprocate. Until now, though, all his efforts had failed. The only piece of news that could be connected to his friend's fate was a vague item about a middle-aged man, forcibly removed from a train by plainclothes security officers on the Czech-Austrian border. But this could be anybody.

Grimaldi couldn't get Kalinin off his mind. What had happened to his friend? Was he still alive? In the small hours of night, when the Operations room was plunged in half-darkness and the late shift operators dozed in their seats, he would bend over the powerful electronic instruments, standing in line against the wall and watch the green hue of the computer screens, the bluish haze of the radar monitors, the transmitters' blinking red lights, signifying that the coded radio call to Oleg Kalinin was being incessantly repeated. A short message, on a secret wavelength, too brief to be intercepted, too smart to be decoded. 'Top Hat contact base' the message said.

And Grimaldi could imagine the electromagnetic wave whizzing across the Berlin Wall and the bleak plains of Eastern Europe, the wheatfields of the Ukraine and the green hills of Bielorussia, the forests surrounding Moscow, the peaks of the Urals, the Siberian taigas and frozen tundras. He hoped that somewhere beyond the Iron Curtain Oleg Kalinin was still a living, free man, eluding the evil force that pursued him. He hoped Oleg would finally hear the voice whispering into his tiny receiver: Top Hat contact base.

Call base, Top Hat, he prayed in his heart. Stay alive, my Oleg. Don't give in, don't let them beat you, my friend. We'll find you, we'll take you out, and we'll bring you home.

Claudia's reaction to his decision to go to Paris surprised Alex. He hadn't expected her to be so possessive. 'I love you, Claud, but I have to go away for a while,' he said to her, explaining his reasons. 'I feel lousy sitting on my butt all week with nothing to do, hoping you'll come for the weekend.'

She didn't want to listen. Since he'd told her about the scholarship in the dining room of the Connecticut inn where they were spending a weekend, she kept throwing at him the same accusation. 'If you love me, why do you leave me?'

'Jesus H, Claud,' he protested, then lowered his voice. 'You're leaving me every second weekend.'

'This is different,' she flared. The only other couple in the dining room, a tanned, handsome athlete and a lovely black girl, turned and stared at them. 'I am with you all the time, I am calling you, I am writing to you, I am coming back.'

'I'll be with you as well,' he said. The black girl smiled at him. 'I'll call you, and I'll write to you, and in a year we'll be back together.'

'Don't count on it,' she snapped, her eyes burning. 'Don't take me for granted.' She shook her head. 'And stop staring at that woman or else.'

They finally reached a ceasefire and agreed that next June, nine months from now, Claudia would join him in Paris and spend the summer with him. They would then have a serious discussion about the future. But Alex could tell this discussion would never take place. Claudia was drifting away, becoming immersed in her own life, growing easily irritated when in his company. A few times, when she had come back from her travels, they had gone out with some of her model friends and their dates. The girls were stunning indeed, but he soon got fed up with their incessant chirping about divine dresses, divine makeup and divine designers, named Lorenzo, Vittorio or Angelo. Not to mention the divine hairdressers, makeup artists and photographers bearing similar names.

'You don't like my friends,' Claudia said that night in Connecticut, planting her fists on her waist with the same sweet, disturbing gesture he remembered so well from the night they first met. But tonight she wasn't smiling.

'No,' he countered, 'I don't.'

'You'd better get used to them, Doctor, because I like them and I'm going to spend a lot of time with them.'

'Suit yourself,' he shot back, losing his nerve. 'I'm not going to spend any time with them, nor with you. I'm going away.'

'That's true,' she said, suddenly reflective. 'You're going away. And you have no idea how far away you're going.'

The fight ended in bed, sex having become a temporary panacea for all their bitterness. But even sex wasn't fun anymore for two people exhausted from hurting each other.

They clashed and argued every weekend they spent together, until the summer heat was blown away by the chilly winds of September. And the day after their last fight, Nina and Claudia drove Alex to Kennedy airport.

At the security check point, in TWA's new terminal, Alex turned back and hugged Nina. The old woman tried to smile at him through her tears. She looked awful, he thought, as he held tight to her frail, brittle body. Her hair had turned completely white, her cheeks had hollowed, and an opaque hue dulled her irises. She wasn't well lately; her ulcer was tormenting her all day long. Since her retirement, she barely left the house except for visits to Doctor Sapirstein. But today she had insisted on accompanying him to the airport, although she had to share him with Claudia, an arrangement she disliked intensely.

'I am happy for you, *golubchek*, really. You'll have a wonderful time in Paris. You did the right thing.' She kissed him on both cheeks and repeated forcefully: 'The right thing.' The old girl was happy he was getting away from Claudia. The ancient rivalry of the two women had erupted again lately, when Nina realized how deeply Claudia had hurt him.

He turned to her. She was pale and upset. Anger showed in her face. She had cut her hair short this morning, and he was sure she had done it to spite him. She knew he loved her hair long and soft. Perhaps she was trying to tell him something, erase the image of a certain Claudia that had existed for him until now. He held her tight, her body was stiff, hostile.

'I love you,' he whispered in her ear. Nina had tactfully taken a few steps back, displaying sudden interest in a long line of magazines on the newsstand rack.

'If you do you shouldn't go away,' Claudia said stubbornly.

He kissed her again, and waved at Nina. He went through security, then proceeded to his gate without looking back. His throat was constricted, he felt a sense of tremendous loss. He tried not to think about Claudia, and concentrate instead on what lay ahead. His flight was already being paged. Alex boarded the 707 and took his aisle seat. He flipped through the in-flight magazine, but Claudia was on his mind, and he had to read the same phrase several times to grasp its meaning. Today I lost Claudia, he thought.

He looked around. There were very few passengers on the flight, but the seat beside him was occupied. His neighbour was a man in his fifties, dandyishly dressed in a blue blazer suit over a flowered waistcoat, a silk shirt and polka dotted bow tie. He was liberally sprayed with cologne. His tanned face, adorned by a Clark Gable moustache, was lit by a pair of cunning green eyes. He wore heavy golden rings on his manicured fingers.

'I guess we're going to travel together,' the stranger said. 'My name is Grimaldi, Franco Grimaldi.'

During the long flight to Paris Alex discovered that in spite of his flamboyant looks, Grimaldi was a fascinating man. Over dinner his new acquaintance told him about his life. He was with the United States Information Service, and had travelled a lot. He had lived in Berlin, London and Paris, and not long ago had returned from a tour of duty in Moscow.

The mention of the city of his birth aroused Alex's curiosity, and he assailed his companion with questions. Grimaldi answered with good grace, slipping here and there a question of his own. Only when their plane started its descent towards Charles de Gaulle airport did Alex realize that he had talked even more than Grimaldi, telling him everything about his parents, his lost brother, his scholarship, even about Nina and Claudia. He attributed this gregarious behaviour to the unusual amount of drink he had consumed. Grimaldi kept ordering double vodkas for both of them, swallowing his in single gulps, the Russian way. Alex had soon joined him in shouting '*Nazdorovye!*' and slapping his back. That had lasted all through the flight. A fine fellow Grimaldi, a real man of the world, and he even spoke some Russian!

They parted at the airport, not before Grimaldi had given him the address of his hotel, the Intercontinental at Place Vendôme, and his telephone number at the embassy. Grimaldi then wrote in his diary the phone number for the Centre for East European Studies. Yes, he had heard of it; a fine institution indeed.

Grimaldi offered to share a taxi to Paris, but Alex politely declined. He had heard so much about the City of Light, he wanted to enter it alone and enjoy its sights to the full. He hailed a cab, a Peugeot that looked very small on the outside, but was surprisingly spacious once he got in. It was early morning, the sky was clear, and the first sunbeams cast a golden hue on the fabulous city. Alex's cab was driven by a stout Parisian with a red face and bleary eyes, who kept growling and lamenting all through their trip. The Frenchman addressed his irate complaints to his huge German Shepherd that sat enthroned on the passenger seat, suspiciously eyeing Alex and ominously licking his lips.

They entered Paris by the Porte de la Chapelle. Alex stared in wonder at the massive old houses, the lively markets set on small squares or branching off into side streets. The autumn was at the peak of its beauty. It had painted the foliage of the trees lining the boulevards in shades of yellow, brown and magenta. The leaves kept falling on the pavements, covering the cobbles with a golden carpet. The Parisians didn't look a very cheerful lot. The men were grave-faced, conservatively dressed; the women slim and graceful, wearing their clothes with a haughty air.

As the cab progressed into Paris, the architecture improved. Brass, glass and lights gleamed from crowded cafes and brasseries; he saw some opulent furniture shops, and a few exquisite boutiques. Small cars, mostly Peugeots, Renaults and Citroens, darted swiftly beside them, displaying a Gallic indifference for the traffic laws. Choleric drivers stuck their heads out of car windows, glowering at each other, and exchanged saucy opinions about their respective mothers and sisters, accompanied by eloquent gestures.

A beautiful church, crowned with domes and turrets, was perched on top of a hill. He had seen it in pictures so many times before; he knew this was the Sacré-Coeur, and the hill was Montmartre, the famous artists' colony. In front of them, the Eiffel Tower sailed through the morning haze. They passed by the Madeleine, a huge grey church modelled after a Greek temple, and crossed a huge square in the middle of which stood a sleek Egyptian obelisk, covered with gold-painted hieroglyphs. On his right, he briefly glimpsed the Champs Elysées and the Arc de Triomphe.

They turned left on the bank of the Seine. The muddy waters of the river were spanned by a succession of beautiful bridges built in different styles. A couple stood kissing abandonedly by the riverfront. A long barge emerged under a vaulted bridge on their right, and Alex remembered with a pang that night with Claudia at the Waldorf Astoria. There had been a watercolour painting of a Seine barge hanging in their suite.

The cab turned into a maze of narrow streets, lined with very old houses and unusual monuments, churches and small *hôtels particuliers*. He was shocked to see a golden horse's head, the trademark of a horse butchery. The cab entered the courtyard of a sprawling mansion whose stone walls had been restored to their original whiteness. A large veranda, paved with rectangular flagstones, led to a double wooden door, painted light brown. Alex knew the place from the brochure he had read countless times back in Brooklyn. This was the Centre for East European Studies.

He carried his suitcase into the building. In the lobby he passed two young men in polo shirts and neatly pressed jeans who were heatedly discussing, in French, the relationship between Lenin and his wife, Krupskaya. The director's office was on the ground floor, guarded by two secretaries busy torturing their typewriters. He introduced himself, and the elder of the two, a silver-haired woman with a receding chin, stared at him stonily.

He repeated his name.

'Oh, Monsieur Gordon,' she finally said, 'we didn't expect you so early.'

She disappeared through an inner door and he overheard a quick exchange; beside the secretary two other men spoke urgently. A door creaked open and slammed shut – apparently a second door to the director's office – and the secretary was back.

'Mr Martineau will see you now,' she said coldly. There were beads of sweat on her upper lip.

Alex knocked and walked into the inner office. Even before shaking Martineau's hand, he cast a quick look about the room. There was indeed another door in the far wall. In the ashtray on the director's desk were two crushed cigarettes of different brands. One was 'blond', American-made, and the other a stinking Gauloise that the French call 'brune'. A package of Kent cigarettes and a lighter lay beside the ashtray. The Gauloise, therefore, belonged to the visitor who had left in such a hurry.

'Monsieur Gordon, welcome to Paris and to our institute.'

Martineau was a thin man with a pale narrow face and limp black hair. His brown eyes, magnified by wire-rimmed glasses, blinked repeatedly, betraying an odd nervousness. The double-breasted jacket of his suit hung loosely on his spare frame. He shook Alex's hand limply. 'We didn't expect you so early,' he said apologetically, and blinked again.

'I took the night flight.'

'Yes, yes, I understand.'

Martineau sat down behind his desk, ramrod straight. Papers, files, magazines, were stacked on the large desk in neat, tidy piles. A narrow wooden tray contained sharpened pencils; another was full of paperclips. A large map of Eastern Europe and the Soviet Union hung behind Martineau's chair.

The director gradually relaxed as their conversation progressed. He explained the institute's rules to Alex, and briefed him on the technical aspects of his stay in Paris. He suggested that Alex might rent one of the apartments the institute's former scholars had used, as they all were in good areas and kept in excellent condition. Alex agreed, and parted from Martineau with a promise to have lunch with him by the end of the week.

Half an hour later he was in a cab again, house hunting through Paris. He was shown a few apartments in different parts of the city, one not far from the Opéra, a couple of others off the Champs Elysées. He picked the fourth for two reasons: it was on the left bank, in the very heart of the student quarter; and it was perched on top of a seven-storey building, its windows offering a breathtaking view of Notre-Dame and the turrets, ramparts and needle-sharp spires of the Ile de la Cité.

He had lunch at the famous Brasserie Lipp, on the boulevard Saint Germain. He got a table on the covered terrace, that commanded a good view of the old church and the crowd of writers, models and movie stars clustered around the Café des Deux Magots, across the street.

He ordered a choucroute – hot sauerkraut with cold cuts – which was the house speciality. The waiter ushered two elderly gentlemen to the table next to his. He estimated their ages as between sixty-five and seventy. He couldn't help overhearing their conversation. His highschool French had been improved and brushed up at Brown, and he found no trouble following the grandfathers' dialogue.

'*Cher ami,*' one of them was saying to the other, his handsome, leonine face glowing, 'I am in love.'

His friend, florid-faced and white-haired, leaned forward. 'Tell me about her.'

The happy lover started describing his Dulcinea – the way she looked, the way her eyes sparkled in the morning, the colour of her hair, the velvety feel of her skin. He talked with passion of the way she spoke, the colours she liked to wear, her taste in books and poems. He painted the sunlight in her face, the play of the wind in her hair as they strolled in the park, the softness of her voice, the magic of her touch. 'She reminds me at times of that verse of Baudelaire,' he said, quoting from memory. His friend countered by quoting another famous poet. The old man – and young lover – spoke for more than an hour, his friend listening, enraptured, interrupting the passionate exposé with an occasional question.

This is Paris, Alex inwardly sighed, as he watched the two grand old men talking with such passion about a love affair. He recalled another conversation he had overheard in a Manhattan restaurant, a couple of weeks ago: his neighbours were two young men, no older than thirty. 'Listen,' one of them had said. He was dressed in an expensive suit and a silk tie. 'Last night I picked up a girl at the Rendezvous bar. She was something, I tell you.'

'Was she a good lay?' his friend asked. They both brayed with laughter, then switched the subject to the Stock Market.

That must be the difference between the French and the Americans, Alex decided, sipping his espresso. The French remain incurably romantic till their last breath, while we get cynical, or perhaps ashamed of our feelings, even before we come of age.

He paid his bill, adding a tip which apparently was too generous, and left, escorted to the door by a very grateful waiter who desperately sought reassurance that he would come again. The air was crisp and invigorating. He felt good on this first day in Paris. He had arrived in the best of seasons, had found a great apartment, and witnessed the French cult of love, brilliantly displayed by two old and forever young Parisians.

Back at the institute, an antique elevator panted and moaned all the way up to the library on the top floor. Here he felt at home. He wandered between the overloaded stacks, relishing the dusty smell of old books, leafing through rare volumes of Russian history. The library was outstanding indeed, a fine collection of Russian history.

On a side shelf he found a book he hadn't known existed: the minutes of the Writers' Trial in 1949. His father's trial. He picked up the heavy volume and was about to take it to one of the desks when a rustling sound behind him made him turn. He took a sharp intake of breath. Before him stood one of the most beautiful girls he had ever seen.

He drank in her beauty, rooted to the spot. Her face was so lovely and yet so full of sadness that he felt the urge to possess and protect her, all at the same time. The face could have belonged to a Greek goddess, with its clear forehead, high cheekbones, and chiselled, passionate mouth. Her upper lip was slightly drawn up into an oval line. It was the mouth of the ravishing little Princess Bolkonsky, as Tolstoy had described it in *War and Peace*. Her skin was white, luminous, bestowing an ethereal glow upon the oval face and graceful throat.

From that pure face stared huge, deep blue eyes, imbued with innocence and unfathomable grief. They made her look so vulnerable, so forlorn, that Alex felt an instinctive craving to do all he could to dispel that profound sorrow. Yet there was something enigmatic in the expression of her eyes, some secret knowledge that made her distant and unreachable.

Her blonde hair was woven in a heavy plait that topped her head like a crown of ancient gold. Her slim, small-breasted body and delicate limbs made him think of an elf. Her black shirt and trousers clung to her skin. The combined traits of ripe beauty, innocence and vulnerability cast a strange spell.

That was how his mother might have looked, he suddenly thought. Blonde, blue-eyed and pure at heart; romantic and innocent, a dreamer child lost in a cruel, cynical world.

'*Bonjour.*' He smiled. His voice was unsteady.

She looked at him gravely. '*Bonjour.*'

'I am Alex Gordon,' he said. 'I arrived this morning from New York. I'm going to do some research here as a visiting scholar.'

She nodded earnestly like a little girl. A bearded student passed by them holding an open book, and greeted her with a smile.

'And you,' asked Alex, desperately racking his brains for a clever remark and failing, 'who are you?'

'My name is Tatiana.' Her voice was clear and pleasant.

'Russian? I am Russian, too.'

A brief smile transformed her face. 'I was born in Paris. My parents were Russian immigrants.'

'What's your last name?'

'Romanov.'

He raised his eyebrows. 'You're connected to the Czar's family?'

'Distantly,' she said, her mouth tightening. Apparently she didn't want to talk about that subject.

'So you really are a princess!' he exclaimed, so spontaneously that she couldn't help smiling. A student wearing glasses and a chequered sweater tried to squeeze by them, and she stepped aside, leading Alex to one of the windows that overlooked the back garden. She walked with a slight limp. It made her even more endearing, enhancing her vulnerability.

He switched to Russian. 'You work at the Institute?'

She shook her head, holding her books against her. 'I am writing a thesis on the Russian Civil War for my degree at the Ecole des Langues Orientales. I only use the library.'

She told him her research dealt with the White Armies, financed by the West, that had tried to smother the October Revolution after 1917. She worked at the library daily, from four pm till closing at eight. She had a part-time job as interpreter for several Soviet companies represented in Paris.

'And the Soviets employ a Romanov?' Alex asked, surprised. 'They don't mind your being related to the Czar's family?'

She shrugged, gave a brief smile. 'On the contrary, they seem to be very pleased to tell everybody that a Russian . . .'

'Aristocrat?' he suggested.

'. . . well' – she didn't seem to like the word – 'that a grand-niece of Czar Nikolai is working for them now. This is the best proof that they won, isn't it?'

Her voice was sarcastic, and he chose to change the subject. 'I've just found a nice apartment in the Latin Quarter,' he said. 'Where do you live?'

'Not far,' she said cryptically.

I would like . . .' he started, but was interrupted by the library clerk who popped up beside them. 'Will you please keep quiet?' he asked angrily. He was a small, mousy man with bad teeth. 'This is a library, not a cafe.'

'Excuse me,' Alex said, then turned back to the girl. Her face had gone red. 'Will you have a cup of coffee with me?'

'I'd like that,' she said seriously.

They found a corner table in the old-fashioned bistro across the street from the institute. An elderly waiter served them two café-crèmes. Tatiana spoke very little. Alex did most of the talking, narrating his life story, describing his quest for his lost brother. When he mentioned his parents' deaths, she paled. 'Many of my relatives were shot by the communists,' she said.

The old waiter started placing cutlery, wine glasses and paper napkins on the tables. Alex glanced at his watch. It was almost eight. 'Let's have dinner together,' he suggested.

She seemed taken aback. 'I can't,' she said. 'I've got to go.' She vanished so quickly that later he wondered if he really had met her or if it had been a dream.

In his new home, that night, he tossed in his bed, bathed in sweat, and threw the long French bolster on the floor. Tomorrow he'd buy a normal pillow, he thought. Tomorrow he might see Tatiana again. He recalled those nights years ago when he was only seventeen and couldn't sleep for thinking of Claudia. Tatiana was the opposite of Claudia in every way – her colouring, her slight build, her vulnerability. Claudia had always been a streetwise kid, aware of her sensuality, exuding an animal attraction. She was cheerful and relaxed, able to take care of herself and have her own way in any situation. She didn't need a man's protection.

Tatiana did. She looked innocent as the newborn day. She made him want to rescue her from real or imaginary dangers. He tried to imagine Claudia's reaction if he told her his head had been turned by a Russian girl with golden hair, but her face had faded from his memory. And out of the Parisian night sailed before him the face of the beguiling, tormented Tatiana.

When she entered the library the following afternoon, he was waiting for her. It was raining outside, a typical Paris drizzle, and she wore a black military-style raincoat over a loose white blouse and tight black skirt. She seemed pleased to see him, but when he mentioned dinner she declined again. 'Perhaps tomorrow,' she finally said, 'when the library closes.'

The following day, which was a Wednesday, he came to the library again. He saw Tatiana at a desk by the window and waved at her, but chose a seat at the far side. He didn't want to make a nuisance of himself. He decided to pass by her desk only after the attendant announced the library was closing.

At five minutes before eight, she suddenly appeared by his side. 'Somebody offered me dinner or a drink,' she said cheerfully. 'Does the offer still stand?'

He looked at her in surprise. Her gaiety seemed artificial, her smile forced. But he was overwhelmed by her accepting his invitation. 'The offer is valid,' he announced. 'Where would you like to go?'

'If you don't mind, I would like to walk a little,' she said. 'It's a beautiful evening.'

At the porch, he looked at the starry sky. Yesterday's rain was gone, the air was cool and dry.

'I bet you haven't strolled through Paris yet,' she said softly. 'It's the most enchanting place in the world.'

'Do you think . . .' he started, involuntarily glancing at her left foot which she dragged almost imperceptibly.

'You mean my limp?' she asked. His face flushed with embarrassment. Damn your big mouth, Alex Gordon, he thought.

But she wasn't embarrassed. 'I am all right,' she said, 'I can walk for hours. I was born with a deformity in my left foot. A doctor tells me all I need is a simple operation.'

'So why don't you do it?' he said, trying to sound casual. They emerged into the street and turned left. Two nuns passed by them, their heads bowed.

'Money,' she said. 'It costs money, you know, and even a Romanova can be very poor nowadays.'

They walked side by side in the quiet streets, and he thought they looked a couple of Parisian lovers, he in a woollen shirt and casual jacket, she in tight jeans and flat-heeled boots. They stopped briefly at the magnificent Place des Vosges. His eyes swept in wonder the thirty-six ancient mansions surrounding the garden and its four foundations. They stood under the statue of King Louis XIII, and she explained the history of the famous square.

'This way,' she said, after describing the famous duel between two groups of French noblemen, fought under the windows of Cardinal

Richelieu in the seventeenth century. They passed by the house of Victor Hugo, the author of *Les Miserables*, reached the Seine and crossed the river by a narrow bridge. Underneath the water dully gleamed and the dark shadow of a barge silently slid upon its wavering surface.

'We are on the Ile Saint Louis now,' Tatiana said, leading the way through a labyrinth of picturesque lanes. They passed by several restaurants with large picture windows; young people were sitting around massive wooden tables, laden with cold meat, raw vegetables and bottles of wine. One of the diners raised his glass to Tatiana. A couple was kissing beside a poster of Jacques Brel.

He took her by the hand. She didn't object but her fingers lay limp in his, unresponsive to his touch. Still, Alex was overjoyed. Here he was, in a beautiful Paris night, walking hand in hand with this stunning girl. Tatiana spoke Russian with a soft French accent that made his native tongue sound like music. She told him a little about herself. She was twenty-two, the only daughter of Vladimir Romanov, and the grandchild of the Grand Duke Evgenyi Romanov, who had escaped the Royal Palace and his cousin Nikolai's fate as a young man. Her mother was ill and had spent most of the last year at the American Hospital in Neuilly.

She abruptly fell silent. He turned back to her but she had stopped in her tracks, staring fixedly ahead. They were in a dark cobbled street that ran alongside the river. There were no shops or cafes as far as he could see, and the place was very quiet, very peaceful. Still, Alex felt vaguely alarmed. What were they doing here? he wondered. There was nothing here but darkness.

'Tatiana,' he started, but she kept gazing into the dark. She suddenly pressed his fingers, very hard, as if trying to convey a message; then she pulled her hand away and took a step back, her eyes still focused on the same spot.

He followed her look. Out of a porch's black shadow, a man stepped forward and stood facing him. At that moment a bâteau-mouche – a pleasure craft, loaded with tourists – passed on the river and its powerful floodlight swept the street, briefly painting the stranger in a ghastly white light. He was of about the same height as Alex, with a shock of black hair, and burning black eyes sunk deep in a very pale, sharp-lined face. He was dressed in a dark suit, and a black coat was thrown on his shoulders. Could he be a bandit, a thief? Would Tatiana lure him into a trap? Ridiculous, he thought. He had nothing worth stealing, and she could have landed fatter prey if she had wanted.

Alex stopped in the middle of the street, undecided. He glanced back at Tatiana; she was leaning on a wall, her arms around herself.

Her head was lowered. In the building on Alex's left, a woman loudly shouted and a man answered. Quite close a car passed by, its engine hoarsely coughing. Then there was silence.

The stranger approached slowly, his footsteps echoing on the pavement, until he came face to face with Alex.

'I am your brother,' he said.

Chapter Twelve

Alex stared at the dark silhouette facing him, his stunned mind failing to digest the single phrase spoken in clear, crisp Russian. I am your brother. A strange chill made him shiver, and he tried to speak but couldn't. His feet were nailed to the cobblestones. The pale young man before him also seemed deeply disturbed. He took a pack of Gauloises from his pocket, and spent a few matches trying to light one. His fingers were trembling in the flickering light of the flame. The man offered the package to Alex, but he shook his head.

'Dimitri?' he managed at last, swallowing painfully.

The young man nodded. 'I am Dimitri Morozov,' he said.

'Dimitri . . . I don't believe it!'

Emerging from his stupor, Alex took a couple of steps forward and clumsily hugged Dimitri. It didn't seem right, though, it was an artificial gesture, like embracing a total stranger. His brother's torso was stiff, unyielding. Dimitri looked embarrassed, and his hands feebly patted Alex's shoulders. Alex had seen this moment in his dreams endless times. He had played and replayed in his mind the reunion with his brother; he had visualized their fierce hug and brotherly kiss, the surge of wild, overwhelming joy. It hadn't happened exactly as he had fantasized it; nevertheless, his quest was over. He had a brother, he had found Dimitri! Or, rather, Dimitri had found him.

'How did you find me?' Alex asked. The last few minutes resurfacing in his memory, he veered round, looking for Tatiana. She had disappeared. He turned to Dimitri again.

'Through Tatiana Romanova,' said his brother. 'We're working together.' He nervously drew on his cigarette. 'Yesterday she told me about you. I was amazed. I couldn't believe my ears. I didn't sleep all night. I finally asked her to set up a meeting between us. I wanted it to be a surprise.' He let out a short, dry laugh.

'Where is she? Where did she go?'

Dimitri shrugged, exhaling white, acrid smoke. 'I suppose she wanted to leave us alone. We have a lot to talk about, Alexander.'

'What are you doing in Paris?' he asked. 'Why didn't you answer my letters?' Now that he had recovered the faculty of speech, the questions were pouring out. He clasped his brother's arms. 'Do you know you have an aunt in New York? Nina, our mother's sister? Did you hear that I was refused an entry visa to Russia?' He paused, shaking his head in wonder. 'I don't believe it. I arrived here three days ago and now here I am, standing in the middle of the street, with . . . with my brother. Do you know that I've been trying to find you for fifteen years?'

Tonya Gordon should have seen her sons now, he thought, alive, safe, meeting after so many years. What would she have said? And his father? He recalled a verse from his father's poem, dedicated to the heroes of Stalingrad. 'Brothers', Victor Wolf had named the Red Army soldiers.

Each ready to die for his brother,
Each willing to give him his life –
With his body to stop the enemy's bullet
That his brother's heart seeks to destroy.
For brotherly love is unselfish and pure,
And brothers forever are one.

Oh, father, Alex thought, if you could only be by my side. You would have understood my feelings. For brothers forever are one.

A car turned the corner into the street and roared towards them. They hurriedly stepped aside.

'Let's go somewhere we can talk,' Dimitri offered.

'Do you know that they killed our mother?'

Dimitri nodded. 'They killed my father too.'

Alex winced. 'I didn't know. How did it happen?'

'Let's go somewhere,' Dimitri said again, 'we have so much to talk about.' He dropped his cigarette on the pavement and crushed it with his heel. 'I want a place with lights, and food, and people. This is a great day. A reunion after more than twenty years. I want to get drunk. Let's celebrate.'

'Yes, let's drink to it,' Alex said. He felt a little uneasy. His brother's words sounded fine, but the reserved tone in which they were uttered didn't quite match up.

They hailed a taxi at the Pont de Sully. By the fuzzy light of the streetlamps Alex studied his brother. Dimitri was one or two inches shorter, with powerful shoulders and strong arms that even the well-cut suit couldn't conceal. His handsome profile, crowned with a thick mass of black hair, carried a romantic air; still, the eyes were hard, even mean. Bitter lines bracketed his mouth. He had a small mole over his upper lip. But there was something else in his brother's face that vaguely disturbed Alex. It was a controlled face, its expression carefully composed, mouth sealed, eyes guarded, refusing to betray any spontaneous feeling.

'You still live in Russia?' Alex asked in the cab.

Dimitri nodded, casting a quick glance at the driver. 'I represent a Soviet company in Paris,' he said.

'Which company?'

Again the short pause. 'Sovtorg, foreign trade.'

'You live in Paris?'

'Yes. And you?'

The taxi double-parked on the bustling Boulevard de Montparnasse. Dimitri paid the driver with a hundred franc bill he peeled from a thick wad of money. The restaurant was a huge, brightly-lit hall, packed with people, most of them young. It hummed with laughter and animated talk, like a giant beehive. People were walking in and out all the time, casually dressed students and unshaven artists mixing with bejewelled women in fur coats and men in expensive suits and bow ties. Overburdened waiters, in black waistcoats and long white aprons, carried trays laden with food, leaving in their wakes tantalizing smells. Dimitri led the way through the bar whose walls were covered with posters of paintings by Picasso, Toulouse-Lautrec and Magritte.

'I like this.' Alex smiled as they sat down at a table by the far wall. 'Let's have some champagne.'

Dimitri hesitated a second, looking around him with a fixed smile; his eyes were watchful, alert. Across the aisle, a waiter uncorked a champagne bottle that spurted white foam, and two long-legged girls in short skirts squealed with delight.

'Champagne it is!' Dimitri announced. They ordered their dinner, each scrutinising the other. In the bright light, Alex drank in every detail in his brother's face. He was a handsome brother, there was no doubt, although rather stiff and reserved. He was well dressed, in a blue suit, snow-white shirt and silk tie. If you looked very closely, Alex thought, you might notice some common traits – the high forehead, the full mouth, the straight nose. There was something vaguely familiar in the shape of Dimitri's eyes. Otherwise they didn't look much alike, not in colouring, features, and certainly not clothes. Alex was casually dressed in baggy light grey tweeds and a comfortable navy blue shirt with an open neck.

The waiter opened the champagne. They raised their glasses, smiling at each other. 'To my dear, dear brother,' Alex said impulsively. He reached across the table and squeezed Dimitri's shoulder. 'I feel I'm in a dream.' He took a sip of champagne.

'To you, Alexander.'

'Everybody calls me Alex.'

'To Alex, then,' Dimitri announced, warmly smiling back. His brief smile made him look absurdly young and mischievous. A group of black men, elegantly dressed and speaking a soft African dialect, settled beside them. Across the aisle sat a middle-aged couple, a woman in glasses and shabby clothes, and a broad-shouldered, balding man with a beer gut. He was struggling with the crust of melted cheese and croutons sealing a bowl of onion soup. A stout woman with a red face and plump forearms was passing between the tables, selling cellophane-wrapped roses.

Alex leaned towards his brother. 'Now, Dimitri, I want to hear everything that happened to you since we were separated.'

'What do you want to know?' Dimitri asked, watching him with a crooked smile over the rim of his glasses.

'Everything,' Alex said eagerly. 'You can't remember me, you were too little when we separated. What is your earliest memory?'

'A stinking orphanage,' Dimitri said viciously, just to test his brother's reaction.

Alex seemed shocked. 'An orphanage?' he repeated, his voice pained. 'Good Lord, Dimitri, it must have been hell.'

So this is my brother, Dimitri thought, studying the tall blond man who watched him with trusting, compassionate eyes. He had never seen such vivid grey eyes, sparkling with intelligence and curiosity. His brother's smile was frank and engaging, yet the strong jaw and dimpled chin revealed a stubborn streak. Alex had an athletic build and looked well even in his old, crumpled jacket. His most striking features, however, were not his good looks, but the warmth and candour he exuded. His smile lit up his entire face; at other times his eyes were veiled, assuming a dreamy look. My brother is a poet, Dimitri chuckled inwardly, one of these innocent well-meaning suckers I used to eat for breakfast.

'Do you ever write poetry?' he abruptly asked.

Alex smiled. 'Once in a while, in my spare time. I think it's a family streak. And you?'

For a moment Dimitri felt a pang of black anger. The bloody sissy can afford to be nice and innocent, he thought, and write poems in his spare time. He's had a cosy and sheltered life since he was a baby, growing up in the affluence and comfort of America, while I was starving in my freezing stable.

The thing he really hated about Alex, though, was his late father's attachment to him. Boris Morozov had taken an enormous risk, back in 1953, to smuggle the boy out of Russia and send him to America. It could have cost Morozov his life. Perhaps it did. Why did he do it? Because of Tonya Gordon? Because he loved her boy? The little Jew landed in New York, Dimitri mused, while I was thrown to the dogs. Watching now the handsome, confident man in front of him, he felt a surge of jealousy.

But his resentment soon simmered down, melted by the disarming warmth of Alex. In a way, Dimitri thought, it was much better to have a nice guy for a brother than to confront a streetwise, scheming bastard like himself. With Alex, he could bring down his guard, he had nothing to fear. He had been embarrassed by his brother's attempt to hug him when they met by the Seine, but it was only natural. Nobody, except for Tatiana and a few other women, had ever shown him any outward sign of affection.

He resumed his narrative, spoke briefly of his father's execution without revealing that it had been caused by Tonya's crimes. Alex seemed genuinely shocked. He spontaneously squeezed Dimitri's hand. 'I'm so sorry, Dimitri. I think I remember him – a tall, dark-haired man.'

Dimitri spoke for a long time, through the champagne, the dinner and the coffee, carefully editing his story, omitting the thefts and the murder in the quarry, substituting a well-rehearsed yarn about university studies and official missions instead of his KGB training and his operations throughout Europe.

He didn't tell Alex either that he had read about him in the *Victory is Near* magazine, and had hurried back to Moscow where, after pulling some strings, he had finally discovered his brother's KGB file, containing some of his letters, his visa applications and reports of agents who had occasionally checked on him in New York. The file was the best proof that Alex was sincere. He had been trying for years to come to Russia and find Dimitri. 'I thought you were dead,' he said to Alex, draining his glass. 'I never received a letter from you, and nobody knew what had happened to you after Mother's death.'

'Somebody must have destroyed my letters,' Alex remarked. 'Somebody very powerful and very evil.'

'They didn't want us to meet,' Dimitri agreed.

'Who are "they"?'

Dimitri didn't answer.

It was a pleasant dinner, and gradually they unwound. They burst into laughter when they both ordered the chocolate mousse, and discovered that both of them were addicted to chocolate. 'This comes from Mother,' Alex said knowingly.

When the ancient clock hanging on the wall chimed three times, and the waiters, looking at them with jaundiced eyes, began piling the chairs upon the tables, they realized they were the last diners left in the restaurant. By that time Dimitri had started to enjoy their conversation. It was Alex's turn now, and he was telling his life story with such passion that Dimitri wanted to hear more.

Besides, for the first time in his life he felt he could relax and talk to the young man facing him, without fearing his intentions. He could turn his back on him – what a luxury – without risking a knife. Everybody else he knew was a potential enemy. The agents of the Western services would riddle him with bullets if they knew he was the assassin who left behind a trail of bodies with broken necks. His colleagues at Department Thirteen would tread on his corpse without thinking twice, to climb higher in the KGB hierarchy. His mentor Oktober could send him to his death with as much remorse as he felt stepping on a cockroach.

Alex was different. With him Dimitri felt even safer than with Tatiana; and Tatiana was the only human being he had ever loved. But with Tatiana he had to be careful, and watch his mouth; after all, she was from an emigré family, and on top of that a Romanov!

Alex, he knew, wouldn't plot behind his back; he didn't want anything from him, and wished him well. He was family, he was his brother. It was a strange feeling, that both confused and pleased Dimitri. A feeling reassuring because it was safe and yet upsetting because it was a secret he had to conceal from the KGB; a feeling tempting and scaring, soothing and disturbing, like a secret sin, forbidden and yet delightful.

When they left the restaurant, he told Alex, 'If you meet other Soviet citizens, don't tell them you're my brother.'

He frowned. 'But I mentioned you in all my letters and my visa applications.'

'I know. It must be the reason you didn't get a visa. Anyway, they might know I have a brother in America, but they shouldn't know I met him in Paris. In our foreign service fraternization with non-Russians isn't encouraged, and you are an American now. I could be recalled home for less than that.'

'Fine,' Alex said. 'Let's say that I needed some figures for my research, I called Sovtorg, and we met.'

Dimitri nodded. They crossed the street and turned left.

'But what about Tatiana?' Alex said.

'I'll take care of her.'

Dimitri took Alex to a small all-night bar on the Rue Vavin where they continued their conversation over a bottle of cognac. In the background, concealed loudspeakers diffused cool jazz arrangements by Jerry Mulligan.

Dimitri didn't mention, of course, his hatred for the Jews, and most of all for Tonya Gordon. Still, when the liquor had slightly eroded his defences, he pointed to the Star of David hanging on a chain from his brother's neck. 'You wear this all the time?'

Alex seemed surprised. 'Of course,' he said. 'It's Mother's. We are Jews, aren't we?'

'My father was Russian,' Dimitri said quickly.

'It doesn't make any difference,' Alex remarked. 'According to the Jewish faith, it's the mother who counts.'

Dimitri clenched his teeth. He was aware of the Jewish tradition, although he had been trying to bury that infuriating knowledge in the deepest recesses of his mind. Before leaving Moscow, he had formed a secret KGB cell of the Pamyat antisemitic group. Quite a few officers had joined the group. He could imagine what his comrades would say if they knew his mother was Jewish. He would be kicked out of the organization he had founded! He swallowed his glass of cognac in a single gulp. 'If you know so much about being Jewish,' he slurred, 'why don't you grow a beard and sidelocks too? And wear a soft hat, like a . . . a . . .'

'A Hassid?' Alex smiled cheerfully. 'Oh, but I did,' he said, 'for a while.'

'What?' Dimitri stared at his brother incredulously.

'Yes.' Laughing, Alex told him about one summer when he had grown fed up with the WASPY ambience of Brown. He had set out on a search for his roots that had led him to a building in Brooklyn's Crown Heights, housing the headquarters of the Lubovitcher Hassidim. 'They taught me to pray, and took me to the *yeshiva* – their religious college – across the street. I even started wearing a skullcap, and tried to grow a beard.'

'You've got no beard now,' Dimitri pointed out.

Alex shrugged. 'I didn't last very long. I regard every religion as a burden. I saw the abandonment of the Hassidim when they prayed, and I got scared. I was afraid that if I got hooked I could turn into a fanatic.' He paused. 'Those people weren't real fanatics, though. They were very kind, they had wonderful songs and dances, a kind of simple love of life. But it was too late for me. If they had got to me ten years earlier, you might have met today a guy with sidelocks and a fur hat, wearing a long silk caftan.'

'Thank Jehovah for that,' Dimitri snapped with sarcasm.

They parted at dawn, exchanging promises to meet again the same evening for a drink and perhaps dinner.

Dimitri was living on the fifth floor of a massive eighteenth-century building overlooking the Park Monceau. He took a cab straight home. At least in Paris he didn't have to go through the routine of sanctuaries, changing cabs and living in hideouts. He had an official position, he represented a Soviet company, and his status was perfectly legal. The French Sûreté guessed, of course, that he hadn't been sent over to promote the sales of Russian *matrioshka* dolls, but as long as they hadn't caught him red-handed, he was free to carry out his clandestine operations.

He unlocked the apartment door and walked into the small vestibule. The scent he knew so well lingered in the dark apartment and he was suddenly fully awake. He didn't turn on the lights. He took off his clothes, then stepped into the bedroom, approached the large bed, and with a sharp movement pulled the covers aside.

Tatiana woke up with a start, and peered at him in the dark. Then she lay back on the pillows and opened her arms, her naked body offered to him, belonging to him, eager to satisfy his wildest fantasies.

When Alex returned home, dawn was breaking. He picked up the phone and dictated a telegram to Nina in New York.

'Wonderful news. Dimitri is in Paris. Met him tonight. You have another good-looking nephew. Letter follows. Love, Alex.'

He hung up, opened the high French windows and stepped on the narrow balcony of his rooftop flat, watching Paris slowly wake up. The air was limpid, and the black, twin-towered hulk of Nôtre Dame hovered ominously over the slated roofs. A narrow strip of sky, low over the horizon, was slowly turning from grey to purple, with a touch of gold. It was a magnificent sight, but his thoughts were elsewhere. Dimitri's striking, passionate face was vividly etched on his mind. After so many years, he thought, he had found his brother. Dimitri was a winner; a self-made man, he had climbed out of poverty and hunger to a high position in the Soviet hierarchy. His brother was handsome and intelligent.

And a bloody liar.

He sat behind his desk and wrote a long letter to Nina, narrating in detail his reunion with Dimitri. 'Ninochka, dearest,' he then added, 'there's something else, not so pleasant, that I must tell you. I don't buy a word of what my brother told me.

'You taught me, Nina, never to believe in coincidences. When I recovered from the shock of meeting Dimitri on the Seine embankment, I started to think. I can't believe that it was just by coincidence that I got a scholarship to the institute in Paris, where by pure coincidence I met Tatiana Romanova, who by sheer coincidence happens to work for my brother, who by a wonderful coincidence happens to be posted to Paris. It seems to me that everything was planned from the start: the grant, the Paris letter, the meeting at the library. Apparently Dimitri found out about me – perhaps from my visa applications – and conceived a clever scheme to lure me to Paris. Not that I care, as long as it was for a good cause.' He underlined the last sentence twice.

The sunshine painted in bright yellow the growing pile of handwritten pages. He put down his pen, ran the back of his hand over his unshaven face, and went to the kitchen, to brew some coffee. He was thinking of his conversation with Dimitri.

'Have you been to the institute?' he had innocently asked his brother.

Dimitri had shrugged. 'I only heard about it from Tatiana. She told me she was doing some research there.'

He must have thought me a fool, Alex told himself now. *I devoted seven long years to the study of the Soviet Union. I know enough about my native country to recognize a KGB operation when I see one, damnit!*

He carried his mug of coffee to his desk, and sat down, absently staring out of the open window. The institute, now that he thought about it, looked exactly like a front institution, one of many that the KGB had established throughout the free world – cultural centres, peace movements, friendship leagues, travel bureaux – all of them providing cover for clandestine operations. He remembered that on arriving he had overheard a conversation in Russian in Martineau's office, and in an ashtray on his desk had seen a crushed Gauloise cigarette, the brand his brother smoked. Could Dimitri have called on Martineau to make sure Alex would be properly manipulated?

He picked up his pen again. 'I'm afraid, Ninochka, that my brother doesn't look very kosher. In the cab, taking us to dinner, he admitted he was working for Sovtorg. But I know, and you know, that Sovtorg's envoys abroad are almost exclusively KGB agents.

'At the restaurant I also noticed that Dimitri insisted on finding a table close to the exit, with his back to the wall; he carries neither a credit card nor a chequebook and pays for everything in cash. During dinner he kept checking and studying everyone who approached our table. He has travelled all over the world, which as you know is also unusual for a Russian.

'And what do you say to Tatiana? Dimitri has on his payroll the daughter of notorious emigrés, a member of the Czar's family! Now, Ninochka, you know that any bona fide Russian wouldn't touch a Romanov with a ten-foot pole. The most innocent contact with such a people's enemy could earn him a one way ticket to a sub-Arctic gulag – except if he had been explicitly authorized to do so.

'There can be no doubt, I'm afraid, that my brother has KGB written all over him.'

He drained the last bitter drops from his cup and leaned back in his chair, rubbing his fingers over his face. KGB spy or not, Dimitri was his brother. He had gone to all the trouble of planning such an intricate operation just to meet Alex. It must mean Dimitri cared about him, had never forgotten him, perhaps was even risking his own career by bringing Alex over to Paris. He felt a renewed surge of warmth towards his brother and recalled his affectionate smile in the restaurant, the way he raised his glass: 'To you, Alex!'

Perhaps Dimitri had no choice, perhaps he had to lie to protect his own skin. It didn't change the fact that Tonya Gordon's two sons were together again.

Tatiana had first met Dimitri one Thursday, eighteen months previously, when she was walking down the Rue de Lille, after her evening seminar at the Langues O'. She wasn't used to walking the streets of Paris alone; she had recently broken up with Louis, her boyfriend, a fellow student. A black car had stopped beside her at the dark corner of the Rue de Beaune, two strong arms had grabbed her from behind and thrown her on to the back seat, then the car had bolted forward. She had fought and tried to scream, but a hand was clamped over her mouth.

'Nobody will hear you, Tatiana Borisova,' a cool voice said in Russian, and she stared into Dimitri Morozov's black eyes. 'Besides, we mean you no harm. I just want to talk to you. If you misbehave, your relatives in the Soviet Union might be harmed.'

She shook her head violently.

'Oh, yes,' Dimitri said. 'You do have relatives in Russia. They don't call themselves Romanov today. But I know all about the Golitzins in Moscow, the Zvetayevs in Kiev, and the Yulins and Daniloffs in Odessa. Now, may I take my hand off your mouth?'

She nodded, vanquished. What could she do? The dark man and his cronies knew about her relatives who had hesitated too long when her grandparents had fled Russia. Their children were still living, under assumed names, in the Soviet Union.

'Who are you?' she asked after he had removed his hand.

'We work for the Soviet Government,' was the answer, and she realized that her blackest fears had come true. This man belonged to the KGB.

The driver of the black car was a scrawny man with two steel teeth. He left them in another dark street and Dimitri led her to a cafe crowded with workers. They were in the dormitory suburb of Bagnolet. After they had settled at a corner table and ordered coffee, Dimitri leaned closer.

He spoke matter-of-factly. 'We know all about you, Tatiana Borisova. We know that you're related to the Grand-Duke Peter, that you play the piano, that you left your boyfriend a month ago. We know your father is an architect, and your mother is very ill. We also know what your father is doing after hours.'

She listened in mounting panic to Dimitri's discourse. This man knew all their secrets! He mentioned her father's ties with the emigré organizations, and a close friend of their family who had become a CIA expert. Then he brought up the most devastating secret of them all: the story of her cousin Igor who had infiltrated the Soviet Union posing as an Austrian journalist.

'How do you think Mr Egon Kunzle' – he pronounced Igor's assumed name with disdain – 'so easily got his visa to the Soviet Union? And so easily found an apartment in Moscow? We knew all about him from the beginning. We actually planted the idea of going to Russia in his head.'

'Why?'

'Because we wanted him in our power there, and you in our power here,' Dimitri helpfully explained.

He told her all those things in a low, casual voice, while sipping his coffee. He seemed certain that she wouldn't run away. She could escape, but for what purpose? The man who had kidnapped her could bring death upon her relatives in Russia and tragedy upon her parents in France by a snap of his fingers. Therefore she stayed and listened to him.

She revolted only once, when he calmly threatened her father with death.

'Boris Romanov is a French citizen,' she flared. 'He came to this country at the age of three. He is protected by the French government.'

'So were several others,' he said placidly, throwing a batch of photographs on the table before her. 'Emigré leaders,' he said, matter of factly, 'prematurely deceased.'

He pointed at the photographs, announcing the names of the assassinated dissidents. 'You wouldn't want us to add your father's picture to this collection, would you?'

She stared in horror at the photographs, some of which she recognized, then raised her eyes. Morozov was watching her with a sarcastic grin. There was something so deadly, and yet so triumphant in his eyes, that she guessed he had been involved in some of those murders; perhaps he even was the murderer.

'So, Tatiana Borisova, what do you say?'

She couldn't believe the conversation was real. She had often participated in emigré meetings in her family's house in Saint Germain, or accompanied her father to conferences out of town. To her it had been nothing but vain talk, hollow declarations, pompous nonsense about the liberation of the motherland. She had never taken all this seriously, not even the departure of her cousin for Russia.

All of a sudden she had awakened to the cruel reality of the secret war. The KGB had infiltrated their organization, it probably controlled the emigré societies all over Europe. She had to choose between cooperating, or condemning her friends and family to death. And from that moment she was in Dimitri's power.

That night he coldly blackmailed her into working for him. She had no choice but to accept the crude barter he offered; the lives of her family and friends in exchange for the information she would provide. The cover chosen for her contacts with Dimitri was the position of interpreter at Sovtorg. 'And remember,' he said later, when the black car was speeding back towards Paris, 'a single word to your father will be his death sentence.'

'And if I went to the police?' she asked. The car was crossing the Ile de la Cité.

Dimitri ordered the driver to stop the car. 'Why don't you?' he said. 'The police headquarters are right across the street. What will you tell them? They won't believe you. In the unlikely event they do, they may expel me to Russia. I'll survive. But you – you'll start worrying for your family. And for your own life.'

He gave his short, dry laugh, and left her on the streetwalk.

That was how she started to work for him. A month later, she became his mistress.

It was a rainy Sunday and he had summoned her to his apartment. After closing the door behind her he steered her to his bedroom, undressed her with deliberate slowness, and threw her on the bed. She didn't lift a finger. Then he started unbuckling his belt while she watched him, immobile, holding her breath. It wasn't rape; they both knew she wouldn't fight. He thought she feared him; he couldn't guess that she was fascinated by his raw power, and his absolute domination oddly excited her.

That first time she had let him do as he wished. She had been docile and passive, obeying him like a robot. And then, gradually, she reversed their roles. During the following weeks she learned to satisfy his sexual urges, using her body, her mouth and hands, to make him reach new peaks of orgasm. And when this powerful man groaned and panted in abandon, when his body grew taut with passion or went slack in her arms, she felt she was in total control. She played him like her piano. And she loved the music.

She knew she belonged to him and accepted that; but she didn't love him. In their bizarre relationship there was no place for her emotions. She enjoyed having sex with him, and didn't feel debased. She was far more affected by her role as a spy inside her father's organization. She came daily to the Sovtorg building, and went to Dimitri's office, staring straight ahead, her shoulders hunched, avoiding the avid looks and the lewd smiles of middle-aged Russians in grey suits and brown shoes.

Once a week she would bring Dimitri her report. It contained the names of people who participated in emigré meetings, summaries of the topics discussed, details of future activities. Dimitri showed special interest in the contacts of emigrés with the CIA. She felt disgusted with herself. Even the knowledge that she saved her relatives' lives didn't appease her sleepless nights.

The arrival of Dimitri's brother troubled her deeply. She had been ordered to strike up a conversation with Alex, the day he turned up at the Centre. She did as she was told; it was easy. But she didn't expect the brother of her sinister, brooding lover to be so charming. She wasn't ready to deal with a man she could like, not fear.

The afternoon they had spent together had been delightful. She was drawn to the young man, the only natural, real person in the world of deceit in which she lately moved. Alex Gordon was so much like her, she thought, or rather like her as she used to be: an honest, candid young man who liked music and poetry, and cared about people. The poor guy had no chance if his ruthless brother turned against him. Dimitri could destroy him if he wished. She had wanted to warn Alex the night she led him to the meeting. Beware of your brother, she had wanted to scream, beware of his deadly hug, beware of his kiss.

But she had only dared to press his hand, fast. Then she ran back to Dimitri's apartment, to await his pleasure.

She met Alex Gordon again the following evening at the Bofinger Brasserie, and old Parisian eatery with a magnificent stained-glass ceiling. She came with Dimitri and watched Alex closely when Dimitri told him she was his girlfriend. Alex paled, staring at both of them; finally he managed a smile. 'Congratulations, Dimitri,' he said. 'Tatiana is a ravishing woman. I think Mother looked like her when she was young.'

Dimitri didn't like the comparison, Tatiana remarked; she was familiar with the tightening of his jaw which indicated his anger. But he didn't say a word. They spent the evening together; after dinner they went to an old Parisian night-club, on the Montmartre hill, where young artists sang old French songs on a small stage. They ended their night out over an assortment of oysters in an all-night bistro at Place Clichy.

In the following months they spent a lot of time together, eating out, going to the movies, night-clubs, even driving to the countryside for an occasional weekend. Getting to know each other better, the two brothers also discovered the profound gap that separated them. Alex was infuriated with the trite communist slogans that seemed to dictate his brother's views. He resented Dimitri's suspicious attitude towards the Western way of life.

As for Dimitri, he couldn't cope with the degree of personal freedom in America; for him it was a dangerous phenomenon, bordering on anarchy. In August, Nixon had resigned following Watergate. The Americans must have gone mad, Dimitri said, to kick their president out of the White House for such nonsense. He failed to understand the functioning of a society that was not tightly controlled from above.

Tatiana was fascinated by the development of the brothers' relationship. At first, there was genuine affection and curiosity on both sides; she was surprised to discover how charming Dimitri could be. But after a few weeks the brothers' honeymoon turned sour. Dimitri raising his defences again. Tatiana had the feeling that her lover had become scared by his own behaviour. He had become too much like Alex, too carefree, spontaneous, obviously enjoying a different life from the one he had chosen.

Henceforth, Alex's openness was countered by Dimitri's reserve. Whenever Alex made a political remark about the Soviet Union, Dimitri would clam up. Alex's attempts to bring up the death of their parents were also met by sullen silence. Finally these subjects dropped completely out of their conversations. The brothers preferred to discuss food and movies, sport and international events. They debated the fall of Saigon, the French presidential election that brought Giscard d'Estaing to power, Gerald Ford's chances in 1976. Russia became a subject they tackled very rarely and very cautiously.

It seemed artificial, Tatiana thought. The only subjects that bound Alex and Dimitri together, their background, their family, their native land, had turned into a taboo they wouldn't touch.

Several times Dimitri had to stay late at the office because of some last-minute emergency; Tatiana and Alex were left alone. These nights they would go to a concert or a ballet performance, which Dimitri intensely disliked.

Whenever she was alone with Alex, Tatiana felt an awkward tension rising between them. Their conversations were strained, interspersed by uneasy silences. When he touched her, helping her out of a cab or holding her coat, she felt a current shooting through her flesh. Later, she could remember every smile, every look they exchanged. She caught herself watching Alex's mouth, the fire sparkling in his eyes, the lock of blond hair that so endearingly fell over his forehead; and she felt an overwhelming desire to reach and touch him, feel the contour of his lips with her fingers; taste them, softly, with her mouth. It slowly dawned on her that she was being drawn into a dangerous, obsessive infatuation with Alex Gordon.

She suspected he felt the same way about her. She could tell by the way he looked at her, by his metamorphosis into a different, happier person when they were alone. Yet it was an impossible love. Dimitri inspired her with tremendous fear. If she ever cheated on him, he would kill her without thinking twice. He might even kill his brother. Therefore she went out with Alex, whenever Dimitri told her to, but was always on her guard. She never gave Alex the opportunity to hold her hand again.

She made sure always to be at home before Dimitri returned, lying naked on the large bed the way he liked, ready to please him. Like a modern Cinderella, she left Alex wherever they were, at least half an hour before Dimitri's supposed time of arrival, and rushed home to undress and perfume herself for him. The last few times she cried while combing her hair before the mirror and watched the tears run down her face.

But then she came home one night at the beginning of February and found Dimitri waiting for her. He was fully dressed, sitting on the single armchair in the hall.

'I . . . I didn't expect you before midnight,' she stammered.

He nodded, lighting a cigarette. 'I know. How is my dear brother?' The tone was cynical, with no trace of the former warmth.

'We went to a ballet. We saw *Romeo and Juliet* at the Opéra.'

'Good,' he said absently. 'Look, I got an urgent phone call from home. I have to fly to Moscow tonight. Something unexpected has popped up.'

'When will you be back?'

'I don't know.' He stepped into the bedroom and was back in a moment, carrying a light suitcase and a black briefcase. He put on his heavy overcoat. 'In two or three weeks, I suppose.'

He pulled her to him and kissed her mouth hard. 'Wait for me,' he said, his hand hungrily exploring her breasts, slipping down her body. 'Keep this for me. And don't make mistakes.'

The black eyes were intense, watchful.

Romeo and Juliet, performed by the principals and corps de ballet of the Opéra Company, had been magnificent. After the performance Alex helped Tatiana into a taxi, then walked down the Rue de la Paix, crossed the opulent Place Vendôme, and strolled along the river bank toward the Pont des Arts. The streets were almost empty, and the fierce cold had driven away even the lovers and the derelicts who roamed the Seine embankment. A light snow started falling. He shivered in his light coat, raising his collar and wrapping his woollen scarf more tightly around his throat; but he didn't want to go home yet. He knew he wouldn't be able to sleep, not after he had spent an evening with Tatiana. She had bewitched him completely, and he was desperately in love with her.

He had never felt this way before. He wasn't the same man who had arrived in Paris five months ago. His life had become a long wait for the few hours he would spend with Tatiana, mostly in Dimitri's company, sometimes alone. They got on so well together, speaking the same language, enjoying the same artistic interests, stemming from the same roots. They understood each other by a look or a smile. And she was irresistible with her multifaceted personality changing in a flash from mischievous youngster to inquisitive scholar, sensitive art lover or stunning young woman.

He could think of nothing but Tatiana. He ate badly, slept little, dressed carelessly. He knew he was being unfair to Claudia by courting another woman, but had she been fair to him? They could have been married by now. He felt a deep resentment towards her for refusing to go along with him at the time when he needed her so. Tatiana was more sensitive, she wouldn't have refused to marry him if they were so deeply in love. He stopped writing to Claudia; compared to his obsession with Tatiana, his love for her now seemed nothing more than a mild affection.

Tatiana had enticed him to the point that nothing else mattered; neither his research, nor his relationship with Dimitri. He courted her assiduously, but very subtly, letting his eyes speak, refraining from any straightforward word or gesture. He knew he was breaking a moral code, and abusing Dimitri's confidence; coveting his brother's woman was wrong, but he couldn't help it. His affection for his brother had given way to a blinding jealousy. He couldn't stand the way Dimitri treated the girl, as if she were his property. He couldn't stand watching Dimitri touch her, stroke her hair, or possessively kiss her.

Tatiana wasn't the only reason for his drifting away from Dimitri. Since they first met, Alex's suspicions had been confirmed. He noticed the strange rendezvous places his brother would propose –

mostly street corners where he would be picked up by a chauffeur-driven car; he noticed Dimitri's unusual hours, his use of public phones only, his sudden disappearances. His brother seemed involved in something very fishy indeed.

Dimitri contributed to their drifting apart by entrenching himself behind walls of reserve, sudden outbursts of anger, or embarrassing, stubborn silences. Alex knew that he was also to blame; still, being with his brother wasn't fun anymore.

Alex had mentioned Dimitri to Grimaldi whom he was seeing quite often lately. A week after their arrival in Paris, Grimaldi had left him a message at the Centre. Alex had called him back, and his flamboyant friend took him out to lunch in an exquisite seafood restaurant off the Champs Elysées. Since then they had met often, mostly for lunch or dinner. Grimaldi knew the best gourmet restaurants in Paris, was a personal friend of the chefs, and always picked up the tab. 'Uncle Sam is paying,' he said once, 'the USIS is very generous, so don't worry.'

He always appeared in a different attire, strutting like a peacock in his flowery waistcoats, silk ties and kerchiefs, his lively eyes shining from a deeply tanned face. Alex suspected a sun-lamp contributed to his friend's healthy complexion. He liked Grimaldi's animated way of speaking, and enjoyed watching the sparkle of his golden rings and chains as his bejewelled hands accompanied his fascinating stories. Grimaldi was a great story-teller, an amusing bon-vivant, and Alex liked his company. Besides, he was a never-ending source of information about life in Russia.

Alex had told Grimaldi about Dimitri, but didn't share with him his suspicions that his brother was a KGB employee; he didn't want to harm Dimitri. Besides, Grimaldi didn't seem to care about Dimitri's line of work; he was fascinated by the human angle of the story, which he regarded as a triumph of poetic justice. 'You and your brother are Tonya's revenge on the system that murdered her,' he once said. Alex wanted the three of them to have dinner together; he thought Dimitri would be amused by Grimaldi's extravagance. But his friend didn't think it was a good idea.

They were going to have lunch tomorrow, Alex remembered. He crossed the Seine by the Pont des Arts and plunged into the picturesque Latin Quarter. As he passed by the King's Club disco, a couple came out, passionately kissing. The girl was blonde and slender. He clenched his teeth. A group of black musicians was leaving the Bilboquet, and he thought of his favourite jazz club in Greenwich Village. At Saint Germain's corner, the wind was whipping an old poster from the presidential campaign, showing Giscard d'Estaing confidently looking at the future. A street vendor was selling hot grilled chestnuts, and Alex yielded to the temptation.

The entrance to his building was dark. He took the lift to the seventh floor. As he stepped out, chewing a chestnut, he saw a woman's figure huddled by his door. His heart missed a beat as he recognized the silken mass of blonde hair, and the soft sheepskin Dimitri had brought her from Moscow.

'Tatiana!'

She stood up. Her face was chalk white.

'What happened? What are you doing here?'

She stared at him, suddenly so close, so accessible. 'I came . . .' she started, then bit her lip. 'Dimitri left for Moscow tonight, he won't be back for two or three weeks.'

He wanted to say something, but couldn't find the right words. The paper bag with the chestnuts slipped from his fingers. They looked at each other for another moment, then he stepped forward and gathered her in his arms. Her face was cold, but her lips were soft and burning, feverishly trembling under his mouth.

'I love you, Tatiana,' he said. Her eyes lit up with happiness, which soon melted into dark, boundless fear.

Oktober was a night person, Dimitri thought, as he climbed the dark, winding stairs to his office. It was past two am on the second night after his return to Moscow. He had spent most of the day sleeping in his apartment on Pushkinskaya Street. In the afternoon he had dropped into his office where he had read a few reports. He had dinner at the KGB club with a couple of friends from the Department. Nobody knew why Oktober had called him back. There was a lot of talk of the Italian Brigate Rosse and the French Action Directe, two left-wing guerrilla organizations that had lately been infiltrated by the Department. But nothing unusual had happened these last few days that could require Dimitri's presence.

He returned home and browsed through the John Barron book about the KGB that had just been published in New York. At one-thirty a car picked him up and took him to the black mansion that Oktober had turned into the Wet Affairs headquarters.

'Come in, Dimitri,' Oktober's cracked voice called when he knocked on his door. What would he say if he knew that Dimitri had just left his brother in Paris? Could Alex be the reason for his sudden recall? Dimitri felt a pang of anxiety.

He walked into Oktober's tiny den. The files were stacked in neat tidy piles all over the place – on the desk, most of the chairs, even on the floor. His chief perched, like a raven on a straight-backed wooden chair behind his massive desk. Oktober hated armchairs.

'Take off your coat,' he croaked again. 'Sit down. What's new in Paris?' Dimitri peered at him through the thick cigarette smoke that hung like an opaque veil in the gloomy, cold room. Oktober had grown even more gaunt and skeletal since he had seen him last. The sharp nose curved down like the beak of a bird of prey; the cheekbones bulged, tautening the wizened skin. Oktober's burning eyes had sunk deeper in their dark sockets, and his scrawny neck couldn't fill the collar of his black pullover. His long white hair was getting yellow and curled at the edges.

'In Paris . . .' he started, and shut up, realizing that Oktober had asked his question by rote. He didn't seem to want a report on Dimitri's activities.

'I called you back, my boy,' Oktober was saying, lighting a fresh cigarette with the stub of another, 'because a year ago you carried out, almost single-handedly, a very important operation. The Saint-Clair affair. The time has come for the next stage.'

Dimitri stared at him, puzzled.

'I wanted you to meet somebody,' Oktober rasped. 'Right here.'

He went to the door connecting his den with his secretary's office, and opened it. 'He's here,' he said to somebody in the office, 'you can come in now.' He stepped aside.

'Good evening, Dimitri,' said a pleasant, familiar voice.

A man in an elegant suit appeared in the doorway, the contours of his body outlined against the dim light from behind. Dimitri squinted. The man stepped inside, turning towards him. He was smiling.

Dimitri recognized the handsome, scarred face of Oleg Kalinin.

Chapter Thirteen

In her fantasies, Tatiana had countless times imagined the moment when Alex collected her in his arms. She had anticipated the fire lighting his grey eyes, the softness of his full lips against hers, the blond head snuggling into the hollow of her neck. Alex's voice saying, I love you, Tatiana. And she murmuring, I am yours, Alex. Since the first moment I saw you. There was nobody else before you, just an illusion. She had visualized his carrying her to his bed, feverishly undressing her, then sinking into her as she clung to him, trembling. It could have been like that, it almost was like that, had not terror of Dimitri gripped her. His was a blood-chilling presence that clung to her even when she pulled Alex inside her and whispered her love.

Even in these moments of absolute love, she remembered Dimitri's warning. 'Don't make mistakes.' Memories of his face never left her, his menacing hint ringing in her ears, and the fear of his revenge clinging to her skin like a cold, wet shroud. 'Keep them for me,' he had said as his hand had swept over her breasts and thighs, 'and don't make mistakes.' An hour later she had made the worst mistake, for which she might pay with her life. But she couldn't help it. Only the thought of Alex had driven her mad. He was so close, alone, yearning for her; she had gone to him knowing she might be sentencing herself to death. And Alex as well. She shuddered.

'Something's wrong, my love?'

'Nothing,' she said, stroking his hair. 'Nothing. Hold me, Alex, *lyubimi*, make love to me.'

The fear of Dimitri's revenge haunted her throughout the following week, which otherwise was the happiest of her life. She spent every single moment with Alex. She needed him beside her, she had to be sure that whenever she reached for him, he would be there. She didn't go to Sovtorg; they probably didn't expect her to come when Dimitri was away. Alex didn't go to the Centre either. He didn't return phone calls, didn't open the letters that came from America, sent by a woman called Claudia Benevento. 'She used to be my girlfriend,' he said to Tatiana. 'Ages ago.'

They explored Paris the way only lovers can, and she was amazed to discover how people and places, sights and sounds, smells and tastes she knew so well, seemed so different to a person in love. The Parc Monceau and the Luxembourg Gardens, the gravel paths of the Tuileries, the forests of Fontainebleau and Rambouillet, even the stone-paved banks of the Seine, looked as if they had been conceived for the two of them, and them alone.

Even the occasional clochard under a Seine bridge, the wildly kissing couple under a tree in the middle of a furious rain, a love song by Piaf or Brel played on the radio, seemed as if staged for them by a brilliant director.

Theirs were the crooked streets of the Latin Quarter and the Marais, Montmartre and the Bastille, the little cafes of the Place de la Contrescarpe, the chansonniers and the literary night clubs, the small Vietnamese and Italian restaurants behind the Saint Sulpice church; theirs were the crisp, starry Parisian nights and the dreamy dawns, hailed by generations of poets, when a gauzy mist rose from the Seine and invaded the adjoining streets, turning the city into a living legend, slipping into the porch where Tatiana stood with Alex, passionately kissing.

'I want to marry you,' he said to her one cool, clouded afternoon. They had spent the night in a small inn in the Vallée de la Chevreuse, and now walked hand in hand beside a lazy, narrow stream. He was wearing a white turtleneck sweater.

'No, it can never happen,' she said, oddly disturbed. A family was having a picnic by the water, the children chasing each other in the grove. A tiny black dog furiously barked at their approach, then scurried to safety, its tail between its legs.

Alex looked at her. The wind was playfully blowing her hair across her face.

'We love each other, Tatiana. I want to marry you and take you with me to America.'

She stubbornly shook her head. Poor Alex, he didn't even suspect who Dimitri was. When she spoke again, despair had crept into her voice. 'Dimitri will never let this happen.'

Dimitri's out of your life for good,' he said. 'It's just you and me.'

But Dimitri was with them all the time, an unwanted but persistent companion, his invisible presence terrorizing her, and tormenting Alex's conscience. They avoided speaking about him, but she could tell Alex was deeply troubled; he couldn't forgive himself for having stolen his brother's girl. Their love, however, was so deep, so consuming, that nothing else seemed to matter.

But one night she awoke screaming, bathed in cold sweat. In her nightmare she had seen Dimitri coming for her with a rope, calmly tying the noose around her neck. Cold fire was burning in his eyes, and his mouth was bitterly drawn. 'I warned you,' he said softly, before strangling her. 'No mistakes.' She awoke suffocating, gasping for air.

'It's all right, my love,' Alex whispered to her, gently stroking her forehead, 'it was only a dream. Calm down, all right? Look at me.'

She lay on her back, staring at the fluttering curtains.

'What's the matter, my love?'

'He'll kill us,' she whispered. 'Dimitri will come back from Moscow and kill us both.'

He stared at her in dismay, then shook his head. 'What are you talking about?'

'Alex,' she murmured in despair, 'we must leave before he comes back. If he finds us, we're as good as dead.'

In the soft light of dawn she saw he was smiling. 'Don't be silly,' he said. 'He's my brother. I'll talk to him and . . .'

'You don't know your brother,' she said. 'You don't know what he can do. You don't know who he is.'

Alex rolled away and sat on the bed, looking at her closely. His face grew serious and he softly touched her cheek with his fingertips. 'Who is my brother? Tell me.'

And she did.

His phone call awakened Grimaldi. 'You must be out of your mind,' his friend groaned into the receiver. 'It's not seven yet. What happened? The Russkies attacked?'

'I'm sorry,' Alex said, his eyes glued to Tatiana's face. She sat across the table, huddled in his bathrobe. 'It's urgent.'

They had spoken of Dimitri until daybreak. Alex had suggested that he met his brother on his return, and explain that he and Tatiana had fallen in love. She refused to hear of it. She seemed scared to death. 'He will kill us,' she kept repeating. 'If you go to him, he'll kill you, and then he'll find me and kill me too.'

Alex proposed that she flew to America and stayed with Nina. Tatiana refused again. Dimitri's thugs would find her, she said.

'Alex! Hey, Alex!' Grimaldi's voice brought him back to reality. 'What's wrong? What about lunch?'

'Yes, that's a great idea. Something came up, and I need your help.' Alex was speaking like a robot, disjointed thoughts flashing through his mind. A murderer, Tatiana had said, his brother was a murderer. He had guessed Dimitri was a spy, but hadn't suspected him of any violent acts. Not his brother, not Tonya Gordon's son.

'What kind of help?' Grimaldi sounded reserved.

'I told you about my brother. Meeting him in Paris, I mean?'

'Yes.'

Alex felt disgusted with himself, as if he were betraying Dimitri. Let's hope it's a false alarm, he thought, let's hope Tatiana is imagining things, that he is just a second-rate spy paying his stay in Paris with some chickenfeed about imaginary emigré conspiracies.

'Alex, are you there?'

'Listen, you work with the embassy, you know quite a lot of people. My friend Tatiana . . .'

'Your friend?' Grimaldi sounded amused. 'You told me she was your brother's girl.'

'My friend Tatiana,' Alex repeated, irritated, 'is afraid Dimitri might try to hurt her, and I thought she might need protection.' From across the table she stared at him, her eyes wide with fear. Somewhere, very far away, a churchbell was ringing.

'Tell her to go to the police,' Grimaldi said impatiently. 'This has nothing to do with the embassy.'

I must not incriminate Dimitri in any way, Alex thought. He phrased his words very cautiously. 'Tatiana thinks Dimitri might try to hurt her with the help of the Soviet . . . services. I'm sure she's wrong, I don't believe he's involved in anything illegal. But just to be on the safe side, I'd like you to find out if your embassy friends suspect Dimitri of any unusual activities.'

'If we have a file on him, you mean? As a Russian agent?'

Alex didn't answer.

'His last name is Morozov, isn't it?'

'Yes,' Alex murmured. 'Dimitri Morozov.'

'I'll see what I can do,' Grimaldi said. 'Let's make lunch at one-thirty, the Closerie des Lilas.' He paused. 'And another thing – come alone. Don't bring the lady along.'

Grimaldi entered the famous Parisian restaurant fifteen minutes before the agreed time.

'*Ah, Monsieur Grimaldi, vous êtes déjà là!*' The owner of the Closerie ceremoniously shook hands with him and motioned to the Maître d', who led him to a secluded corner table. '*La table de Monsieur Ernest Hemingway,*' he disclosed knowingly, fussing with the gleaming cutlery.

Grimaldi chuckled inwardly. Each table at the Closerie became Monsieur Hemingway's when the patron was an American tourist.

The truth was that Hemingway mostly sat on the terrace, but who cared about the truth anyway? He settled on the padded bench, ordered a champagne kir, and again rehearsed his story. He was closer than ever to achieving his plan. Alex was coming to him, to ask for help against his brother. Grimaldi hadn't taken into account the appearance of the Russian girl, and her infatuation with Alex. But this was for the best. The brothers' rivalry over Tatiana was a welcome development; the girl could unwittingly turn Alex Gordon into his tool against Morozov.

'Hi, Franco.'

He raised his eyes. Alex stood before him, in a pair of freshly pressed jeans, a snow-white shirt and a smart light-grey jacket. His face was pale; he had cut himself shaving.

'You look worried,' Grimaldi said. 'How's Tatiana?'

Alex hesitated a moment. 'Scared,' he said. A striking Spanish-looking woman sitting by the next table turned back and stared at him with smouldering black eyes, smiling slightly.

'Sit down before the señora rapes you,' Grimaldi grunted, 'and let's order. Then we'll talk.'

After their order had been taken, and he had tasted the Nuits Saint Georges, Grimaldi leaned forward. His eyes carefully swept the restaurant then concentrated on Alex.

'Did you . . .' he started impatiently.

'Let me tell you something first. You didn't call because I work at the US Information Service, right?'

Alex hesitated, then nodded.

'From the very beginning you suspected I was more involved with intelligence gathering than I cared to admit.'

Alex nodded again. 'Yes. You spoke to me about your life in Moscow, London, Bonn . . . You seemed too knowledgeable and too smart to spend your life mailing pamphlets about the American dream. But I preferred not to ask. Besides, I didn't care.'

'I accept that. But I want to be frank with you.' He clammed up abruptly when a silver-haired waiter deferentially placed a plate of smoked salmon before Alex, and half a dozen sizzling snails in garlic butter before Grimaldi. '*Attention, c'est chaud,*' the waiter chanted, poured some wine into their glasses and vanished.

'I have been a CIA agent since the Company was established,' Grimaldi said bluntly, watching Alex who winced. His fork froze in mid-air, then returned to rest on his plate.

'And our meeting on the plane . . .' he started.

'. . . wasn't fortuitous, no. We knew who you were, and we knew that the Centre for Eastern European Studies was a KGB cover organization. We wanted to find out if you were working for them.'

Alex stared at him reflectively. 'Very smart.'

'You know why?' Grimaldi said. It was the moment to plant the first seed, he thought. 'Because we wanted to make you an offer. We wanted to ask you to join the Company. We think you're one of the best experts on the Soviet Union today, Alex.'

But he totally ignored the cue. 'You wanted to check me out, you said. And what did you find?'

Grimaldi let out a short laugh. 'We found out you were a bona fide scholar who had nothing to do with their clandestine activities. So, we asked ourselves, why did they bring Boris Morozov's stepson over here? You see,' he lied, 'we didn't know Dimitri was your brother. Only when you told me about meeting him here, did I understand that he had masterminded the scholarship.'

'So you came over to spy on me,' Alex summed up.

Grimaldi spread his hands, palms up. 'Yes, I flew here to spy on you and found you were clean.'

'I thought you were my friend.'

'We became friends, but that's another matter.'

'Sure,' Alex said and looked away. It had started raining outside and the first drops made sinuous patterns on the terrace windows. A cosy darkness crept into the restaurant.

Grimaldi leaned back, deftly extracting a reluctant snail from its brown-purple shell. 'Still, I didn't find out what Dimitri's real intentions were. Perhaps he wanted to recruit you?'

Alex shook his head.

'Not yet,' Grimaldi said, munching with pleasure, 'but I'm sure he'll approach you sooner or later.'

'He's my brother, for Christ's sake,' Alex said stubbornly. 'He wanted to meet me.'

Grimaldi reached for his briefcase and took out a pale yellow file. 'Do you want to meet him?' he asked gently.

A half hour later, Alex raised his eyes from the file. He hadn't touched his food, and the waiter, after returning several times, had finally taken away his plate. On Grimaldi's whispered orders, he had brought them two double glasses of Hennessey cognac.

'This . . .' started Alex, and his voice broke. Grimaldi handed him the brandy, and Alex gulped it down. His eyes were out of focus. Grimaldi signalled the waiter for another drink.

'All this is true?' Alex asked, his fingers nervously raking through his hair. A vein was throbbing feverishly at the base of his throat. He started to get up, then sat down again, his left hand fidgeting with his shirt buttons.

'As far as I can tell, yes,' Grimaldi said.

'According to this file,' Alex started in a low, almost inaudible voice, 'my brother is a cold-blooded murderer. He has killed at least three people, perhaps more, with his bare hands.'

Grimaldi lit a cigarette with deliberately slow gestures and blew out the match. 'You know about Department Thirteen.'

'Of course I do. I've read everything published about the KGB. But it says here that Dimitri kills his victims with his bare hands. That's not KGB procedure.'

The waiter brought another cognac and placed it beside Alex.

He was staring fixedly at a glossy photograph of a woman's body, her head twisted in an impossible angle. Her skirt was torn, revealing white thighs. 'If all this is true, how come he moves freely throughout Europe and even enjoys special privileges?'

Grimaldi exhaled a long puff of smoke. 'These are only conjectures, Alex, we have not a shred of solid proof.'

'So you might be wrong!' He drained his second glass.

Grimaldi shrugged. 'I know how you feel. You want so badly for us to be wrong.' He drew on his cigar. 'But I trust our sources.'

He suddenly felt he had beaten around the bush too long and leaned forward. 'What do you want, Alex?'

'I want to take Tatiana to the States and marry her. I want her to be safe.'

'All right. Listen to me, and listen to me good. Tatiana's life is in danger, and so may yours be.'

Alex made a deprecatory gesture with his hand.

'I know you're a big hero,' Grimaldi said acidly, 'but Tatiana is right. If Dimitri comes back and finds out about you two, he might kill both of you. Do you understand?

'We can offer Tatiana safe passage to America, and a new identity. We'll guarantee her protection. But' – he raised his hand as Alex was about to say something – 'first she must be debriefed by us, here in Europe. She has worked for Morozov for eighteen months, and must know a lot about his operations.'

'No,' Alex said, 'no debriefing.' He fell silent, then seemed to change his mind. 'Where do you want to debrief her?'

'Not here,' Grimaldi said. 'Paris is too risky. In Brussels, or London, perhaps Frankfurt. We have safe houses in these cities.'

'How long will it take?'

'About two weeks. That's also the time needed to prepare her papers.'

Alex was slowly coming to himself. 'I want to talk it over with Tatiana.' He got up, gauchely pushing back his chair. 'I'll call you in a couple of days.'

'No way,' Grimaldi said. 'It's yes or no, and you decide now. If you leave, you leave tonight.'

'Why, what's the hurry?'

'The hurry is,' Grimaldi picked up the murdered woman's photograph, 'that if your brother returns from Moscow before you call me, your precious Tatiana will look like this. You understand, *tovaritch? Ponimayesh?*'

Alex stared at him, his jaws locked in fury, then bolted out of the restaurant.

Just you wait, golden boy, Grimaldi thought, sipping his cognac. One day I'll make you dance to my tune. I'll make you destroy your brother for what he did to me. And to Oleg.

In Oktober's dark den, Dimitri Morozov and Oleg Kalinin were facing each other, with their dark-clad host restlessly pacing around, telling a strange story of deceit. Dimitri was holding a lukewarm glass of tea between his palms; he still hadn't recovered from the shock he had experienced on seeing Kalinin.

The stunned silence that had followed his appearance was broken by Oktober's rasping voice. 'You didn't expect to see this one here, did you? You expected to meet him at the Lubyanka, in chains or facing the firing squad. Well, Dimitri, don't you remember what I told you? Never trust what you see and what you hear. Deceit, deceit, deceit' – he accompanied his words by thumping his fist on his desk, a black-draped, white-haired conjurer wickedly grinning through the smoke – 'that's the essence of the secret war. Remember that, Dimitri!'

Kalinin settled in one of the chairs while Oktober, waving his cigarettes like a conductor's baton, his predator's eyes glued to Dimitri's, revealed to him the secret of Operation Top Hat.

It had started shortly after the war, Oktober's story went, when he was stationed in Berlin, charged with infiltrating the American OSS circles. He had detected a certain weakness in an American officer, Franco Grimaldi, and concluded he was ripe for establishing emotional contact with another man. Captain Kalinin had been chosen for the job and performed brilliantly. He had succeeded in winning Grimaldi's total devotion.

Dimitri's eyes shifted from Oktober to Kalinin and back. Kalinin seemed ill at ease, scowling at Oktober then crushing his cigarette in the ashtray before lighting a new one. He avoided Dimitri's look. What is Oktober trying to tell me? Dimitri thought, bewildered. Does he mean that the American was a homosexual and Kalinin was ordered to screw him and get screwed just to gain his confidence? Not that Oktober was unable to conceive such a plan; Dimitri knew his chief wouldn't stop short before any legal or moral rule when he wanted to achieve his goals.

Kalinin's friendship with Grimaldi was very helpful for a while, Oktober's narrative went on, but it was cut short by Kalinin getting himself shot and wounded in the Austrian Alps.

'That's where I got my scar,' Kalinin said almost shyly, and wiped his forehead with a light blue handkerchief.

By the time Oleg had recovered, Oktober croaked, Grimaldi had been posted to Pullach with Gehlen's BND.

'Grimaldi's job made him even more valuable to us,' Oktober said. 'I tried the same approach again. On three different occasions my men tried to seduce Grimaldi. We had quite a few people on the job. But Grimaldi was very careful. He knew that if he were caught he would immediately be thrown out of the service.'

Dimitri nodded. The CIA didn't employ homosexuals for fear they could easily be blackmailed or yield unwittingly to their sexual urges.

Yet Grimaldi's sexual urge had finally vanquished his caution. The American had slipped, and become involved in a homosexual affair. He had been caught and immediately kicked out of Pullach. Ironically, he hadn't been seduced by Oktober's commando of irresistible queers, but by a local boy, absolutely innocent, unaware of the tragic consequences of his short-lived affair with the swashbuckling American officer.

Grimaldi had been recalled to America and disappeared. 'We thought he had been forced to resign from the CIA, and we closed his file,' Oktober said. 'Oleg Kalinin, as you might know, came back home and made a fine career in the GRU.'

And in 1966, Grimaldi had suddenly surfaced. A local KGB stringer had identified him in London where he was posted as liaison officer for the CIA with the British SIS. He had somehow survived the Pullach scandal, and was still on active duty. And Oktober had decided to revive the wartime operation.

Dimitri grimaced sceptically. 'The real liaison between the two services is carried out in Washington,' he said. 'What could you get from the man? Grimaldi couldn't sell you anything.'

'Yes, but he could buy! We could turn the tables, and use him to feed the CIA with first-class *disinformatzia*.' He let out a rasping laugh. 'A man in love is ideal for that purpose. They say that love is blind. Have you ever been in love, Dimitri?'

Oleg Kalinin had been recalled to active duty. He had contacted the CIA representative in Vienna, and offered the Americans their best deal since the war: a high-ranking agent in the Kremlin. At first

Kalinin had pretended that he wanted to defect, but had let the Americans convince him to stay in Moscow and spy for them. On one condition, though: that his case officer would be his friend from the Berlin days, Franco Grimaldi.

It had worked perfectly. Grimaldi had come to Moscow, under cover, and for seven years had been fed a cautiously blended cocktail of true and false information.

'In Moscow it was a totally platonic relationship,' Kalinin quickly said, and Dimitri nodded, amused by the man's embarrassment.

'I wanted Grimaldi here because of his ties with Oleg,' Oktober said coldly. 'When somebody feels, he doesn't think; when he is emotionally involved, his judgment is muddled. He disregards the occasional inconsistency, he feels he has to protect his agent, not control him. Grimaldi blindly believed Kalinin, and guaranteed the authenticity of his material. Anybody else would have checked and double-checked the product. Not Grimaldi. He was in love with Kalinin. He still is.'

That was how Top Hat had become the best American agent in Russia since the war, even more trusted and respected than Colonel Penkovski. The American assessment of Soviet missile and nuclear power, submarine deployment, active tank divisions, was based mostly on Kalinin's phoney reports.

'It could have continued for many years to come,' Oktober said, 'if during a routine surveillance exercise, a KGB trainee named Dimitri Morozov hadn't chosen to follow Grimaldi and hadn't seen him meet Kalinin at the Bolshoi.'

'Saint-Clair,' Dimitri whispered.

'That's right,' Oktober nodded. 'Saint-Clair.'

'But why didn't you tell me?' Dimitri shouted angrily, rising from his seat. He turned to Kalinin: 'Why didn't you tell me when we met in Paris?'

'Sit down,' Oktober snapped. 'Kalinin had no right to tell anything to anybody. He was a double agent under deep cover. By the time he contacted me, you had taken action and the hunt for Kalinin and Saint-Clair was on. I tried to stop you, remember?'

'I thought our men had captured him on the Austrian border.'

Oktober shrugged. 'I planted that item so the Americans could stop looking for him. I didn't want them to find out that Top Hat was our mole not theirs.' He sighed. 'You unwittingly blew the best operation I have conceived, Dimitri.'

When he was summoned again to Oktober's lair, a few days later, Kalinin wasn't there. It was late evening. Oktober was seated behind his desk, the table lamp casting bright light on the papers that lay before him. His face was in shadow.

'I called you because we have to decide what to do with Kalinin,' he said quietly.

Dimitri raised his head. 'What to do with him?' he repeated.

'Yes. Operation Top Hat is over. Kalinin's face is known to the Americans. One of their agents might identify him in the street, or in a cinema, a restaurant. If they find out he's alive, they'll start asking questions. How come this most dangerous spy is walking free on the streets of Moscow?' His long white fingers lightly drummed the rough surface of the desk. 'We must decide if we should keep him alive or kill him.'

Dimitri slowly sat down and lit a Gauloise. 'Why do you ask me?' he said. 'Can't you decide alone?'

'I can never decide alone.' Oktober went into a bout of coughing. 'Any decision to kill a man should get the approval of the Politburo, you know that.'

'Yes, but you are the one who advises the Politburo what should be done.' Dimitri smiled wanly. 'Except if it is an accident. If it so happens that Kalinin is run over by a car, or falls from his balcony, the Politburo will not need your advice.'

There was a short silence. Oktober's hands moved closer in the circle of yellow light. 'What do you think?'

It was not a game, Dimitri realized. In this dark lair, tonight, Kalinin's fate will be decided. But why him? Dimitri had the strange feeling he was being tested. Not for his operational capacity. If he were ordered to kill Kalinin, he could do it easily. But he was asked to think, to think and advise. Oktober didn't need his advice, yet he was asking for it. Why?

He remembered that day at Panfilov, when he had seen Kalinin for the first time with the KGB Committee. He had spoken for him, and Dimitri had known he had a friend. The next time he had seen him was at the Bolshoi, then in Paris, and finally in this room. Kalinin had quietly swallowed the humiliation imposed upon him by Oktober. He had been forced to divulge a most intimate secret, his homosexual experience, to a practical stranger. And all of a sudden Dimitri wanted to help him, save Kalinin's life.

'You want to kill Kalinin to remove the danger of the Americans discovering they have been deceived,' he slowly summed up. 'We already had a case like that in Frankfurt when you sent me to kill one of our men. He died because he had done a good job.'

'Killing Lyubimov paid off,' Oktober pointed out.

'Perhaps it did, but Kalinin's case is not the same.'

'Oh, really?' Oktober's voice was sceptical. 'Tell me why.'

'We can kill Kalinin,' Dimitri said, trying to sound indifferent. 'The news will reach the West.'

Oktober nodded. 'Of course.'

'They'll deduce that we killed him because he passed secrets to Saint-Clair. Therefore they'll assume that everything he reported is worthless now. They'll assume we are going to modify our strategic development, knowing that they've had access to our plans. All our efforts during the last six years, operation Top Hat, will go down the drain.'

'Go on,' Oktober said.

'We have some other options. We can put him on trial, sentence him as a spy, and throw him in prison. The result will be the same. On the other hand, we can reinstate him in his old position. But then the CIA will get suspicious. Saint-Clair will not . . .'

'Grimaldi,' Oktober corrected.

'. . . Grimaldi. He won't forget our meeting at the airport, the day he escaped. He won't believe it was a false alarm.'

So what's your conclusion?'

'Leave them in the dark. Let them guess what happened to him. Make Kalinin disappear. Send him to a place where nobody would recognize him. Baikonur, or Kazan, Tashkent. We have facilities there. But keep him alive. We might still need him.'

'What for?'

'Grimaldi,' Dimitri said. 'We used Kalinin twice to bait Grimaldi. We might use him another time.'

For a long time Oktober didn't speak. Somewhere in the dark, silent mansion a clock chimed nine times. Oktober bent forward, and his predator's profile invaded the circle of yellow light. His eyes were narrow black slits, dully gleaming. 'Good,' he finally said. 'Very good, Dimitri.'

He stood up. 'Wait,' Oktober said. 'There is another matter I want to talk to you about.' There was a knock on the door. 'Come in,' he said.

Tamara Fedorova, Oktober's stout, middle-aged secretary, peered inside. 'There is an urgent phone call for *Tovaritch* Morozov,' she said. 'From Paris.'

He left Oktober's room, closing the door behind him. On Tamara's desk the receiver was off the hook, lying on a heap of files. 'Morozov,' he said. He immediately recognized the voice of his deputy, Nikita Srebrov. He sounded unhappy. 'It's about Tatiana Romanova, Comrade Morozov.'

'What about her?'

'She's left your apartment.' Srebrov fell silent.

'Where did she go?' he roared, and Tamara jumped from her seat. He sharply waved his hand at her, then put it over the mouthpiece. 'Get out!' he hissed at the woman, who ran out of the office, her face white.

'Where did she go?' he shouted again into the mouthpiece. 'Speak, man, speak!'

'She was followed to the apartment of a man you know, Alex Gordon, where she spent the last few nights.'

The cruel words hit him harder than a physical blow, and he swayed. The bitch! Black fury formed in the pit of his stomach, swelling in his chest, and his hands clawed with hatred. She was cheating on him! With his brother. His own brother, the American Jew-boy. I trusted him, and he stole my woman. If I could only lay my hands on you, brother, if I only had hold of your throat, I'd make you choke with your damn' chain!

'I'm flying back,' he said. 'Tell everybody I'm taking tomorrow's afternoon flight, and I'll be there in the evening.'

'Yes, Comrade Morozov.'

'And stick to her, wherever she goes. I want a full report.'

'Yes, Comrade.'

He slammed the receiver on its cradle. 'Tamara!' he yelled.

Oktober's secretary darted in immediately, she must have been listening by the door. 'I have to fly to Paris, tonight. Find me a flight. I don't care how many connections I have to make.'

'I thought I heard you saying you were flying tomorrow.'

'You'll reserve a seat for me on Aeroflot for tomorrow, and inform everybody about it, understood? And then, very quietly, you'll put me on the first flight that leaves tonight. Use an alias if you want. I'm flying back right away.'

Deceit, he thought, always deceit. Tatiana has a couple of women friends at Sovtorg. She'll find by them that I'm coming back tomorrow. Let her think she has one more day.

He stepped back into Oktober's office. His knees felt as if they were made of cotton.

Oktober stood by his window, overlooking the Bichevski Park, smoking one of his pestilential cigarettes.

'I have to fly back to Paris,' Dimitri said casually, 'some minor problems.'

Oktober nodded. 'Fine. But there's something I want you to do for me.'

'Of course.'

'I want you back here,' Oktober said, without turning. 'We are in a difficult period and I need somebody beside me. I want you here as my deputy. You've been in Paris long enough.'

So this had been Oktober's motive in bringing him over. Not only to tell him about Top Hat, but to test him and prepare for his return. At a different time he would have been overwhelmed. Oktober was making him his right-hand man. It meant he would become department chief in a few years. It was a good reason for rejoicing.

But tonight Oktober's words seemed to concern somebody else, not him. Right now he was obsessed with maddening thoughts of Alex and Tatiana naked, her licking and sucking his brother's body as she did to him. He could hear her panting and screaming with abandon. He wanted to kill her, kill Alex, see the horror in their eyes as he squeezed out their lives with his hands! He didn't care for Oktober or the promotion. His brother had stolen the only woman he had ever loved! Alex had all the women he wanted in America, but he had chosen to steal Dimitri's Tatiana. All that mattered now was getting back to Paris.

'I'll finish my business in Paris as soon as possible,' he heard himself saying.

'Good,' Oktober said, as he reached for the door. 'That's good, Dimitri. Do whatever you have to do, and come back.'

Tatiana and Alex strolled hand in hand by the pond in Parc Montsouris, and watched a few children shove their toy sailboats away from the shore, screaming gleefully. A few grandmothers were sitting on white-panted iron chairs, huddled against the morning chill. A young mother in corduroy pants and high heels clumsily chased a toddler who scurried too close to the water.

'I'd like to have your child,' Tatiana said, offering her mouth to Alex who bent over and lightly kissed her.

'So why don't we go into the bushes,' he suggested, 'and make one?'

She raised her face, but her smile froze, her eyes shifting to a point beyond his shoulder. He turned back. Two men were striding towards them, followed by a sturdy young woman. She was wearing a navy blue jacket, jeans and flat-heeled shoes. The men were more conservatively dressed, one in a black overcoat, the other in a tan mackintosh. The man in black was in his forties, while his burly friend seemed at least ten years younger.

'Mr Gordon, we must talk to you,' the older man said in American English, softened by a southern accent. He had drooping eyes, a thick blond moustache and a pointed chin.

They could be Dimitri's men, Alex thought. He took a step back, grasping Tatiana by the arm. The woman was trying to approach her from the other side.

'We are friends of Grimaldi,' the younger man said.

'Prove it,' Alex said, pulling Tatiana towards the group of Frenchwomen who stared at them suspiciously. He threw a glance behind his shoulder. Nobody approached from the back except for an elderly couple feeding a flock of plump Parisian doves.

'It's true, believe me,' the young man insisted, while his friend raised his lapel and whispered something into a tiny microphone.

'Don't come any nearer,' Alex said, 'or we'll start a commotion. You don't want that.' If the strangers were armed, they would have the upper hand anyway, he thought. The old women, smelling trouble, were already beating a disorderly retreat. Even if we yell, nobody will interfere, Alex realized. He didn't feel afraid, though, and coldly assessed their chances to escape.

'Look!' The man in black pointed towards the park entrance, where Grimaldi had materialized. He stood there, cool and elegant in his dandyish camelhair coat, nonchalantly smoking his cigar.

Thank God, Alex thought. 'This is Grimaldi,' he said to Tatiana, whose eyes darted frantically about. 'He's my American friend, it's all right.'

They walked towards Grimaldi, the three strangers forming a compact group around them. The stout woman fell in step with Tatiana, and smiled at her. 'My name is Jane,' she said.

'Leave her alone,' Alex said fiercely. He was seething with anger. 'How did you find me?' he asked Grimaldi as they reached the CIA agent. 'How did you know we were here?'

Grimaldi's face was drawn. 'We must leave immediately,' he urgently said. 'There's no time to waste.'

I asked how you found us,' Alex repeated. 'You've been spying on us since we parted at the Closerie.'

'Yes, and so have your Russian friends.' Grimaldi gestured towards an ivory Fiat, parked by a billboard praising Dim tights. The old couple who had been feeding the pigeons in the park were hurrying towards it, not looking so old anymore.

'I told you . . .' Alex started, but Grimaldi cut him short impatiently. 'We have no time for arguing. Dimitri is back and he's looking for you.'

'This is not true,' Tatiana interjected in her French-accented English. 'My friend Natalie said that he's coming back only tomorrow.'

'Yes,' Grimaldi said, 'that's what he wanted us to believe. Thank God I had people posted at both airports. They spotted him at Orly passport control. Now let's move!' He pointed to two cars, a tan Citroen and a silvery Mercedes, parked by the curb.

'Will you come with me, please?' Jane said to Tatiana, who shot an anguished look at Alex.

'She's coming only with me,' he said.

Grimaldi shrugged. 'Burt, you and Jane take them,' he said, nodding towards the Fiat, then ran to the Mercedes. They crowded into the silver-coloured car, Grimaldi, Tatiana and Alex in the back, the man in black beside the driver. The two younger agents got into the Citroen, the girl taking the passenger seat. As she bent to enter the car, Jane's jacket opened, and Alex glimpsed the butt of a handgun protruding from her belt.

'Where are we going?' Alex said. The Mercedes darted forward up the narrow street. The Citroen was next, followed by the Russians' Fiat. As they reached the intersection, the driver of the Citroen following them braked suddenly, sharply turning the wheel. The car skidded on the road, running askew, tyres screeching. It finally came to a stop, barring the street. The Fiat, trapped behind it, braked as well, furiously honking.

'Good,' Grimaldi said as the Mercedes turned the corner and darted down the Boulevard Jourdan. 'If there's no car ahead as well, we're home free.'

'Where are we going?' Alex asked.

The driver, a young man with an acne-ravaged face and a rebellious forelock of red hair, changed lanes a couple of times, plunged into a side street, made two right turns and emerged on the avenue again, taking the opposite direction. 'No car ahead of us,' he said confidently. 'We've lost them.'

Grimaldi leaned back. 'Do you have your papers on you?'

'My passport,' Alex said, and turned to Tatiana.

She fumbled in her bag. 'I have my Carte d'Identité.'

'That's all you need to cross the border,' Grimaldi said.

'Wait a minute,' Alex said. 'Wait. I want to stay here and talk to Dimitri, I think he'll listen to me.'

'Sure,' Grimaldi chortled, 'and then he'll wring your neck.' Tatiana pressed his arm, shaking her head. The Mercedes took the Boulevard Periphérique, the ringlike highway circling Paris.

'You said we're crossing a border. What border? Where are we going?' Alex asked.

'You're in danger, we're taking you out of the country.'

'What are you talking about?' Alex was fuming. 'First take us home, then . . .'

Grimaldi's voice was furious. 'There's no going home,' he said. 'Dimitri is probably there, waiting for you. There's no place in Paris you'll be safe. If you're hungry, we'll buy you lunch later. If you need clothes and cosmetics, we'll provide them. But if you want to save your girl's life, Alex, please shut up, relax and enjoy the ride.'

They changed cars at a discreet garage in Le Bourget, where a black Peugeot was waiting. At the border, Belgian immigration officers waved them through without even glancing at their papers. In the late afternoon, they drove into Brussels.

Ten days later, chased by a furious rain, Alex barged into the Café du Brabant, on Brussels' Grande Place. He took off his new raincoat – another present from Uncle Sam – and sat down by the large bay window overlooking the magnificent square. His eyes swept the tall houses with their gabled roofs and exquisite turrets. An obsequious waiter wearing a short white jacket with golden epaulettes bowed his narrow head. '*La même chose pour Monsieur?*'

'Yes, Alfred. A large café-crème, and two croissants.'

'*La même chose*, then. Right away, Monsieur.'

La même chose, the usual, as for an old, regular customer. How quickly his life had entered a new routine, he thought with wonder. Every morning, at nine o'clock sharp, a Company car would pick up Tatiana at their apartment and take her for the debriefing session that lasted until six pm. Their apartment was in the Rue Gaspard, one of the narrow streets behind the Grande Place. It was a large, cold flat with standard furniture, and they hated it.

They hated the new clothes and toiletries they'd had to buy to replace what had been left in Paris. They also hated the constant presence of armed agents: the girl, Jane, who stayed twenty-four hours in the apartment, sleeping on a camp bed in the sitting-room, and the younger male agent, Burt, positioned in a car parked across the street. Their guardian angels stuck to them even in the rare evenings they went out, to a restaurant or a cinema. Last night, Grimaldi had agreed to ease off the security measures and leave them alone in the apartment. Jane had left, after hugging Tatiana; in spite of it all, they had grown accustomed to each other. Only Burt remained in the car outside, still watching the house entrance.

At this hour, the Cafe du Brabant was almost empty except for a couple of elderly ladies who were devouring two huge slices of chocolate cake. Alex ordered another coffee, and sank back into his thoughts. Thank God the damned flat and the bodyguards were only temporary. In two days Tatiana's debriefing would be over, her papers would be ready, and they would fly back to the States. He had already written to Brown, accepting the offer of a teaching position for the following year.

He had phoned Nina – from a public phone, Grimaldi had forbidden any use of the phone in their apartment – and told her of his plans. 'I am bringing you a bride, Ninochka. A *krassavitza*, a beauty. And, besides, a real *Prinzessa*. You'll love her.' He hadn't told her, of course, about the imbroglio with Dimitri. He was going to marry Tatiana and settle in Providence. 'You'll live with us, we might soon need a babysitter.' Nina had sounded stunned, but pleased. He was sure she and Tatiana would like each other.

He put down his empty cup, thinking of Claudia. He didn't want their beautiful love affair to end like that, with him running away, not answering her letters. But what could he do? Bewitched by his new love, he had become a hostage to his own emotions.

Most of all, he felt lousy for what he had done to Dimitri. He had never imagined that he could so despicably betray his brother. For a betrayal it was, an abuse of his brother's trust. All my life I've looked for Dimitri, he thought miserably, and when I finally found him, I seduced his woman. Now he was condemned to be haunted for the rest of his life by a guilt feeling toward Dimitri.

Not that Dimitri was a saint, quite the contrary. His brother was a spy and a ruthless killer. While reading his file Alex had felt, instinctively, that the accusations against him were true. During the months they had spent together, he had learned to know him. His brother was very cunning, and had a violent streak. One night, at the ancient Flo Brasserie, they had discussed Kim Philby, the notorious Soviet mole inside the British Intelligence service. Alex had spoken of the frustration of Philby's colleagues, who had suspected him for years, but didn't have any proof against him. 'Proof, no proof,' Dimitri had smirked, 'if I were in their place, I would have killed him long ago.'

Alex indignantly objected. 'But perhaps he was innocent.'

Dimitri chuckled. 'So what?' he muttered.

The rain turned into a downpour, and the antique square all but disappeared behind a swaying grey curtain. Alex thought of the life he would have with Tatiana. He could get a nice cottage in Providence, perhaps Tatiana could teach as well, they would have a couple of kids. Not much excitement, but a happy, pleasant life. If he wanted excitement, he thought, he should have accepted Grimaldi's offer. The CIA man had been lunching with him almost every day, pressuring him to join the Company. He was the best Soviet expert they knew, he was bright, smart . . . that kind of rubbish. At first he had been flattered by the offer, but Grimaldi's insistence had finally got on his nerves. Yesterday he had turned down the offer in the bluntest possible way.

'All I want,' he said to Grimaldi, who watched him while looking unusually pale, 'is to live with my lovely wife in a quiet neighbourhood, raise her lovely children, and teach at a good university. That's final, Franco, so leave me in peace, okay?'

'And Dimitri?' Grimaldi blurted. 'Will he leave you in peace?'

'If he doesn't find me, he will,' Alex said. 'Anyway, that's another reason I don't want to join your organization. Dimitri is my family, we are of the same blood. We're brothers, dammit! And I don't want to have to fight my brother!'

He had angrily bolted out of the restaurant, leaving his steak untouched. Once back in the States, he swore, he would never approach Grimaldi or any other CIA agent again. And perhaps, with time, Dimitri would forgive him.

Gazing out of the window, he saw two young kids scurrying in the rain, protecting their heads with a soaked newspaper. They had their arms on each other's shoulders and were laughing. As they passed by the Cafe du Brabant, they turned for a second and he saw the physical likeness between them. Brothers, he thought.

'For brothers forever are one,' his father had written. If Victor Wolf was alive, he thought, he wouldn't forgive me. Lately he thought quite often of his father, and tried to guess how he would have reacted to his acts. But this time he didn't have to guess. Victor Wolf was a pillar of morality; he could never have done, or condoned, what Alex did to his brother.

He suddenly had an idea. It was crazy, true, but perhaps it could work. He got up and descended the steps to the lower level of the cafe. He stepped into a phone booth bearing the sign 'Interurbain'. He knew it meant long distance. He had enough coins to call Paris. He took his notebook out of his pocket and dialled.

'Sovtorg,' a sweet Russian voice chirped in the receiver.

'Dimitri Morozov, *pojalost*,' he said, his throat suddenly dry. He knew they wouldn't ask him for his name. KGB standing instructions were to let anyone from the outside establish direct contact with resident officers.

'Morozov.' He heard his brother's voice.

He took a deep breath. 'Dimitri, it's me,' he said.

There was silence at the other end of the line.

'I must talk to you. Please don't hang up.'

Dimitri didn't speak.

'Dimitri, I wanted . . . I wanted to tell you how sorry I am.' He was suddenly at a loss. What could he say to him? That he was sorry he stole his girl? 'I am sorry, very sorry, for what happened with Tatiana. I didn't want this to happen. I was the happiest man on earth when I met you. I have no family but Nina and you. I thought perhaps we could meet and talk things over? I didn't want to hurt you. I don't want to lose you.'

Silence again, that same hostile quiet. But Dimitri was listening, Alex could hear his hushed breathing.

'Dimitri, that night on the bank of the Seine, I . . .'

'I wish I'd never met you.' Dimitri's voice, hoarse, hate-filled, uttered the final abnegation before severing the last link between them.

'For me you're dead,' he said.

While Alex was speaking to Dimitri, Grimaldi was sipping a bitter espresso barely a hundred yards away, in the elegant Café des Anglais. He didn't know that Alex was so close, but Alex was the subject of his thoughts and the reason for his ill temper.

Grimaldi's plans for Alex Gordon had turned sour. Everything had worked to perfection, including the disclosure of the ugly truth about Morozov at the Closerie des Lilas and the timely escape to Brussels. Gordon had every reason to join the CIA and the battle against his brother. But the bastard had refused. He didn't look for excitement in life. All he wanted was a middle-class existence, with his little house, and his little wife, and his little mortgage, and his little babies. And probably a new little car every two years, lace mats on the television set, and a barbecue brunch in the backyard on Sunday, wearing a stupid smile and a pink apron adorned with embroidered little piggies.

The entire operation was a failure. Gordon wouldn't join the CIA and wouldn't fight his brother. The only man who knew the Soviet Union so well, who was familiar with Dimitri Morozov's way of thinking, refused to assume the role he had been assigned. Grimaldi had misjudged Gordon. The man was much meeker than he'd thought. He wouldn't hurt a fly unless he had a very good reason. He would fight Dimitri only if he felt overwhelming hatred towards him; only if he was motivated by a blinding lust for revenge.

Revenge, he thought, but for what? Dimitri had done him no wrong. Alex had no reason to be bitter. In a couple of days he would fly back to the States and live happily ever after with his Tatiana. Nothing could prevent him from building his own paradise. Except . . . except if it didn't happen, if he lost Tatiana forever, and the reason for that loss were Dimitri.

He put down his cup. The idea swiftly budding in his mind was appalling, but it had its own inner logic. If he could only play it right! If it worked, Alex would be on his knees, begging Grimaldi to let him tear Dimitri to pieces.

He got up and walked out into the rain, feeling like in a dream. He took a cab to the main Brussels post office. The place was teeming with people. That was good. He entered a phone booth, wrapped his handkerchief around the mouthpiece and dialled long distance. The line was busy. He waited a moment and dialled again.

'Sovtorg,' a voice said.

'Dimitri Morozov,' he grunted in the mouthpiece, and a moment later he heard Morozov's voice. It sounded disturbed.

Grimaldi assumed a low, strained voice. He spoke French. 'Tatiana Romanova,' he rasped. 'Tomorrow, nine o'clock. Thirty-seven, rue Gaspard, Brussels. Apartment seventeen.'

'Hello? Hello?' Dimitri's voice roared in the receiver.

He hung off and walked out, using his handkerchief to wipe the cold sweat off his forehead. There was no reason for remorse, he thought. The girl's debriefing was over, she was expendable anyway.

From his rented Taurus, parked on the corner, Dimitri watched Alex leave the building and enter a black Peugeot. Nikita Srebrov, who sat beside him, had seen the car earlier, and reported there was someone inside, waiting. For a moment Dimitri had thought it could be a trap, but quickly dismissed the idea. If somebody wanted to kill or kidnap him, they would rather do it in Paris, where his address was known and his routine habits were no secret. They didn't have to lure him to Brussels for that. He had no idea who had telephoned him, but the tip was worth exploring. As he saw Alex, his heart leapt with savage joy. The driver of the Peugeot kicked the engine into life, and the car drove away.

'Wait for me,' he said to Nikita, then crossed the street and entered the building. The entrance lobby was cold and sombre. He didn't take the lift, it could turn into a deathtrap. Instead, he stealthily climbed the staircase. There were four apartments on each floor, and apartment seventeen was on the fifth.

Moving in the dark, he thought he heard the pounding of his own heart. In a moment he would be facing Tatiana. What would he say to her? That he loved her more than anything in the world? That he had never loved anybody else? And that she had betrayed him? He suspected that she didn't love him, only feared him, but it didn't make much difference. She was his woman, he had trusted her, taken care of her, and she had stabbed him in the back.

He reached the fifth floor. Apartment seventeen was on the right. His fingers explored the lock on the door. It was child's play for a KGB agent. He fished in his pocket for the tiny kit of tools. It took him less than a minute to let himself in. He stepped inside, softly closing the door behind him.

'Alex?' He heard Tatiana's voice.

He stopped in the middle of the sitting room, breathing heavily. His heart leapt painfully in his chest. It was unreal, he couldn't take one more step.

'Alex?'

She appeared in the doorway, breathtakingly beautiful in a white skirt and loose white shirt, a smile dancing on her lovely mouth. He froze, petrified. He couldn't move. She could have walked past him and he wouldn't have been able to stop her. She could have pulled a gun on him and he couldn't have defended himself. She could have talked to him, and he would have talked back, and done anything in his power to bring her back to him.

But she cried out in horror, and ran back into the bedroom, helplessly limping. That shook him out of his torpor and he darted after her. The sight of the bed made his blood boil. The bitch had fucked his brother here, perhaps minutes ago. She had pulled his cock inside her. She had scratched his back, she had whispered that she loved him. He turned toward her, his hands clawed.

Tatiana stood by the bed, trembling. Her face was livid, and tears streamed down her cheeks. She was trapped, with nowhere to hide. As he approached her, she didn't even raise her arms to protect herself. Her eyes stared at him dully, a strange look in which he read deep despair and listless resignation. She waited for her death, realizing it was all over, there was no hope left.

He took another step towards her. She didn't move, bitterly crying, biting her lips. He impulsively reached for her, hugged her with all his force and pulled her towards him, burying his face in her hair. He breathed the fresh smell, and held the frail, beloved body that shivered in his arms. He raised her head towards his. She closed her eyes.

The telephone rang, a shrill, loud scream that filled the apartment. She winced, but he held her tight. The phone rang a few times, stopped, then started ringing again. The noise of running steps suddenly rose from the stairway, and he felt her body tautening with hope. It could be Alex, coming back to rescue her.

But the ringing stopped and the steps faded away. He bent toward the face, so defenceless, and kissed the trembling mouth. Tears were welling in his own eyes. 'I loved you so much, Tatiana,' he gasped. His eyes swept the whiteness of the bed behind her, and black fury heaved in his chest. His hands closed on her slender, milky neck, and he pressed, his thumbs digging deep into the yielding flesh, feeling the girl's frantic convulsions, hearing the gurgling sounds escaping from her throat. And then she went limp in his arms and he let her collapse at his feet.

He fell on his knees and gathered the girl's corpse in his arms. He rocked her gently, kissing the still face, wailing in agony.

Chapter Fourteen

Alex unlocked the door and stepped into the apartment. 'Tatiana,' he called. 'Where are you? I've got your passport.' He threw his coat on an armchair. The US consul had been less efficient than he had expected; it had taken Alex more than a hour to get Tatiana's papers. Anyway, the formalities were over now. Tatiana's debriefing had been completed yesterday so they could spend the day at their leisure. Tomorrow they would fly to Washington aboard a US Air Force plane. He hoped they need never see Grimaldi again.

'Tatiana?' The apartment was absolutely still. She never turned on the radio or played a record; she loved the silence. He crossed the living room and stepped into the bedroom. She wasn't there. 'Tatiana?' Receiving no answer, he turned towards the bathroom. Out of the corner of his eye, he saw a strange white heap on the left side of the bed. He started, then uncertainly trod towards it, his instincts already screaming in terror.

Her inert body lay before him, her head oddly twisted and her huge eyes wide open, frozen in dread. At first he couldn't grasp the meaning of the gruesome sight and stood awkwardly by the bed, staring down. No, she couldn't have fainted. He had left her happy and laughing only an hour ago. But the sad little heap lay still at his feet, and hopeless comprehension gradually seeped into his benumbed brain. She was dead.

He crouched beside her and his throat contracted, his breath bursting from him in short, painful gasps. He was shaking uncontrollably. A feeling of *déjà-vu* sneaked into his mind. Her corpse was spread on the floor the way he had seen it in his nightmares. She was dead. Tatiana was gone.

He bent over and touched her face. Her skin was cold. Incoherent ideas rushed through his mind. He shouldn't have left her alone, it was his fault, they shouldn't have come to Brussels, what would he do with her passport, where was Grimaldi, for God's sake! Tatiana knew she would die like this, she had warned him . . . Still, from all this confusion, one thought emerged, clear, obsessive, gaining total control over him. 'Dimitri,' he murmured. He stood up, and turned away from the body. Dimitri.

He ran down the stairs and into the street. Burt was sprawled luxuriously on the driver's seat of the Peugeot, smoking. A bossa-nova blared from the car radio. Alex yanked the door open. 'Get out,' he managed. 'Out!'

'What's the matter with you, man?' Burt showed no intention of complying. Alex grabbed him by the lapels of his jacket and dragged him out of the car. 'The keys,' he snapped. 'Where are the keys?'

'What the hell . . .' Burt started, and Alex hit him viciously in the stomach. Burt doubled up in pain, then raised his fists. 'Hey, you wanna fight?' he muttered. He was a big man, towering over Alex. But Alex hit him in the face with such savage power that Burt fell by the car, blood trickling from his mouth. Alex kicked him like a madman, and Burt tried to protect his face with his hands.

'The keys!' Alex yelled. A couple of elderly men stopped on the pavement, watching them in horror. 'Police!' one of them called urgently. 'Help!'

Burt shakily pointed towards the car and Alex looked inside. The keys were dangling from the ignition.

'Papers,' he breathed.

'In the glove . . . compartment,' Burt gasped, getting on to his hands and knees. Alex shoved him aside, jumped into the car, started it, and drove off, the tyres screeching on the asphalt.

He gunned the car through the city centre, ignoring red lights and approaching vehicles, chased by the shrill whistles of police officers. Following the signs posted at the major intersections, he soon reached the international highway heading for the French border, and beyond it Paris. His mind was blank except for one thought. Find Dimitri and kill him.

Later, he couldn't remember how long it took him to drive to Paris or what happened on the way. He didn't remember much of the eerie voyage except the long columns of cars along the road, the fog rolling down the slopes of the Belgian hills, then the torrential rain as he approached Roissy. At the border he must have shown his papers; but he remembered nothing. He came out of his torpor only when, having parked his car on Boulevard Pereire and tried to barge into Sovtorg, he was beaten senseless by the two Russian guards. He regained consciousness lying in a gutter, soaked in the ice-cold water that quietly flows at night in the deserted streets of Paris.

During the next few days – or was it weeks? He never kept count – Alex embarked on a quest for Dimitri. He was determined to avenge Tatiana's death. He didn't shave, didn't sleep, kept drinking heavily in the neighbourhood bars. He occasionally collapsed from fatigue on the back seat of the black Peugeot.

Most of the time he wandered in the streets like a ghost, or lay in wait outside the Sovtorg offices. At night he hid in a porch facing Dimitri's house, his eyes glued to Dimitri's black windows. Twice he sneaked into the house, climbed the staircase and pounded on Dimitri's door, but there was no answer. He haunted Dimitri's usual hangouts, the restaurants and bars where they had spent so many nights with Tatiana. No, Monsieur, we haven't seen the gentleman who had dinner with you. Yes, we remember him perfectly, a handsome young man. How is the lovely lady who came with him? Une beautée. Quite exceptional, don't you think?

Nothing mattered anymore, nothing but finding and killing Tatiana's murderer. He didn't know how he would do it, he had no weapon and barely held on his feet. Nevertheless, there was nobody on the face of the earth who could stop him if he only succeeded in finding his brother. But Dimitri had vanished.

One night he tried to climb the wall surrounding the Sovtorg building, and was beaten up again by the guards. One of them was a tall, bitter-looking man with a widow's peak crowning his narrow, expressionless face; the other was blond, good-looking, with a bull neck and wrestler's shoulders. The blond man was wearing a black polo shirt and a leather jacket; he punched and kicked Alex with a lopsided grin on his face. They didn't call the police, though; perhaps Dimitri had ordered them to avoid any contact with the authorities. A few times he glimpsed Soviet officials walking in and out of the building. One foggy afternoon he thought he saw his brother at an office window, staring down at him.

But he couldn't be sure he wasn't having delusions. When he dropped in a bar for a drink, the barman refused to serve him and two waiters threw him out. While struggling with them, wriggling in their arms, he slipped and fell head on against a wall mirror. He saw before him a filthy, bleary-eyed wreck, face covered with bristle and caked blood, lips parched, hands trembling.

That night, as he lurked by the wall surrounding the Sovtorg building, he was startled by the roar of a powerful engine. A black sedan, headlamps blazing, darted towards him at full speed. He tried to run, but he was too slow. He hurled himself towards the wall, lost his balance and fell heavily. The car climbed on to the pavement and rumbled towards him. The sedan's left side hit him with tremendous power, throwing him against the concrete. He felt the swish of hot air and the smell of rubber when the wheels hissed by his side; then everything went black.

He woke up in his apartment, ages later, lying on his bed. He couldn't move; he was in terrible pain. Somebody was applying a cold towel to his forehead. He opened his eyes, but everything was blurred. He tried to speak, but no sound came out of his mouth.

'Don't move,' a woman said softly, and he recognized the warm, musical voice of Claudia Benevento.

During the last few weeks Claudia had become deeply worried. Alex had stopped writing, and didn't return her calls in spite of the messages she left on his answering machine. She didn't know why he ignored her. She wanted to hear his voice, visualize his smile as he said 'Hi, Claud.' Only now that he was away, oddly inaccessible, she realized how much she missed him.

Claudia had reached a stage in her life when she could look in the mirror and see herself the way she really was. She knew she was proud, possessive, fiercely independent. She was a one man woman, and that man was Alex Gordon. There had been nobody else in her life since that balmy evening when the sixteen-year-old brat that she was had fallen for the boy who helped her carry her load of skirts and petticoats. True, she had experienced a couple of inconsequential flirtations while she was away – a disastrous dinner with a basketball star in Dallas, a violent evening with Ronnie Havermeyer in Indianapolis, when she had to kick the oversexed brute out of her suite, a brief kiss with a handsome designer who turned to be gay anyway. But that had nothing to do with the passionate attachment she felt for Alex.

She was deeply hurt when he left for France. It was partly her fault, she conceded. She had been intoxicated with her budding career as a designer, and instead of making Alex a part of it, had chosen to show him how successful she could become on her own. Refusing to marry him had been a mistake; they could have decided not to have children for the first few years, and she could have travelled as much as she wanted. Besides, as her mother always told her, the ring on her finger could have kept quite a few bumblebees away from her honeypot.

When Alex vanished behind a wall of silence, Claudia sensed something was wrong. He was a handsome, romantic young man, neglected by his sweetheart, alone in Paris, enjoying his new freedom in the world's love capital; it was a dangerous combination, whose bottom line spelled another woman. One Sunday afternoon she went to see Nina Kramer.

'Oh, it's you, Claudia,' the white-haired woman said dryly. 'Come in.' She led the way into the living room. On the wall hung a large photograph taken on the Champs Elysées in Paris. There was Alex, his arm thrown around the shoulders of a dark-haired young man. They were both smiling at the camera. The dark man hugged with his other arm a lovely blonde girl with huge, sad eyes and an expressive mouth. She was dressed in white.

'That's Dimitri?' Claudia asked.

'Yes, and the young lady is girlfriend of his. He is also my nephew, you know.' Nina sat on the edge of a chair, very erect, her gnarled hands on her knees. 'Sit down, please. Anything the matter?' She didn't even offer her a cup of coffee, but Claudia was immune to such hostility.

'I see you're reading,' she said politely, to break the ice. On the small table beside Nina's chair lay a new book. It was entitled *The Chief – The Real Story of Sasha Kolodny, The Greatest Spy of World War Two*. Beside it lay an old English-Russian dictionary. Claudia had seen lots of Russian books in the house but only once before had she seen Nina read something in English. It was when the old woman painstakingly went through Alex's doctoral thesis, word by word. That time, too, she had used a dictionary.

Claudia nodded towards the book. 'It is good?'

'Yes, yes, very good,' Nina said, her face colouring slightly.

'I didn't know that you read spy stories,' Claudia observed.

'This is not story,' Nina corrected severely, 'this is true.' A brief smile flashed across her face. The old girl was behaving very strangely, Claudia remarked, she seemed almost happy.

Nina pushed the book aside and became her old self again, cold and grave. 'Please tell me how are you, Claudia,' she said, her tone in total contradiction to her words.

'I wanted to ask you,' Claudia said, taking out her cigarettes, if . . .'

'I ask you not to smoke here,' Nina said sternly.

'Sorry. I wanted to know, is Alex okay?'

Nina looked at her strangely. 'Okay? Of course Alex is okay. Why not?'

She spread her hands. 'Well, he doesn't write to me, doesn't answer my calls.'

'He answers mine calls,' Nina said. 'Did you have fight?'

'No, it's just that I don't know what's going on.'

'Perhaps he is very busy,' Nina said coldly, 'he is writing an important work on the trial of his father.'

'I know, but he never calls me.'

'I thought you were never in New York.' There was a note of rebuke in Nina's voice.

Claudia stood up. 'Well, if you write to him, tell him I miss him.'

Nina got up too. As the apartment door closed behind her, Claudia had the impression that Nina knew much more than she cared to reveal. Anyway, she wasn't worried, and Alex was writing to her; that confirmed Claudia's suspicions.

She didn't give up, though. In the evening, she called a friend of hers who was a flight attendant with TWA and flew to Paris regularly. 'Karen, would you do me a favour? When are you flying to Paris again?'

'On Tuesday night. Why?'

'I'd like you to take Alex a small present, okay? He had his birthday a couple of weeks ago.' It was a lie, but what the hell?

'Sure, if it's not too heavy.'

'Of course not, it's a cashmere scarf.'

Karen had called her back only two weeks later, profusely apologizing. On arriving in Paris, she had been offered the opportunity of taking her vacation right away, and there was this French guy with a chalet at Avoriaz in the French Alps, you know, these snowbound peaks and valleys, and the fur carpet in front of the fireplace, and that delicious champagne . . .

'Did you see Alex?'

Karen seemed embarrassed. 'All men are pigs, you know.'

'You talking about your Frenchman?'

There was a long silence. 'Well, honey, don't get upset. I went to see Alex before leaving for Avoriaz. But just as I was getting out of the cab, he came out of his house with a girl. A stunning blonde. They seemed very . . . very friendly, I'd say.' She paused. 'I'm sorry, Claudia, I really am.'

A stunning blonde. She could be the girl in the photograph at Alex's house. But Nina had said she was Dimitri's girlfriend. Claudia angrily slammed down the phone. She had taken the call in her office at Havermeyer's. The entire floor was in turmoil. People were running in and out of her office, spreading out colourful fabrics, belts, jewellery. She was in the middle of preparing her autumn collection, the first 'Claudia' collection that Havermeyer was to present to the chain stores' buyers in a couple of weeks.

Launching her own collection was the realization of all her dreams. Still, Claudia didn't hesitate for a moment. She wasn't the kind to give up easily; she wouldn't miserably sit in her room, wringing her hands and dabbing her tearful eyes while the man she loved was being stolen from her. Life was a perpetual fight, and she was going to fight for Alex. There was nothing she could do in New York. For a moment she considered calling Nina; the old woman had phoned three times during the last week, leaving messages. But she finally dropped the idea. The conversation she had had with Nina, when she visited her three weeks before, was all the humiliation she could take. Let her simmer, she decided. Claudia picked up the phone and reserved a seat on the evening flight to Paris. And the hell with the collection, she thought. There would be other autumns, but there was only this opportunity to win back her man.

The Boeing landed in Paris in the early morning. On her way from the airport, she dully stared out of the cab window. In different circumstances, she would have been thrilled; she had been looking forward to the summer she was going to spend here with Alex. But now she felt indifferent to the views that unfolded before her. She thought of her forthcoming confrontation with Alex. Her future, she reflected, depended on the next few hours.

The cab took her directly to Alex's house. It was eight-fifteen in the morning, he was probably still at home. She picked up her overnight bag – she had no intention of staying in Paris more than a couple of days – and walked into the building. The entrance was neat, the floor covered with black and white tiles. The names and apartment numbers of the tenants were inscribed on a plan of the building that hung on the concierge's door.

She took the lift to the seventh floor, and pressed the brass button by Alex's door. Her breathing was shallow, and she was very tense. The blonde girl in the photograph was constantly on her mind. It was ridiculous, she thought, there were other blondes in Paris. But Dimitri had a blonde girlfriend, and Alex was seen with a blonde girl. She had rehearsed several times, during the flight, the things she would say to him – or to them, if the girl was there – but they had faded away, and her mind was totally blank.

Nobody came to the door. She pounded on the door, with the same result. 'Alex, are you there?' she called. There was no answer. What should she do? She was alone, in a faraway city, unable to speak the language. Suddenly another door opened on the opposite side of the landing. A small old woman stared at her. She was wearing a brown woollen nightgown and padded felt slippers. 'I'm looking for Alex Gordon,' Claudia said.

The old woman shook her head and said something in quick French from which Claudia picked up only the word 'concierge'. She took the lift back to the ground floor and knocked on the concierge's door. She expected an old, choleric woman, hissing and puffing, like in all those novels about Paris; she was surprised therefore when the door was opened by a plump but pretty young woman with red cheeks, who held a baby in her arms. 'I am looking for Alex Gordon,' Claudia said slowly, 'perhaps you could help me.'

The girl's face turned sombre. '*Oh, Madame,*' she said, '*je regrette à vous dire Monsieur Gordon fût blessé dans un accident. Il est à l'hôpital!*'

Claudia missed a heartbeat. 'Hospital?'

The girl nodded miserably.

An hour later she was at the American hospital in Neuilly, staring at the unconscious, heavily bandaged young man, burning with fever, turning and tossing on his narrow bed and incoherently rambling about a girl named Tatiana.

As Alex stirred and gazed fixedly at the crimson curtains in the bedroom of his apartment, Claudia bent over him. 'Alex, are you awake? Can you hear me? It's me, Claudia.'

She saw him moving his lips, a flicker of recognition in his reddened eyes. 'Don't try to speak,' she said. 'You're too weak. Just nod if you understand what I'm saying.'

For a long moment there was no response, then he painfully moved his head, a bare fraction of an inch.

'You were at the hospital,' Claudia said. 'The police found you in the street. You were hit by a car. Do you understand me?'

A slight nod again.

'You remember the accident?'

There was no reaction.

'You remember the car that hit you?'

He stared at Claudia's face, and with great difficulty moved his left hand towards her. He looked terrible, an emaciated, wrinkled man with sunken yellow-tinged cheeks, cracked lips, saliva running down his chin; his face was covered with a two-week-old beard. Her eyes filled with tears when she recalled the handsome young man he used to be.

'When you were brought to the hospital, you had three broken ribs, and a broken arm. Don't move your right arm, it's still plastered. All your body was cut and lacerated. You had lost a lot of blood, and you were very weak. You spent a week in a coma, and the doctors thought you would never make it. Wait, don't move.'

From the kitchen, she brought a bowl of chicken soup, which she had been keeping warm since Alex had started shifting in his bed. She slipped a pillow behind his back and carefully pulled him up. He was light as a child, a bag of loose skin hanging from a heap of bones. She started spoon-feeding him, like a baby.

'I brought you over from the hospital five days ago. You were still unconscious, and you are under very strong medication. We disconnected the infusion only this morning. I've been injecting you six times a day, a nurse taught me how to do it.' She patiently fed him the soup, although most of it dribbled down his chin.

'You must sleep and rest, and I'll feed you when you wake up. The worst is over now.'

He nodded, this time more distinctly, and closed his eyes. For the first time in five days, she let out a sigh of relief. Now she could perhaps take a shower, and even doze a little bit. She hadn't had a moment to herself until now. She had spent ten days and nights at the hospital, drowsing once in a while on a bench in the corridor; since their return to the apartment she hadn't left his bedside except when the nurse came.

But her troubles were not over yet. In the following nights, Alex kept waking up, hoarsely screaming, in spite of the heavy sedation. He was bathed in cold sweat and his body was shaking. In the muddled stream of words and phrases erupting from his mouth, Claudia again discerned the girl's name: Tatiana. Each time he pronounced it, in infinite love or in intense pain, she felt as if somebody was plunging a knife into her heart. Alex also repeated the name Dimitri, which she knew was his brother's. His utter torment reached its peak when the word 'murder' emerged from his mouth and he wildly tossed on the bed, kicking away the covers, crying, choking, his good hand fiercely clawing at something in the dark.

As these fits seized him, Claudia would gather him in her arms and rock him gently until his convulsions subsided and he sank again into an agitated sleep.

When he was asleep, she restlessly wandered through the apartment. Everywhere she found traces left by the other woman. The toothpaste, the comb and cosmetics in the bathroom, the clothes hanging in the wardrobe, between his suits, or mixed with his shirts and underwear; a couple of books, a handbag, some blonde hairs sticking to his clothes. She often stood in the dark, watching the bed where he now lay, feverish, and couldn't help imagining him with Tatiana, naked, wildly making love. She tried to escape these obsessive thoughts, and would seek refuge on the narrow balcony, staring unseeingly at the sleeping city, letting the cold wind lash her face. But the image of Tatiana wouldn't fade away.

When she washed him and changed him, she thought of Tatiana's hands, lovingly stroking his naked body. Jealousy and anger churned inside her. She felt she was slipping out of her mind. He was hers, he had been a part of her for years, and he had betrayed her so willingly.

My God, Alex, she thought, looking at his pitiful figure, how could you do this to me?

From the bits and pieces she could put together, she roughly worked out what had happened. He had become infatuated with Tatiana, and they had become lovers; the girl had been murdered afterwards. Alex held Dimitri responsible for the murder. Nina, whom she phoned from the apartment, broke down and admitted that Alex had indeed spoken to her a few weeks before and announced he was coming back to New York with Tatiana, whom he was about to marry. Yes, Tatiana was the blonde girl in the photograph. She used to be Dimitri's girlfriend before. Alex had said she was a real princess, Nina added. He had called from Brussels.

Brussels, Claudia thought, what was he doing in Brussels? And how did he get into the car accident in Paris? Nina didn't know, and there was nobody she could ask. Alex had been found in the street by the police, and brought to the hospital unconscious. She had called the Institute of East European Studies, but a sour woman's voice answered that Mr Gordon hadn't been seen for several weeks. No, they didn't know that he had been involved in an accident. How terrible indeed.

The riddles that haunted Claudia were solved by a swarthy man with a trim moustache and green eyes who came to see her one morning. 'My name is Franco Grimaldi,' he introduced himself. He was in his fifties, ostentatiously dressed in a blue cashmere blazer and bow tie, velvet waistcoat and grey trousers. Solid gold rings glimmered on his fingers. 'Alex told me a lot about you.'

'You know him?' They were sitting in the living room, with the door to Alex's room closed.

'Very well.' Grimaldi lapsed into uneasy silence, then frankly admitted: 'I work for American Intelligence. I flew over to Paris on the same plane as Alex.'

She eyed him suspiciously. He didn't exactly fit her idea of a secret agent.

Grimaldi told Claudia a harrowing story about Alex's brother, a killer in the service of the KGB; he described Alex's infatuation with a girl of Russian origin, Tatiana Romanova, and their flight to Brussels for fear of Dimitri, her former lover. Grimaldi had made arrangements for their return to America in a few days.

'Dimitri tracked them down. He followed them to Brussels. He succeeded in breaking into the safe flat where Tatiana was in hiding, and strangled her.'

Claudia winced. An image of Dimitri hugging Tatiana on the Champs Elysées flashed before her eyes.

'I shall never forgive myself,' Grimaldi said, looking away. 'I was in charge of her safety, and I failed to protect her. She died because of my negligence.'

Claudia clenched her jaw. The story was tragic, indeed, but she couldn't forget, for a single second, that the man was speaking of Alex's mistress. The one who had taken him away from her.

Grimaldi then told her how Alex had jumped into a car and driven to Paris, seeking revenge. He had tried to force his way into Dimitri's office, determined to kill him. 'What happened to him on that street was not an accident,' he said, his eyes holding Claudia's in bleak focus. 'The Russians tried to do away with him, and he was lucky to survive.'

'Where were you when the car hit Alex? You had promised to protect him.'

'We tried,' Grimaldi said, 'but there was no way to control him. He acted like a madman. Besides, our people are instructed to stay away from Russian compounds. That could create international complications.'

Claudia frowned. The excuse sounded phoney. She decided she didn't like Grimaldi, he was too sleazy for her taste.

Grimaldi said that the following week he was returning to Washington, and suggested that Claudia take Alex back home. 'Paris is still too dangerous for him,' he warned. 'We think that Dimitri Morozov has gone back to Moscow, but we can't be sure. Even if he has, I'm certain he could send his agents to assassinate Alex. This apartment is being kept under our surveillance, but so was the flat in Brussels that Alex shared with Tatiana.' Grimaldi offered his help in Alex's safe transfer to New York.

Claudia listened in stunned silence. Here was this green-eyed dandy, telling her of the wild passion of her lover for another woman, describing how he had almost died because of it. He would never have done that for me, Claudia thought. He never fought for me, he always took me for granted. She had never been so humiliated, but she was not going to show it. She stared defiantly back at Grimaldi when he spoke of her lover's betrayal. She didn't need anybody's pity.

'Thank you,' she said finally and got up. Grimaldi hesitated a moment, then stood up as well. 'I'll stay here with Alex until he recovers, then I'll take him back home. Thank you for your help, but I'll manage by myself.'

Three weeks later, a cab took Claudia and Alex to Charles de Gaulle airport, where they boarded an Air France flight to New York. Alex was still very weak. He kept silent most of the time, answering Claudia's questions in monosyllables. He had behaved like that since he had started to recover. Their former closeness had vanished. She avoided any mention of Dimitri and Tatiana; nevertheless, his answers were cryptic. His spontaneity, his infectious laughter, had faded away. There was no more warmth in his smile. His eyes had acquired a hard look; two bitter lines framed his mouth.

This is the end of our love, Claudia thought. Watching the stranger beside her, she realized they had nothing left in common. He had hurt her and humiliated her. True, she too had been to blame for the way she had treated him before. But she had done everything in her power to redeem her mistake and bring him back. She had left her work, jeopardizing her career, and flown to Paris, to find him. She had saved his life. She couldn't save their love. There was no use trying to resuscitate something dead and gone. He didn't belong to her anymore; even now, his feelings were with the dead Tatiana. As soon as they reached home, she would turn a page and spend the rest of her life trying to forget Alex Gordon.

From Kennedy airport Claudia took Alex to Nina's house. When they arrived in Brooklyn, she had the cab driver unload Alex's luggage on the pavement then kissed him lightly on the cheek, and drove away. He made no effort to stop her. She watched his immobile figure until he disappeared from her sight. From her life as well, she thought, and clenched her teeth, holding back the tears.

'*Golubchek moi, lyubimi*!' Nina received him with hugs and tears, but he was reserved, remote. Something had broken inside him, and he recoiled from any sentimental effusions. She had prepared a real feast for his return, but he barely touched the food, skipping even his favourite chocolate mousse. After the coffee, he retreated to his room. He heard her pacing restlessly outside his closed door. His poor aunt, she loved him so much. But he couldn't talk to her now. All he wanted was to be left alone.

For the next few months he barely left the house, mostly sitting by his bedroom window, staring at the blank grey wall across the yard. He spoke very little; Nina's attempts at conversation shattered against his silence. He didn't even react when with starry eyes she brought from her bedroom the book about Sasha Kolodny, and showed him several passages. 'He is alive, you know, perhaps I meet him some day,' she said.

He only nodded, and mumbled some niceties, as in all their conversations. She was deeply hurt by his apathy, but he couldn't help it. Nothing mattered now, nothing had any meaning. He was at home in Brooklyn, but his mind was away, and the grisly scenes from

Brussels and Paris kept flashing through it, like an endless tape of horror, perpetually replayed.

As time passed, though, nature gradually took over. He started eating, and slowly recovered his health. When he emerged from his torpor, he threw himself into physical activity with a febrile determination. He jogged every morning, worked out at home, then practised at the Fitness and Spa Club. He started visiting Jack Macmillan's boxing school again, although Jack was long dead, and mercilessly tortured the punching ball, night after ferocious night. His body recovered before his mind; he regained weight which turned into taut sinew and stone-hard muscle, powerful arms and tapered legs.

It was weird, a kind of escape, or perhaps his own way of regaining his sanity. Yet it took a long time before he could read newspapers, make phone calls or open letters. The only letters he wrote were returned unopened; the only phone calls he placed were unanswered. Both were addressed to Claudia Benevento.

Four months after his return, in the early fall of 1975, Alex flew to Washington. He was slowly surfacing from the nightmare. He could think of Tatiana without breaking into a cold sweat or starting to shiver. His obsession with revenge wasn't gone but it had metamorphosed into a cold, ruthless determination.

He landed at Washington National, rented a car, and drove to CIA headquarters at Langley Woods. He had called ahead and was expected. At the main gate he got a visitor's tag and was ushered to a conference room in the main building. Grimaldi was waiting for him, smoking a black Swiss cheroot. Alex took a chair facing the peacockish agent and impatiently brushed off Grimaldi's attempts at small talk. 'You're still fighting the KGB?' he asked.

Grimaldi nodded. 'Somebody must do the job,' he said, tilting his head. 'What about you? First they killed your mother and father, then your girl. And you still want to hide in some goddamn campus and let others avenge your dead?'

Alex quietly said: 'That's why I came. I wanted to find out if your offer still stands? If the Company wants me, I'll join.'

'We want you all right,' Grimaldi said.

From Langley Woods Alex drove to Baltimore. He swallowed a tasteless hamburger and a beer at a diner, then parked his car behind the Excelsior Hotel. He crossed the lobby and went down the stairs to the Grand Ballroom. Rhythmic pop music filtered through the closed doors. He found a chair and patiently waited until the doors opened and a group of thin, long-legged models emerged, chirping and laughing, swinging their bags. Claudia was the last to come out. She had lost weight, and looked slim and elegant in a blue suit. She was laughing, a throaty carefree laugh. 'Tomorrow at five,' she called after the departing girls, then she saw Alex and stood still.

He got up and approached her.

'What are you doing here?' she breathed. She nervously ran her fingers through her hair.

He ignored the question. 'How was the rehearsal?'

She hesitated. 'Fine. The fashion show is tomorrow.'

'I know. I checked with your office.' He paused. The silence was awkward, tense. 'Will you have a drink with me?'

She looked at her watch and nodded indifferently.

The hotel bar was polished mahogany, leather, gleaming copper and subdued lights. In the background Johnny Cash lamented a lost love. A middle-aged couple were holding hands in one of the booths, the woman throwing anxious glances over the man's shoulder.

Alex ordered a chilled vodka. Claudia asked for champagne, then changed her mind. 'A glass of white wine will be better,' she said.

'I came to talk to you,' Alex said. 'I can't go on like this, Claud. You don't answer my calls and my letters, but we must talk.'

She shrugged. She sat perched on the edge of her chair, her back ramrod stiff.

'You saved my life in Paris, I'll never forget that. But I didn't come here out of gratitude. I love you. I don't think I can live without you.'

'I thought you couldn't live without Tatiana,' she said scornfully.

'I became obsessed with her, that's true. I don't deny it. But you're the woman of my life.'

'Don't give me this bull!' she angrily threw at him. Looking over her shoulder, Alex saw the barman, who was polishing glasses, turn his head towards them.

'It's true, though,' he said patiently. 'We had a wonderful love story, you and I. Then I went away, and had a dream. That was Tatiana, a dream that turned into a nightmare. Now I'm waking up, and it's not always easy.'

She lit a cigarette with angry, disjointed gestures, without looking at him. 'What do you want, Alex?'

'I want to marry you, Claud.'

'What for?' she threw at him, leaning over the table. 'To hold your hand? You lost her, so you remembered your fall-back girl? What do you think I am, a consolation prize?'

'No, you're not,' he said forcefully. 'I told you, Claud, I love you, and I want to marry you.'

She shook her head. 'It's too late.'

'Why? Is there anybody else?'

She shook her head again. 'I am seeing somebody, but that's not it.' She drew on her cigarette and slowly let out the smoke. He had the feeling she was making a tremendous effort to control each of her movements. 'By the way,' she said, 'before I came to Paris, I was faithful to you. I never cheated on you.'

'Which isn't the case now.' He completed her thoughts. 'I understand. But that isn't cheating. You left me, but only after I left you.'

'You wrecked my life,' she said forlornly, suddenly off guard.

'I know. And I don't know if I can help you rebuild it again. I've changed, Claud. My whole outlook on life has changed. I don't want to teach anymore, I am going to work for the CIA.'

She smiled bitterly. 'So you're still seeking revenge, are you? You're still after your brother.'

'I guess so. I don't want to lie to you. And I'll tell you something else – I still think quite often of Tatiana. I can't take her out of my mind. But I don't think of her as I did before. It's like something from another life. I don't know if we would have been happy together.'

She raised his eyes and looked at him sceptically. Her mouth was bitter. On the jukebox, Johnny Cash had ended his ballad, and some young boy was softly killing Roberta Flack with his song.

'I told you,' Alex went on, 'I was obsessed with Tatiana, it was an infatuation.' Memories flooded his mind and muffled his voice. 'A cursed infatuation that brought only misery and death.'

'You're telling me that you want to marry me, but Tatiana will always be between us.'

'No,' he said, leaning forward and taking her hand. It was cold, inert. 'I love you, I dream of you, and I want to build my life with you. I'm ready to beg your forgiveness if it will help. I hurt you terribly, I know. You're extremely beautiful, Claud, you're a proud woman, and' – he smiled wanly – 'you're Italian. You must have gone through hell because of what I did to you. I can't think of a worse humiliation.'

'Well, I was to blame, as well, at the beginning,' she spontaneously admitted, softening a little.

'You mean for my leaving for Paris? Yes, it was your fault. But I don't want to talk about it. I want to talk to you about the future, not the past.'

She leaned back and crossed her legs, exhaling a long puff of smoke. 'Did you tell Nina that you were coming to propose to me?'

He nodded. 'She was very pleased. She's sitting now in her old chair by the stove, praying that you say yes.'

Claudia frowned. 'That's new.'

'She speaks of you like a saint. She knows you saved my life. She says what you did was very Russian.' He beckoned to the pretty

Hispanic waitress for another round of drinks. 'The reason she didn't want you before was because she knew you would take me away from her. She was right. Now she knows that I'll be unhappy for the rest of my life without you. And she knows I'll never meet anybody like you again. Anyway, Nina's position in this doesn't matter.'

'Alex . . .'

'You're going to say no, aren't you?'

She nodded gravely. She was more relaxed now, the old, confident Claudia. 'Alex, we've changed, both of us. You're not the same boy I was in love with when I was sixteen. You betrayed my trust. And I'm not the same, either. I was cheerful, then, I was a happy person. I grew up in a warm family, with great friends and lots of love. You opened up a new world for me, and our love story was a great adventure. But that adventure ended badly. I've become cynical now, even bitter. I don't trust declarations of love anymore, Alex, even yours.' She looked into her empty glass. 'I don't want to get hurt again.'

'Please don't say no. Think it over. Remember, Claud, I love you. It's a different love now, deeper, more mature. It's not a teenage passion anymore.' He let out a deep breath. 'And don't forget – I'm your man, Claud. I always will be. Even if you reject me, you can never forget what we had together. We can't get away from each other. We still can be very happy. You loved me once. Don't you love me now? Tell me, I must know. Don't you?'

She bit her lip and stubbed out her cigarette with abrupt, angry gestures.

'Why are you so upset?'

'Because you make me unsure,' she said frankly, 'and I hate it. I had everything organized and decided. You were out of my life, for good. I had made up my mind. And here you come and buy me a glass of cheap wine, and there's this music and the lights that make me sentimental, and things are not so clear and final anymore. I don't want to melt again, Alex, I'm still hurting.

'Perhaps I'll stay here and we'll meet for breakfast, to talk it over again?'

She stood up. She was so lovely, he thought, with the shadows under her high cheekbones and her head proudly raised. Her voice was calm, sensible. 'No. Go back to New York. I can't answer you now, Alex, and I won't answer you tomorrow. If you insist upon an answer right now, it will be no. I hated you when . . . when all this happened. I don't hate you now, but I still feel betrayed. Humiliated. Leave me alone, let me be with myself for a while.' She refused the second glass of wine that the waitress brought. 'They say,' she turned to him, picking up her bag, 'that time heals all wounds. Do you believe that?'

Claudia gave him her answer on New Year's Eve, calling him long distance from Seattle, laughing and crying over the phone.

Six weeks later, in a modest ceremony in Washington, she and Alex were married. Only a few friends and relatives assisted at the wedding.

A year after their marriage, shortly after Alex completed his training course at the CIA, their first child was born. The baby was a blonde, blue-eyed little girl, and they named her Tonya.

But deep in his heart, and never aloud, he called her Tatiana.

Part Three
WAR
1977–1991

Chapter Fifteen

A new surge of rain violently splashed against the glass panes as Dimitri, standing by the high window, gazed at the morose greyness of Boulevard Pereire. He was in his old dusky office at the Sovtorg building in Paris. It was March 15, 1977. Exactly two years ago he had hurriedly escaped from Paris, after his return from Brussels; today was the second anniversary of Tatiana's death.

He had stubbornly avoided Paris since, not because he feared the authorities. The Belgian services had failed to establish any link between him and the dead girl; the French had no grounds to accuse him of the hit-and-run accident that had almost killed his brother. Actually, the man who had hit Alex was Evgeni Zaitzev, one of Dimitri's agents in Paris. The accident had occurred almost a week after Dimitri had returned to Russia. The French Sûreté couldn't know, of course, that he had cabled the instructions in code to Zaitzev from Oktober's black mansion in Moscow.

No, the reason for his skipping Paris was different: for him Paris was Tatiana. Everything in this city – the rainswept streets, the parks, the restaurants and cafes, the language, even the people – reminded him of her. It was a tormenting memory that he vainly tried to chase away. He had loved Tatiana with a savage passion that he had never experienced before. No other woman had excited him like her, no other woman had driven him to the same peaks of ecstasy. And no other woman had awakened in him such intense feelings, such desire to share his life.

During the last two years he had slept with many women. It was rough, mean sex, always on the verge of violence; it left him spent but angry, dissatisfied. Perhaps it was an attempt to overcome the haunting memories of Tatiana. But the attempt failed. The sad, slender girl with the golden hair was the only woman he had ever cared for. The open wound she had left inside him was still burning with pain, vivid and fiercely intense. As was his hatred of Alex Gordon.

He had made a mistake about him, though. Revenge didn't mean murder necessarily. If Zaitzev had succeeded in killing Alex that night, his brother would have suffered for a split second, then given up the ghost. That was not enough for what he had done. He should make Alex suffer for years, make him live in torment and fear, turn his days into a nightmare and his nights into hell. 'Revenge means hitting our enemy where it hurts most,' Oktober had croaked one night, 'and making him wish he never saw the light of day.'

Revenge, however, was a double-edged sword. It hounded the victim, but it also haunted the avenger with ugly, overwhelming obsession. Alex Gordon was constantly on Dimitri's mind, surfacing in his memories, a hated yet faithful companion. Standing now in his old Paris office, Dimitri strove to drive his brother from his thoughts and concentrate on his present mission.

When he had left Moscow, a couple of weeks ago, he hadn't intended to come to Paris. His destination had been Oslo. Since becoming Oktober's deputy he was on the road most of the time, supervising Department Thirteen's operations. He had gone to the Norwegian capital to set up the assassination of a KGB mole, code name Greta, a Foreign Ministry secretary who had been supplying Moscow Centre with secret documents for the last twenty-five years. Greta had recently drawn the suspicion of the Norwegian services and had to be silenced before revealing the tremendous scope of her betrayal. Dimitri's plan was to kill the woman at home and dress up her murder as a heart attack. But an urgent message from Oktober had cut short his preparations and summoned him to Paris.

Two Russian dissidents, living in Switzerland, and a CIA team, dispatched from Langley, were about to meet in Paris, Oktober's cable said. The purpose of the meeting was to establish an overall plan of dissident activities inside the Soviet Union. Oktober wanted all those who assisted at the meeting dead, Americans and Russians alike. It was the first time in years that Dimitri had been ordered to kill American agents.

Since Jimmy Carter's inauguration, America was becoming an active enemy again. The weakling president who kept blabbering about world peace was openly scorned by Moscow Centre; but his quixotic crusade for human rights was alarming. He had just exchanged letters with the notorious dissident Andrei Sakharov and welcomed in the White House another dissident, Vladimir Bukovski. This had to be stopped. A good juicy hit would warn the CIA to leave the dissidents alone.

The phone on Dimitri's desk discreetly buzzed and he picked up the receiver. It was Monsieur Doriot, the owner of the antique firearms shop Le Mousquetaire on Quai Voltaire. He had been Dimitri's main supplier when he used to live in Paris, and was the first he had called on his arrival.

'I've got what you want, Monsieur Morozov,' Doriot happily chirped. 'Two duelling pistols from the early seventeenth century. They belonged to the Marquis Bussy d'Amboise who was killed in a duel under Cardinal Richelieu's windows in 1627.'

'Very good, Doriot,' said Dimitri, excited. He was proud of the ancient firearms collection that occupied an entire room in his Moscow apartment. He spent hours a week dismounting and cleaning his guns, pistols and ornamented muskets. 'They're certified authentic?'

'Of course, Monsieur. When can I expect you?'

Dimitri glanced at his watch. It was ten thirty-five, and he had nothing to do before lunch when his agents would report at his office. 'Why not right now?' he said.

'I'll be delighted. *A tout à l'heure, Monsieur Morozov.*'

His car, a black Citroen, was waiting by the main entrance, driven by Murad Islamkulov, a Turkoman with a broad, fleshy face. The use of drivers' jobs as cover for high-ranking operatives was a routine practice. Islamkulov was one of Dimitri's top agents. 'Quai Voltaire, Murad,' he said.

The car emerged out of the driveway, its roof battered by the fierce rain. In front of them the outer gate began to open. As the Citroen reached it, a blinding white light suddenly flashed in the car windows. Lightning, Dimitri though, but then a tremendous force heaved the car off the ground and tossed it towards the wall. Its left side crushed against the gatepost and it overturned heavily, landing on its roof as a deafening noise rumbled behind.

Islamkulov slumped over Dimitri, his arms limp, his liquid black eyes wide open.

He crawled out of the wrecked car via the shattered windshield, amidst a hail of debris that rained all over the place. His left thigh hurt terribly and he leaned on the wall. His trouser leg was torn, he had lost his shoe. He felt a stinging pain along his jaw, and ran his hand over his face. There was blood on his fingers. A familiar odour wafted about, but he couldn't place it. The Citroen lay on its roof with its wheels in the air, like some giant beetle. Dimitri still didn't understand what had happened, then he turned back and gasped in astonishment.

The Sovtorg building had vanished. In its place rose a heap of rubble, stones, broken beams and pieces of furniture. A couple of human figures painstakingly crawled beside the ruins, like giant, gawky crabs. Of the entire building, only one wall was still standing, crisscrossed with fat grey lines that marked the former emplacement of walls, floors and a staircase. A bidet and a lavatory seat, miraculously intact, hung at the wall's upper left corner; they made the ruins look oddly obscene.

Dimitri, dumbstruck, took a couple of steps towards the building, the rain furiously whipping his face. The wall of sirens rose behind him, and suddenly the place was full of cars, police, ambulances, firemen. A few medics carrying stretchers darted past him, heading for the ruins. A woman was shrilly screaming. Somebody threw a blanket on his shoulders. '*Monsieur, vous êtes blessé!*' a concerned voice called, but he shook his head and kept trudging towards the ruins.

His numb mind started to clear and he worked out what had happened. An explosion had blown the house to pieces; the blast had overturned his car, killing Islamkulov. Still, his own life had been saved because he was in the car. If Doriot hadn't called, and he hadn't decided to leave unexpectedly, he too would be buried under the ruins now like so many of his men.

A police officer was bent over a heap of torn papers. Dimitri winced. 'The archives!' he called, and beckoned to one of the Sovtorg guards, a blond guy who wandered about, eyes wild, jaw slack, apparently unscathed. 'You – are you all right?'

He had to repeat his question for the guard to understand.

'Yes, I'm looking for Grisha.'

'Forget about Grisha,' Dimitri hissed. 'The French will take care of him. You go and find all our people able to walk, and collect all the papers scattered around, understand?' The man showed no intention to comply, a dumb expression painted on his face. Dimitri yelled at him: 'The papers, the documents, you idiot! The French shouldn't put their hands on our papers.'

'But Grisha . . .'

'I am Lieutenant-Colonel Dimitri Morozov, and I am ordering you to collect all the papers from these ruins, you half-wit! Now go and do it, on the double!'

'Yes, Comrade,' the guard mumbled, still dazed, and scurried towards the house.

Dimitri's head was spinning. He slumped down on a block of masonry. A sharp pain repeatedly pierced his chest; every time he took a breath, he felt as if a dagger were ripping his lungs. He must have been flung against the dashboard when the car overturned. People were running beside him, carrying immobile bodies on their stretchers. He heard moans and one of the bodies stirred; the man was alive. Most of the people inside the building had probably been killed. Thank God some of his men were out, looking for the dissidents and their CIA contacts.

A couple of firemen half-carried him to a cafe across the street where he was laid on a bench. His clothes were soaked with rain and he shivered violently; but the pain in his chest subsided, turning into a dull throbbing. He struggled to a sitting position. The owner served him a bowl of beef bouillon, laced with brandy. The warmth spread through his body. He gazed dully at a Toulouse-Lautrec poster of the Moulin Rouge hanging on the wall. Tatiana had loved Toulouse-Lautrec. Once she had said to him that he looked like Lautrec's portrait of a poet called Aristide Bruant.

After a while a police officer came to him and asked for his address. He gave the name of his hotel, the huge Concorde-Lafayette at Porte Maillot. In large hotels, foreigners were less conspicuous; operational units never stayed in small hotels, where they were easily remembered. A police car took him to the hotel where a doctor dressed his wounds and sedated him.

He woke up in the late evening, to an insistent pounding on his door. He got up. He was still dizzy, but the pain had subsided. He limped to the door. A police officer had come to interview him. Dimitri ignored his questions. 'What caused the explosion?' he asked. 'A bomb?'

The Frenchman was surprised. 'No, of course not,' he said. 'It was a gas leak. A ruptured gas conduit leaked a huge amount of gas that accumulated in the basement. Then some electric spark, or a match . . .' He shrugged, spreading his hands. 'A tragic accident, Monsieur.'

Dimitri recalled the sharp odour he had sniffed after the explosion. It was gas indeed.

'Do you think it happened otherwise?' the officer asked.

He stared at the Frenchman's face. 'Oh, no,' he said finally. 'I'm sure it was an accident as you said, a gas leak.'

Suddenly, unable to control himself, Dimitri laughed bitterly. The officer stared at him in bewilderment. Yes, Dimitri thought, they'll find nothing else. No bomb, no explosives, no dynamite. Just a gas leak. A tragic accident. That's what they would diligently write in their reports before closing the file.

But he knew it was not an accident. Not on the anniversary of Tatiana's death. Not on the date when he had snapped her neck. Not with him, Dimitri Morozov, cunningly lured back to Paris, his own base of operations. Now he was sure there would be no meeting between dissidents and CIA agents, it was a red herring. The story had been cooked up and leaked to Oktober just to bring Dimitri to Paris and set him up for the kill.

The killers had meticulously planned everything, except for one small detail: Doriot's call had saved his life. Dimitri was sure that the French would find no clue as to the identity of the man who had ruptured the gas pipe after sealing the basement. It might have been somebody wearing the uniform of Gas de France or the electrical company. He would never be found.

But Dimitri could identify the fingerprints all over the operation. The unmistakable mark of the man who had volunteered to the CIA in October 1975, completed his training last winter, and right away – according to the reports piled on Dimitri's desk in Moscow – joined the Soviet Division of Clandestine Operations. The man who knew the Soviet obsession with subversion was so intense that a report of CIA agents meeting with dissidents in Paris would bring Dimitri running. The man who had sworn to destroy him. This had been his first strike, and others would certainly follow when soon his enemy found out that he had survived.

Alex, you're behind this, I know it. This is a declaration of war, big brother. Now it's my turn. You'll live to regret the moment Tonya Gordon brought you into this world. If I don't kill you first, that is.

On the plane, on his way back, Alex felt strangely elated. The plan had worked smoothly, and the uniforms of the Electricité de France had served perfectly the team of three agents who had infiltrated the Sovtorg building under his orders. He should keep using uniforms and official papers in the future – people respected them, especially the Russians. And he should always act as swiftly. The entire operation – the puncturing of the rusty gas pipe, the sealing of the basement, the installation of the plastic timer, which would be pulverized by the explosion – had all taken less than fifteen minutes. It had been easy, almost too easy.

But his brother had escaped again. He clenched his jaw. He had been so close, dammit! Dimitri had no reason to leave the building, he was supposed to be there when the house blew up. The sonofabitch won't be so lucky next time. He thought of the bodies they had dug from the rubble. The fact that he had killed so many people didn't bother him. Why should it? After all, nobody had forced them to join the KGB. Two year ago he would have been appalled by the death of nineteen people, refused to believe he might cause it. But that was in another life, before Tatiana's murder. He was a different person then. A romantic, he thought, with a surge of self-contempt. Still, the pictures of the maimed corpses he had seen in the newspapers kept flashing before his eyes.

Grimaldi picked him up at Dulles International, drove him to Langley, and proudly paraded him in the seventh-floor Executive Lounge where all the Clandestine Services barons came 'for their pint of blood', as he used to say.

'We're very proud of you,' he beamed, sticking his thumbs in the pockets of his paisley waistcoat. 'It was a superb hit. And what counts most – it's untraceable. They can never prove it wasn't a gas leak.' He ordered a double vodka for Alex, a cognac for himself, and started rolling a big cigar between fingers and thumb. 'That was a beaut, Alex. You've got a great future ahead of you. You go on your first operation abroad – and wipe out the entire Department Thirteen headquarters in Western Europe. It will take them ages to recover. All their archives gone, nineteen agents blown up . . .'

'Except the one I wanted,' Alex said bitterly.

'You'll get him next time.' Grimaldi blew a whiff of smoke to the ceiling. 'You've just started.'

Alex nodded. He had just started, indeed. He had gone through a preparatory course in Washington, and a shortened physical training at the Farm. He was a few years older than the other trainees, but he had an edge over them – his burning motivation. The course in Washington had been routine – espionage techniques, coding, transmitting, decrypting; the seminars on geopolitical questions and foreign services were disappointing. At the Farm, on the other hand, he had enjoyed the physical exercises, the firearms practice, and most of all the hand-to-hand combat.

On completion of his training, Alex had joined the discreet Redwood Unit where Grimaldi served. Redwood was a part of S/D – the Soviet Division of Clandestine Services, operating against Soviet targets. Alex had been offered a better position as an analyst with the Office of Current Intelligence, but had turned it down. He was determined to go after Dimitri Morozov, and could do it only as a field agent. His brother's face didn't leave him for a single moment. At night he would often wake gripped by murderous, black hatred.

His appointment as an operational agent, so early in his career, was an achievement in itself, but he had nobody to share it with. Claudia wasn't happy with his career at the CIA. She suspected he had embarked on a vendetta to avenge Tatiana's death. She was right, of course. They had a tacit agreement not to discuss the job, and that blew a chill over their relationship. Nevertheless, their marriage was successful. Claudia wasn't travelling so much as before, she had taken a couple of years off to be with the child; she was painting now, mostly delicate aquarelles that reminded him of the French artist Marie Laurencin.

Nina, on the other hand, had become overtly hostile. She told Alex she couldn't understand how he could ever raise his hand against the land of his birth. He hadn't admitted that he worked for the CIA. He told her a vague cover story about a research section at the State Department, but she had seen through his bluff. She often telephoned Claudia, they got along well at last, and sometimes he felt they created a common front against him.

He felt very lonely in spite of his love for Claudia. He couldn't mourn his lost love on his wife's shoulder. The only person with whom he could share his agony was Nina, and she was drifting away from him.

Since joining the Company, he had lost his peace of mind. He couldn't concentrate on reading; he rarely listened to music. His only relaxation, when he returned to his Chevy Chase home, was the time he spent with little Tonya, grimacing and clowning before the baby, changing her, feeding her, and searching in the clear blue eyes for the poignant vulnerability of Tatiana.

'Congratulations, Napoleone,' a slim black man said. His voice brought Alex back to reality.

'Thank you,' Grimaldi said, 'it's not official yet, Ned, but thanks anyway.'

'What's not official?' Alex asked. Ned chuckled, moving away.

'Well,' Grimaldi said with studied indifference, 'old Vince Morton is leaving the Soviet Division, and I am going to succeed him. I guess it's partly because of you, Alex. There was another candidate, Ralph Rusk. You know him.'

Alex nodded.

'But after Paris they didn't want to hear of anybody but me. So I'm taking the skipper's seat, thanks to your gas leak. And you' – he pointed his cigar at Alex like a king's sceptre, green eyes glowing – 'as soon as you complete your first year in the division, you are going to become my deputy. Which will give you all the power you need to crush your beloved brother.'

'I've got another plan,' Alex said, staring intently at Grimaldi. 'I want to bring Dimitri to Bonn in a couple of months. I've thought of a bait, and this time he won't escape.'

Grimaldi stared at him, his smile slowly vanishing. 'You don't waste time, do you?' he said. 'Did you ever think that while you're planning Dimitri's funeral, he might be preparing yours? He might hit you where it hurts most, you know.'

The telephone in the living room rang at midnight. She had just fallen asleep. She woke up with a start and hurried in the dark, shivering in her nightgown. Even before picking up the receiver she had a presentiment that something unusual was gong to happen. A faraway woman's voice asked: 'Nina? Nina Alexandrova?'

'*Da*,' she said in Russian, her body shaking. Alexander was her father's name in Russian. Nobody had called her Nina Alexandrova for more than fifty years.

'Somebody wants to speak to you,' the woman said, in Russian as well. 'A friend of yours. One moment, please.'

A man's voice, old and cracked, filled the receiver. 'Nina? Ninochka, is that you?'

Her knees buckled and she collapsed in the nearby chair. The voice was old, but she would recognize it always. She had been waiting for it since she was a young girl.

'Sasha?' she whispered. 'Sasha?'

'Yes, that's me, Sasha. *Lyubimaya*, how are you?'

'Sasha! My God, I don't believe it, you're alive.' He had called her '*lyubimaya*', his beloved. 'Where are you?'

'In Moscow, and I feel fine. Are you all right?'

'Oh, yes,' she managed, crying and laughing at the same time. 'Yes, I feel fine too. How did you find me?'

She could swear by his voice that he was crying as well. He said something she didn't understand.

'Who is that woman?' she asked, bracing herself for bad news.

'What woman?'

'The one who called me?'

He laughed. 'Oh, she is my neighbour. I was afraid to cause you a shock, we are not very young anymore, so I asked Maria Fedorova to speak to you first. She's gone now.'

'Thank her for me,' she blurted, laughing with relief. 'Can you speak or do you want me to call you back? International calls are expensive, you know.'

'No, it's all right, I don't mind spending all my savings on this call.'

'Tell me, Sasha my dear, what happened to you?'

He would tell her, he said, but not over the phone. He had finally received the book about himself almost three years after it had been published in England, and found her name. He had got her telephone number from the writer. Yes, he had phoned London. No, actually London had phoned him. The publishers were very excited that they had found him at last. They were going to produce a special programme about him on British television, and they were flying him over to London. And – brace yourself, he said, brace yourself tight and don't say no – his publishers wanted to bring her too, from New York, so they could meet, almost sixty years after they had been separated.

She was dumbfounded. 'They'll pay for my trip to London?' And he said yes, her trip, and her stay, for a week in January. They wanted her to appear with him on television and be interviewed about their youth together. Was that all right? And she said yes, she would come to London in January, she wanted so much to see him. She was pinching herself. She thought that it was a dream, and expected to wake up at any moment.

He laughed, then asked her to be discreet about their plan. The English publisher wanted their appearance on television to be a surprise to the viewers. She agreed, it made sense indeed. 'They'll sell your book all over the world after they see you on TV,' she giggled. 'You'll become rich, a capitalist.' After exchanging some more words of affection, they hung off.

She didn't sleep that night, and didn't want to. She sat by the window, in the dark, thinking of him. Their conversation had filled her with tremendous joy, an overflowing happiness she hadn't expected could exist. Everything seemed different. Life was beautiful. She felt young again, even softly intoned a few measures of *Ochi Chornaya*, a love ballad about a pretty black-eyed girl that he used to sing to her. 'It's a bourgeois song, but that's the way I feel about you,' Sasha used to say, smiling.

Stop that nonsense, Nina, she humorously scolded herself. You're an old woman, almost seventy-five years old, and he's eighty! But for her he was still the handsome young Red cavalryman with the shock of blond hair and the mischievous eyes. The years that had passed since their separation, her life with Samuel, her miserable times in Russia, Palestine and America – suddenly all that didn't matter anymore. What counted was that she was going to be with Sasha, her Sasha again.

Was he married? A widower? Did he have children? He hadn't said. But it really didn't matter. Each one of them had lived their own life. What counted was that after all those years he had called her 'my love'. And he had cried, they had both cried with happiness.

She felt an urge to call somebody and tell them the great news. She started dialling Alex, then on second thoughts replaced the phone on its cradle. No, she thought, she shouldn't tell him. He was with the CIA, he might make a fuss about the whole thing and spoil her wonderful adventure. She decided not to tell anybody. It could reach the newspapers and harm Sasha. She would only tell Alex and Claudia that she had decided to go on vacation to Europe, just once in her life. After all, she had the right to such a small luxury.

Her plan worked perfectly. Alex didn't suspect anything when she told him she was going to Europe for a week or two. On the contrary, he and Claudia encouraged her. 'That's wonderful, Ninochka,' Alex said over the phone, behaving nicely for the first time in more than a year. 'Take a vacation, enjoy yourself!' He offered to give her some money, for expenses, but she proudly refused. Claudia also seemed very happy for her. She was a sweet girl indeed. They had become very close after she had saved Alex's life; the past was forgotten. Besides, Claudia had given them little Tonya, a cute little devil, exactly like her grandmother.

In mid-December Nina got a phone call from British Airways. Her ticket had arrived, the nice girl said, a return ticket to London, departing on January 21, return open. Could she come and pick it up at the office?

Their office was on Fifth Avenue in Manhattan. And a few days before Christmas, dressed in her best clothes, her new patent leather shoes and the new beige coat she had bought for the trip, she took the subway to New York, walked into the British Airways office, and picked up the plastic pouch they had ready for her. Later she had lunch at a nice Chinese place off Fifth Avenue where she examined her ticket thoroughly.

Sasha called once again, to make sure everything was all right, and on January 21 she took a cab to the international terminal at Kennedy airport. 'I feel like a million dollars,' she happily confided in Alex, who had flown from Washington to say goodbye.

'Take care, Ninochka,' he said, kissing her warmly. 'And beware of the men in London. They are dangerous – they crave for older women.'

Oh, boy, have I got news for you, she thought.

The first hitch occurred on her arrival at London airport. She was tremendously excited by the thought that she would meet Sasha, in a few minutes. Would he like her? She had been to the hairdresser yesterday, and for the first time in her life, to a beauty parlour. The girls at the parlour had told her she looked great. Still, when he had left her she was a young girl, with soft white skin and long, abundant hair. Today she was an old woman. Would he remember the girl who had given him her love?

She couldn't wait to see him, her patience had run out. The line before the immigration counters seemed to be the longest in the world, as was the wait for her bag which a nice young man loaded on to her trolley. But when she was finally outside, in Heathrow's arrival hall, Sasha was nowhere to be seen.

She stood undecided in the middle of a crowd of harried passengers, welcoming parties, drivers, porters and airline employees. In the loudspeakers a mellifluous voice announced the departure of an Alitalia flight to Rome, gate 27, then repeated the announcement in musical Italian. On the newspaper rack before her, fat headlines announced the forthcoming meeting between Presidents Carter and Sadat, and Israel's Begin.

'Madame Nina Kramer?'

She turned sharply. Before her stood a florid-faced British gentleman, in a dark suit, stiff-collared shirt and striped tie. He held *The Chief*, Sasha's biography, in his left hand.

'Yes, I am Nina Kramer.'

He bowed slightly. 'Derek Sloane, from Graham and Dickinson. We published the book about Mr Kolodny.'

'Oh, yes, how are you?' She shook his hand.

'I hope you had a pleasant flight?'

'Yes,' she said mechanically. 'Yes, thank you.' She looked over his shoulder, dark foreboding invading her thoughts.

'I'm awfully sorry,' Sloane said, 'but Mr Kolodny has been delayed. He has been a little indisposed the last few days.'

'He is ill?' she asked anxiously.

'No, not really.' Sloane took hold of her trolley and pushed it towards the exit. 'He is supposed to arrive today with the late Aeroflot flight from Moscow. I'll take you to your hotel so you can eat something and rest. You must be very tired.'

'Yes,' she said. 'Thank you, sir.'

In the funny cab, like she had seen in the English movies, she sat silent and erect during the long drive to London. She stared with curiosity at the double-decker buses, the police officers with their unusual helmets, and the House of Commons that she glimpsed from a distance when they crossed the Thames. The hotel was in Hampstead Heath, a neat establishment called the Tudor Arms. Her room was small but pleasant, decorated in light colours. She hesitated for a long while before finally she gathered all her courage and called room service for a couple of sandwiches and a glass of milk. Then she switched on the television and watched school programmes for a couple of hours. She was just about to lie down for a nap when somebody knocked on her door.

It was Derek Sloane again. 'A small problem, I'm afraid,' he admitted. 'Mr Kolodny cannot come, he is too weak to travel.'

Her disappointment was immense. She wasn't going to see Sasha, after all! 'So . . . so I came for nothing?' she stammered.

'Not necessarily.' There was another possibility, Mr Sloane pointed out, that was perhaps even better than the one they had planned. If Mrs Kramer agreed, they could arrange for her to fly to Moscow tomorrow, and meet Mr Kolodny there. The BBC had some local TV crews in Russia, and they could film Mrs Kramer and Mr Kolodny in Moscow. 'Just imagine,' he said, 'you two talking to the camera with the Kremlin as a backdrop.' If she agreed, they could arrange everything. They had good connections with the Soviet consulate and could get her a visa in a matter of hours.

'I don't know,' she said uncertainly. But her imagination was already galloping wildly, and she knew she would give anything to be there, to fulfil the dream that had been burning inside her for the last fifty years. The temptation was tremendous: walk in the streets of Moscow, stroll in Red Square, see the Kremlin, Lenin's mausoleum! Suddenly she had a golden opportunity to visit Russia before she died. Yes, she thought, she wanted to go. But would Sasha agree? 'I want to speak with Sasha first,' she said, 'on the telephone.'

'Very wise,' approved Sloane. 'We'll make the arrangements.' He left fifteen minutes later with her passport, 'to get you a visa in any case', and she stayed in her room, waiting for Sasha's call. It came in the early evening. Sasha's voice was tired and rasping, but he was very enthusiastic about her coming to Moscow. 'It's only a three hour flight, Ninochka. I'll be delighted to show Moscow to you. Come! Come quickly!'

The next afternoon, exhilarated yet gripped by profound trepidation, she landed at Sheremetyevo airport. The sun was setting, its last beams painting in pale gold the snowbound fields on both sides of the runway. She was in Russia, on Soviet soil! The terminal was a huge, modern building surrounded by scores of airliners from many countries. She felt she was coming home, or else like an aging mother meeting her child after years of separation, amazed by the way it had grown up. Walking along the vast concourses, she stared with wonder at the showcases full of Russian artifacts, the colourful posters of Ostankino and the Lenin Museum, the bust of Brezhnev, carved in black stone. She smiled at the handsome officers, clad in green uniforms and shining boots, who stood guard in the arrivals hall; she spoke in Russian to the immigration clerk, who seemed pleased and said to her, grinning: '*Dobro pojalovat, tovaritcha.*' Welcome, Comrade.

He waited for her by the exit from the customs hall, a very grave old man, not so stocky anymore but still erect, broad-shouldered, dressed in an old dark suit, a white shirt and a tie, his leonine head proudly raised, his mane of white hair neatly combed, the sharp eyes nestling under thick eyebrows. He was holding a bunch of fragrant red roses. And she started crying even before he collected her in his arms. She smiled through her tears. 'Roses in January,' she said, and burst out crying again.

'*Nu, nu*, Ninochka,' he said gently, softly caressing her hair.

'It was black when you left me, remember?'

'What?' He smiled. His teeth were stained by nicotine.

'My hair. It was jet black. And you had blond curls.'

'Well, we're both the same colour now,' he said. 'White. Let me look at you.'

She stepped back, blushing like a little girl, feeling the warmth rising in her skin, setting her cheeks on fire. She stared back at him. His jaw was still strong, and his mouth full and determined, as in the picture the English writer had brought to her.

He reached over and took off her glasses. 'Wonderful,' he said, 'you look wonderful. I would have recognized you anywhere. My Nina.'

She wiped away tears, but they kept coming. 'I should have gone with you to Palestine when you asked me,' she said. 'Our lives would have been different.'

He nodded.

'Oh, Sasha, how childish I was. How foolish.'

'Come on now, don't cry. We can't change the past. Let's go.' He took her by the hand. She held his roses close to her face, breathing their perfume.

'Where are we going?'

'We'll leave your bag at your hotel, we'll have dinner, we'll drink a little, and we'll talk.'

'You're not married?' she blurted. 'There was nothing in the book about your marriage.'

He smiled, a wistful, inward smile. 'I was. That's a sad story. I didn't want them to print it.'

Later, when they were seated in the Kiev Restaurant, in her hotel, they spoke a little, and drank a little, and cried a lot, about the years they had wasted, about their going their separate ways, which no reunion could ever bridge. She knew a lot about him from what she had read in the book, and he filled in the gaps. Yes, he had married, in Spain, during the Civil War, to a Russian girl named Irina. They had returned to France together, and there were born their two daughters, Katya and Nina. 'Yes, Ninochka, I named her after you. I told Irina it was my way of remembering you.'

When the war had broken out, Irina and the children had returned to Russia, and he had been left behind to direct the Soviet espionage network in occupied Europe. 'I suppose you know all about that,' he said, lighting a black cigarette, 'it's all in the book.' But when he had returned to Russia after the war, and had been thrown in the Lubyanka, Irina had divorced him and taken the children away. She had even testified against him, denouncing him to the KGB as an English spy. The KGB inquisitors, who had tortured him in prison, had shown him her declaration, couched in studious, neat handwriting on four pages of a child's exercise book. 'Well, I was in prison, and she wanted to save her hide, so she signed all they told her to.'

But when he had been released, she hadn't even called, and his letters to her were returned. She was dead now, and he didn't mind. But his daughters were both married, one in Orel, the other in Kazan, and he had four grandchildren whom he loved dearly. 'Nina might come to Moscow while you're here,' he said. 'She wants to meet the other Nina.' When he smiled, his eyes became slanting slits, surrounded by tiny wrinkles, and he looked like an old Chinaman.

But then the smile would vanish from his face, and he stuck out his chin aggressively, eyes burning, and suddenly he became a formidable, brutal man. She could feel the power he had once exuded. Here was the Chief, the man who had ridiculed the Gestapo, broken the Nazi codes, and scared the KGB so much that they threw him into an underground cell for eleven long years.

After his release, he said, he had been reinstated in the KGB, but a few years ago had retired. He lived on his pension now. 'I also was decorated,' he said with undisguised pride. 'Better late than never. Lenin's Order, the highest decoration of the country. I am a hero of the Soviet Union.'

'Hero of the Soviet Union,' she repeated, transported, then raised her glass. She couldn't believe she was doing this. 'Let's drink to the hero.'

He swallowed his vodka in a single gulp, then put his hand over hers. 'Now let's hear about you, *lyubimaya*.'

She leaned forward and clasped both his hands. 'I don't want this to end, Sasha, I don't want to wake up. It's a dream.'

A dream it was indeed, for a full week. They spent practically all their time together, strolling in the streets of Moscow and on the banks of the Moskva river, touring the city monuments, visiting the Bolshoi and the Maly Theatres, sitting on a bench in the park or in some ancient cafe before an order of *blinis* and *kvas*, and talking. They had a whole lifetime to talk about.

They also spent their nights together. 'I am an old man,' he admitted to her the first evening, with his disarming smile. 'I am too old for lovemaking. But at least let me sleep beside you, and hold your hand.' She had blushed and said yes, she wanted that very much.

This is not you, Nina, she told herself when she undressed in the bathroom, put on her nightgown and slipped under the covers at his side, this is another woman. You would never do that. And as he turned off the light and reached for her, she smiled to herself. Yes, indeed, she was another woman.

She had never been happier. If they could only stay together, she thought, if they could only finish their lives together. But she knew this was impossible.

It was a wonderful week, although there were a few distressing moments. One afternoon they crossed Dzerzhinski Square and she almost fainted, staring at the Lubyanka where her sister had been shot. She said that to Sasha, who sadly shook his head. Yes, he knew about Tonya and Victor and all the others. Stalin, he said, was the tragedy of the revolution.

Nine also grew upset during the television interview, which was very strange with three stone-faced Russians filming them in front of the Kremlin and St Basil's Church while a fourth man asked them stupid questions in high-school English. She had seen interviews on television. This wasn't an interview. But Sasha said the questions didn't matter, actually, the BBC people would edit the film and leave the questions out.

There was also the matter of Sasha's morose mood, which she perceived after sobering up from her initial elation. Most of the time he was rather sullen and ill at ease, although he was very gentle and loving towards her. At times, when she caught him off guard, his eyes had a grim, almost desperate look. She asked him if something worried him, and he denied it with unusual vehemence.

On their last night together he cried when she told him about their little boy who had died. At the airport, he hugged her hard and kissed her very softly, very lovingly, on the mouth. 'Ninochka,' he murmured, 'dearest, I love you. I've loved you all my life.' He added cryptically: 'Remember that, come what may.'

She remembered that on arriving in New York when two FBI agents who had been waiting for her at the airport arrested her for espionage and assistance to a foreign agent.

'It's quite conclusive, I'd say,' FBI Special Agent Norman Neave muttered, spreading the contents of the thick file on the desk, placing documents and photographs in neat rows as if playing a game of patience with oversized cards.

'Conclusive my foot!' Alex Gordon grunted, bending over the desk. They were in the headquarters of the CI-3 counterintelligence squad, on the eleventh floor of the FBI's Washington field office. It was late at night, and the large agents' room with its thirty metal desks, was all but deserted. A lone agent sat by the window, reading some material under a bulletin board covered with postcards of girls in bikinis. The smell of stale tobacco hung in the air. Agent Neave had his own office, separated from the squad room by a glass partition.

'See for yourself,' he said, pointing at the tidy rows of glossy papers. 'Photographs of Nina Kramer and a KGB officer, Sasha Kolodny, known as the Chief.' He repeatedly struck the glossy photographs with the back of his hand. 'Here they are by the Kremlin. Red Square. Gorky Park. Sheremetyevo airport.'

'The man was her former lover, for Christ's sake!' Alex snapped angrily.

'When? Sixty years ago?' Neave glowered at him, picking up a report. He had pink, plump hands. 'Did she tell you that she was going to Moscow, when she left the country?'

'No,' Alex said, 'so what?'

'What did she tell you?'

'She said she was going to London for a holiday,' he reluctantly admitted.

'And what is she saying now? Did you see her?'

Yes, he thought, he'd seen her. His Nina, broken, humiliated, held in the women's detention centre on 11th Avenue, with the junkies and whores of New York's West side. 'She says she went to London to tape a joint television interview with Sasha Kolodny who had phoned her from Moscow. But in London she found out the man was sick, he is eighty years old, and couldn't travel. So his publishers flew her to Moscow, and the interview was taped there.'

'Oh, really?' countered Neave, smoothing his brown moustache. He stuck his round paunch forward. 'I know those answers by heart. I questioned her, remember? Well, let me tell you, there is not a word of truth in what she says. First of all, there was no television interview, not in London and not in Moscow.'

'But she said . . .' Alex started, then fell silent.

'The BBC never planned such an interview. ITV never planned such an interview either. The publishers of the book are a very respectable London firm. They never invited him or Nina Kramer to London. No representative of theirs ever met Nina Kramer at the airport. She didn't pay for her flight ticket. It had been prepaid in London and cabled to New York. We traced the source. It was paid by cheque by the Russian trade mission there.'

'Sovtorg,' Alex murmured, a chilling doubt slipping into his voice.

'Same with her hotel,' Neave went on triumphantly. 'Sovtorg paid for it. And for her flight to Moscow. She had a Russian visa waiting for her in London. Nobody gets a visa for Russia the same day, it takes at least two weeks to process an application.'

Alex took a deep breath and paced around the desk. On the wall was a photograph of a thinner Neave and three other men, looking elated, surrounding two terrified young boys. Under the photograph was an inscription in handwriting: 'Boyce and Lee. The Falcon and the Snowman, January 1977.'

'And what does your aunt say about this?' Neave asked, handing him a batch of photostats. Alex shuffled through them. They were sequences of letters, in unintelligible groups of four and five. He looked questioningly at the CI-3 agent.

'Microdots,' Neave said. 'We removed them from a guidebook of the Kremlin, in Russian, that she carried in her suitcase. We haven't decoded them yet, but that's only a matter of time.'

'The book was a present from Sasha,' he muttered.

'Of course,' Neave sneered. 'What more do you want? She's a communist, she was investigated in the fifties, she secretly flew to Moscow and met with one of the greatest spymasters of the KGB, she came back carrying a book full of coded instructions, she lied every inch of the way, and you say she's innocent?'

Alex shook his head. 'I say she was framed.'

Neave eyed him sceptically. 'By whom?'

Alex walked to the window and looked outside. Before him stretched the dull waters of the Anacostia River. Between a large junkyard and an empty field, their ugliness mellowed by a thick layer of snow, rose the stark bulk of an electric power plant, spewing thick smoke. A train passed close by, sadly hooting.

The last days had been tough. He was in Bonn, working with the West German service on a scam intended to entrap Morozov. A high up German official, known for his ties with exiled minority leaders, was to approach the Stasi, East German Intelligence, and offer it secret documents about the Armenian underground in Russia. It was a bait Dimitri couldn't ignore; a few months before, three Armenians had bombed the Moscow subway. They had been arrested, tortured and shot, but hadn't revealed the names of their accomplices.

In the middle of a meeting, Alex was called to the telephone. On the other end of the line was Claudia; she sounded hysterical. Nina had been arrested last night, on her return from Europe. All the New York papers carried her photograph on their front pages. They described Nina as a Russian mole, planted in America fifty years ago. One headline proclaimed: 'Red Nina Was Red Spy.'

Flabbergasted, Alex had cut the meeting short, and flown back home. Claudia met him at Kennedy; she had left Tonya with her mother. Bail had been denied, she told him on their way to town, they said Nina was a danger to the security of the United States.

In the women's jail, they met his aunt who looked like a ghost. Because of his position with the CIA, they were allowed to talk in a separate room. Nina kept crying and wringing her hands. Claudia hugged her closely, and Nina gradually regained control over herself. Bit by bit, she described her trip to London and Moscow. But suddenly she broke down and doubled up in a foetal position, weeping and mumbling unintelligible words in Russian, her eyes glassy, her clenched fists trembling. When he tried to hug her, she screamed and turned to the wall. Leaving Claudia with her, he flew back to Washington to meet the man who had arrested her.

Sovtorg had paid for her ticket, Neave had said, and for her hotel. Dimitri . . . His devious brother could easily have made the payment untraceable, of course, by paying cash and leaving a phoney address. But he had chosen to leave Sovtorg's prints. He had wanted Alex to know it was him. Nina's ticket was Dimitri's signature. The damn' snake had chosen to hit Alex by destroying Nina.

He turned back. 'Let me ask you a few questions,' he said to Neave, making an effort to control himself.

He was stuffing a big meerschaum pipe. 'Shoot,' he said. Too many action movies, Alex concluded.

'How did you get all these pictures from Moscow?'

'That's classified information.'

In two steps Alex was upon him, shaking him by his lapels. 'Don't give me that shit, do you hear me?' Neave's pipe fell on the floor, the tobacco spilling on the brown carpet.

The FBI agent grabbed his wrists. His face had turned white. 'Let me go! You crazy or what?' His eyes darted towards the telephone.

Alex grabbed the phone and stuck it in Neave's face. 'Go ahead, call your boss, ask him if you should answer my questions. Ask him! Tell him I threatened to bust your face before he kicks you out of the service.'

'Me? Why me?'

'Because, brother, you're in big trouble. This little old lady has been set up, with your active cooperation. This is a KGB scam, and you've fallen for it. When the truth is revealed, they'll need a scapegoat for that blunder. You.'

Neave glowered at him, then stepped back. 'Okay, okay,' he muttered with wounded dignity, 'don't get excited. I can't disclose the modus operandi . . .'

'I don't give a damn about your modus operandi,' Alex threw at him. 'I want to know if your people took the pictures, and why.'

Neave kept dallying, denying, eluding the issue, but finally, cornered, he admitted that yes, the FBI had been tipped off before Nina Kramer's departure that her destination was Moscow; and, yes, she had been under FBI surveillance since she left Kennedy. He had alerted the security people at the American embassy and they were waiting for her in Moscow; they took the pictures of the couple. He didn't know who had tipped them off. No, he didn't know either who had furnished the newspapers with the details of Nina's past.

It all figured. 'As I told you,' Alex said, 'it's a frameup all right.' Dimitri, you scum, he thought, did you have to involve her in this? This poor old woman, your mother's sister. Did you have to pillage her last dream? Her one moment of happiness?

'Frameup?' Neave had regained some of his confidence. 'Why would they frame a harmless old lady?'

'Because they wanted to get at me,' he said.

'Who's they?'

Oh, hell, Alex groaned inwardly, what should I say? My brother? My brother, who is a KGB priest, wanted to hurt me by framing his aunt? He shrugged in silence and turned to leave. He was by the door when the telephone on Neave's desk rang. The agent picked it up. 'Neave,' he said. He listened for a moment, then turned towards Alex, glaring malevolently. 'It's for you.'

It was Grimaldi. 'I knew I'd find you there,' he said. 'We just received a flash from Moscow. Sasha Kolodny committed suicide today in front of the Lubyanka. He shot himself in the head. Hundreds of people saw him do it. Your brother won't be able to cover it up. Kolodny is a hero of the Soviet Union, you know.'

Alex quietly replaced the receiver and stared at the dark window. Dimitri's ploy was falling apart. He had apparently forced Kolodny to play out that despicable farce with Nina. The old man, probably remorse-ridden, had cracked and killed himself. At least the suicide proved Nina had been framed. Then he suddenly realized that he would have to break the news to his aunt. How shall I tell her? he thought in anguish. It will kill the old girl.

But when he arrived at the detention centre, Nina wasn't there. She had been taken to the hospital during the night. A stroke, the warden said. He found her at Bellevue hospital, lying motionless on her bed, a small gaunt woman, her white hair spread on the pillow, looking like death. There was, though, a strange tranquility about her, as if she had departed the world of the living, without regret, and quietly waited for her hour to strike. She didn't recognize him. Massive brain damage, the doctors said.

Two weeks after she suffered her stroke, a letter arrived at her home. It had been posted in Vienna. The address had been written in block letters on an old air-mail envelope. Alex opened it. The letter was in Russian. It was signed by Sasha Kolodny.

My Nina,
When you receive this letter I won't be alive anymore. I cannot live after what I did to you. And what use is there in staying alive? I had my greatest moments of happiness when you were here, in my arms. I'll never experience such happiness again, even if I lived to a hundred years.
   Before you left I told you that come what may you should always remember that I love you. This is the truth, but not the whole truth. I was blackmailed into framing you by the classic method that, I must admit, I too used to practise in the past. I was threatened that if I didn't take part in the plot intended to incriminate you, I would never see my daughters or my grandchildren again. I'm an old man, my love. Katya and Nina and their children are all I've got. I couldn't allow any harm to come to them. I had no choice but to comply.
   I lied to you. About my British publisher inviting us to London, and about the television interview. But I didn't lie to you about my deep love for you. Ninochka, we both made a tremendous mistake in our youth, in choosing our new religion, in parting from each other. We should have gone to Palestine together and built a new life for ourselves. But we can't change the past, and we paid for our stupidity. I'm dying, a sad and disillusioned man. I hope this letter will at least bring you some solace, by letting you know you were the only woman I ever loved.

The last line, scratched and twisted, bore witness to Sasha's terrible agony. 'I didn't betray you,' he wrote.
   Alex rushed to the hospital and broke into Nina's room. Perhaps, he prayed, that letter would shatter the blank wall that her disrupted brain had erected around her. He squatted by her bed and read the letter aloud, several times, stroking the old woman's forehead. But Nina stared fixedly into space, unseeing, unhearing, a dead soul in an extinguishing body.
   She died two days later, without surfacing from her coma.

Chapter Sixteen

Shortly before dawn on December 27, 1979, Dimitri Morozov landed at Kabul International airport, in Afghanistan, aboard a military Ilyushin aircraft. With him were twelve agents from his department and sixty KGB commandos, trained at the Special Operations School at Balashikha. They were all dressed in uniforms of the Afghan Army. They immediately boarded Afghan jeeps and trucks that had been prepared beforehand, and headed for the presidential palace. At the palace gate, the convoy was stopped by an Afghan roadblock. As the sentries approached the vehicles, Morozov's men opened fire on them, riddling them with bullets.

Dimitri led the assault on the palace, firing his submachine gun at anything that moved. In the splendid lobby, furnished with crystal chandeliers and precious silk carpets, three Afghan officers barred his way. They were apparently amazed by seeing soldiers in Afghan uniform attack the palace. After a short hesitation, one of the officers pointed his pistol at Dimitri. He was a colonel, burly and balding, with a thick black moustache. Dimitri mowed him down. The other two raised their hands in surrender. He shot them as well. Oktober's orders had been succinct: no witnesses should survive.

More Afghan soldiers appeared in the doorways, and his men hurled themselves upon them, shooting and throwing hand grenades. From the corner of his eye he saw two Russians slump to the floor. Fuck your mother! he thought. We didn't expect so much resistance. Firing madly, he ran up the marble staircase to the President's living quarters. Frightened screams, thuds, bursts of machine-gun fire echoed throughout the palace. Scared servants scattered before him, trying to hide in bathrooms, closets, under the beds. He fired at them, short, accurate bursts, and dashed through the long succession of rooms, reloading his weapon.

He heard his soldiers' running steps behind him. He hesitated in a narrow, dark passage, then crouched by an open doorway, spraying the room before him with bullets. It was the presidential bedroom. Parade uniforms, civilian clothes, women's silk robes, were strewn on the large bed and the white carpets. A bottle of perfume had overturned, spilling a golden liquid that spread a sweet, musky odour.

He darted up the steps to the top floor, kicked open a locked lacquered door and broke into an obscure room. It was not a room, he realized, but a bar, with mirrors, round stools, a rosewood counter. Behind the counter, several racks were loaded with bottles of imported spirits. Glasses of various sizes and shapes stood in two cupboards. That was how a Muslim President broke the Islamic ban on alcohol, he thought in a flash. He heard a muffled sob on his left and swerved, simultaneously squeezing the trigger of his Kalashnikov. Two figures, closely entwined, collapsed on the floor. He bent over. Before him lay President Amin and a young, dark-skinned woman, probably his mistress.

Dimitri straightened up, his breathing shallow. His face was on fire, his forehead covered with sweat. He stepped behind the bar and poured himself a tall glass of cognac. He had accomplished his mission.

The next morning the Soviet protégé Babrak Karmal was sworn in as President of Afghanistan, and asked the Soviet Union for the assistance of her troops.

At a modest ceremony in Moscow, Dimitri Morozov was promoted to full colonel.

After the Afghan coup, Dimitri was assigned to train PLO guerrillas at Balashikha. He disliked Arabs, but enjoyed the thought that by training the Palestinians he would be indirectly fighting Israel and the Jews. He loathed the State of Israel, although he had to concede it had a fine army and an excellent intelligence organization. But Jews had always been good spies, he thought, because of their sly, treacherous nature.

In the early fall, he was back in the department mansion. On Oktober's orders, he reluctantly showed the department's poison research laboratory to four Bulgarian visitors, members of their secret service. When he had taken over Thirteen, Oktober had transferred the poison laboratory to the mansion.

Dimitri led the Bulgarians to the cellar where the research facilities were located. The scientists moved silently between the visitors. They were not allowed to talk to foreigners. Dimitri knew several of them, including an old, bald gnome of a man with a wizened face and bright blue eyes; Oktober claimed that he had worked in the notorious poison chamber of the Stalin era.

When the tour was over, the Bulgarians specified what they wanted. Dimitri had to comply. These were Oktober's orders. He regretfully parted with the laboratory's latest invention, half a dozen tiny poisoned pellets that could be noiselessly fired from the tip of an ordinary-looking umbrella. The Bulgarians later used the weapon to murder two of their dissidents in Western Europe.

In 1981 he was in Warsaw, advising the Polish Army on the techniques of seizing power and imposing martial law; the Kremlin thought this was the best way to contain the dangerous Solidarity Movement. Dimitri had a different opinion. He thought the Polish services should assassinate Lech Walesa and the other Solidarity leaders. The movement would be decapitated and fall apart. But the Poles feared that such a step might lead to a revolt.

On his return to Moscow, he clashed with Oktober in their most violent confrontation ever. Oktober wanted Dimitri's operational team to assassinate Pope John Paul II, whose origins and outpourings had turned into a threat against the Polish regime. Dimitri refused. 'We can do it,' he threw at Oktober. 'But if it ever became known that Soviet Russia assassinated the Pope, the political consequences would be devastating.'

They brought their opposing views before a secret Politburo board, which ruled in favour of Dimitri. The attempt on the Pope's life was taken off the hands of the KGB and entrusted to Mehmet Ali Agca, a Turkish terrorist, who was manipulated by the Bulgarians. All connections with the KGB were carefully severed.

That summer, in Rome, Agca managed to approach the Pope's open car in St Peter's Square, fired and wounded him in the stomach. But John Paul II survived. The identity of the assassin was eventually exposed. Former KGB chairman Yuri Andropov, now an eminent member of the Politburo, invited Dimitri to his Kremlin office and warmly thanked him for his foresight. Oktober's disgrace was only a matter of time, Dimitri realized. With Brezhnev's death, in November 1982, Andropov was crowned as the new Soviet leader. A few weeks later, Oktober was ordered to resign. At thirty-two, Dimitri Morozov became the youngest ever chief of Department Thirteen.

Dimitri stuck to Oktober's tradition of keeping his department separate from the rest of Moscow Centre. He refused to move the headquarters to the new complex at Yasenevo, where all the other branches of the First Chief Directorate were grouped. Department Thirteen stayed in its black mansion, impregnable to the outside world, a maverick fiefdom.

Dimitri's new position bestowed upon him a variety of privileges. He was offered a large apartment on Kutuzovsky Prospect, complete with well-stocked pantry and bar, and a full-time cook and housekeeper. The apartment was in the same luxurious building where Andropov lived. With his new job came a dacha at Porechie for the weekends out of town. A shiny Volga limousine with driver was also assigned to him. He gained admittance to several exclusive stores and clubs, reserved only for the upper crust of the Soviet *nomenklatura*. The orphan from Panfilov, who had stolen food in order to survive, had made his way to the top.

But the orphan from Panfilov didn't want this kind of life. He turned down the dacha and the new apartment. As time went by, Dimitri's tastes had grown ascetic, utterly rigorous. He disliked other people's company, and never attended official dinners and receptions. He now dressed in black, a rough *rubashka* with tight, buttoned collar, black belt and boots; he carried a gun at all times under his jacket. He looked more and more like his tutor, the austere Oktober. Like him, Dimitri worked mostly at night.

He took no interest in art and music; he rarely visited his apartment, and transformed Oktober's former den into his dwelling. He ate little, and preferred simple, basic food. His body grew spare and lean, his cheeks sunk, and his full shock of black hair prematurely acquired a grey colour. His features became sharper, angular, the nose beaked, jutting forward, the lips thinner, colourless; only his eyes burned with a wavering, restless fire.

Women were attracted by his tormented good looks; his brusque manners and his indifference didn't discourage them. He used them to satisfy his sexual needs, then retreated into his black shell. He was unable to develop a deeper relationship with a woman; something had died inside him, together with Tatiana. Besides, what could he give a woman? Nothing but a bare existence in the shadow of a cold man, dedicated to his secret schemes. The only luxuries he afforded himself were the occasional glass of cognac and cheap cigarettes, soldier's brand. And, of course, his collection of ancient weapons which he treated with infinite care.

Dimitri's colleagues could criticize, even ridicule, his black monkish figure, his unusual behaviour and strange tastes. They could guffaw behind his back, calling him Oktober's bastard. But nobody could deny that Oktober's bastard was the most dedicated of the Centre's department chiefs.

Dimitri became the Wet Affairs chief when alarming winds of war were blowing through the Kremlin. Ronald Reagan's ascension to power in Washington had plunged the KGB into fear – rather paranoid, in Dimitri's opinion – of a sudden nuclear attack. Reagan's speeches about 'the evil empire' and his decision to embark upon the

Star Wars project enhanced suspicions. The entire KGB was mobilized to carry out a huge operation, code named RYAN. RYAN stood for the initials Raketno Yadernoye Napadenie – Nuclear Missile Attack. Dimitri was charged with violent operations against American scientists involved in the Star Wars project.

It was a risky, challenging undertaking, Dimitri thought. But RYAN, Afghanistan, Poland, Star Wars, were for him nothing but pawns in the only contest he really cared about: the deadly game he played against his brother.

A year after assuming his functions as chief of Department Thirteen, Dimitri drove to the small farm Oktober had chosen for his retirement. Oktober's house was an old, low structure of rough brown wood on a high bank of the Kliazma River, north-east of Vladimir. It was a cold, windy day, with a low sky and the tang of rain hanging in the air. Oktober was in the backyard, tilling the soil. He was wearing a faded brown tunic over his baggy trousers, and old cracked boots. His frail body, bent from the waist, and his long limp hair falling over his face, reminded Dimitri of a Russian serf from the pre-Revolutionary era. Oktober's resigned body, bowed to the ground, symbolized the eternal submission of the Russian peasant to the rule of Mother Earth, and the whims of his masters in Moscow and Petrograd. Nothing had changed after all.

'Growing your own cabbages now, Oktober?' he inquired dryly.

Oktober glowered at him, and kept hoeing the moist *chernozem*.

'I want you to come back to Moscow with me,' Dimitri said to the old man, 'as my personal adviser.'

Oktober straightened up and leaned on his hoe. 'You don't need me,' he lashed out. 'You've taken away my department, what more do you want?'

'To tell you the truth,' Dimitri admitted, 'I don't think highly of your political judgment. But I can still use the devious brain of a crazy old Chekist.'

Oktober stared at him shrewdly. 'You need me for your brother, don't you?' he finally asked.

I need you for myself, Dimitri thought. You're my only friend. I've got nobody else but you.

He shrugged and looked away. To the south, beyond the immense corn fields, the antique Church of the Intercession towered over the village of Bogolyubovo.

'I was born there, you know,' Oktober suddenly said. Dimitri stared at him with surprise. He knew nothing about Oktober except for the rumours wafting about Moscow Centre. In his youth, the rumours said, Oktober had been a fanatical inquisitor. He'd had his own wife shot for deviationism, and his entire family had perished in Stalin's gulags. Others maintained that Oktober was a priest's son, and had massacred his family to protect himself from exposure. The communist regime had always considered religion its vilest enemy, and Oktober's link to the church could have cost him his life.

'You had a big family?' Dimitri asked cautiously.

Oktober reached down and picked up a lump of dirt, crushing it between his fingers. 'They're all gone. There's nobody left.'

'Did you have a wife, children?' Dimitri pressed on.

'They're all gone,' Oktober repeated.

'What happened to them? They were killed?'

Oktober wiped his pale forehead with his sleeve. 'Let's go and eat,' he said.

They silently lunched on black bread, potatoes and smoked sausage. There was a half-bottle of vodka on the table, but they didn't touch it. After the meal they walked on the river bank, overlooking the muddy waters of the Kliazma. The current carried branches and logs. The spring rains had caused a few floods in the area. The corn stalks to their right were still green. A few heavy drops of rain splashed on Dimitri's face and he glanced at Oktober. His face reminded him of the sharp profile of an Indian chief he had seen once in the *Ogoniok* magazine. He had the same leathery, hollowed cheeks, a predator's cruel mouth, and long wispy hair. We are quite similar, Dimitri suddenly thought. We are both lonely men, with nothing left but our work.

'He's got under your skin, I see,' Oktober said.

'Who?'

'Your brother. You can't live without him. In a way, hate is very similar to love. It's a bond between you, even stronger than love. Your war makes you inseparable.' A thin, defiant smile lingered on the old man's lips.

'His wife had another baby last month,' Dimitri said. 'A boy. They called him Victor.'

Oktober picked up a blade of grass and chewed it thoughtfully. 'What do you think about Gorbachev?' he suddenly asked. Mikhail Gorbachev had become Russia's leader a few months ago.

Dimitri stared at him for a while then said bluntly: 'He is a disaster. He must be removed.'

Oktober glanced at him with irony. 'Who will remove him? The party? The KGB?'

'Some people you know at the KGB, perhaps,' Dimitri cautiously suggested. 'Will you come back, Oktober? I need you.'

The rain caught up with them by the river bend. They walked back in a furious deluge, water streaming down their faces and soaking their clothes; it was no use running, it was too far. When they reached the house, sloshing in the mud, Dimitri repeated his question. Darkness was imminent, the last diffuse light filtering through the murky clouds in the west. 'Well,' Oktober finally said, gesturing at the open spaces around him, 'I always had a dream of living in the country. Perhaps I should keep it like that. A dream.'

They left, together, the following morning.

Oktober was the only one to share Dimitri's secret and take an active part in the planning of his coup against Alex Gordon. He seemed to delight in devising ever more ruthless, more diabolical schemes in the brothers' war. It had been Oktober who had advised Dimitri to hit Alex by setting up Nina Kramer.

'Your brother is emotional, he's a family man,' Oktober had said. 'He loves his wife, his child, his aunt. Perhaps he has relatives in Russia. Hurt them – and you'll hurt him. Each time you stab one of them he'll scream as if you were drawing pins in a voodoo doll.'

Oktober had been right. The Nina Kramer scandal and her death had dealt an agonizing blow to Alex Gordon. His emotional link to his family was definitely the chink in his armour. Yet there was another reason for Dimitri to go after Alex's family. The bloody bastard had one.

For most of his life he'd had Nina, who loved nobody but him; he had his wife, Claudia, who looked very striking in the pictures Dimitri's agents had dispatched from Washington. He had his lovely little daughter, and now a boy. Dimitri never said it to Oktober, but he secretly envied his brother for being surrounded by a loving family. Dimitri was a lone wolf, he had nobody. Alex had stolen the only person who had been dear to him. Well, now it was his turn to hit back. Nina Kramer's death was a foretaste of his revenge. Other hits like that would come in the future.

It was a very complicated task, however. Alex must have guessed, after Nina's death, that Dimitri might go after Claudia and the children; therefore he kept them under constant protection. Dimitri's men reported from Washington that Claudia, her daughter and son were always escorted by armed bodyguards.

Dimitri tried to find other members of Alex's family in Russia. Tonya had a brother, Professor Gordon, but he had died in Leningrad. Perhaps Alex's father, Victor Wolf, had brothers, or sisters? Dimitri recalled how insistently Alex had questioned him, back in Paris, about Victor Wolf's family. Alex had seemed so eager then to find all his father's relatives.

Fine, Dimitri thought. He would be delighted to help his brother in that endeavour, locate the bunch of Jewish aunts and cousins, then take good care of them. He knew how to make them scream. He instructed Ivan Sereda, his orderly, to find Victor Wolf's file in the KGB archives. If he had relatives, their names would figure in the file. The KGB often used relatives as tools for blackmailing its targets.

In the meantime, Dimitri had chosen more traditional weapons for their duel. After failing to kill Alex in Paris, he embarked with equal resolve on a secret offensive intended to outwit his brother, sabotage his operations and sap his credibility. Which was exactly what Alex was trying to do with him.

After Nina's death, Alex had been long preparing his counterattack. He finally hit back at Dimitri, by exposing a KGB plot to assassinate Mexico's president, Gomez y Diaz. The assassination had been thwarted at the last moment, and the rumours said one of the conspirators had crossed the lines shortly before the attempt on the President's life.

Alex found out that Dimitri had visited Mexico a week before the coup was to take place. He then coldly worked out a plan for setting up his brother as the Russian agent who had betrayed the KGB. The scheming Jew, Oktober reported, had deposited sizeable sums of money in Morozov's name in several Swiss banks; then he planted doctored evidence that pointed at Morozov as the CIA's informer. Two KGB networks in Mexico City were destroyed, their members arrested, and the role of the Soviet embassy exposed in the world press. With a lot of embellishment, of course. All the clues pointed to the chief of Department Thirteen as the turncoat. In normal conditions, Dimitri thought, this was more than enough to have him dragged to the Lubyanka and shot for high treason.

The KGB established an internal board of inquiry to investigate Dimitri. For the first two weeks the evidence against him, planted by Alex, kept piling up on the board's desk. Dimitri felt his life was hanging by a thread. But then the tide turned. The board couldn't ignore Dimitri's immaculate record, and his solid position inside Moscow Centre. The testimony of Oktober, who had come back from retirement to work with him, helped in convincing the board of inquiry that Dimitri had been framed by the CIA.

'Your brother is trying to pay you back for Nina's death,' Oktober told him that night. 'All right, let's play the game by his rules.'

'How, Oktober?'

'Don't come to your office for a while. Don't go home, either. Hide somewhere, disappear. Let him assume that he scored, that you're in jail, perhaps even dead. And while he rests on his laurels, we'll hit back.'

Morozov's name disappeared from CIA reports coming from Moscow. By suddenly vanishing, Dimitri gave his brother reason to believe that he had won. Dimitri and Oktober let Alex delight in his success for a few months, before striking back. Alex Gordon was now deeply involved in supplying operational intelligence to the anti-Soviet rebels in Afghanistan. 'Fine,' Oktober said, 'let's give him a victory there, if he so wishes.'

On March 15, 1985, in a rocky gorge in Afghanistan, Mujaheddin rebels pillaged the wreck of a Soviet Antonov aircraft that another guerrilla unit had destroyed with a Stinger missile. In that wreckage they discovered a briefcase full of documents that soon reached Alex Gordon's desk in Washington. Most of the papers dealt with the supply lines for a summer offensive against the rebels. The detailed plan described a two-pronged attack in the semi-desert region of Kandahar in the south-west. Alex flew personally to Karachi, crossed the border into Afghanistan, and passed the information to the chiefs of the Mujaheddin, who started preparing to repel the offensive.

Suddenly, a month before D-Day, the Russians attacked in force, following a totally different plan. Instead of Kandahar, they stormed Zebak in the rocky mountains three hundred kilometres to the north, by the Pakistani border. The rebels suffered a tremendous defeat. Alex was devastated. A week after the offensive started, he received a postcard from Brussels, bearing the photograph of the Manneken Piss – the peeing mannikin, the tiny statue of a naked boy which is the city's symbol. The postcard carried a single phrase: 'Never believe good news on March 15.'

March 15 was the date of Tatiana's death.

'I'd love to have seen Alex's face,' Dimitri said to Oktober, 'when he realized I was the one who fed him the phoney plans.'

'I'd love to see your face right now,' Oktober retorted, and took a rectangular envelope from his briefcase.

Dimitri looked at him sharply.

Oktober spread a few photographs on the desk. 'These arrived with the diplomatic pouch from Washington.'

Dimitri shuffled through the photographs. He recognized his brother, in a crowded restaurant, in the company of a corpulent man who seemed vaguely familiar. He looked questioningly at the old man.

'Remember Saint-Clair?' Oktober said.

'Saint-Clair? You mean . . . Grimaldi? This is Grimaldi? I can't believe it.'

Oktober nodded. 'He vanished after he escaped Moscow twelve years ago. We thought he had retired from the service. We were wrong. He is the Director of the Soviet Division.'

'The Director?' Dimitri repeated, amazed.

Oktober nodded. 'Actually, he's Gordon's mentor.'

'Good God,' Dimitri rasped. A smile spread over his face. 'This seems to be my lucky day, Oktober. We can use him for our plan.'

He buzzed his orderly, Ivan Sereda. His voice was hoarse, charged with contained triumph. 'Vanya,' he said to the short, wiry Ukrainian, 'get me the GRU Electronic Intelligence Centre in Alma Ata on the phone. I want to speak to its commander.'

Grimaldi, holding his glass of champagne in his left hand, worked his way through the crowd. The Gordon party had attracted about fifty spooks, mostly from the Company, the rest from the other branches of the Intelligence community and the State Department. He bumped into Claudia beside one of her paintings, an aquarelle of two women on a beach, the outlines of their graceful bodies barely suggested by light, gentle strokes in grey, black and pale blue. Claudia was dressed in a low-cut bottle green dress, that enhanced her dark beauty. She was explaining something about the painting to Rudy Sullivan from DDP/CA, the Covert Action staff, and his fat, white-haired wife who looked five years his senior.

'Hi, Claudia,' he said.

Her smile lacked warmth. 'Hi, Franco.' She had never liked him. He supposed she couldn't forgive him the role he had played in Alex's affair with Tatiana. He had met Claudia in the most humiliating period of her life. Grimaldi had seen Alex both with her and with Tatiana; he knew that she was only the second woman in her husband's life. Claudia couldn't forget that. She was a jealous, proud woman. But what a woman! She reminded him of a tigress, a graceful, fierce animal, devoted to her mate but determined to use her claws to defend what was hers.

Rudy and the old lady mumbled something about the great party, and congratulated Claudia again, then disappeared into the crowd. She turned to Grimaldi.

'You look absolutely smashing,' he said.

'You look very well too. I like this velvet jacket. Nobody would guess that you're retiring.' He read a hint of triumph in the dark eyes. She was glad he was stepping out of their lives.

'Well, I'm not exactly retiring. I'll stay with the division as a consultant.'

'Says who?' she asked. At least she wasn't a hypocrite, he thought, amused.

'Says Alex,' he answered. 'He claims he can't run the place without me. Which, of course, is absolutely true.'

'The same modest old Franco,' she said sarcastically.

'Mommy, Mommy!' Tonya emerged beside them, her lovely cameo face flushed. She had a fair skin and a rosy pouting mouth. 'May we have some ice cream, Ronnie and I?' A dark, mischievous little face peered over her shoulder.

'Ronnie is my brother's son,' Claudia explained. 'Okay,' she said, 'it's in the freezer. But take Victor with you to the kitchen.'

'Mommy, he'll spoil everything,' wailed Tonya.

'I don't want to hear you speak like that about your brother,' Claudia said quietly. 'Off you go.' The little girl shrugged and dragged her brother to the kitchen. Victor followed obediently, then turned back, smiled and waved at his mother.

'I still have to congratulate you officially,' Grimaldi raised his glass and assumed a solemn tone. 'A toast to the new chief of the Soviet Division, and to his gorgeous lady! Cheers.'

'Cheers,' she said absently, and finished her drink.

'I hope you're pleased with the promotion,' he said. 'I was fifty-eight when I got the division, Alex is barely thirty-seven.'

'Yes,' she said without enthusiasm, 'I am pleased. I'll see him even less than before. Great, isn't it?'

Her bitterness surprised him. 'Perhaps you'll have more time for your painting.'

She shook her head. 'It's not the time I need, it's the peace of mind.' She picked up another scotch from the tray of a passing waiter. 'I am going back into fashion design.'

A silver-haired man, possessively holding a stunning blonde by the waist, passed by, raising his glass, 'Congratulations, Claudia,' he said. 'The right man in the right place.'

'Thank you, Irv,' she chirped, with the same fake smile.

Grimaldi was watching her closely. 'Back to fashion design?' he repeated. 'So you'll start travelling again?'

'Probably. It won't make any difference to Alex. He doesn't see much of me anyway.' Her lips twitched slightly.

Before moving away, Grimaldi noticed that her glass was empty again, and she was looking for another. She would be drunk as a skunk before the party was over. Claudia was in bad shape, her marriage was definitely on the rocks. It was rumoured at Langley that Alex and Claudia had hoped a second child might save their marriage, but it hadn't worked.

He couldn't blame her. Claudia was a passionate woman who needed a lot of attention. But Alex was almost never at home, and when he was, his mind wasn't there. He was so obsessed by his schemes, so enthralled with his crusade against Morozov, that nothing else mattered. Grimaldi wouldn't be surprised if Claudia was seeing somebody on the side. A sexy, desirable woman, she could have any man she wanted. She could go crazy at the thought that she was wasting her youth and her beauty while waiting at home for a husband who didn't even care for her.

He waved at Alex, who was earnestly talking to the Deputy Director of Plans. Alex looked very cool and self-possessed in a dark suit, striped shirt and Lanvin tie. The warm, gentle boy Grimaldi had met on the Paris-bound plane had grown into a confident, ruggedly handsome man. He had shed the warmth and the gentleness, however, somewhere along the way.

Grimaldi gave his unfinished drink to a waiter and made his way to the back porch. He needed a smoke, but smokers had lately become the lepers of the free world. He preferred to catch a cold outside than light a cigar in the Gordons' living room and provoke an enraged assault by some health nut, screaming bloody murder.

There was nobody on the porch. He lit a Corona and stared into the darkness. So this is it, Frankie, he thought. You're sixty-six, and you're retired. You can stop pretending. You're out, in spite of all this crap about the consultant's job.

He sighed and let out a long puff. Alex wouldn't need his services, though perhaps he would reluctantly throw him a bone once in a while. Alex didn't like him, probably blamed him for Tatiana's death although he never spoke about that. At least Alex didn't suspect that Grimaldi was the one who had delivered the girl to Morozov. He, too, would never learn that Grimaldi had been his informant. That call from the phone booth in Brussels was a secret Grimaldi would take to the grave.

He had no regrets, though. The girl's death had made Alex fall into his hands like a ripe fruit. The phone call had been a brilliant move: it had triggered the brothers' war which gave him eleven more years of scheming, and promotion to the top slot. He had been right to bet on Alex Gordon. And setting him against his brother had been a stroke of genius.

A cold wind was rising from the nearby creek. What would he do now? he thought in sudden panic. What would he do tomorrow, next week? He had no life outside the Company. He had nobody to share his anguish, his pain, his feelings. Or his bed. He'd had a few lovers during the last few years, very brief affairs, mostly one-night stands in New York where he could pick up a boy in a gay bar. But with the AIDS scare he couldn't afford even that anymore. Besides, his sexual powers were dwindling. He was getting old in spite of his dyed hair and moustache.

He shuddered at the thought of the bleak years ahead, alone in his apartment, waiting for a phone call from Langley that never came. He would be forced to give in and buy a condo in Florida with the inevitable trimmings – shuffleboard in the afternoon, early bird dinners, shaky swims in the oceanside pool. And foolish conversations with brown, dried-up old people in bright clothes, obsessed with their bowel movements and warming their ancient bones in the sun, waiting for death. It was maddening.

He threw away his cigar, crossed the crowded living room and left, without parting from his hosts. He quickly walked to his car, shivering in the chilly autumn air.

He unlocked the door and opened it, but the light didn't come up. He bent, surprised. A fuse, perhaps? Then he saw the immobile figure on the passenger seat.

'Hello, Franco,' the dear, familiar voice said and his heart leapt in his chest. 'Don't turn on the light. You know my penchant for dark and cosy cars.'

'Oleg?' he gasped. 'Oleg, is that you?'

Shortly after midnight there was a discreet knock on the door of unit 132 at the Rockville Skyways Motel in Maryland. Grimaldi turned off the lights and opened the door, letting Oleg Kalinin sneak into the room. He bolted and chained the door, checked the curtains, then turned the lights on. He affectionately patted Kalinin's shoulder. He still couldn't believe he wasn't dreaming. His friend, whom he had believed dead for more than twelve years, was here, alive and apparently well.

Alex Gordon rose from his armchair by the coil-shaped radiator that cast a red glow upon his grave face. He was wearing a pair of jeans and a heavy woollen pullover.

'Oleg Kalinin.' Grimaldi gestured. 'Alex Gordon.' He anxiously watched the two men. It had been his idea for Oleg to meet the new chief of the Soviet Division.

Alex firmly shook Kalinin's hand, but his eyes were watchful, reserved. 'Grimaldi told me a lot about you,' he said in Russian, 'and I know what you did for us. But I didn't expect that I would ever meet you. We thought you were dead.'

'Whisky?' Grimaldi said, smiling at his friend. 'You like it straight, no ice, no water.'

Kalinin smiled back and nodded.

'And an iced vodka for you,' Grimaldi said to Alex. He opened the mini-bar and fixed the drinks, choosing a Bailey's Cream for himself.

He opened a cellophane bag of roast peanuts, and placed a chocolate bar beside Alex. He knew his weaknesses.

'Cheers!' he said and raised his glass.

'*Nazdorovya*,' Oleg echoed.

Alex picked up his glass, his eyes glued to Oleg's face. His reserve made Grimaldi uneasy and he nervously fidgeted with his bow tie.

'Grimaldi told me,' Alex said slowly, 'that you arrived last week with the Soviet scientific delegation to the Space Congress.'

'The Fourth International Congress of Astrophysics,' Kalinin corrected. He hadn't changed much, Grimaldi thought. The same smile, the same confident voice. His skin had acquired a deep dark tan, though, and his waist had thickened. Still, he looked very distinguished in his elegant charcoal suit, light blue shirt and knitted silk tie.

'What is your capacity with the delegation?' Alex went on.

'Deputy Administrative Director.'

'And your real function?'

Kalinin shrugged. 'I am a brigadier-general in the GRU . . .'

'General? Well, Oleg, congratulations!' Grimaldi raised his glass and Kalinin acknowledged the greeting with a grin. Alex remained impassive.

'My field,' Kalinin went on, 'is electronic intelligence, and I am interested in all the lectures and papers concerning satellites. Surveillance, photographs from outer space, signals, telecommunications, this sort of stuff.'

Grimaldi stared at him in surprise. Oleg hadn't told him anything about his functions when they met in his car. He had only asked for a meeting later that night. He was leaving Washington the following morning.

Alex was perched on the edge of his chair, very intense, his back stiff. 'When Grimaldi escaped from Moscow, twelve years ago, you were a wanted man. The KGB hunted you all over the country. Now you're here, a general and an expert on electronic intelligence. Tell me about this comeback, Top Hat.'

Kalinin smiled again at the mention of his code name. 'I was hunted, but not by all the KGB. There was this young officer, Morozov' – Grimaldi cast a quick glance at Alex, noticing the tightening of his jaw – 'who stumbled upon my ties with Grimaldi. In Moscow Franco called himself Saint-Clair, you know.'

Alex nodded, sipping his drink.

'Morozov had nothing tangible against me, only suspicions. He confronted me in Paris, then went after Grimaldi in Moscow. I advised him to leave, then decided to lie low until I could get in touch with Morozov's superiors. I finally succeeded in meeting Morozov's boss, the chief of Department Thirteen . . .'

'Oktober?' Alex asked, diligently writing on a yellow pad.

'Oktober, yes.' Oleg Kalinin leaned back in his armchair. 'I had known him since the war. I found him and convinced him that I was innocent. He stood by me like a rock, he virtually saved my life. Morozov had me brought before a KGB inner court. I spent several months in prison, during the investigation.'

'Morozov tortured you?' Grimaldi quickly asked.

'It was not a picnic,' Kalinin said coldly. 'Morozov himself was most of the time abroad, but some of his cronies did the dirty work. Oktober testified on my behalf, however, and I was finally released and reinstated.'

'When?' Alex watched him with his head thrown back, his eyes narrowed in suspicion.

'Grimaldi left Moscow in February '74. I was arrested in April, and released the following February.'

'You spent ten months in prison? The Lubyanka?'

'No. Morozov held me incommunicado at Lefortovo prison. It is in the south-western outskirts of Moscow.'

'I know where Lefortovo is,' Alex said, scrawling a note on his pad. Then he raised his head. 'By what you're saying, I understand that Grimaldi, I mean Saint-Clair, was also cleared?'

'Oh, yes, absolutely. He is not suspected of any wrongdoing. He represented a respectable Canadian company in Moscow. He had to leave in a hurry because of the unfortunate death of his mother, that's all.' Kalinin smiled a lot, like in the old days.

'And you?' Alex persevered. 'Were you totally cleared?'

'"I was finally rehabilitated,' Oleg cautiously said, 'but there was, how shall I say, a cloud of mistrust around me. Morozov had spread the word that I was a traitor. Oktober thought it would be better for me to get away from Moscow. That way nobody could accuse me of maintaining contact with American agents.'

'Where did he send you?'

'Alma Ata, in Kazakhstan. I was appointed commanding officer of the GRU Electronic Intelligence centre there. On January 1 this year I was promoted to brigadier-general. This meant I was in good odour again. Last month I was transferred back to Moscow, to the Science and Technology Division. This is my first trip abroad. There are also three KGB people with us, besides the scientists.'

Alex stepped to the mini-bar to pour himself another drink. 'Why didn't you contact us during all these years? We've been looking for you since you disappeared.'

A slightly condescending smile flashed across Kalinin's face. 'Do you really think that was the right thing to do? I was exiled, suspected, watched, with Morozov breathing down my neck . . . You think I should have risked my life and gone looking for some American agent who might also be a decoy?' He shook his head. 'Come on, Mr Gordon.'

Alex bowed his head, rebuffed. Good, Grimaldi thought, that was the answer you deserved. He raised his glass to his lips. The Irish Cream was smooth and velvety.

Alex picked up the chocolate bar, but on second thoughts put it back on the table beside him. 'And on arriving in Washington, the first thing you thought of was finding Grimaldi?'

The sarcastic smile appeared again on Kalinin's face. 'Something wrong with that, Mr Gordon?'

'You can call me Alex,' he said coldly, then started pacing about the room, his hands clasped behind his back. 'You followed Grimaldi to my house and got into his car. How did you get in?'

'Waiting in dark cars is Oleg's speciality,' Grimaldi said, and they both laughed.

Alex abruptly changed the subject. 'What do you think of your Secretary General?' he asked Kalinin.

'Gorbachev? I like him. He's a dreamer.'

'Do you know him?'

'I met him in the seventies, when he came to Moscow as a member of the Supreme Soviet, and later in Alma Ata. He arrived with a Politburo mission. He is a maverick. He has some very naive ideas about rebuilding the Soviet Union, retreating from Afghanistan . . .'

'You think he means it? He'll abandon Afghanistan?'

'He means it, but he won't stay in power long enough to do it. He's losing his hold on the country.'

'Seen from Washington, he doesn't seem so weak,' Alex remarked. 'Gorbachev has been Secretary General for almost two years already, and seems quite popular.'

'Do you know any Soviet leader who wasn't popular? Frankly, I am surprised Gorbachev's survived for so long. Take my word: the old guard in the party will kick him out very soon, perhaps before the end of this year.'

'What does the KGB think of him?'

'At first they liked him. Now they loathe him. Morozov wants him dead. The KGB barons think he wants to curtail their power. This feeling is shared by the army and the party machine.'

Grimaldi lit a cigar and stepped to the window. He slightly parted the curtains and looked outside. The street was calm and peaceful.

The two Company cars parked by the opposite pavement were dark, but he noticed the glowing tip of a cigarette in the closer one. There were two agents in each car, equipped with walkie-talkies and handguns, watching the motel entrance. His eyes swept the street and rested for a moment on the huge abstract mural painted on the exterior wall of the Savings and Loans building. It was the work of some Spanish artist, he vaguely recalled.

He turned back. Alex was pacing back and forth, frowning in thought. 'You're in electronic intelligence,' he pointed out. 'What do you know about the KGB bugging of the American embassy?'

'It's the greatest coup of Moscow Centre in the last decade,' Kalinin said.

You bet, Grimaldi thought, sucking his black cigar. The Moscow fiasco was one of the worst scandals in Langley's history. Two stupid Marines, serving in Moscow as embassy guards, had been sexually entrapped by KGB whores, the so-called 'skylarks'. The bozos had started by letting the girls in at night and screwing them all over the deserted embassy. The girls had then convinced the Marines to let in 'some friends' who had bugged the embassy, planted a microphone in the ambassador's desk, and opened the CIA resident's safe. The KGB agents had photographed a list of American deep-cover agents in Moscow. Most of them had disappeared during the last two months; they had probably been tortured to death.

And those idiots called themselves Marines, Grimaldi bitterly thought. The Russian whores just had to pull off their panties for the Marines to lose their heads. The KGB penetration had been a tremendous blow to the CIA networks. At least three boards of inquiry were investigating the disaster, and the State Department had already rushed two assistant secretaries to Moscow. There was talk of replacing the ambassador.

'This will get Morozov his general's stars before his fortieth birthday,' Kalinin was saying.

'Morozov?' Alex stopped in his tracks. 'What has he to do with this?'

Kalinin grimaced. 'Everything,' he said. 'It was a Morozov operation from start to finish, didn't you know?'

'I thought that the bugging . . .' Alex started. He still seemed stunned. Morozov's name always produced that effect on him, Grimaldi noted.

'He didn't give a damn about the bugging. All that he cared for were the networks. And he got most of them. He knows how to make his prisoners sing, believe me. It's a matter of months before he rounds up the remaining agents you've got.'

Alex stood with his back to the window, his face stamped with hatred. 'So we're left with no agents in Moscow,' he said hoarsely. 'How can we restore our networks there?'

'Somebody must start again, from scratch,' Kalinin said.

'You, for instance?' Alex looked at him suspiciously, but Kalinin shook his head.

'No, I am too well known for these cloak-and-dagger games.'

Alex looked at Grimaldi. A mixture of fear and sweet anticipation flowed through his veins, as he realized what was going to happen. And even before Alex Gordon asked his question, he knew he was going to answer yes. Definitely yes, I'll do it.

Alex Gordon said, watching him closely: 'Franco, I know that you're looking forward to your retirement. But we're in trouble, and we can't let Morozov get away with it. You know Russia, you've served there for years. Will you go back to Moscow and rebuild our networks?' He paused. 'I know it's risky. Kalinin can help you. Think it over, you don't have to answer me right now.'

'No need to think, Alex,' Grimaldi said. 'I'll go, I'll do it.' And he thought, Thank you, Oleg. God bless you, my friend. Thanks to you they won't get rid of me so easily. They still need me! A triumphant feeling swelled in him. Franco Grimaldi wasn't finished, he kept repeating inwardly, Franco Grimaldi is still in the game, alive and kicking. And Florida can wait.

Most of the elation he had felt that night at the Rockville Skyways Motel had evaporated by the time of his arrival in Moscow, three months later. Still, in spite of the jabs of nervous fear that sporadically pierced his gut he was confident that no harm would come to him. Moscow was not so sinister as before, Russia was becoming a free country, the press was drunk with the newly acquired *glasnost*; the KGB was no more the evil power lurking in every shadow. He had a few years' exciting life ahead of him, with the help, and perhaps love, of Oleg.

Arrival in Moscow couldn't have been smoother. Using his old Saint-Clair passport, he boarded the flight at Toronto. The plane was full of Canadian businessmen, reporters and tourists, who treated the employees of Sheremetyevo airport with amused irreverence. He went quickly through customs and immigration, hailed a cab outside, and less than an hour later checked into the magnificent Cosmos Hotel. His room, offering a beautiful view of the Mir Avenue, was equipped with a colour television, a radio and a modern telephone. Russia had definitely changed since he had left twelve years ago.

He took off his coat and turned on the radio which was playing extracts from Tchaikovski's *Evgenyi Onegin*. There was a knock on the door. His luggage had arrived. He took a few one-rouble notes out of his pocket and opened the door. He winced, then stood still.

Three men waited outside. He immediately recognized Morozov, a gaunt, ominous figure in black attire. He didn't know the white-haired man who stood beside him, but could guess he was the man he had feared all along, Oktober. The face of the third man was momentarily blocked by Morozov.

'Welcome to Moscow, Mr Grimaldi,' Morozov said.

He was panic-stricken. Morozov knew his real name! Then the Russian stepped inside and behind him he saw the grim, unsmiling face of Oleg Kalinin.

Kalinin softly closed the door behind him and leaned on it. He was wearing a long coat and a Russian fur hat. Grimaldi retreated to the window, his eyes nervously shifting from Morozov to Oktober. He couldn't look at Kalinin. Incoherent thoughts darted through his mind. Was Oleg on their side? Perhaps he had been captured? Had he betrayed their friendship? And those two men, Dimitri and Oktober, what would they do to him? He shuddered. He thought of the Lubyanka cellars, and of the KGB torturers. He couldn't withstand pain, he was an old man.

Morozov placed his briefcase on the bed. He opened it with swift, efficient gestures and took out several files that he neatly arranged beside each other on the bedspread. He laid down one blue file, and put beside it three brown ones marked with Roman numerals, I to III, and a black file, fastened with two clasps.

'Let's see,' he said in English, 'what we have here.' He picked up the blue file and opened it. It was full of old yellowing documents, written on an ancient typewriter. He absently leafed through them, and the brittle sheets rustled dryly. 'These are the minutes of the conversations you had with Kalinin in Berlin in 1948,' Morozov said matter-of-factly. 'All the information he fed you, and you passed to the OSS and the CIA. All false.'

He threw the file on the bed and picked up the second one, bound in brown paper. 'This file and the two others,' he gestured at them gravely, keeping the same low tone, 'contain the copies of all the reports Kalinin delivered to you in Moscow, during the years '67 to '74 when you were here under the name of Charles Saint-Clair. A few of them, unimportant of course, were accurate, and were given to you only to establish Kalinin's credibility. All the rest are fake. First-grade *disinformatzia*. For seven years you have been feeding the CIA with lies, Grimaldi.'

He blinked as the stunning meaning of Morozov's words seeped into his mused mind. Everything was fake – all the reports, all the documents he had risked his life for. But how could that be? Kalinin was their best agent, he was Top Hat, for God's sake! Unless . . .

Morozov handed him the fourth file. 'I don't think you would like to open this one in our presence. Inside you'll find some explicit descriptions and photographs of your intimate activities with Oleg Kalinin.'

Grimaldi stepped back, feverishly shaking his head, refusing the black file. His breathing was shallow and a nerve twitched uncontrollably in his left cheek. His eyes held Oleg in desperate focus. He tried to speak, but his throat was too tight. 'Oleg,' he finally managed, his voice raucous and rasping, 'you were part of this? You betrayed me? Oleg, it was all a lie?'

Kalinin stared back at him, speechless. A sickly pallor had spread over his face. He didn't deny it, didn't proclaim his innocence. 'You traitor!' Grimaldi cried out and hurled himself at Kalinin. 'You bloody, lying, sonofabitch!'

Morozov blocked his way and clamped his arms, pushing him back against the wall. A standard lamp fell over and the bulb shattered to smithereens. Stinging beads of sweat rolled down Grimaldi's forehead. Morozov's fingers were hard and sharp, like iron hooks. 'Calm down!' he hissed. 'This is not a lovers' quarrel, this is serious.'

Morozov nodded to Kalinin, who turned and scurried out of the room. 'Sit down!' he barked at Grimaldi, who obeyed, staggering to the bed and slumping heavily on it between the files. His heart was beating unevenly, and his mouth was sticky.

'Now listen to me,' Morozov said in the same firm commanding voice. 'We can arrest you for espionage. We have ample evidence against you, from 1948 until today. We can put you in prison for the rest of your life.'

He paused. 'Or we can shoot you and dispose of your body. Nobody will ever know what happened to you.'

Morozov took a sturdy cigarette from a soldier's cigarette case made of battered metal sheets and lit it. 'We can also send you back to your country and release all these files to the newspapers. All these fake reports. If your bosses at the CIA take them seriously, you'll be accused of being a double agent who betrayed his country for years in league with the KGB. If they have any sense of humour, you'll become the joke of your Intelligence community.'

Morozov sucked the cigarette and let out some grey acrid smoke. Oktober still hadn't said a word, watching him with narrow evil eyes. The romantic music of Tchaikovsky kept flowing from the radio until Oktober brusquely turned it off.

'You'll be portrayed by the world media,' Morozov said, 'as a gullible homosexual who misled the CIA for forty years, causing irreparable damage. And for what? To screw a Russian ass.'

He chuckled. 'Even if they let you go, there would be no place where you could hide. Look at him, all the secret services in the world would say, look at this old stupid queen. He was chief of the Soviet Division! What a joke, the CIA.'

Grimaldi stared at Morozov, speechless.

'So,' he said, 'which alternative would you prefer, Grimaldi?'

He averted eyes that were welling with tears. His world had crumbled. There was nothing left. Nothing but shame and disgrace. What choice did he have? Rot in some stinking Lubyanka dungeon, or be covered with ridicule? How could he face the public humiliation? He was a proud man, he had dedicated his entire life to the Company, he had made a brilliant career. And now he would become the laughing stock of America.

'Well?' Morozov coldly enquired, looking at his watch. 'I don't have all day.'

Grimaldi swallowed and licked his dry lips. 'What do you want?' he asked Morozov.

Alex's brother smiled thinly and sat beside him.

Chapter Seventeen

As the balmy May night softly invaded the peaceful city of Geneva, Nikita Srebrov sat immobile by his hotel room window. The Grand Hotel Mondial faced the silvery lake, and Srebrov's eyes were glued to the city's symbol, a graceful plume of water spurting high above Geneva's skyline. His clothes were hung in the wardrobe, his toilet articles neatly laid on the marble work surface in the bathroom. Books and papers were tidily stacked on the small desk by the telephone. He was already dressed in a conservative blue suit, a plain cream shirt and paisley tie. He stole a look at his watch. It was seven forty-eight. In twelve minutes exactly, abandoning all his belongings, he was to leave his room, sneak out of the hotel, and defect to the United States.

He was a man of forty-three now, rather plump, balding, looking at the world through huge sad eyes of a deep brown colour that some women found utterly disarming. His English was excellent, his French adequate. He had spent most of the last sixteen years as a close assistant to Dimitri Morozov. He had been with him in Paris, then back in Moscow; he was always close behind him when their Wet Affairs team carried out its spectacular coups, in Helsinki, Kabul, Frankfurt or Mexico. A resourceful chief of staff, he made the machinery work to perfection, smoothly orchestrating the arrivals and departures of agents, the prompt supply of forged passports and documents, the timing of the operations, the swift dispersal of the escape vehicles. Pedantic as a German and an excellent organizer, he saw himself as a contemporary Atlas, who carried on his shoulders the entire Thirteen. Morozov held him in high esteem although he was a bad shot and a source of desperation to his karate instructors.

In his younger years, he had enjoyed the adventure and the danger. He had relished the sensation that he belonged to the upper crust of Soviet society. He drove a 1988 Volga, lived in a spacious apartment off Gorky Street, owned the traditional dacha south of Moscow, and his two boys went to an elite school. His wife Katya was fat and plain, with a trace of a moustache on her upper lip, but she was an able anaesthetist and earned a fine salary of 220 roubles a month at Moscow's Lassov Hospital. He must have loved her once, he thought, but couldn't remember when and why. He didn't love her anymore, actually he couldn't even stand her, she was too vulgar and nagging for his taste. He found refuge in his fascinating work and his rare stamp collection. The love he denied Katya he wholeheartedly gave to his country. Even Gorbachev's reforms and the disintegration of the Soviet empire didn't influence his views, or so he thought.

But all that was before his trip to America in the early-autumn of 1989. Dimitri Morozov had sent him to Florida to supervise the assassination of a Cuban exile, Miguel Garcia. Garcia's extremist organization was apparently financed by the CIA. According to certain sources, it planned a coup against Fidel Castro.

Srebrov had arrived in Miami at the end of September, and for twelve days had done nothing but stalk Garcia and prepare the operation. He carried an Australian passport which introduced him as a Czech-born engineer who had emigrated Down Under in 1982. He had brought over his hit team, briefed the agents on the operation, traced their escape routes, and equipped them with weapons that had been smuggled over by another unit. But on the eve of the coup a cryptic message had arrived advising him to wait. The day after, a second message had ordered him to be ready for immediate action, but a third one cancelled the previous orders and instructed him to stay put.

Srebrov understood that a power struggle was being waged at Moscow Centre, perhaps even at the Kremlin. His suspicions were soon confirmed by a Department Thirteen courier, an old buddy of his, with whom he held a crash meeting in the cocktail lounge of Fort Lauderdale airport. 'This motherfucker Gorbachev objects to your project,' his friend the courier said bluntly. 'He actually objects to all our projects. All he wants is détente with America. He thinks we should stop all wet operations against Americans. He'll sell us down the river without a second thought. There are rumours he even wants to disband Department Thirteen.'

Srebrov was angered, but not surprised. Gorbachev's betrayal was the main topic of the gloomy conversations in the Department canteen. Morozov, who had supported Gorbachev initially, was ready to wring his neck now. Morozov had said it, in so many words, and even added that something should be done before it was too late.

Srebrov now leaned toward the courier who was blissfully sipping a frozen margarita. 'What's the bottom line?' he asked. 'The men are waiting, what should I do?' In the loudspeakers, a voice was chirping something about Florida's clean air regulations.

'Wait,' was the answer. 'Until they decide what to do, wait. Stay in Orlando, Miami, Fort Lauderdale, but don't come back. As long as you're here, Dimitri can pressure Gorbachev into action. He can say that the team is in place, and it's too late to call the project off. But if you come back to Moscow, Gorbachev will kill the entire operation. And kill Thirteen as well.'

Srebrov, therefore, had waited. For three long weeks, which were the first holiday he'd ever taken, and his first long stay in America. And during these three weeks he fell desperately in love with America, with her sweet, tempting way of life, the beautiful beaches, the rustling palms, the happy hours, deep-sea fishing, cable TV, tequila sunrises, grass, football, Pontiac Transams, Disney World, and a golden-haired and brown-skinned sex goddess who had been born in Indiana and was a waitress at a seafood place and whose name was Heather but whom everybody called Cookie.

He never found out if Cookie had been served to him by some devious scheme of Thirteen's arch-enemy, Alex Gordon. As a matter of fact, he didn't care. He wasn't one of those famished sex maniacs who gladly discard their principles and betray their country for a young juicy girl. He was a cool-headed, conscientious Soviet agent. Yet Cookie's ravenous sexual appetite and her astounding expertise in bed amazed him; he'd never suspected women could be so inventive. He also had a great time discovering some of South Florida's hot spots with Cookie, and spending on her thick wads of Gorbachev's money.

But most of the time, wherever he went, he thought how wonderful his life could be in this warm, sunny paradise. He thought of weekends in the Keys, and fishing expeditions to Bimini and the Grand Bahama, seafood dinners on the waterfront, wild nights in the glamorous discos and nightclubs. He visualized himself and Cookie, dressed to kill, being shown to their table in a gourmet Boca Raton restaurant by a pompous headwaiter wearing a tuxedo and a European accent. It didn't have to be Cookie actually, South Florida swarmed with Cookies and other delights from all over America. He stared with tremendous envy at the young Americans, certainly less gifted than him, parking their shiny new cars in their driveways and entering their neat, beautiful houses facing the Intracoastal, the ocean or just a limpid, shimmering blue pool. And at night screwing their leggy, sexy American women.

What have they got that I haven't? he kept asking himself. Why can't I live the same kind of life? I can make a fortune with the publication of my memoirs, on top of a fat bonus from the CIA. I can spend the rest of my life working on my stamp collection. I can escape from Katya and never see her again. Communism is the only gospel, that's certain, but in communist Russia I will never have this kind of life. And besides, Russia is falling apart. Anarchy and famine will invade the country in a matter of months.

He let himself indulge in the fantasy of so many unhappily married men entering middle age, to start everything over again, in a new world, with a new woman, and do all the things he had wanted but hadn't done in his life. For most men it was just a fantasy; but for him, a high priest of the KGB, a coveted prize for the CIA, it was within a hand's reach.

Obsessed by these thoughts, he almost felt relieved when he was approached by a friendly couple in a crowded North Miami bar. It was his last night in America. The following morning he was about to return to Moscow via Mexico and Havana, as the Garcia project had been definitely shelved. After a couple of drinks, his new acquaintances started blabbering about a friend of theirs, a magazine publisher, who wanted to print interesting stories in his magazines, and . . . 'my goodness, you are such an interesting man!' He understand immediately what nice Mr and Mrs Ozack wanted; they had CIA stamped all over them. He agreed to meet their friend in Europe, in a few weeks. He had no doubt the publisher friend was one of Alex Gordon's men. When he went home to pack, that night, he thought Mr and Mrs Ozack had saved him a phone call. If they hadn't contacted him, he would have called Alex Gordon himself. He had already memorized Langley's phone number.

It took another six months to prepare the operation. He didn't tell Katya a word, of course. He stealthily emptied his stamp albums into numbered glassine envelopes, which he stacked at the bottom of his suitcase, under his clothes; they were the only memento from his former life he was going to take with him in a money belt he had prepared for his escape. He knew he would miss the kids, but as they grew up they took more and more after their mother, and this thought would dispel his longings. One day, perhaps, he would bring them over to America, just for a visit.

He had flown into Geneva last Monday for a routine meeting with the Thirteen resident. The Americans made a final contact with him: their operational team was in place. Today, in his hotel room, he ranged the envelopes containing the stamps in his money belt and wrapped it around his flabby waist, under his body shirt. The first thing he would do in America, he thought, was diet and work out in a physical fitness club. That decision taken, he shaved and combed his hair across his skull, to conceal the expanding bald area. In America they had lotions against balding, and if those didn't help there were hair transplants. A hair transplant was very expensive, but with the CIA money he could afford it. Perhaps he could even require it as part of his new identity. He sprayed his face with Gucci aftershave, took his time dressing, then lit a cigarette and sat by the window, waiting for H-hour.

He glanced at his watch again. One minute before eight. He got up, put his key in his pocket and left the room. A film of sticky sweat formed on his palms and nervous spasms squeezed his stomach. He took the lift downstairs. His mouth was dry, and he almost jumped when the lift stopped at the third floor and another man got in. The elegant lobby was full at this hour, many of the guests clustering around the concierge desk and the main entrance, on their way to dinner, theatre or a concert.

He went to the newspaper stand and bought the *Journal de Genève*. Perhaps one of Dimitri's watchdogs was in the lobby, secretly stalking him. Dimitri often sent people from the inner security unit to shadow his own operatives, for fear of defection. But Srebrov couldn't attract anybody's suspicion. He was coatless, he wasn't going out, and he had made it a habit, the last four days, to buy the *Journal de Genève* before dining alone at the hotel's Alpine restaurant.

He stepped behind the newsstand, and turned the corner into the shopping arcade. It was deserted, and the shops were closed. He walked quickly toward the men's cloakroom. The barber shop faced the door marked *Hommes*. It was dark. He boldly approached it and turned the handle. The door was unlocked. He breathed the smell of oils, shampoos and lotions hanging in the air. The two chrome and leather thrones looked in the dark like monsters from outer space. The second door, in the back of the shop, was also unlocked. He stepped into a narrow corridor, came down three steps, pushed another door, and found himself in an inner court. The cool evening air was a caress against his burning cheeks. A cab was waiting in the courtyard, its engine droning. He opened the back door and sat down beside the immobile figure that huddled in the far corner.

The cab smoothly sailed into a narrow, quiet street. At the corner it turned right into a brightly lit avenue and merged into the stream of identical-looking Geneva cabs. A few minutes later, they were on the highway leading to the French border.

All that time the passenger beside him didn't say a word, watching the cars following them. As they left the outskirts of Geneva, he turned. He was blond, very handsome, with ice cold, calculating eyes. 'Good evening, Vladimir Ivanovitch,' he said in soft, impeccable Russian. His handshake was strong but brief. 'My name is Alex Gordon.'

Alex was determined to start Srebrov's debriefing without delay. That same night, in a secluded farm south of Grenoble, he held the first session with the defector. Srebrov's name meant 'silver' in Russian, yet Alex swiftly realized that the man was a gold mine. Gifted with the memory of a computer, Srebrov produced an endless string of facts about Thirteen's operations, assassinations, forgeries, blackmail, agents abroad. He disgorged concise reports about the modus operandi, the weapons used, the poison labs, the three revolving hit teams, the bank accounts abroad, the department's hierarchy, its plans for the future.

But for Alex, the most precious information was the detailed portrait of his brother that Srebrov drew, trait after intimate trait, starting with his taste in clothes and food, and ending with his strange relationship with the dying, cancer-ridden Oktober.

For two full weeks, the defector spoke softly, soberly, to the delight of Alex and his interrogation team. Except for his repeated requests for a new identity and a new home in Florida, Srebrov performed flawlessly. But it wasn't until the last day that he disclosed his most explosive secret, one which left Alex astounded.

They were sitting over coffee and chocolate cake in the dining room, sipping the steaming brew from earthenware mugs. At Alex's elbow, a tape-recorder was noiselessly turning. The lights were on, despite the early afternoon hour. Outside it was raining, a warm, late-spring rain that gently drummed on the window shutters, while feeble gusts of wind wailed in the chimney shaft.

'So he hates Gorbachev,' Alex was saying.

'Hates him? He wants to kill him,' Srebrov snapped, munching a mouthful of the rich cake. Noticing the amused smile on Alex's lips, he added: 'I'm serious, Alex, he is going to kill Gorbachev.'

'What are you talking about, Nikita?'

Srebrov wiped his mouth with the back of his hand. 'I'm not part of this affair,' he said cautiously, 'and I don't know all the details. I've only put together some bits and pieces I happened to overhear during the last few weeks. You'd better listen to what I'm saying, though: Dimitri is going to bump Gorbachev.'

And so it was, in a farm lost in the lush French countryside, with the last spring shower falling, that Alex Gordon learned of his brother's devious scheme.

In the last years, Srebrov's story went, a secret group headed by Dimitri Morozov had formed inside the KGB. It spilled into the army, the party, even some stray intellectuals. The movement was named *Pamyat*, which meant memory, the memory of eternal Mother Russia. It was a hard-line, reactionary group, whose tough communist ideology was laced with Russian nationalism and harsh antisemitic feelings. Their ideas were similar to Stalin's wartime blend of communism and nationalism, which he had used to stir patriotic feelings among his countrymen.

Alex nodded. 'I've heard about *Pamyat*. But I didn't know it had anything to do with Morozov.'

Srebrov chuckled. 'Some say that even *Pamyat*'s black clothes were introduced by Morozov. He dresses only in black, you know.'

Alex was intrigued. He had seen, in English and German newspapers, several stories about the black-clad *Pamyat* activists. Interviewees spouted gibberish about the purity of the Russian race. The interviews, interspersed with hard-core communist dogma, were accompanied by pictures of long-haired men with burning eyes, photographed against a background of ancient weapons, religious icons, Russian flags from the Napoleonic Wars, and pictures of Lenin and Stalin.

The KGB inner circle of *Pamyat* leaders, Srebrov went on, was deeply worried by Gorbachev's reforms, and believed he was leading the Soviet Union towards a civil war. 'They say communism and Western democracy cannot mix together. A communist state and a communist economy cannot coexist with free political parties, free elections, and free press.'

Alex nodded. 'They're right.'

'But that's exactly what Gorbachev is trying to achieve. Morozov believes Gorbachev is a disaster for Russia. He has already lost Eastern Europe, Nicaragua, Angola, Ethiopia and Iraq. He agreed to the reunification of Germany. He is responsible for the revolts in the Baltics, in Georgia and Armenia. Russia isn't a world power anymore, but a country on the verge of anarchy that begs food from the Germans and the Americans. That's Gorbachev's fault, and that's why Morozov thinks Gorbachev must be stopped.'

'By assassination?' Alex was still sceptical. Srebrov's story seemed rather farfetched.

Yes,' Srebrov said gravely.

'Who knows about this?'

'Very few people. Even Morozov's closest assistants are kept out of this affair.'

Alex tried to think objectively about the idea. In Gorbachev's Russia, indeed, the KGB was the great loser. If détente brought freedom, democracy and friendship between Moscow and Washington, nobody would need the KGB spies, assassins and torturers anymore. The KGB barons regarded Gorbachev as the cause of all their troubles. From their point of view, the assassination plot made sense.

'What are their plans?' he asked Srebrov.

'As far as I know, Morozov intends to carry out the assassination on foreign territory, so that it wouldn't be linked to the KGB. The murder will be disguised as an accident.'

'Foreign territory, you say?' Alex stepped to the window, looking out through the slits in the shutters. Grey clouds were clustered around the Alpine peaks, a dark mass pressing against the white-capped mountains. 'Where? What country?'

'Your country, of course,' Srebrov said mildly.

Alex veered back sharply. 'What are you talking about?'

'Gorbachev will visit the United States in the spring of '91. The assassination will take place during this trip.'

Alex watched him over the rim of his mug. 'This is ridiculous. Gorbachev will be under our protection from the moment he sets foot in America. The KGB can't operate in the States.'

'Well,' Srebrov apparently enjoyed Alex's bewilderment, 'Morozov, it seems has a trump card in his sleeve: a secret ally in the United States. A rich, very powerful American.'

Alex frowned. 'But you won't tell me who he is, of course?'

'I don't know who he is. No name was ever mentioned, and I understand that Morozov has a private channel of communication with this man. The rumours say he is an industrial tycoon, heavily invested in the Star Wars project. He is going to lose billions if the détente between Moscow and Washington prevails. If the Americans keep disarming, they won't need the Star Wars' gadgets anymore.'

Srebrov finished his chocolate cake, and clicked his tongue, contemplating his clean plate. 'You see,' he chuckled, 'our right wing and your right wing have a common interest. Get rid of Gorbachev. May I have some more of this cake, please?'

Srebrov's revelations still echoed in Alex's mind when he boarded the early Air France flight from Paris to Washington. Srebrov himself was flown to the States on a Company jet, bound for the CIA airfield at Fort Leary, Virginia. He was to spend a couple of months there, for a detailed, in-depth debriefing.

But Alex doubted if Srebrov knew more about the plot against Gorbachev. He had only heard a rumour. Yet, if the rumour was true, it could change the history of the Soviet Union, and perhaps the world. If Gorbachev was assassinated, the hardliners would seize power in Moscow. The Soviet Union would fall in the hands of his brother and a ruthless junta. The détente would be drowned in blood, Russia would become an evil empire again, and the Cold War would rise as a phoenix from its ashes.

There was no time to lose. Alex's mind, already geared, was swiftly tracing a plan of action. He could cancel all existing operations. He would set up an emergency headquarters far from Langley, in Washington or New York. He wouldn't inform his superiors yet. He would work outside the framework of the CIA. Dimitri's mysterious ally was involved in the Star Wars project; therefore he must be a leading figure in the aerospace industry. Alex's men would fan over the country, and screen owners and presidents of aerospace companies; then, when the search narrowed down to a few names, he would tap their phones, and place them under surveillance. That would mean breaking the law, but he had an emergency on his hands, so the hell with the law.

He should also alert Grimaldi in Moscow, and instruct him to find out more about *Pamyat*'s intentions. Top Hat must have his own channels to the inner KGB circles. On the other hand, Grimaldi shouldn't be informed of the plot against Gorbachev. Alex had never completely trusted Grimaldi. And that night, at the Rockville Motel, he had felt strange vibes, watching the looks Grimaldi and Kalinin exchanged. There was something between those two he didn't fathom. He thought for a second of a homosexual relationship, but discarded the thought. It was too risky.

The flight attendant brought him an iced vodka, and the thread of his thoughts was broken. He raised his eyes. Across the aisle sat a lovely blonde girl in a white mini-dress, with long flaxen hair and graceful shoulders. She was tenderly embracing the young man who sat beside her. He had long fair hair, the lean, sensitive face of a dreamer and a passionate mouth. She was about Tatiana's age at the time of her death. They looked very much in love.

Alex was oddly perturbed; he stared insistently at the couple, unable to take his eyes off them. Feeling his intense gaze, the girl turned towards him, then stiffened, smiling uncertainly, and averted her eyes. Alex felt a pang of raw envy. They were so happy, dammit, so much in love! They seemed to belong to another world, another life. What has happened to me? he thought. This young man across the aisle, that was me, not so long ago. Passionate, romantic, desperately in love. I liked music, poetry, I trusted people, life was fun. And now there's nothing left.

What kind of life have I got? It isn't mine anymore, it belongs to my brother. He's the one who fills my thoughts and stirs my emotions. His picture hangs in my office, the most intimate details of his life fill thick files that I keep in my safe. I know more about him than about myself, I know what he likes to eat, drink and smoke. I'm more interested in one of his casual paramours than in my own wife. I spend my days and nights with him, following his steps, striving to penetrate his mind and guess his thoughts. I'm with him when he confers with Oktober, when he brutally enters a woman's body, when he snaps an emigré's neck, riddles with bullets an Afghan President or an Ukrainian dissident.

He closed his eyes, pressing the cold vodka glass against his cheek. Tatiana was the cause of this blood feud. But Tatiana had retreated from his life long ago. And his revenge, trailing in the wake of her memory, had become his unique purpose in life.

When he was a little boy, Nina had told him the story of the Taj Mahal. The beloved wife of an Indian prince had died, and he had decided to build around her coffin a splendid shrine. His architects and engineers toiled for many years, and raised a beautiful palace around the black coffin of his defunct wife. But when he stepped inside the palace, the prince realized that the coffin didn't belong there; its small, grim shape offended the pure beauty of the marble-paved dwelling. The prince turned to his slaves, pointing at the coffin. 'Take this thing away,' he said.

That's me again, he conceded. I built a black Taj Mahal, a redoubtable machine of revenge around my lost love; I dedicated my life to avenging her death. But now it is the revenge, and not Tatiana's memory, that haunts my mind. Tatiana doesn't matter any more. I've removed her from my sinister Taj Mahal long ago. My feud with Dimitri has become an end in itself, the essence of my life. And it has already consumed my youth, and Claudia's love.

He arrived home late at night. The house was dark. The children were apparently with Sandra, a friend of Claudia's who lived two streets away. They often spent the night there when Claudia was on a business trip. Sandra had two girls of approximately the same ages at his kids. But something was wrong, Claudia wasn't supposed to leave until the end of the week.

His bodyguard turned on the lights and started his routine tour of the ground floor, checking the rooms thoroughly. Alex entered the living room, to fix himself a drink. He immediately saw the letter, lying on the silver tray beside the cognac decanter. And even before he tore open the envelope, and unfolded the single plain sheet of paper, he had already guessed the ominous news it concealed, a verdict long delayed but no less cruel.

'I am leaving you,' Claudia wrote.

Claudia had done her best to make her marriage work. She had swallowed her pride after Alex had betrayed her in Paris. She had given him another chance when he proposed to her that night in Baltimore. She had given up her career, she had carried his children, she had been at his side whenever he needed her.

But he hadn't needed her. Perhaps in the first year of their marriage, when he was still a trainee. That was their best year, and she had naively believed that the nightmare was behind them. She made a lot of new friends, most of them young CIA wives. She and Alex spent a lot of time together, she had the baby, they moved into a pleasant house at Chevy Chase. They never spoke of Tatiana.

Then Alex completed his training, became an operational agent, and started travelling. She didn't know where he went and what he did. He didn't tell her, for security reasons.

But Washington had other means of communication: it was the CIA wives' tom-tom, broadcasting with lightning speed any scrap of information concerning their husbands' dark trade. That way she learned that Sandra's husband had blundered in Nicaragua, and Susan's husband was being transferred to Covert Operations, and Caroline's husband was involved in the Iran-Contra affair – and that her husband had tried to assassinate, in Paris, a KGB baron named Dimitri Morozov.

A surge of bitterness had swelled inside her. He hadn't forgotten. His first step, fresh out of the training centre, had been to rekindle the strife with his brother. Because of Tatiana.

And her nightmare had started again.

'Time heals all wounds,' she had said to Alex that night in the dark Baltimore bar. But time hadn't healed his wounds. Instead of trying to forget, he had embarked on a bloody quest for vengeance. He didn't care about her, he cared only about Tatiana. Claudia was convenient, tucked in the house, cooking his meals, pressing his shirts, raising his children, while he travelled the globe, fighting his crazy brother for a woman they had both lost.

The maddening frustration didn't leave her for a single moment. Did he really love her? or was she only a substitute for his Russian princess? When he smiled at her, and talked to her, he probably thought of Tatiana. When he made love to her, his eyes closed, he must be making love to Tatiana. She was jealous even of Tonya. When he held the child against him, caressing her blonde hair and touching her milky cheeks, he must be hugging Tatiana.

Her Alex went through an ugly metamorphosis before her eyes. The sensitive, decent young man for whom she had fought so desperately, gradually withdrew into himself. His natural curiosity faded away, his sense of humour dried up, his cheerful smile changed into a guarded expression. His casual clothes were replaced by strict, dark suits and ties. He turned into a cold master-spy, fanatically dedicated to his private war. He raised a wall between them, and didn't want her to get too close. He travelled abroad often, and when he was in Washington came home late. He had little time for the children, he had no time for her. Her rival was dead but her shadow still obsessed Alex.

For years she had suppressed her pain, avoiding a confrontation. Her foolish pride, she reckoned. She couldn't go through another humiliation. She was afraid to talk things over with Alex; he might deny everything, and accuse her of unfounded jealousy. She tried to develop other interests, started painting, returned to the fashion business. She smoked a lot, and began drinking in secret. Finally, after Nina's death, she couldn't play games any more.

'Alex, what's happening to us?' she softly said one night after they had made love. He had performed mechanically, without passion; he now lay immobile beside her, his profile etched against the white curtains. 'Our marriage is falling apart, and you don't care. Does Dimitri matter more than your family?'

'I don't know.' He even didn't deny he was fighting a private war against his brother. 'I can't help it, Claud. I won't have peace before I destroy him. He's an evil man.'

'I don't know if you'll destroy him,' she said. 'But you've already destroyed us. You don't care about me or the children. You're obsessed with revenge. You're still fighting your brother over a dead woman.' She averted her eyes, she felt so degraded.

'No,' he said, 'it's not her, it's him.'

'This madness has already cost Nina's life,' she went on. 'Isn't that enough?'

'No!' He jumped out of bed, trembling with fury. 'No, on the contrary! That's one more reason to get rid of him. You don't know what kind of man he is, Claud. He hates our mother, he hates my father's family, he is a compulsive murderer.' She had never seen Alex like this, his eyes burning, his face distorted, the words pouring from his mouth. 'There is nothing sacred for him. He would go for you and the kids if he only could. That's why I have people watching you all the time.'

'But I can't live like that,' Claudia shouted. 'All these bodyguards make me sick! I haven't got one private moment in my life.' She tried to control herself. 'Alex, let go, for God's sake! There is a wonderful life out there, and it's passing us by.'

'Later,' he stubbornly said. 'We'll have a great life later, after I get rid of Dimitri.'

But you never will get rid of him,' she said wearily. 'You're two old, scarred fighters, circling around each other, staggering, bleeding, unable to win and unable to call it a draw.'

'No,' he said, 'no.' His eyes still burned with that strange fire. 'I have a plan. Trust me, I know what I'm doing.'

She got out of bed and ran downstairs. She spent the night on the living-room couch, smoking and getting drunk. She couldn't make him change his mind. She should have left him that very night. But she still loved him. She couldn't bear the thought that their wonderful love had turned into a torment.

Lately, she would often stand before the mirror and watch herself. She was still very attractive, she could perhaps find somebody to care about her, not about a dead Russian girl. Men turned their heads when she passed; she was often accosted – at the supermarket, in a department store, even in the street. A couple of days ago a handsome boy, much younger than her, had approached her at a Washington gallery and she had accepted his invitation to a drink the following afternoon. But at the last moment she decided not to go. She could guess what was bound to come afterwards. Not that she didn't want it. She did. She yearned for a fervent embrace, for a body burning with passion, for someone making love to her hungrily, all night long, proving to her she was wanted. But she had decided that the day she wanted another man, she would leave her husband.

Actually, the episode with the young man had been the last straw. Time to move away, Claudia, she said to herself, time to start again, old girl. She packed a couple of suitcases for herself and the children, collected her paintings, and drove to Sandra to say goodbye. On the porch, Sandra hugged her tight. She was crying. 'Take care, Claudia,' she said, 'you deserve a little happiness.'

She reached her mother's house in Brooklyn after midnight. Her insistent knocking woke up Mrs Benevento, who appeared at the door, grey hair dishevelled, an old dressing gown thrown around her shoulders. 'Claudia,' she gasped. 'What's happened?'

She hugged her mother. 'Now, don't say anything. I've left Alex and I'm here with the children – they're in the car, asleep. I want to leave them with you for a while. I have to find a small apartment in New York and a job.'

'The kids are in the car?' her mother repeated, her hand darting to her chest.

She nodded.

Her mother shook her head. 'I saw that coming, God is my witness. Didn't I tell you, Claudia, you shouldn't have left Stevie in the first place?'

'Mother, don't. Please.' It was so humiliating.

The old woman stared at her with compassion then nodded, letting out a deep sigh. 'I'll help you with the kids.'

She left Brooklyn at dawn, after the children were sound asleep. She drove into the awakening streets of Manhattan. The city was peaceful in this early morning hour, the pavements empty, the roads deserted. The sky was limpid, and the first rays of the rising sun painted the towers of the World Trade Centre in liquid gold. She rolled down the window. The air was still, cool and pure. Arriving in New York, alone, was a strange feeling for her, scary and yet thrilling, full of uncertainty but also of promise. A new beginning which she so desperately wanted to be the final one.

Dimitri's agent, who followed Claudia to New York, reported to him every move she'd made since her separation from Alex. After a couple of weeks spent in a small East Side hotel, he stated, Claudia Gordon had rented a loft in SoHo and returned to work with Havermeyer. The press announced her comeback, with a new collection to be presented the following spring. Simultaneously, she toured the Greenwich Village galleries, trying to exhibit her paintings, but without success.

A couple of months later, Dimitri's men witnessed another development in Claudia's life. At a party in the village, she met a handsome English businessman, Robin Westlake, who was a dedicated art collector. They were seen together at restaurants, Broadway shows, and mostly at art exhibitions. One night, Claudia was seen entering Westlake's apartment building in his company. She came out late the next morning. The same thing happened the following night, and the next.

'Claudia Gordon and Robin Westlake have become lovers,' the agent's report solemnly concluded.

Dimitri smiled to himself. After all, Westlake was one of his best field operators.

Chapter Eighteen

Alone in a black Company sedan, unshaven, shivering with cold, Alex Gordon watched the entrance to Claudia's house in New York. It was the third night in a row he hadn't slept, waiting for her to come home. It was already two forty am, and she hadn't shown up, like the previous nights. Now he had to face the inevitable conclusion: she was spending her nights with a lover. A stab of raw jealousy pierced his gut. Who was the man she had left him for? Who was the one who undressed her, held her in his arms, kissed her mouth? Claudia was part of him, they had grown up together, they had spent half of their lives together. She had saved his life once, and been at his side all through his adult years. How could she conceive the rest of her life without him? How could she now be so close, so intimate with somebody else? He missed everything about her: her spontaneity, her stubbornness, her passion, even the scenes of jealousy. She had got much deeper under his skin than he had ever thought.

His throat constricted with bitterness and a feeling of loss. He strove to chase the maddening thoughts from his mind, but the distressing images kept parading before his eyes. He had been betrayed and humiliated. His Claudia was right now in bed with another man. Who was he? Alex could put his team on her trail, of course, and in twenty-four hours find out all the lurid details. But he wouldn't use his official position to settle his private affairs. Besides, he couldn't bear the thought that his marital problems would become public knowledge.

The only person to whom he had spoken was Sandra, her friend. He had spent a long evening with her, a month after Claudia had left him. Sandra had been astounded by his distress. 'I didn't think you loved her so,' she admitted.

'I didn't say that,' he said defensively.

'You didn't have to.'

Sandra had agreed, after long hesitation, to give him Claudia's address and he had called several times. She was very restrained, very civil, but cut short his hints about reconciliation. 'Don't even think about it,' she said bluntly. They reached, though, an agreement about the children, for the time being. They would have them in alternate custody, she during their holidays, he during the school year. When they were with him, Claudia would fly to Washington once a week, to spend the afternoon with them. But she refused to see Alex alone. 'There's no use,' she said, when he asked to meet her for a conversation. 'It's over, Alex.'

He had been surprised by the intensity of his own pain. Perhaps he wasn't as cynical as he thought, perhaps his family mattered much more to him that he cared to admit? He couldn't imagine life without Claudia at his side. He kept replaying in his mind scenes from their past, since the day he had met her in Brooklyn. It was torment. He was unable to speak to the children about their mother, at a loss before Tonya's frank cruel questions. 'Don't you love each other anymore, Daddy? Are you going to divorce? What will happen to me and Victor?'

With Claudia gone, he had lost his peace of mind. He couldn't stay home, and couldn't carry on with his office routine either. He hired the widow of a former agent, Brad Cunningham, to take care of the children, and escaped to New York.

His new project, the search for Morozov's secret American ally, came at the right time, he thought; he would be so deeply immersed in the operation that he wouldn't have time to feel sorry for himself. He had a bed brought to the operational headquarters he had established at New York's Rockefeller Centre and slept there at night, while the reports from all over the country arrived by fax, phone and teleprinter. But he couldn't stop thinking of Claudia, and of the danger of losing her for good. That was why he had gone to Sandra, to beg for Claudia's address.

And it was tonight, while he was waiting in vain in his car for Claudia to show up, that he learned about the breakthrough in the investigation.

The radio in his car suddenly came to life in an outburst of static, then Angel Soltero's voice filled the receiver. Soltero was a young, irreverent agent of Puorto Rican origin, with a slight body, a birdlike face and dark veiled eyes. 'Robocop to Rambo,' he announced, 'Robocop calling Rambo.'

Soltero had a mania for using his private code of film heroes. Besides Robocop and Rambo, he had in his glossary, Rocky, Batman, Ghost, Flatliners, and of course Pretty Woman.

'Go ahead, Angel,' Alex said wearily. He had instructed Soltero to put an end to his childish game, but didn't intend to start his reeducation at three in the morning.

'Wherever you are, you'd better fly back to base, Rambo,' Soltero solemnly announced.

'Why, what's the matter?'

'We found your man, Rambo.'

'You did.' He was suddenly wide awake. 'You personally?'

'With the help of the Flatliners, of course.' The Flatliners, in Soltero's jargon, were several FBI agents of the CI-3 counter-intelligence squad that Alex had commandeered, thanks to the good relationship with their New York bureau.

'Who is he?'

'I give you three guesses, Rambo.'

'Jesus, man, will you stop that stupid game?'

There was a short pause, for effect. 'Devereaux,' Soltero breathed finally.

'You're sure?' Bingo, he thought, my hunch was right.

'Positive.'

'How did you find out?'

There was a silence.

'Angel? Angel, do you read me?'

Soltero's voice came on the radio waves again, strained, strangely subdued. 'I'm afraid you won't like the answer.'

'I'm on my way,' Alex grunted, started the engine, and gunned the car in the empty streets of New York. Soltero's message, if it was true, crowned months of strenuous work which had seemed at the beginning like looking for a needle in a haystack. Alex's men had spread around the country, vetting chairmen and owners of companies specializing in space hardware, radar, lasers, rocket and missile research. The first list consisted of more than a hundred names, but a couple of months later, after a thorough check of the tycoons' political opinions, it had dwindled to twenty-five.

The list was eventually narrowed to five names. Alex's suspicions had focused on an elderly Georgia millionaire, Alfred Devereaux, one of the major Star Wars' contractors. He was a right-wing man, with murky Ku Klux Klan connections; he had several times declared that after Gorbachev Russia would become America's worst enemy again. Therefore, the Star Wars project should be maintained.

Alex was ready to bet on Devereaux, but he had not a scrap of evidence to support his suspicions. And here was Soltero, calmly announcing that he had positively identified him as the man conspiring to assassinate Gorbachev. He wondered how the boy could be so sure. 'You won't like the answer,' Soltero had said.

Soltero was waiting for him by the skating ring at Rockefeller Centre. He was wearing studded jeans, a leather jacket, high-heeled boots and a mischievous smile. Alex suspected he was dressing like that on purpose, to fit the stereotypical image of a Puerto Rican as seen by his colleagues. 'Will you buy me a cup of coffee, *gringo*?' he asked. Thank God he had put Rambo and Robocop to sleep.

Alex nodded. He was in no mood to enter his gloomy lair, up on the seventeenth floor, and start looking for a clean spoon and an unused plastic cup. They crossed the street to an all-night diner, and ordered some coffee and chocolate cake. The aging waiter, who only spoke a few words in English, had trouble understanding them, and Alex repeated his order twice. He then turned to Soltero.

'I'm listening, Angel.'

'Two weeks ago,' Soltero started, 'I had a long talk with Josh Caldwell of the Flatliners. He thought that we should look into the time employ of our suspects.'

'Which suspects?'

'All of them.' He passed his fingers through his hair. 'We assumed there must be regular contacts, at least once a month, between Morozov and his buddy over here. We decided, therefore, to check the time employ of all our suspects during the last two months, looking for any unusual contacts. Which we did. It turned out to be' – he swallowed his last forkful – 'a piece of cake.'

'What is it that I won't like?' Alex asked impatiently.

Soltero raised his hand. 'Alex, let me tell it my own way.'

'Okay, go ahead.' He beckoned to the stooping waiter, who refilled their cups. 'Where do you come from?' Alex asked.

The man smiled, revealing decaying teeth. 'Odessa,' he said. 'Russia.'

Angel raised his arms in mock despair. 'The Russkies are here already,' he said, 'why don't we just give in?'

But noticing Alex's cold stare, he hurriedly continued. 'We verified the time employ of our clients, as I said. And we found out that six weeks ago Devereaux had made a three-day trip to New York. He had a few bona fide appointments, and one non bona fide meal. He lunched at La Côte Basque with a stranger, a man the Flatliners couldn't identify. But I have his description for you.'

He took a sheaf of papers from his jeans pocket, and leafed through it. 'Here it is,' he said. His voice had suddenly acquired the same ring as before – pained, and very serious. 'The party who met Devereaux was a man of about sixty-five to seventy years of age. Deep tan, green eyes, dyed hair and moustache, striped shirt, silk tie, double-breasted blazer with two rows of gold buttons, grey twill trousers, Gucci loafers. Wearing a lot of flashy golden jewellery, several rings, and a bracelet.'

Alex took a sharp intake of breath. There was only one man he knew corresponding to that description.

'When was that?' he managed, a wave of fury swelling inside him. He made a tremendous effort to control himself. Grimaldi had been here and met Devereaux. Devereaux was suspected of being Morozov's partner. Grimaldi was posted in Moscow. Where he had ample opportunities to meet Morozov. He had all the qualities for becoming the ideal courier between Morozov and Devereaux. There was only one logical explanation for Grimaldi's meeting with Devereaux: he was Morozov's agent. Napoleone had crossed the lines.

He frantically racked his brains, trying to conceive a different explanation, but to no avail. Grimaldi couldn't have met Devereaux by coincidence. In his trade, Alex said to himself, coincidences never happened.

Soltero was looking at him oddly. 'When was that lunch?' Alex repeated.

'Six weeks ago. We checked. It corresponds with Grimaldi's last home leave. He had crossed the border by car from Montreal, flown from Buffalo to the Farm, and after debriefing, returned to New York for two weeks.'

Alex shook his head, his feelings a mixture of disbelief and resignation. 'What's your source?' he asked, his voice strangled.

'The Maître d' and two of the waiters at the Côte Basque. He spoke to the Maître d' in French. The man was a gourmet, knew his way around French cuisine.'

'Did you show them pictures of Grimaldi?'

Soltero nodded. 'We came back three days after the first interview, with a few photographs. The waiters picked Grimaldi's photograph out of the display. Sorry, Alex.'

He was nodding mechanically. Yes, there could be no doubt who the rotten apple was. The bloody turncoat, he thought, how could he betray his country at the end of such an impressive career? And Dimitri, how did he recruit Grimaldi? What had been Kalinin's game when he came to Washington?

His devious brother was playing a dirty game, he thought. But then he remembered Srebrov and Cookie, and slumped back on his chair. He had stolen Dimitri's man, and Dimitri had stolen his. He and his brother were back in the ring again, bleeding and exhausted, locked in absurd combat. What had Claudia said? Two old fighters, stumbling and staggering, but still punching each other, unable to win and unable to call it a draw.

'Keep on with your work as usual.' He pointed a finger at Soltero and got up, leaving a note on the table. 'I'll have to double-check your report with Moscow.'

'Why?'

'Perhaps Grimaldi has a logical explanation,' he said. 'Perhaps it was an innocent lunch.'

'Innocent?' Soltero's voice was heavy with sarcasm. 'You've got a spy in Moscow who's been fooling the KGB dummies for years. Your own Scarlet Pimpernel. Your spy sails unscathed through all the KGB traps, comes and goes from Moscow at will, without anybody even bothering him. What is his secret? Your answer is – the man's a hero. And your hero happens to come on home leave, and happens to know our prime suspect, and happens to have lunch with him. Innocent my foot, Señor Alex!'

'Perhaps he has a legitimate explanation,' Alex stubbornly repeated.

'Do you believe that? Really?'

Alex stared blankly at him, and turned to go.

Morozov was waiting for Grimaldi on the back seat of his Volga, at Tatarskaya, a gloomy street off Lenin Square. It was getting late, a dry wind was rising from the east, and people were hurrying home, chased by the fierce onslaughts of the dying year. A long line for vodka snaked around the block, the men shivering and stamping their feet. As he saw Morozov's profile in the car window, enveloped in the smoke of his soldier's cigarettes, Grimaldi clenched his teeth in disgust. He hated the young sonofabitch, his mannerisms, his black clothes, his ascetic habits. Morozov had made him admit his own weaknesses, and turned him into a traitor.

But what else could he do? Refuse, that day at the Kosmos Hotel, and be exposed, kicked back to America and covered with ridicule? Admit before his peers that his lust had blinded his senses, and for the last forty-five years he had unwittingly served as a tool of the KGB? He'd rather die than face them, hear their cynical remarks and mocking laughter, imagine what they said behind his back. The story would have ended in the papers. No, he had to lie low, keep passing Kalinin's phoney reports to Washington, complete the present project with Morozov and Devereaux – then retire somewhere very far away, where they'd never find him.

What a mess, he thought. He was identified with Top Hat, the greatest American mole of the last fifty years. Some mole! For years Oleg had been feeding him first-rate rubbish, concocted in the Lubyanka *disinformatzia* workshops. And he had gullibly swallowed it, because he loved Oleg. He hadn't seen him since the Kosmos meeting. He clenched his fists. If he saw Kalinin again, he might strangle him with his bare hands. He'd never suspected people could be so ignoble. They had been lovers, and Oleg had betrayed him. Perhaps had never loved him, only used his body to draw him into that sordid trap.

He opened the car door and slid into the back, beside Morozov. The Thirteen chief touched the driver's shoulder, who switched the engine on. The car darted forward.

'Where are we going?' Grimaldi was very jumpy lately.

Morozov shrugged. 'Nowhere. We'll just drive around town a while, it's safer that way.' His voice sounded tense.

'Why the precautions, Morozov?'

The younger man stared at him, his black eyes gleaming in the falling dusk. 'Gordon is after you,' he said. 'He is investigating your connections with us.'

A chill descended upon him, a terrible fear, and for a moment he was speechless. 'What are you talking about?' he finally managed. His throat was dry, rough. 'Who told you that?'

Morozov didn't answer, absently looking out of the window.

'What is your source?' Grimaldi repeated.

'I have good sources,' Morozov said. 'Gordon must have smelled something. Srebrov, perhaps.'

The interior of the car was suddenly hot and stuffy. Grimaldi wiped his perspiring brow, then unbuttoned his collar and rolled down the window. The wind whipped his flushed face. He saw a long line of cars waiting outside a service station.

'I don't believe it,' he mumbled. His tongue was thick and sticky. 'Srebrov is a fool, and besides he doesn't know a thing. You told me that yourself.' There was no way Gordon could have found about him. Nobody in the KGB, except Morozov, knew of their connection. Still, if Gordon discovered his role in the plot, he was a dead man.

'How do you know he's investigating?' he asked again.

Morozov kept his eyes on the window. 'He's sent three coded cables to the political officer at the embassy, to inquire about your contacts with Soviet officials.'

The political officer was the CIA resident. He didn't know anything about Grimaldi's assignment. But if Alex had instructed him to investigate Grimaldi – Charles Saint-Clair, as he was known – it meant he suspected something very fishy indeed.

'How do you know? You broke the embassy code?'

Morozov said nothing, and Grimaldi understood. The man was as cunning as the devil, he still had access to the embassy. After the

Marines scandal, and the debugging of the entire building, Morozov still found ways to penetrate the embassy strongrooms, or perhaps he had planted new bugs in the political section.

'You must stop him,' he said, mopping his forehead with a silk handkerchief. 'You must stop Gordon.'

Morozov grimaced. 'Easy to say. The man is well protected, even more so than your President.'

'You have to smoke him out,' Grimaldi said urgently. 'Lure him to . . . Paris, or Havana, bring him here. You must get him under your control. If he really finds out about the Devereaux affair, it will be my funeral. And yours,' he added viciously.

Morozov glanced at him sideways, lighting another cigarette. 'Any ideas?' he asked.

The Washington purple cab turned the corner and came to a stop before the house where she used to live with Alex and the children. Claudia caught a glimpse of her face in the cab's rearview mirror. She saw two twinkling black eyes glowing with anticipation, a mouth harbouring a secret, mischievous smile. She could barely contain her excitement. In a moment she would hug her children, and then it would be time for the surprise that she had been planning for the last three weeks. She was as thrilled as a little girl about to receive the doll of her dreams.

It wasn't the first time she had come back. Since she had reached her agreement with Alex, the children lived with him several months a year. She kept flying over from New York every week, to spend a few hours with Tonya and Victor. She didn't meet Alex even once, he was busy somewhere in New York. She preferred it that way, didn't want to talk to him and reopen old wounds.

She loved the afternoons with the children. She would take them out, to the movies, a shopping mall or a fast food restaurant. But she couldn't stand the sight of the CIA bodyguard who followed them everywhere. It was the same man most of the time, a bearlike middle-aged agent with heavy jowls, suspicious beady eyes and a brown hairpiece. A cigarette was always stuck in the corner of his mouth. Tonya claimed the bear's name was Babcock, she had once heard her father call him so. Claudia felt like Babcock's prisoner. Wherever they went, she could sense his stare boring into her back. It was infuriating. Another of Alex's manias, she thought, another result of the insane brothers' war.

The afternoons they spent together were too short and the disgusting bodyguard was getting on her nerves. She dreamt of a relaxed, long weekend alone with the kids, somewhere nobody would find them. She spoke to Robin about it, and he encouraged her. 'If you feel like that, love,' he drawled in that fabulous accent of his, 'just do it! Go ahead, be a sport.' She therefore concocted a plan – or perhaps Robin did, she couldn't actually remember – to give the slip to the bodyguard, then sneak away with the children for a weekend in the countryside. She told nobody about it. Robin was the only one in the know.

She prepared everything to the last detail. It was exciting, like planning one of Alex's covert operations. She rented two rooms at the Chesapeake Inn for one night. She bought warm clothes and presents for Tonya and Victor. It had been fun, choosing jackets, sweaters, and shoes, especially for Tonya who was on the verge of becoming a young lady now. Claudia loaded the bags with the clothes, and her own stuff, put them in a Thunderbird she rented at Washington airport, then drove to the city and parked the car behind the Savoy 3 cinema, off Dupont circle. She even wrote a letter to Alex that she would leave with the housekeeper, explaining she had taken the children away for a weekend and they would be back on Sunday night. Anyway, she intended to call him from Baltimore or Chesapeake City, and reassure him.

She then took a cab home. As they reached the house, she asked the cab driver to wait, ran up the steps and rang at the door.

Her plan worked perfectly. The housekeeper, Mrs Cunningham, was very nice, and promised to give the letter to Alex when he came back. Tonya was looking ravishing in a new jeans outfit. She was wearing her hair long now and looked very feminine. She hugged Claudia lovingly. 'Mommy, I have a boyfriend,' she excitedly whispered in her ear. 'His name is Jimmy, he is the coolest guy in our class.' Jimmy, of course, was mad about her and was going to become a rock singer. But he was also interested in space travel.

Tonya's confidences were interrupted by Victor, who jumped on his mother, toothlessly grinning, screaming with delight. He was almost seven, a healthy, merry child who had inherited her complexion and ardent black eyes. He insisted on examining the belly of the small toy robot she had brought him, and of course broke it in thirty seconds flat, which was a record of endurance for the robot. She and Alex used to joke that they should buy Victor a hammer to go with every toy they bought him, and that way he could dispose of it faster.

They piled in the cab that set on its way with the CIA car trailing behind them. Only then did she tell the children about her plan. They were going to spend the weekend touring the Chesapeake Bay area. They would drive to Baltimore by country roads, and spend the night at the Chesapeake Inn. The following morning they would board a round-the-bay cruise, and visit the historic community of Havre de Grâce. Afterwards they would take the car and explore the surrounding rivers, forests and Civil War battlegrounds.

Victor was thrilled. 'Shall we see Indians?' he kept asking, clapping his pudgy hands and shooting imaginary arrows in the air. Tonya was very excited too, but didn't calm down before securing her mother's promise that she could call Jimmy from the hotel. They all agreed it was going to be a fun weekend, but just before leaving the cab Victor spoiled it all by asking if his daddy would join them. Claudia felt a throb of nostalgia, looked away, and stiffly walked to the cashier's booth of the Savoy.

The movie shown today was a rerun of *The Gods Must Be Crazy*, which they had already seen twice. The theatre was full of kids and teenagers, laden with popcorn and giant Cokes. Claudia and the children sat by the exit door. She noticed Babcock take a seat at the opposite side of the cinema. As soon as the lights went off, she prodded the children and they smoothly sneaked out of the dark hall. They were in the Thunderbird and on their way in seconds. 'We did it!' she happily announced. The children cheered, and Victor jumped excitedly on the front seat.

Half an hour later, they had left Interstate 95 and were on a deserted country road, winding through the peaceful Maryland countryside. Claudia was just lecturing the children about the name Chesapeake, derived from 'Chesepiook' – the great shellfish bay – of the Algonquin Indians, when she noticed two other automobiles in her rearview mirror. One of the cars gathered speed and came very near, tailgating her own and turning on its lights.

'Mommy, what does he want?' Tonya cried out in alarm. Victor turned back in his seat and merrily waved at the blazing headlights, Claudia, suddenly terrified, tried to accelerate, but the second car overtook them, sharply cut into their lane and braked, swerving slantways and blocking the road. She hit the brakes, and her car stopped with a shrieking of tyres, inches away from the other automobile.

Four men jumped out of the cars and converged upon Claudia's Thunderbird. Good God, she realized, they're carrying guns! She frantically fumbled with her seat belt. Tonya was screaming in fear, burying her face in her hands. Panicking, Claudia tried to lock the car doors, but she was too late. Two of the strangers, whose faces were covered with ski masks, yanked the right side doors open, and pulled the children out of the car. Another man pointed a gun at Claudia. 'Don't move!' he shouted.

She hurled herself upon him, wildly clawing and kicking. The man seized her by the waist, then slipped and they both fell on the asphalt.

She tried to grab his gun, but he punched her in the belly, a tremendous blow that left her stunned. Their other assailants dragged the wildly resisting children towards the first car. Tonya was screaming and pounding on her kidnapper's chest with her fists. Victor was twisting and kicking, shrilly yelling.

All of a sudden, she heard the roar of another car engine, and turned to the left. A third car appeared and braked beside them. Babcock, whom they had left in the Savoy cinema, jumped out of it, pulling his gun. She hadn't fooled him after all.

With surprising speed for a man of his age, the burly agent fired several shots. The two men holding Tonya and Victor seemed confused. Tonya wriggled free and dashed towards the roadside ditch. Her captor feebly tried to raise his arm, then swayed and slowly collapsed, a dark stain expanding on his chest. The man holding Claudia threw her aside, and aimed his gun at Babcock, but Claudia jumped on him and plunged her teeth in his hand. The man cried out in pain and his gun clattered on the road. He hesitated a moment, then ran towards the first car.

His third companion, holding Victor as a human shield, fired back at Babcock. Claudia let out a hoarse shout and darted towards him. She saw the gun's barrel pointing at her, but she didn't care. The masked man let Victor go, and kept firing. 'Mommy, Mommy!' the little boy cried out, scurrying towards her, his arms open, his little face wet with tears. He almost made it when suddenly he lurched and crumpled, his arms widespread. Claudia was beside him in two steps and gathered him in her arms. The child was gurgling, breathing unevenly, and her open hand, holding him against her, felt the sticky touch of blood.

She heard shouts in a foreign language, and running steps mixed with a few scattered shots. Their assailants dashed to the front car, carrying their wounded with them, then the car took off. 'Mrs Gordon!' somebody hoarsely shouted, probably the CIA agent. Tonya's voice was suddenly very close, and Claudia groped for her daughter, who knelt beside her, hysterically screaming. Then she heard more voices, and car engines, and the place was swept with lights. But she stayed on the narrow road, gently rocking her son's little body, feeling his spasms subside and the tremors in his limbs slowly fade away.

A Company helicopter waited for Alex at Baltimore airport and flew him to the First Memorial Hospital. It was almost midnight. From above he could see the lights of the hospital landing strip glow in the shape of a cross. An icy shiver ran down his spine. The child was badly wounded, they had said to him in New York, but alive. Alive, that was what counted. He jumped on the tarmac, bending before the ferocious wind, and ran into the emergency entrance. God, make him survive, he thought, make him overcome. Victor's toothless smile flashed before his eyes. What the hell were they doing in Maryland? he asked himself for the hundredth time.

A white-haired nurse was waiting for him outside the emergency ward. 'I am Nurse Gannett,' she said. 'The child is in surgery, Mr Gordon. Will you come with me, please?' They ran past an old man in a wheelchair and two young nurses, softly giggling, their white shoes squeaking on the linoleum. A lovely blonde woman with an inflated belly painfully trudged towards them, pushing a stand on wheels from which hung a plasma infusion. Behind a closed glass door, a telephone was forlornly ringing.

A sign over two swinging doors said 'Surgery – Authorized Personnel Only'. The nurse led him into a spacious corridor with gleaming white walls. A heavy odour of antiseptic hung in the air. White beds with green plastic mattresses were lined along the wall. Against the opposite side stood three chairs, and by them, leaning on the wall with a paper cup in her hand, he saw Claudia.

'Here you are,' the nurse said. 'Dr Salpeter will be with you shortly.' She disappeared by another door.

His eyes were glued to his wife. He hadn't seen her since she left him. She was dressed in a beige sailor's coat with large buttons, tan trousers and brown boots. Her trousers were covered with black and brown stains, and were torn over her left knee. Her hair was a mess, limply falling to her shoulders. There were dark smudges under her eyes and a fresh scratch across her left cheek, between her ear and the bridge of her nose.

'Hi, Claud,' he said.

She nodded.

'How is he?'

Before she could answer, the door at the back opened and Nurse Gannett was back, followed by a tall, athletic man of about sixty with grizzled hair and sharp features. He was dressed in a surgeon's green outfit. 'Mr Gordon?' His voice was weary. 'I am Dr Salpeter. Your boy is still in surgery. We are doing all we can. I'm afraid his chances are very slight. He was hit by two bullets in the back. His lungs and some major blood vessels have been severely damaged.'

Alex stared back at him. 'But he's alive?' he asked.

Salpeter looked at him oddly. 'He is still alive, yes. But as I said, his condition is critical.'

Alex turned to Claudia. 'Where's Tonya? What happened to her?'

'We are taking care of your daughter,' Nurse Gannett intervened. 'She is in a state of shock. We've . . .'

'She was wounded too?' Alex hoarsely interrupted, his eyes darting between the nurse and Claudia.

'No,' Nurse Gannett said calmly. 'She is okay, but she has suffered tremendous emotional stress. She was hysterical and we had to sedate her. She is asleep now, she'll be all right.'

Alex turned to Dr Salpeter again. 'What are my son's chances?' he asked.

Salpeter compassionately laid a hand on Alex's shoulder. 'Mr Gordon,' he said, sadly shaking his head, 'you must face the truth. Only a miracle can save your son.'

The surgeon and the nurse hurried back to the operating room. Alex stared vacantly after them. His knees wobbled and he slumped into one of the chairs. His son was dying. Victor might never come out of that door alive. He couldn't let that happen, he should do something. But what? He had done something indeed, for the last fifteen years he had been doing something, and in exchange he was about to receive the dead body of his little boy.

He looked around him. Claudia was speaking to him, but he didn't hear. Right now, his daughter was in some dark room, stuffed with drugs, haunted by a living nightmare that would mark her for life. Claudia stood before him, bruised, battered, lucky to be alive. He suddenly thought of Nina, remembering the glazed look in her eyes the day before she died.

All these people were dead or suffering because of him. Because of his war with Dimitri. Because of his vendetta Nina had died, and Victor was about to die, too; Tonya was tormented by boundless fear. Claudia had run far away. But not far enough.

His grim thoughts were interrupted by Nurse Gannett. 'An urgent phone call for you,' she said.

He followed her to a small cubicle where a telephone stood on a desk laden with papers. He picked up the receiver that lay beside the telephone. 'Yes,' he said.

It was Babcock. 'My findings confirm my initial report,' he stated bluntly.

Alex took a deep breath. Right now he didn't give a damn about Babcock's findings.

'Your wife's car,' Babcock went on, 'wasn't followed by anybody except me. We found the two other cars used for the attack, one on the scene of the shooting, the other outside Baltimore airport. Both cars were rented in Baltimore this morning, long before Mrs Gordon took her plane for Washington. It was an ambush, Alex.'

His mind on Victor, he had trouble following the agent's report, so asked him to repeat it twice. Only when Babcock started telling his story for the third time, did he grasp the startling meaning of his words. 'Wait,' he said leaving the receiver off the hook. He returned to the surgery ward. Claudia stood where he had left her, sipping from her paper cup.

'Claud,' he said, 'I am sorry to have to ask you these questions, but we must know. What were you doing with the kids on the road to Baltimore?'

'What difference does it make?' she asked, without looking at him.

'It's important, Claud. We must find out who attacked you.'

She turned back to him, her face dejected. 'I wanted to be alone with them,' she started, then told him about her plan to spend the weekend with Victor and Tonya at Chesapeake Bay.

'Who else knew about this?'

She frowned. 'What do you mean? Nobody knew.'

'Nobody?'

The blood drained from her face. 'Robin knew, of course. He helped me plan the entire thing. Are you trying to insinuate . . .'

'Robin is your friend?' Even at this moment, he couldn't pronounce the word boyfriend. 'What's his last name?'

'Westlake, why?' She grabbed his arm. 'Alex, what's going on?'

'Come with me,' he said.

She hesitated, looking in anguish towards the doors of the operating room, then followed him to the small office. 'Babcock? Check right away a man called Robin Westlake . . .' He paused. 'You're right.' He turned back to her. 'His name doesn't sound American.'

'He is a British citizen,' she said stiffly.

'Address?' Alex asked, stifling his jealousy.

She hesitated, then gave an address in New York's Upper East Side and a telephone number.

Alex repeated the information. 'The man is British.' he said, 'you'd better check with immigration as well. Call me back.'

He hung up.

'What's all this about?' she flared. 'Do you suspect Robin?'

He took her by the shoulders. 'Believe me, Claud, I pray to God that your Robin had nothing to do with this. Because if he has, I'll never forgive myself.'

He leaned on the window, resting his forehead on the ice-cold glass. He did hope Claudia's lover wasn't involved in the plot. He already blamed himself for not having screened Westlake thoroughly. But he had been held back by his foolish pride, couldn't bear the thought he would be shadowing his rival in the streets of New

York. Besides, he had feared that Claudia might accuse him of interfering with her private life. Yet this was exactly what Dimitri would have done: laid a tender trap for Claudia, then made her lover goad her and the children into a deadly ambush.

Babcock's second phone call arrived an hour later. Claudia stood beside him when they spoke, waiting for the verdict.

And it was grim indeed. Robin Westlake wasn't at home, Babcock announced. A search of his apartment had established that some of his clothes and toilet articles were missing. The doorman had seen him leave the building shortly after six o'clock with a suitcase, and take a cab to the airport. Immigration reported that a Robin Westlake, British passport number 47592845, had left the country aboard a TWA flight to London. The ticket had been purchased four days ago.

Claudia stood petrified, white as a sheet. He took a step towards her but she turned and ran away. Her steps echoed in the long empty corridors. He lost her for a moment at the brightly lit entrance, then discerned her shadow in the parking lot outside. He caught up with her only when she stopped, shallowly breathing, by the fence. She was hysterical, casting frenzied glances about her. He gently took her by the shoulders, but she struggled violently in his arms. 'Let me go!' she fiercely muttered, her whole body trembling. 'Don't touch me!'

The night was bitterly cold. The moan of the easterly winds was interrupted by the occasional wail of an ambulance siren. He stared at her, a broken, betrayed woman shivering with cold and humiliation. He could guess the feelings that were raging in her heart. She had left him, after fifteen years, and fallen in love with another man. Her lover had given her happiness, he had made her feel beautiful and attractive. And now she discovered he was a devious enemy, a man who didn't care for her but had used her to destroy her family. The man she loved had planned the kidnapping, and probably the killing of her children.

'Claud, listen to me,' he said.

'Leave me alone, Alex.'

'Don't blame yourself. You couldn't possibly have guessed.' He looked away. 'This is Dimitri's doing. I'm sure he sent Robin Westlake after you, as soon as he learned that you had left me.'

She didn't answer and he went on, 'There is something I want you to know. I'm leaving the Company.'

She didn't look at him.

'I am in the middle of an operation,' he said slowly. 'It will take me two or three more months to complete. It's an important project, Claud, it might influence the future of this country. As soon as it's over, I'm leaving the Company. I was a fool, I realize that. You were right all along.'

She kept silent. Her mouth was sullen, her eyes hostile.

'Let's go in,' he said, 'they might have news of Victor.'

The mention of his name brought Claudia back to reality. She turned and hurried down the corridors to the surgery ward. There was nobody in the waiting room. She fumbled in her bag, lit a cigarette, then crushed it under her heel.

A nurse they hadn't met, a young black woman with a generous mouth, entered through the swinging doors. 'You are Mr and Mrs Gordon? Your daughter wants you.'

Tonya's room was dark. Alex made out her shape lying in the bed, and the blonde hair spilling over her pillow. 'Mommy?' she said. 'Daddy?' Claudia stepped forward and took hold of her right hand.

'Daddy?' Tonya said again. Her voice was slurred, imploring. 'Where are you?'

'Right here, princess.' He bent over and kissed her cheek.

'Give me your hand.'

He took her left hand, facing Claudia across the bed.

'How's Victor?' Tonya asked.

'We don't know yet, sweetheart,' Claudia managed. She was crying.

'Can we go home?' Tonya said. 'Can we go home, please?'

Victor died at dawn. They had done everything possible. Dr Salpeter said, but the child was doomed from the start. Alex shook his hand. 'Thank you doctor,' he mumbled, then collapsed in a chair, wrapping his coat around him.

'My baby,' Claudia murmured, her voice cracked. 'He's gone, Alex.'

He raised his face towards her, shaking his head. He couldn't speak. No, he hadn't realized it could end like this. An innocent little boy had died because of his foolish games. It had been all his doing. A Russian gun had shot his son, but his own hand had pulled the trigger. A feeling of terrible guilt swelled in his chest.

'Claud,' he breathed, reaching for her. 'Claud!' But he couldn't utter the words that seared his gut like red hot iron. What have I done, Claud? he wanted to say. What have I brought upon you and the children? What have I done to Victor, who bears my father's name?

Victor Wolf suddenly emerged in his thoughts, a powerful, faceless presence. I've failed you, Father, Alex realized. I wanted you beside me, that's why I gave your name to my child. But I gambled with his life and I betrayed your memory. If you only knew that your son's life is dedicated to his brother's destruction! You wrote that 'brothers forever are one'. But these two brothers want each other's blood. And I had to witness my little son's death to realize we've turned into a couple of madmen.

A hoarse moan escaped from his throat, and he turned to the wall, his body torn by violent spasms. He buried his face in his trembling hands, unable to look into Claudia's eyes.

Hesitantly her hand touched his shoulder, his face, then gently she pulled him to her bosom, stroking his hair. Her whole body was trembling, she was probably crying too. She didn't speak, just held him tight, and he felt grateful to her for letting him face alone the demons he had unleashed.

When he raised his head, she was still bending over him, looking at him gravely. 'I . . .' he started, and bit his lip. 'I want . . .'

She took his face between her hands. Her face was puffy and her eyes had a lifeless look. 'Tonya is there, waiting,' she said, her fingers still softly stroking. 'Let's take her home, Alex.'

Chapter Nineteen

Far away, the Kremlin clock towering over Spasskaya Gate struck three times. In the darkness of his small office, Dimitri leaned back in his chair and lit a cigarette. He was used to the blackness of night and loved its soothing, velvety silence. At these predawn hours, when nothing stirred, when even his nightshift orderly slumped exhausted in his seat, Dimitri's mind was alert and sharp as a razor. Night was his realm, solitude his element, and these were the hours when he conceived his best coups, his most devious intrigues.

His cigarette faintly glowed in the dark, and the smoke hovered before him like an old, thick spider's web, swirling in the wind and slowly dissolving. He had learned the advantage of night, like so many of the secrets of his trade, from Oktober who was a night predator too. But he had died a week ago in terrible pain, his skeletal body finally yielding to the cancer that frenziedly devoured his flesh.

In Oktober's cold, monastic alcove, Dimitri had witnessed, appalled, the final phases of the old man's malady. He was at a loss before the agonizing throes. He needed him badly. Oktober was the only human being he felt attached to, the only man whose advice he valued. His only friend. He wanted to help him but didn't know how. Oktober had stubbornly refused to take medicine; his last wish had been to die at his farm, by the Kliazma River, and Dimitri had driven him there in a howling snowstorm. Death, however, hadn't waited. When they arrived at the farm, almost buried in snow, Oktober was already a rigid corpse, his mouth gaping in horror, his glazed eyes staring fixedly into the raging tempest. He had been refused even that last peace, and according to an old peasant superstition was doomed to haunt the bleak lands where he was born, till kingdom come.

Where are you, Oktober, when I need you so? he thought. When I can use your cunning, your intuition, your wicked mind? Dimitri had been so close to breaking his brother, and turning him into his prisoner; yet his foolproof plan had failed, because of an elderly bodyguard and Alex's crazy wife. And because of his incompetent field agents, who had blown their easiest assignment ever.

He hadn't wanted to kill little Victor Gordon, of course. He didn't kill children, and besides, he needed Victor and his sister as hostages. He wanted to kidnap them, and use them to blackmail Alex into abandoning his investigation of Grimaldi and Devereaux. He couldn't let his brother interfere with his project.

Gorbachev was becoming more of a threat with every day that passed. He had let this white-haired demagogue, Boris Yeltsin, usurp Russia, the Balts kick out the Soviet Army, the Germans unite again. He had authorized Jewish emigration to Israel and crawled before Israeli cabinet ministers, receiving them with full honours at the Kremlin. Capitulating before the Americans, he had even joined their pack against Russia's long-time friend and ally, Iraq's Saddam Hussein. Instead of helping Saddam, as in the past, he had meekly agreed to an American offensive against Iraq, which was imminent. Gorbachev had to be disposed of, and if the plot could be kept secret just for another six weeks, he would be.

This had been his goal in kidnapping Alex's kids: a six-week reprieve until Gorbachev came to Washington where he was going to die. Dimitri knew his brother's sentimental side, and his wife's devotion to the children. He had no doubt that if the kidnapping had succeeded, Alex would promptly have abandoned the Devereaux investigation, to save Victor and Tonya.

But at the crucial moment his inept operators had panicked, killed the little boy, and escaped. And the plan had failed.

Help me, Oktober, he thought. I need some other scheme to lure my brother into a trap. Every man has a secret lever that can make him act irrationally, risking everything, even his life. What's your secret, Alex? What's your lever?

He closed his eyes, summoning his conversation with Oktober from the depths of his memory. 'Hit his family,' Oktober had said to him in this very room, his sly eyes burning. 'Hit his relatives, in Russia and abroad. He is obsessed with his family.' That was true, his brother's foolish quest for family relatives was his Achilles' heel. But Nina was dead, Claudia and Tonya well protected – they were living together again – and he hadn't found any relatives of Alex in Russia.

A memory surfaced in his mind, and he reached for the intercom button.

'Yes, Comrade General.' The voice of Sereda, his orderly, was slurred with sleep.

'Come here.' He leaned back, finishing his cigarette, and turned on the desk lamp on his right.

Two minutes later there was a soft knock on the door. Sereda walked in with a steaming cup of tea and a Swiss milk chocolate bar broken into pieces in a small dish.

Dimitri pushed the dish aside. 'I asked you quite a time ago to get me the file on Victor Wolf.' For years he had been requesting the file on Alex's father, hoping to find there the names and addresses of his surviving relatives. The last time had been about six months ago.

Sereda nodded. 'Victor Wolf, Comrade General. I remember that. The Jewish writer, the 1949 trials. I asked for the file several times. I even went myself to the Central archives at the Lubyanka north wing. They say there's no such file. I asked them to check again, but didn't get any answer.'

'No such file?' Dimitri repeated. He had received the same answer in the past. 'How could that be, Sereda? The man was arrested, tried and condemned. He must have not one but half a dozen files.'

'That's what I told them, Comrade General. The only explanation they could offer was that the documents might have been filed in some other section.'

Dimitri took a sip of the strong, fragrant brew. That was Soviet Russia, he thought, his anger rising. Incompetence, bureaucracy, irresponsibility wherever you turned. 'All right,' he said. 'Check under the Anti-Fascist Writers' Committee records. The 1949 trials. The Seventh District Tribunal records. The Vorkuta prisoners' records. The lists of prisoners who died at the camps.'

Sereda was scribbling on his pad, licking his meaty lips.

'It's all computerized,' Dimitri said. 'It's a matter of minutes. You can access this information on our own computer. Do it, right away, and come back with the file.'

But Sereda came back only the following night. He was nervous, fidgeting with his pads and pens. 'I checked everything you told me, Comrade General,' he said, and swallowed hard. 'No file.'

The director of the KGB Central archives was a mousy, middle-aged colonel, with a sallow triangular face ending in a receding chin, a small, bitter mouth and shifty brown eyes. He was apparently terrified by the summons to appear before the formidable chief of Department Thirteen, and nervously perched on the edge of his chair, sweat appearing on his forehead.

'I want to know what happened to that file, Sevliev,' Dimitri said, breathing a long whiff of smoke towards the little officer.

'I have no explanation, General.' Sevliev's shrill voice was wavering. 'We found no trace anywhere.'

'What do you mean, no trace?' Dimitri exploded, and Sevliev winced, as if he had been slapped in the face. 'The man was tried and exiled. He most certainly died. He existed, didn't he?'

Sevliev helplessly spread his arms. 'I could have told you that the file might have been misplaced. But it isn't just one file. There must be quite a few, dealing with Victor Wolf. And if there's nothing left in our archives, that could mean somebody has done a very thorough job. I believe that all the records concerning Wolf have been removed.'

'By whom?'

Sevliev raised his small hands again. 'Somebody very high up, Comrade General. There's no other way files can disappear. We destroy records very rarely, only on explicit orders of the Politburo. This might happen when national security is in danger.'

'Victor Wolf never threatened national security,' Dimitri snapped, killing his cigarette in a pewter ashtray he had inherited from Oktober.

'But if I may, Comrade General . . .' Sevliev raised his hand, like a schoolchild. 'Last night I had an idea.' His voice was uncertain. 'Perhaps . . . perhaps the name is in the restricted list, Comrade General.'

Dimitri frowned. The restricted list was one of several items of ultra-secret information which was available to only a very few top KGB executives. It could be accessed on the office computers by a special codeword, changed weekly and distributed to the KGB generals in sealed envelopes.

'Why the restricted list?' Dimitri muttered. 'He was not a head of state or a party official, just a bloody Jewish scribbler!'

'It was just an idea, Comrade General,' Sevliev muttered and awkwardly got up from his chair. A smile tentatively touched his mouth. 'If you don't need me anymore, I'd like to return to my office. Perhaps my men have found something.'

Dimitri dismissed him with a curt nod. After the diminutive colonel left his office, he turned to his own computer which he used very rarely. He unlocked his safe, and took out an envelope stamped with two purple stripes and marked 'Top-secret'. He tore it open. This week's codeword was '*Nepobedimaya*' – unvanquished. He chuckled. The political commissars didn't miss an opportunity for their propaganda. They'd been pounding into everybody's head that Russia had never been vanquished, which was false of course.

He typed the preliminary orders on the computer keyboard, entered '*Nepobedimaya*', his own code name and secret identity number, consulted the assistance directory, and typed the command for the restricted list.

'Ready,' the computer flashed.

He typed: 'Wolf, Victor, 1949.'

The screen went dark, then a single phrase flashed across its surface, a long string of green, pulsating letters.

'I'll be damned,' he gasped. His mind refused to digest the message. It was amazing, it couldn't be true! But the green phrase was there, announcing the astounding news, waiting for his decision.

As the tremendous meaning of his discovery permeated his mind, a wave of savage joy surged inside him. Now I've got you, Alexander Gordon, he muttered inwardly. I've got you by your bloody balls, big brother. He smashed the intercom button with his fist. 'Get me the Raoul Wallenberg file,' he said urgently.

Angel Soltero entered the small cubicle serving as Alex Gordon's headquarters in Manhattan. 'Grimaldi's last report,' he said, handing him a typed sheet of paper. 'Just arrived by special courier from Langley, the Witches had it decoded this morning.'

The Witches – or decoders – were Soltero's last addition to his glossary. Alex nodded absently. He was bent over his desk, examining the first draft of Gorbachev's itinerary during his forthcoming visit to America. He had underlined, with a red marker, Gorbachev's main stops: the United Nations and the Soviet embassy in New York, then in Washington the White House, the State Department, the Mint (why there of all places, for Christ's sake!), Arlington national cemetery, Capitol Hill, Kennedy Centre. A skilled marksman, positioned by one of the sites on Gorbachev's itinerary, had a good chance of shooting the Soviet President. An army of policemen, FBI and Secret service agents was to be deployed along Gorbachev's route, but still there could be no guarantee against a clever assassin.

He raised his eyes. 'Let's see what Grimaldi cooked up for us this time,' he said, taking in at a glance Soltero's smart suede jacket, gleaming with a dozen or so zippers, shiny buttons and flaring epaulettes. 'Where are you going, to a dance contest?' he grunted.

'Tonight is *salsa* night, *gringo*,' Soltero drawled.

Alex took the report from Soltero, and perused it quickly. Reaching the last phrase, he winced and reached for the desk for support. The room swayed around him, and he sat down heavily, staring at the document in amazement.

'Anything wrong, Señor Rambo?'

He didn't react, his eyes glued to the report. He swallowed hard and took a deep breath, trying to check the wild thumping of blood at his temples.

'Next week,' Grimaldi's report read, 'a Kremlin spokesman will publicly admit that the KGB assassinated Swedish diplomat Raoul

Wallenberg in 1954, when he was kept prisoner at the Vorkuta camp. The execution of Wallenberg was carried out in front of three other prisoners. The witnesses were kept alive, in total seclusion, probably to be used as pawns in the infighting of the Soviet secret services. Wallenberg's execution was carried out by the MVD, that was protected by future Prime Minister Nikita Khruschev and Foreign Minister Andrei Gromyko. The KGB, which was the MVD's main rival in the Soviet Intelligence community, succeeded in getting hold of the witnesses, whisked them to a secret location and has protected their lives for the last twenty-six years. Their testimony could be devastating for the MVD and its political allies. It could prove, if published, that the MVD was a bunch of assassins who didn't recoil before murdering a foreign diplomat and a war hero.

'Two of the witnesses survived, after all the records of Wallenberg's death were destroyed and even the executioners put to death. The third witness, Pavel Michurin, died seventeen years ago.

'With the release of the report on Wallenberg's death, the two surviving witnesses will be set free and confined to the Siberian city of Pecora, located in the restricted zone, beyond the Arctic Circle. The survivors are Genadi Korchagin and Victor Wolf.'

He stared at the paper. Victor Wolf. His father. Alive.

It was too good to be true. It was a trap. It had Morozov written all over. Dimitri wanted to snare him. Dimitri knew of Alex's attachment to his father, of his admiration for Victor Wolf's views and poetry. Dimitri would assume that the report about Wolf being alive would ignite an overwhelming desire in Alex's heart to see his father again. He would have no other choice but to try to penetrate Russia and reach Victor Wolf.

He clamped his jaws in anger. The entire Wallenberg story had obviously been conceived by Dimitri just for him. Grimaldi had then been used to transmit the report to his brother.

On the other hand, he thought, Dimitri certainly knew he would thoroughly examine the information. The KGB knew that Alex had other sources in the Soviet Union besides Grimaldi. If it were a lie or a hoax he would know in twenty-four hours. Dimitri wouldn't throw him such bait if there was no truth in it.

He sat very still. What if the story wasn't a lie? What if Victor Wolf had survived indeed? And if his father had survived . . . he would be a man of seventy-eight today. Not impossible.

He raised his eyes. Soltero was watching him closely.

'Did you read this?' he asked.

Soltero nodded. 'Who is Wallenberg?'

He leaned forward, clasping his hands to conceal their trembling.

'Raoul Wallenberg was a Swedish diplomat posted in Budapest

during the war. In 1944 and '45, in the last months of the Nazi occupation of Hungary, he saved thousands of Jews by giving them diplomatic protection. He disappeared when the Red Army marched into Budapest.'

Soltero puckered hs brow. 'That sounds a bell. He was captured by the Russians?'

'Strictly speaking abducted to the Soviet Union. The Russians apparently wanted him to spy for them, after the war. He had excellent contacts in Switzerland, knew the chief executive of the Red Cross, had met the Pope, and was a man with a great future in Sweden.' He drained the last drops of coffee from his paper cup and grimaced in disgust. 'But Wallenberg refused, and vanished.'

'He was never seen again?'

'Well,' Alex said, recalling the thick files of articles, reports, and letters he had dug out in Langley's archives, 'actually he was. Reports kept reaching the West maintaining that Wallenberg was alive in Russia. These were mostly eyewitness reports, saying that he had been seen in a Russian prison.'

'And what did the Russians say?'

Alex shook his head. His mind was still dazed by the news about his father. He visualized a snowbound field, in the endless night reigning beyond the Arctic Circle, a heavily patrolled gulag, dogs barking, searchlights rotating from watchtowers, a prisoner facing a firing squad, and three people dressed in rags watching the grisly scene. One of them his father.

Soltero's voice repeating his question brought Alex back to reality. 'What did the Reds say?'

'The Kremlin denied everything. They never saw Wallenberg, never heard of the man. But in the meantime, he became a sort of folk hero and a cult grew around him. Jewish survivors' organizations, the Swedish government, Wallenberg's family, and a very active Raoul Wallenberg Society, kept assailing the Soviet Union with letters, petitions, newspaper campaigns. Wallenberg's life became the subject of several books and movies.'

Soltero nodded, half-seated on the edge of Alex's desk.

'I myself believed he had been murdered long ago. The Russians wouldn't keep such an embarrassing prisoner in their secret cells. He could cause them trouble. But lately they've started leaking strange stories to the press. Last year Russian sources spread the rumour that in 1944 Wallenberg had acted as intermediary between Beria, the KGB director, and the chief of the SS, Heinrich Himmler. This year they broadcast another rumour, that Wallenberg had been a personal friend of Adolf Eichmann and other Nazi officers. He was also portrayed as a playboy and womanizer.'

Angel spread his arms. 'They wanted to discredit him.'

Alex nodded. 'Exactly. Which means they had something to hide.' He paused. 'Finally, as international pressure grew, the KGB invited some of his relatives to Moscow, handed them Wallenberg's passport, and informed them Raoul had died of a heart attack in 1947, in Lubyanka prison.'

'No better place for a heart attack,' Soltero agreed.

'And here is this report,' Alex softly said, 'informing us of his murder. One of the two surviving witnesses' – he took a deep breath – 'is my father.'

Soltero stared at him, speechless, utter stupefaction stamped on his face.

The confirmation of Grimaldi's report came in the early afternoon of Friday, shortly before Alex flew home for the weekend. Following his request, the political officer of the Moscow embassy had called the newly appointed KGB spokesman – another sign of Gorbachev's *glasnost* – and was informed that the Soviet government, after a thorough investigation, had finally discovered the truth about Wallenberg's death. Yes, indeed, the affable KGB spokesman said, next Monday it would be officially confirmed that Wallenberg was murdered by the KGB. He had no knowledge, though, of any witnesses to the murder. These were probably just speculations, the cheerful spokesman said.

Alex read the cable again in the car that took him to La Guardia through the bustling streets of Manhattan. With Christmas approaching, the department stores glowed with thousands of electric bulbs, the shops displaying evergreens, trinkets and artificial snow, and Santa Clauses in cotton beards ringing their bells at street corners. The excitement was marred, though, by the grim newspaper headlines, announcing that war in the Gulf was imminent.

That evening, after Tonya had gone to sleep, Alex lit the fire in the living room, poured cognac into two large bell-shaped glasses, and brought them to the couch where Claudia had curled up, staring into the flames. Since that horrible night in Baltimore, they spent as much time together as they could. Claudia stayed in Washington, because of Tonya, but once a week she flew to spend a night with him in New York, and he came home every Friday for a long weekend.

Since Victor's death they both felt a strong need to be close to each other. They talked a lot, went out for long walks together, made love with long-forgotten tenderness. It was like a revival of their former passion. But Alex felt their love was laced with a hidden despair that brought them together. He hoped it wasn't only an artificial closeness, caused by the death of their child. He was determined to do all he could, to win back Claudia's love.

'I have something to tell you,' he started, sitting beside her. She snuggled against him, warming her cognac between her palms. He told her about Grimaldi's report. When he mentioned Victor Wolf, he felt her stiffen. She turned to look at him with eyes full of anguish. Her face was deathly pale.

'Your father,' she managed. 'Your father's alive?'

'Do you see what this means, Claud?' he said softly. 'It's a trap, I know. This is my brother's ultimate weapon. He's found my father and he's going to use him against me.'

'I can't believe it,' she said. 'Your father is alive. Can you imagine what this means? Think of the two of you meeting, hugging each other . . .' She stopped suddenly, looking at him in horrified understanding.

He nodded. 'That's exactly what Dimitri has in mind. He believes that after I learn the news, I'll become obsessed with one idea – finding my father.'

She got up and went to the window, looking down at the dark street. 'You think he knew all along that your father was alive?'

He didn't answer right away, trying to figure out his brother's strategy. 'No,' he finally said. 'If he'd known Victor Wolf was alive, he would have used him long ago to bait me. He wouldn't have attempted to kidnap the children.'

She looked at him sharply. 'Why not?'

'The kidnapping was a desperate attempt, carried out on foreign soil, involving tremendous operational and political risks. He wouldn't have done that if he had had in his hands such an asset as Victor Wolf. I guess he found out about him only lately.'

'How could he find out?'

'Perhaps he stumbled upon my father's name while reviewing the Wallenberg file. The Wallenberg affair is still a pain in the neck for the KGB. They're always having to repel new accusations by world leaders. Finding that Victor Wolf was still alive, Dimitri probably convinced his superiors they should publish the truth about Wallenberg's murder and release the surviving witnesses. I bet that he personally chose this city, Pecora, where my father lives now.'

'Where is it?'

'In Siberia, close to the Arctic Circle. It's deep in the military zone. Civilians from other parts of Russia are not allowed to come near it.'

'Why?'

'The area is full of gulags and military bases.' He paused. 'Dimitri probably chose it to make sure I'd be completely in his power if I tried to rescue my father. He'd probably laid his trap, transferred the old man to Pecora, then dictated the report to Grimaldi. Dimitri might be in Pecora already, waiting for me.'

She returned to the couch and sat beside him again. 'He is sure you'll come?'

He nodded. 'You see, Claud, this report is my death warrant.'

She frowned. 'If you play his game. He wants you to go to Russia, to save your father.' She puckered her brow in thought. 'Only a madman would rise to that kind of bait.' She left her glass on the carpet, then took his face between her two hands and looked at him, very sadly, very lovingly. 'You're going, aren't you?'

He didn't answer.

'I'm coming with you,' she said.

He looked at the waxen face, the stubborn mouth. 'You must be out of your mind, Claud.'

'I'm coming with you,' she repeated.

He shook his head. 'No way. This is a risky business, Claud, it might become very nasty.'

But seeing the defiant look in her eyes, he realized it wouldn't be easy to dissuade her. He had to reason with her, but how could he, when his own reaction was so utterly devoid of reason, so emotional? Still, what could he do? Leave his father to rot there, in that lost Siberian village? He had no choice, he had to go, but if he rejected Claudia now, he might not find her when he came back. If he came back.

'When Victor died,' he started, 'I swore to myself that I'd never leave you again. And I'd never again give you a reason to leave me. Do you believe me?'

They spoke for a long while, and only after midnight, when the logs in the fireplace had long turned to ashes, did they reach a shaky compromise; Claudia would accompany him to the point of entry to the Soviet Union, and wait for him there.

The next morning he called Angel Soltero. 'Hi, Señor Rambo,' his incurable assistant chirped into the receiver.

'I want you to find out how one can get to Pecora,' Alex said.

Chapter Twenty

The ferry was full of boisterous jolly Finns on their way to Leningrad for a weekend of cheap drinking and gambling in the hotel lobbies that had been turned into casinos. They had boarded the ferry in their cars and buses, huddled in warm parkas and tasselled hats; they had started drinking and singing even before the boat had set out on its short voyage.

Alex, too, was dressed in a bright blue, fur-lined jacket and knitted ski hat with white, red and blue stripes. He was carrying a Swedish passport in the name of Arne Blom. He had meticulously prepared for his trip, spreading misleading rumours, setting decoys, using every trick in the book.

His Austrian resident had leaked a report to a KGB stringer in Vienna, saying that Alex Gordon was arriving in Moscow on a Tarom flight from Bucharest; he was carrying a Yugoslav passport. Other reports placed him on a train coming from Prague, a tourist bus that had left Berlin the night before, a car crossing the Polish border, a physicians' delegation bound for a congress in Odessa. Simultaneously, a dozen Company veterans, carrying questionable papers, had arrived in the Soviet Union, using different ports of entry. Each of them could be Gordon; each was submitted to a long and tedious interrogation by the authorities. They had been dispatched with a single goal – to draw Morozov's attention, and allow Alex to make his way into Russia undetected.

While his agents were busy playing hide and seek with Morozov's men, Alex had devised his own paths of approach and escape. He had decided to enter Russia by sea, coming from Finland on the Helsinki-Leningrad ferry. The north-eastern seashore was the least guarded of Russia's borders; the passport control at Leningrad's Pier 14 was a mere formality.

He had left Claudia on the snow-covered pier at Helsinki. He stared for a long while at her dark, tall figure, beaten by the north wind, standing on the edge of the pier as the ferry ploughed the black waters of the Gulf of Finland. He couldn't help thinking that he might be seeing her for the last time. For a moment, the rosy-cheeked face of little Victor surfaced in his mind, gratifying him with a toothless, mirthful smile. And his hands clawed in his pockets, as so many times in the past. Oh, Dimitri, he thought, if I could only lay my hands on you. If I could only make you pay for all that you did to me.

As the flat coast of Finland disappeared in the feathery patches of mist behind them, most passengers deserted the windswept decks to seek warmth in the cosy cafeteria below. But Alex couldn't stand the company of people. Not now, when he was approaching for the first and probably the last time the land of his birth. It could be the land of his death as well; Dimitri was certainly waiting somewhere behind the curtain of fog and low clouds that had settled on the Russian coast.

He stood alone on the freezing deck, peering into the greyness, and his whole life unfolded before him. He thought of the years he had spent in the CIA, devoting his energy, his knowledge, his ideas, to the endless combat against Soviet Russia. Was it worth it? he pondered, then blocked his mind to this maddening question. For the answer was an unequivocal no. No, it hadn't been worth it. Nothing had been worth the cost and the deceit and the bloodshed. Neither this foolish secret war, waged ruthlessly for almost fifty years, nor the sacrificed agents, the bought spies, the double-crossed dead, the false traitors and phoney heroes. And for what? The Russians themselves had destroyed their empire, while the West, with all its sophisticated weapons, alliances, missiles and satellites, had little to do with it.

An icy wind blew at him from the south, and the grey fog wavered, breaking into trembling patches, then fusing again. The contours of the Russian shore gradually emerged out of the mist, and his father's poem echoed in his mind. 'I'll gladly die a thousand deaths . . .' He, too, would gladly die a thousand deaths to see his father just once in his life.

He dreamt of publishing his parents' poems one day, in English translation. He already had the book's title: *The Pures at Heart*. He was going to dedicate it to his living Tonya and his dead Victor. But was the other Victor, his father, alive indeed? Would he see him again? Would he hear his voice? How would it feel to call somebody 'Father'?

A lonely seagull dived low over the deserted deck, then disappeared in the fog. His heart was pounding a merciless beat and he bent forward, gazing into the receding grey wall. Where are you, Dimitri? a voice forlornly called in his heart. Where are you, my brother, my enemy? Are you waiting for me at Leningrad's pier, in some dark alcove over the arrivals hall, watching the berthing of the Helsinki ferry with a pair of binoculars, ready to whisper the order to shoot in your walkie-talkie? Or will you lie low until nightfall, then sneak into my hotel room and snap my neck as you did to Tatiana? Will you stalk me on some lost highway in the frozen wastelands of Siberia, lying in ambush by a roadblock with a team of assassins, armed to the teeth?

Stop this, he said to himself. Think, Alex, think! You know him, you know you're heading into his trap, you know his perverse method of playing with his victims like a cat with a snared mouse, luring them into his lair, delaying the kill until the last moment. He will let you get in, he'll make you feel secure, he'll let you cross all the obstacles – and at the very end of the road he'll be waiting to destroy you.

They sailed into Leningrad harbour, preceded by black waves that shattered against the tall piers in clouds of murky spray. Small harbour tugs passed close by, spooky shadows gliding in the thick fog, sadly hooting their warnings. The sky was low and sombre; he strained his eyes, looking for the famous landmarks of Leningrad – the rostral columns and towering Peter and Paul fortress – but the thick fog hovered over the noble city like a dark curtain. A huge sign, in Russian capital letters, proclaimed from the top of the arrival building: 'Eternal Glory to the Heroic City of Leningrad'. The scarred waterfront was deserted; the bitter cold had driven away even the dockhands and customs officials.

As the twin engines of the ferry roared in reverse shift, a half-dozen men in worn-out parkas and boots ran out of the customs building and spread along the wharf, busy with the boat's ropes and chains. Alex didn't see any KGB officers, in uniform or plain clothes. But the KGB was pretty invisible these days, he thought. One didn't see them in the streets and the airports, didn't run into them when attending an opposition rally in Moscow's avenues and even the Kremlin Guard had been handed over to the city police.

The only KGB officials one heard about were a handful of clowns, busy improving the public image of their murderous organization. They published second-rate, outdated secrets as proof to their good will: they starred at press conferences claiming their innocence, conducted organized tours in the Lubyanka, or feted on TV the newly selected 'Miss KGB', a pretty, big-breasted 23-year old lass named Katya Mayorova, who was supposedly very good at the firing range, the karate gymnasium and the kitchen.

All that made good public relations, while the real KGB, the four hundred thousand officers, agents and spies of the organization, made themselves scarce, waiting for their hour to strike. They hadn't been affected by the wave of poverty and hunger that swept Russia. Their privileges were intact, their apartments and cars untouched; their special stores still offered plentiful food and high-quality clothing. In the middle of the chaos that devastated Russia, the KGB kept its iron grip on the army, the church, the communist party. It secretly supported *Pamyat*, and other nationalist organizations. The KGB waited for Russia to collapse, weak, famished and exhausted, and would then step in, grab the reins and raise the whip again.

The only KGB employees he was to see this morning were four overwhelmed officers in the immigration booths, busy stamping the tourists' passports. The morose clerk who inspected his papers waved him through without even gratifying him with a single glance. Alex had no luggage, just a vinyl overnight bag. His maps, weapons and alternate IDs had been smuggled into the country by other means. His bag was haughtily ignored by the customs officials, a few middle-aged men in grey uniforms, clustered around a samovar that dripped steaming drops on the cement floor. Their transistor radio was broadcasting a news bulletin from Geneva, announcing the failure of the talks between the American and the Iraqi foreign ministers. War was inevitable, a Kremlin spokesman concluded.

Outside the arrival building, black marketeers were selling tins of caviar and fur hats, and buying American dollars. A tan cab, driven by an unshaven lad with a running nose and pointed ears, took him to the Pribalteiskaya Hotel on the windy western beach.

He patiently waited in line until he reached the check-in counter. The reservation in his name had been made by Finntours, a big agency which handled most of the tours originating in Helsinki. He received a card with his name and the number of his room, 1134 on the eleventh floor. He didn't get any key, though. According to the Russian system, where surveillance was more important than the tourists' convenience, he was supposed to receive his key from the 'floor matron', the supervisor of his floor.

Instead of taking the elevator, he strolled in the modern lobby, studying the displays in the duty-free shops. By the Beriozka showcase, he bumped into another tourist, dressed more or less like him. He was of the same height as Dimitri, with blue eyes, a blue bag, and a knitted ski cap. They smiled and apologized. Nobody noticed the quick exchange of cards both held in their palms. As the other tourist turned away, his hand slipped a small package into Alex's unzipped bag.

In a corner of the crowded lobby, he studied the card his contact had handed him. It was in the name of Leif Svedelid, another Swede, staying at room 872 at the Moskva Hotel, off the Alexander Nevski church. He checked the package that had been dropped in his bag. It contained a Swedish passport, duly stamped in the name of Leif Svedelid. Alex went out of the hotel and took a taxi to the Moskva. The first cut-out move had been flawlessly performed. There was no more connection between him and Arne Blom, who was probably walking right now into his room at the Pribalteiskaya. Henceforth he was Lief Svedelid, another perfectly legitimate Swede who had already checked into the Moskva Hotel.

That night he couldn't sleep. Without thinking twice he breached the golden rule of behaviour in enemy territory and set out to explore Leningrad. The city was anything but enemy territory for him. He knew he might die tomorrow, perhaps even tonight. Still, this was his first night in the land of his birth, his first night in a city which his parents had visited and loved. He walked along the broad Nevski Prospect, stopped for a light meal at the Literaturnoye Cafe, where Pushkin had been challenged to the duel that would cost him his life; he strolled along the frozen canals, and stood alone at the centre of Palace Square, where a handful of soldiers and workers had massed before storming the Winter Palace and launching the Bolshevik revolution.

He got lost between the squares, palaces, theatres and mansions that gave the city its noble allure. A tram took him across the Neva, to the two rostral columns standing guard on both flanks of the towering Naval Museum. Across the bay loomed the spire of the Peter and Paul Fortress. A poster of the Leningrad ballet announced a performance of *Swan Lake* at the Maly Theatre. A group of teenagers passed by him, merrily chatting in soft Russian. Some of the girls had pink and baby-blue ribbons woven into their flaxen hair. He was in Russia, he kept saying to himself. After all those years he had returned to Russia. The land of his fathers. And of his vilest enemies.

Shortly before dawn, cold, tired, but deeply moved, he returned to his hotel for a couple of hours' sleep.

His travel alarm clock woke him up at seven thirty am. He bought a ticket for the organized tour to the Hermitage Museum, boarded the tourist bus and left his bag on the rack above his seat. Their guide was a middle-aged blonde woman who told them in heavily accented English that she was a member of the communist party, but thought that Lenin's mausoleum should be burnt to the ground and the city of Leningrad should resume its ancient name of Petrograd. He left the bus together with the other tourists and for the next two hours strolled through the magnificent museum where some of the world's masterpieces were on display. At the end of the tour, he boarded the bus and took up the same seat. When they arrived at his hotel he picked up his bag, added his contribution to the driver's tip, and walked into the hotel.

The bag he held looked exactly like his own, but its contents were different. The switch had taken place while he was exploring the Hermitage galleries. He locked himself in a cubicle in the rest room and unzipped the bag. Inside he found, neatly packed, the uniform, cap and boots of a major in the Red Army. In the bottom of the bag lay two leather pouches. One of them contained the identity papers of Major Lavrenti Selukin: his orders, his permit to travel in restricted areas, and an Aeroflot ticket for the afternoon flight to Murmansk. Alex's photographs were stapled to the military booklet and the officer's pass.

In the early afternoon, wearing his major's uniform, he took a taxi to Leningrad airport and boarded the Murmansk flight. Forty minutes later, the Tupolev landed at Murmansk. Alex briefly glanced at the huge naval base. His department had paid a heavy price for a set of photographs taken by a Polish officer who had spent a year at the submarine basin. At the terminal he waited in line for fifteen minutes before locking himself in the rest room again, and switching identities one more time. From the second pouch in his bag he took the identity papers, lieutenant's bars and artillery insignia of Lieutenant Vladimir Zolotov, and a ticket for the Aeroflot flight to Uchta, which left at 6.30 pm and landed in the snow-covered steppe in the middle of a roaring storm.

In the parking lot outside the rudimentary airfield stood a huge army ZIL truck. The keys in Alex's pouch opened the driver's door and started the ignition. The truck had a full tank and the oil level was satisfactory. The heavy duty heater coughed twice, then slipped into a reassuring drone, the headlights paved a bright path into the darkness, and Alex was on his way.

A blizzard swept the frozen tundra. Across the bleak plain, the howling winds chased opaque clouds of swirling snow that covered the flat wastes and piled on the narrow asphalt road. Visibility was almost zero.

Bent over the steering wheel of the military truck, Alex slowly drove east, the headlight beams breaking against the white wall swaying before him. He'd been on the road for six hours already, heading north in a landscape of white desolation, his progress slowed by the fierce tempest. He was all alone in the frozen wastes of Siberia, assailed by clouds of snow and sheets of ice, accompanied by the savage roar of the Arctic winds. He had come all that way, slipping through Dimitri's net. He was going to reach Pecora if it was the last thing he did on earth.

Pecora was deep in the restricted zone, exposed to the icy breath of the Arctic Circle. The towering chains of the Ural Mountains loomed over the frozen flatlands. Several gulags were strewn through that desert of snow and ice, and the region was out of bounds for civilian travellers. That was why Alex was using the army truck. One or two travellers in a civilian car would certainly raise suspicion, while an army supply truck would be waved through the roadblocks. His men had stolen the truck a week ago, substituted its registration plates, and equipped it with food, petrol, warm clothes and blankets. In a secret compartment under the driver's seat were hidden two virgin passports for his father, a camera for his passport photographs and two Tokarev handguns.

He had spread the map of Pecora on the dashboard. His men had pinpointed the location of the released prisoners' house, and highlighted it with a green fluorescent marker. They had checked the information and confirmed its authenticity. Victor Wolf was alive. He had been released a few days ago, as the report said. The disclosure of Raoul Wallenberg's murder had come later in the week. It all held together.

Nevertheless, Alex was haunted by a dark premonition. Everything had been too easy. His men had obtained the information without any particular effort. He hadn't been bothered, not even once, since his departure from Helsinki until this very moment. Even when he had landed in Uchta, six hours ago, with a planeload of military personnel and government officials, nobody had asked for his papers. The two KGB officers at the gate waved him through, barely glancing at him. That was strange. He knew the Russian mania for papers, permits and official authorizations. They should have checked him, at least for the record.

Perhaps it was all Dimitri's doing. Perhaps he had managed to penetrate that far inside Russia only because his brother had wanted him to. Alex was almost certain that in Wolf's house, Dimitri Morozov was waiting. And if he was, then Alex was heading for certain death. But he had no choice. What else could he do? He had to try and rescue his father, even at the risk of his life.

On his right, a row of dim yellow globes flickered behind the white snow curtain. He leaned further down, until his forehead touched the cold windshield, and peered outside. Behind the lights, large rectangular shapes loomed in the dark. Houses.

He was in Pecora.

Barely a mile away, in a car parked behind an apartment building, Dimitri Morozov was waiting. Tonight he was wearing his general's uniform. The engine was running, to heat the interior. Grimaldi was slumped in the back, huddled in a wolfskin coat.

Dimitri hadn't even tried to interfere with his brother's journey. His people had received the warning signs, and the operations room at Yasenevo had been flooded with bogus reports. Excited agents breathlessly reported they had sighted Gordon crossing the Polish, German or Czech border. Dimitri had ignored them all. What was the use? he thought. Gordon was bound to surface at Pecora. All Dimitri had to do was wait for him there.

He had arrived in Pecora last night, and set up his command post at the local militia station. His staff, and the KGB assault units that he needed for the operation, were stationed at the Inta cavalry barracks, twenty-eight kilometres to the north. They had joined him after nightfall. An hour ago, he had received a report about an army truck, driven by a lieutenant, that was cleared to pass through a roadblock east of Uchta. That must be him, Dimitri thought, that was his method. Alex Gordon and his agents always used official vehicles, uniforms and papers for cover. In Russia people respected authority, and sentries never checked military papers too zealously. Alex's advantage, Dimitri thought, is that he knows us better than anybody else. His flaw is that I know him.

He leaned back, briefly closing his eyes. He could visualize his brother, clutching the steering wheel of his vehicle, fighting the storm on the way to Pecora. It must have cost him a tremendous effort to infiltrate Russia, obtain military papers and uniforms, steal a military truck, penetrate the restricted zone. And all of that, just to enter the trap that was laid for him.

In an hour, maybe less, their private war would come to its end. Dimitri had planned this moment for years, dreaming of his revenge, tasting in advance the humiliation of the Jew who had stolen his woman. It was a useless victory, though. When the brothers' vendetta had started, American and Russian agents were fighting a bloody war all over the globe. Today, however, nothing could change the ugly truth. The Soviet Union was falling apart, the empire was collapsing, the Cold War had been lost – and here he was dealing the CIA one of the most painful blows ever, the capture and destruction of its most glorious baron.

Dimitri glanced at Wolf's windows. They were still dark, there was nobody home. The old man was across the corridor, visiting his friend Korchagin at his apartment. These old prisoners were all the same. They had grown used to living together and couldn't stand being alone. Besides, Wolf didn't suspect that he was so popular with the KGB tonight. He certainly hadn't noticed the military vehicles that had taken up position around the block. The storm and the snow had come just in time. Dimitri had thought of visiting Wolf earlier in the evening, but had finally decided to wait for Alex. It would be more interesting that way.

A shadow materialized by the car window. Dimitri recognized his orderly. He rolled down the window, letting in a gust of glacial air. A few snowflakes landed on his sleeve.

Sereda's broad Ukrainian face was flushed. 'He's coming, Comrade General.'

Alex parked the truck, locked it and trudged in deep snow towards the housing block. The icy wind whipped him mercilessly, and he doubled up, holding on to his cap. He straightened up only when he stood in the small entrance lobby of number 19. It was cold and neglected, bathed in crude yellow light from a bare bulb hanging on the ceiling. The cement floor was cracked and dirty. A small mound of litter was piled in a corner; the paint was peeling from the walls in large flakes.

From the dark well of the staircase a clumsy figure came towards Alex. He immediately recognized the heavy gait.

'Grimaldi,' he said. He hadn't expected him here. By coming to meet him in Pecora, Grimaldi was admitting his betrayal. It was a senseless thing to do. In a flash, Alex recalled their operations together; he had hoped, like a child, that the sad story of Grimaldi's betrayal would fade away and Napoleone would become his ally again. Still, seeing him now, Alex felt neither surprise nor disappointment only a dull lassitude.

Grimaldi stood before him, tilting his head slightly. 'Hello, Alex. I guess this is the end of the road.'

Alex stared back, ignoring the trite formula. If Grimaldi was here, Dimitri couldn't be far behind. The place was probably swarming with KGB troops. It had been a trap, as he had suspected all along. There was no way out for him, and even if there were one, he wouldn't run away without seeing his father. Dimitri knew all that. The game was over, and Dimitri had won.

'It's not what you think,' Grimaldi said incongruously. His hand came out of his pocket, holding a cheroot.

'Isn't it?' Alex said.

'I wasn't a traitor,' Grimaldi said quickly, aggressively. 'I didn't tell them anything. You can check, Alex. Just . . . just this Gorbachev affair. He is a danger, Alex. for all of us.'

Gordon looked at the staircase. There was nobody there. He knew he would be arrested; he wasn't going to leave Russia alive. At least, he hoped, they'd let him see his father.

'You and I, we belong to a dying species,' Grimaldi went on, his lips curling in a wan smile. 'We are the last of the samurais, the princes of the Cold War.'

'Quite poetic tonight, aren't you, Franco?'

'Under Gorbachev Russia is no longer the enemy,' Grimaldi was saying. 'So they won't need the Company anymore, don't you see?'

Alex didn't answer, watching him light his cheroot.

'They won't need us,' Grimaldi went on. 'You, me, anybody. We'll have to end our lives in some dusty government office, stamping building permits or tracking drug peddlars . . . whatever. It's the end, Alex. The end of the big game. If Gorbachev isn't removed, we're all washed out. No more thrills, no right to exist. They'll sell Langley Woods to some insurance company, and turn the Farm into a vacation resort.'

'So you did it for the Company, did you?' Alex pushed him aside and stepped towards the staircase.

'Alex, wait! We should talk.' Grimaldi made a few steps after him, then stopped.

He climbed the staircase to the first floor. At the landing he turned into a drab corridor, faintly illuminated. There were doors on both sides. On the third door on his right, a small rectangle of cardboard was fastened. 'Victor Wolf', it said.

He took a deep breath. He didn't know what awaited him behind that door. He turned the handle.

The apartment was dark. The silhouette of a man sitting on a rocking chair was outlined against the bare window, and the smell of pungent tobacco hung in the air.

'Welcome, Alex,' his brother chuckled. 'Nice uniform. Take a seat. Your father will join us shortly.'

Alex lingered for a moment on the threshold, then stepped inside. The room was stuffy, and he unbuttoned the collar of his uniform. He was suddenly disgusted with this masquerade. He would have discarded the Russian uniform if he could have. How stupid he had been to think he could outwit his brother in his own backyard. The game's outcome had been decided from the start.

As his eyes grew used to the darkness, he pulled a chair from under the table that stood in the middle of the room and sat down crossing his arms. Morozov kept rocking in his chair by the window. They waited in silence, without exchanging a single word. There was nothing to talk about. Alex felt that any exchange of words between them would only lead to a murderous fight. What could he ask? 'Why did you kill Tatiana? Why did you kill my son?'

The best thing is to remain silent, he thought. Silent and resigned. Morozov had laid a trap and he had knowingly walked into it. Still, there seemed to be a tacit agreement between them that nothing would be done until the meeting with Wolf was over.

A few minutes later the door opened, and a stooping figure appeared in the doorway. Alex stood up, holding his breath. A light switch was flipped and weak yellow light spread through the poorly furnished room. Both Alex and Dimitri stepped towards the door. Alex's thighs were stiff and trembling. He couldn't help thinking how ridiculous they must look in their uniforms. The uniforms that for the old man represented humiliation, cruelty and death.

The man was hollow-chested and completely bald. His gaunt face was wrinkled, the skin carrying the greyish tinge caused by heart disease. He had a thin, delicate nose, and his parched lips badly concealed broken, uneven teeth, a few of them missing, a few crowned with some black metal. From his scrawny neck protruded a large Adam's apple. Victor Wolf was wearing thick glasses, fastened to his bare skull with an elastic band. His black suit, made of cheap wool, hang loose on his skeletal frame. His grey shirt was collarless. My God, Alex thought, is this Victor Wolf? The romantic poet who bewitched Tonya Gordon? The passionate, handsome man Nina had described, with the rebellious shock of hair, the sensuous mouth, the bold charisma? Is this the author of 'A Thousand Deaths'? The man who wrote 'brothers forever are one', my father?

The old man didn't seem surprised to find the two officers in his room. He squinted in the raw light, peering at both of them. 'Yes?' he said. He had a rasping, tremulous voice.

Alex's heart was beating wildly, an iron ball swinging inside his ribcage. 'My name is Gordon,' he managed, impulsively unbuttoning the tunic of his uniform. He shouldn't face his father in this outfit that he hated. 'I am Alex Gordon.'

'I am Dimitri Morozov,' his brother said.

The old man's hand darted to his chest, and he swayed, reaching back to the wall behind him for support. He stood breathing shallowly, his black eyes darting between the two brothers. His lips were trembling. Finally he straightened up again and approached them, dragging his feet on the floor. He was staring closely at Alex. His face was cracked into wrinkles that snaked through every inch of his skin. Wolf took a step towards Morozov, then turned back to Alex.

'Tonya Gordon was my mother,' Alex said. 'I am your son.'

Wolf was studying his face. His eyes were intensely black. He reached for Alex with his right hand and gently touched his face.

'No,' he said, and pointed at Dimitri Morozov. 'He is my son.'

In the stupefied silence that invaded the room, Alex and Dimitri froze in their tracks, two pillars of salt, unable to move, unable to utter a sound. Only their eyes followed Victor Wolf who shuffled painfully on the bare wooden floor towards Dimitri. 'He is my son,' he repeated, looking at Alex over his shoulder.

Alex was the first to regain his senses. 'What are you talking about?'

'I told you,' Morozov said in a shrill voice. He cleared his throat. 'I am Dimitri Morozov. I am Boris Morozov's son.'

But the old man was shaking his head again, and Alex could swear he discerned a faint, strangely amused smile on his cracked lips. 'I didn't expect us to meet this way,' he said. 'I didn't expect us ever to meet, actually. But you are my son.' He took another couple of steps towards Dimitri. 'You're not Dimitri Morozov. You are Alex. Alex Wolf. Or Alex Gordon, if you wish.'

'You must be out of your mind,' Dimitri muttered, taking a step back as if he feared the old man.

'No, I'm not.' There was still power in that frail body, and the black eyes were suddenly alive, burning. He was speaking to Dimitri. 'Why don't you look at yourself in the mirror? You'll see the resemblance.' His hand fluttered in the air, outlining the contour of an imaginary face. 'Same chin, same frame, same mole over your upper lip.' He touched his own face, his voice warming slightly. 'You're my son all right. You're not Dimitri, you're Alex. Little Alex, Aliosha. You're my son, and I never laid eyes on you before. God, how I longed to!'

Alex followed their conversation, utterly bemused.

'Nonsense,' Dimitri's voice quivered, and he planted his fists on his waist. 'Outward resemblance means nothing.'

'Of course.' The old man nodded. 'Of course.' He seemed unsteady on his feet and leaned on a nearby chair. He was silent a moment, catching his breath. 'You see, Aliosha,' he finally said in his rasping voice, 'I met Boris Morozov before his death, back in 1953. We shared the same cell for a couple of weeks.'

'I don't believe you,' Dimitri snapped. He was white as a sheet. 'That's too much of a coincidence. There were one million prisoners in Siberia at that time.'

Wolf was nodding repeatedly. 'I didn't say it was a coincidence, Alex.' It was so strange, thought Alex, to hear the old man address his brother by that name. 'It was no coincidence at all. Morozov still had some connections in the KGB. Old friends, people who owed him favours. He asked to be brought to my cell. He was going to be shot, and wanted to meet me. He had nothing to lose.'

He paused, breathing quickly, his hand clutching his throat. Alex quickly crossed the room and entered the miniscule kitchen. There were no glasses, just an earthenware mug drying by the sink. He filled it with water, and carried it to the old man. Wolf gulped it, some of the water trickling down his chin. 'Thank you,' he said, patting Alex's shoulder, then turned back to Dimitri.

'Morozov told me what had happened to your mother,' he went on. 'He said to me that when he saw her die – he actually saw her die, you know – he swore to save her boy. His only son. He knew that somebody at the KGB might order the child's death. They often murdered the families of traitors, you know. Or, if they let the boy live, they would make his life miserable.'

He spread his thin arms. 'He couldn't foresee that Russia would change, you understand? And besides, he was so bitter, so deeply disappointed with Russia. He was a communist, a believer, and where did he end? Waiting for death in a sordid camp, his wife shot, his family destroyed, his life wasted. He swore to give his boy a chance to grow up free in America.'

Alex Gordon swayed in sudden realization. 'He gave his child your son's name,' he whispered.

'Exactly,' the old man said. 'He was sure Nina would take care of the boy as if he were her own child.'

Dimitri was shaking his head, his fingers ploughing his hair, his eyes focused on the old man. 'Rubbish,' he spat furiously.

'It was easy, don't you see?' Wolf slumped heavily in a chair. 'It's very hard to tell a two year old from a three year old. He brought you, my boy' – he was looking at Dimitri – 'to the orphanage, and registered you under the name of Dimitri Morozov. He didn't care very much what happened to you there. It was convenient for him that the child at Panfilov would be known as his real son, Dimitri Morozov.' He took a deep breath again. 'While the real Dimitri was sent to America, under the name Alex Gordon.'

Alex's eyes shifted from Wolf to Dimitri. Everything was reversed. Black was white and white was black. He was the Russian, the Gentile. His brother, the Russian nationalist, the fervent antisemite, was the Jew.

Strange thoughts assailed him. If Dimitri had been the one sent to America, would he be a different man today? And himself? What kind of man would he have become if he had grown up at Panfilov? Dimitri might have loved poetry if he had grown up with his parents' poems by his beside. He might have abhorred violence had he not been forced to live by it. He might have been gentle and warmhearted if he had been raised by Nina, instead of going through the hell of Panfilov. He might have been proud to wear the Star of David on a chain around his neck; he might have loved his Jewish mother if he hadn't considered her the source of his misery.

And he, Alex, if he had been in his brother's place, might have become a killer.

Dimitri stood still, gazing at the snowflakes that fluttered past the window. On a night like this, his mother had stood before her cell window, watching the snow fall, waiting for her executioner. She had died because she was Jewish. He was Jewish too, he was one of the people he hated most, those he held responsible for all his suffering.

It had all been the other way around. It was his Russian stepfather who had kicked him into Panfilov, to save his Russian boy. Could Boris Morozov have been so devious? The man he admired, whose picture he carried in his wallet, could he have been so cynical, so heartless? He shuddered. No, it couldn't be true. Wolf was lying through his teeth, trying to hurt him because he was Morozov's son.

But what if the old man was telling the truth?

He could never get used to this sudden reversal in identity. He recalled a story Alex had told him in Paris about an Argentinian Catholic, one of the pillars of the church in Buenos Aires. He had accidentally discovered that he was a Marrano, a descendant of converted Jews, and had shot himself.

Next week he was to chair a meeting of *Pamyat* in Moscow. What would he say to them? That he was Jewish? That he was resigning? Perhaps he shouldn't return to Moscow. Perhaps he should run away. But where? He was not running away from somebody; his pursuer was inside him. There was no place on earth where he could hide from the confrontation with the Jew residing in his flesh.

No, it couldn't be true. The old man must be lying.

'You're crazy,' he threw at Wolf. His voice was cracked, wavering. 'You've lost your mind. That's what the gulags did to you. You shouldn't be here, you belong in an asylum. Forty-one years in the gulags drove you mad. Nobody would believe you. I don't believe a word you say.'

'I do,' Alex said quietly.

The old man suddenly smiled, a sad, bitter expression. 'There is an old question, very ancient actually, that has always haunted my people,' he said. 'Who is a Jew?'

He stood up and faced both of them. 'Who is a Jew? Who is my Jewish son? You?' He pointed a trembling finger at Dimitri. 'Or you?' He turned to Alex.

Laboriously breathing, he took a neatly folded handkerchief from his pocket and wiped his brow. 'Alex and Dimitri,' he said in wonder. His voice was so low, he seemed to be speaking to himself. 'You are both my sons. One of you carries me in his blood, and one in his soul. It's more than I could hope for.' His legs gave way and he slumped back in his chair, his chest heaving, his breath coming in quick, short rasps.

Dimitri took a step towards the old man and briefly raised his hand, reaching for him. But he regained control of himself and turned away.

Alex stood behind Victor Wolf, gently placing his hands on his shoulders.

Finally Dimitri spoke. 'You still want to take him away?' he asked Alex, without turning back.

Epilogue

Alex Gordon and the old man crossed the border into Finland forty-eight hours later. Claudia was waiting for them in Helsinki. The same day the three of them boarded a plane bound for New York. On arrival, Alex signed his letter of resignation from the CIA, and applied for a teaching position at Brown.

Two weeks later, Dimitri Morozov disappeared from his Vienna hotel. Rumour said he had defected to the West.

On January 16, war broke out in the Persian Gulf. As a result, President Gorbachev's visit to Washington was postponed. He visited the United States a few months later, but Dimitri Morozov, the driving force behind the assassination plan, had vanished; the plot against Gorbachev's life was therefore aborted. The KGB and the Red Army hawks adopted a different strategy, and on August 19 they seized power in Moscow, removing Gorbachev from his position. Dimitri Morozov's name was not mentioned in the Soviet media.

The dramatic events in Moscow justified a decision taken by the United States on the eve of the Gulf War. In a widely acclaimed speech before both houses of Congress, in January 1991, President Bush announced he would maintain the Star Wars project. He was following the assessment of some White House experts that *perestroika* might backfire, and the Cold War break out again.

A few days after the KGB coup, Franco Grimaldi was killed in a hit and run accident in Moscow. The reckless driver was never found.

General Oleg Kalinin retired from active duty. His life story, discreetly censored, was described in a best-selling book by Valentin Begoyev. The book was made into a movie entitled *Secret Warrior for Peace*.

Claudia Gordon's exhibition opened in a SoHo gallery in June. Victor Wolf proudly posed beside his portrait, painted by her. His memoirs, *To Die a Thousand Deaths*, were scheduled for the following spring.

The guests at the opening of Claudia's exhibition noticed that the artist's waist had thickened slightly. She was expecting a baby in the late autumn.

You have been reading a novel published by Piatkus Books. We hope you have enjoyed it and that you would like to read more of our titles. Please ask for them in your local library or bookshop.

If you would like to be put on our mailing list to receive details of new publications, please send a large stamped addressed envelope (UK only) to:

Piatkus Books, 5 Windmill Street
London W1P 1HF

PIATKUS

The sign of a good book